STRANGE TOMBS

SYD MOORE

POINT
BLANK

A Point Blank Book

First published in North America, Great Britain & Australia by
Point Blank, an imprint of Oneworld Publications, 2019

ISBN 978-1-78607-448-5
ISBN 978-1-78607-449-2 (eBook)

Typeset by Fakenham Prepress Solutions, Fakenham, Norfolk NR21 8NL
Printed and bound in Great Britain by Clays Ltd, Elcograf S.p.A.

Oneworld Publications
10 Bloomsbury Street
London WC1B 3SR
England

[definition] Strange /streɪn(d)ʒ/

Adjective: strange
1. Unusual or surprising; difficult to understand or explain.

Comparative adjective: stranger; *superlative adjective:* strangest

Synonyms: Odd, curious, peculiar, funny, bizarre, weird, uncanny, queer, unexpected, unfamiliar, abnormal, atypical, anomalous, different, out of the ordinary, out of the way, extraordinary, remarkable, puzzling, mystifying, mysterious, perplexing, baffling, unaccountable, inexplicable, incongruous, uncommon, irregular, singular, deviant, aberrant, freak, freakish, surreal, alien.

PROLOGUE

Graham Peacock was surprised that his guests had pegged out so early. After all, it was the beginning of a week-long residential for wannabe ghost story and mystery writers and this evening, many would agree, was the most mysterious and spookiest night on the British calendar – Halloween. All Hallows' Eve. The time of year the veil between worlds grows thin and kickstarts the season of the witch, the annual opportunity for motivated dead to hoick themselves up from the grave and walk the earth again.

So, you'd have thought, on such a night as this, the writers would have stayed up into the small hours, hunched around the great fire in the drawing room, exchanging tales of horror and intrigue. But no, they'd all tucked into the wine, then downed a whisky or three and made their excuses. Even the young ones of whom he'd expected a little more tomfoolery.

Youth of today – no stamina.

Even so, truth be told, he was pleased.

His old bones were feeling the cold. He was tired and weary and looking forward to the cosy nest of his bed. This afternoon's workshop in the unheated church, amongst the taciturn effigies and sepulchres, had chilled him. St Saviour's was not a warm place at the best of times: its central heating was notoriously unreliable.

But it was the murky and devilish legends that had, over centuries woven themselves into the fabric of the building, that cooled and unnerved Graham whenever he found himself under its high echoing roof. They were nasty. Devilish. Unsettling. And difficult to forget as one sat amongst the pews with their monstrous mythical beasts carved onto the ends by some perverse patron. No doubt their intention was to keep the peasants on their toes, focused on Jesus Christ, their only salvation, the light in this vaulted darkness. But, though Graham would call himself a saintly man, never one to stray far from the path of righteousness unless he'd had a pint too many down at The Griffin, the atrocious figurines would often pull his thoughts into childish dark places inhabited by Cthulhu, Krakens, creatures from the black lagoon and other demonic beasts. Entities, he believed, that had no place in a church.

Nor had the workshop helped his jitters. With the title 'On Fear and Building Suspense', he supposed it was never meant to.

It had, though, been very evocative and at several points during those ninety minutes he had thought about making his excuses and pelting back to Ratchette Hall. When one of the participants – the woman with the blue hair and New Age name – had called out the words that she swore summoned forth spirits from the tomb, much to his surprise he had felt a prickle of real fear crawl down his back, and a bleak sense of foreboding stole into his stomach. It had taken him quite a while, in the comfort of his study, to convince himself that the invocation had raised no more than the hairs on his neck.

'How silly,' he muttered as he drew the curtains in the day room. 'Of course it wouldn't have done.'

Having said that, it was a revelation to discover that fear and excitement were remarkably infectious if one opened one's mind to them. How the mystery writers lived like that was anybody's guess, he pondered, as he turned off the lights. They must be constantly jumpy, bags of nerves. He was glad he wasn't one. Especially not tonight. Still, All Hallows' Eve was nearly over and done with for the year. Thank goodness. They'd had quite a lot of those tiresome trick-or-treaters this time. Though it was just gone 11:30 now. There wouldn't be any more, thank goodness. They were well into the witching hour when naughty little children should be tucked up in bed. And grown-ups too.

He closed the door firmly.

In the large panelled hallway, a flickering sliver of tawny light was inching across the tiles.

Someone was still up in the sitting room. Fancy that. And he was so sure they had all retired. Now, which one of this motley crew were likely to be up? He'd put money on Nicholas, the young fop. Probably still at the whisky too. That lad had a wicked gleam in his eye, which Graham noticed, often roamed across the lithe form of the dark girl, Jocelyn. She was certainly lovely, with bright eyes, and a sparkling wit that betrayed her high IQ despite her attempts to conceal it. Yes, indeed, if he was younger and of the inclination, he might have lost his heart to her too.

But he was neither and wanted to go to bed.

One last job, then.

He put his hand to the brass door knob rubbed dull from centuries of use and entered the dimly lit room. The fire in the hearth was out, but someone had left a candle burning on the coffee table. Very irresponsible. He tutted. Halfway across the room he noticed a pair of slippers protruding from the bottom of the curtains. Strange.

Was someone playing a prank?

Had they concealed themselves behind the weighty fabric?

Perhaps they were about to jump out on him with a shriek, and laugh when they had succeeded in frightening him to death?

Graham craned his head. The footwear was smallish, fashioned from felt with a paisley pattern over the toe. Female, he thought. Which was also curious. For he couldn't imagine the older guests Tabitha, Imogen nor Margot might possibly be bothered enough to stay up alone and cold for the sake of a good joke.

No, he thought. That would be quite out of character.

Darn. He would just have to go over there and see who it was.

The caretaker took a deep breath and summoned his resolve.

Padding as quietly as he could, Graham reached the drapes.

If I whip them back without warning, he thought, this young comedian's trick might just backfire. They will be the one caught on the back foot, not I.

He grinned at the strategy and with nimble fingers caught hold of the velvet. Then in one swift continuous movement he jerked back the curtain.

To reveal ... nothing.

It was just a pair of slippers.

With no feet stuck into them.

Though relieved, he felt an immediate sense of irritation fire his stomach. Who would leave them there? Why? Had they intended to scare him?

He looked up and out the window towards the gates at the bottom of the drive and sighed. It was his imagination going into overdrive.

That was the problem with mystery-writing residencies. They got to you. So much more than the weekends with the literary luvvies, though those were not without their own set of vexations and prissy requirements. He didn't even mind the intense psycho-geographers and the creative non-fiction lot. Though he liked the ghost-writer courses most of all. That lot were always practical and straightforward. Normal. Thank goodness Write Retreats, the management organisation, didn't consider horror residentials. There was quite enough of that around the place already.

And, as he finished that thought, he realised his gaze had sailed out through the window to the darkness beyond the lawn, the murky and damp night. A spray of mist was curling in the distance. At least he thought that was what it was.

There was certainly something moving around out there. Greyish, he thought, or white like bone.

He shivered.

Best not to dwell.

His imagination had already played enough tricks on him today. He drew the curtain and went and snuffed the candle out.

It was as he was closing the sitting room door that he became aware of an odd irregular sound. A sort of scraping and clanging, like something metallic was being scratched along the walls of the house.

He stopped in the hallway and bent his ear as the unseen object grated on the bricks of the sitting room.

Good grief, what was it?

The jangling discordance of notes and textures was really quite horrible. And now seemed to be over in the drawing room too.

'Oh,' he realised with a shudder of apprehension. The drawing room. Not the sitting room any more. That meant what or whoever was making that infernal racket was getting much closer to where he stood.

His head darted to the door he had closed. Was that a cackle he heard in amidst the scraping? Somewhere under the window?

No, surely not.

But someone was responsible for that godawful racket.

Though who?

And, more to the point, why?

At this time of night?

Within a few seconds he realised that whatever was producing the din had turned the corner and was now screeching along the front of the house.

Towards the vestibule.

The entrance.

Only metres from where he stood.

Graham swallowed noisily. If this was some trick-or-treater he would find out who their parents were and report them first thing tomorrow morning.

Somehow, however, part of him knew no child could make that sound. There was too much, he paused to find the right word, too much blasted volume.

And it was coming from the portico now.

He heard the rattle of metal upon the stone steps as something heavy clattered to the ground. A deep and throaty howl went up somewhere outside.

Good grief – what a terrific noise. Why weren't the others waking up?

He looked up at the staircase expecting to see a gaggle of faces. But it was empty. Only a sudden silence now filled the space around him.

Graham became cripplingly aware of his solitude.

What if there was a burglar out there? Someone with malevolent intent?

He had never been a big man and knew he was unlikely to come out the victor should things turn physical.

But he could call the police, couldn't he? For backup? He felt in his jeans for his phone. Yes, it was there. He tapped it, reassured somewhat, and cast his glance to the front door.

To his horror a resounding boom, sudden and loud, vibrated through the hallway and all over the house.

Someone out there had swung the metal knocker. And hard too. They were strong and powerful.

Graham swallowed again.

And they were requesting to be let in.

He froze to the spot, unsure of what to do. If he opened the door, he risked letting an intruder into the hall.

If he let it remain closed then it was a slight upon the visitor. And what if the sounds they were making were born of despair? What if they needed help?

There came the rap again.

This time it prompted Graham into an almost Pavlovian reaction: he was the caretaker, the administrator, the guardian of Ratchette Hall, the famed Essex Writers Retreat. This is what he did: meeted, greeted, hosted, introduced. He opened doors, he welcomed in.

With tentative feet Graham went to the latch.

As his fingers fumbled with the key he heard a low spiteful groan. It was so loaded with belligerence it caused his heart to contract and skip a beat then gallop irregularly.

Though every nerve was jangling, every instinct within telling him to turn back the lock and run into the house, another voice in his head told him to be bold. 'This is your job. Your job.'

He took a steadying breath and, summoning the remnants of his bravery, he positioned his features to meet the stranger outside.

Shivering, he bit down on his fear and threw back the door.

Mist flooded in through the doorway.

As it began to clear, the sight on the porch clotted his blood.

Abject horror fastened itself upon him.

'No,' shrieked Graham and clutched at his throat. 'It cannot be.'

But it was.

And with one fearful frantic last splutter Graham's heart stopped dead.

CHAPTER ONE

'Earth to earth, ashes to ashes, dust to dust.'

Karen, the reverend, picked up a handful of soil and threw it over the small wooden box in the bottom of the grave. It made a quiet scattering sound. 'We therefore commit our sister and brother, Anne and Bartholomew's bodies to be buried.'

She gestured for Sam to repeat the gesture, which he did, and tossed a bouquet of roses into the grave.

I followed Bronson and then went and stood between Sam and Hecate, our Witch Museum cat, who had come out to oversee the proceedings. Gently I grabbed a handful of earth and threw it over the box. I too had assembled a bouquet: calla lilies for purity, chrysanthemums for loyalty and love. I threw in one of each flower. The rest of the bouquet would keep for the graveside.

'Trusting in the infinite mercy of God through Jesus our Lord. Amen,' said Karen finally.

We all said 'Amen', or mouthed it, then Karen sent a signal to Bronson who exchanged the bucket he was holding for a spade and began to shovel the earth into the grave.

I smiled at the group of twenty or so villagers and said, 'Okay, if you'd like to follow me we have light refreshments in the museum.'

To be honest I was quite impressed by the turnout. After all, Anne Hewghes and Bartholomew Elkes had died over 350 years ago, and weren't related to anyone present. As far as we knew. She was alleged to have been a witch and he had been a kind of astrologer, which was why they were being interred here, in the memorial garden of the Witch Museum rather than the churchyard in the village. Karen, our rev, was really quite cool, but higher up people still had funny views on this kind of thing.

But I didn't and neither did Sam, the museum's curator, nor Bronson, the caretaker. In fact, we were quite happy to look after these remains if no one else cared to. And we were a witch museum. Now complete with witches. Or at least those accused of the crimes of witchcraft. We were starting to like the fact we were a haven of sorts. Someone had to be, right?

Our little party made our way into the back of the museum to the Talks Area where the chairs had been arranged round tables, and Vanessa, one of our regular employees alongside her mum, Trace, were ready to serve teas, coffees, sandwiches, cakes, plus wine and beer for those who needed a bit of the strong stuff. One of whom was me.

I was about to go over and get a glass when I was intercepted by Karen. She was a middle-aged woman with coarse grey hair and kind blue eyes. I thanked her for saying a few words. She hadn't been too sure about it first of all. Mostly because she wondered if Anne and Bartholomew would have wanted a Christian burial. We'd decided, after a very long discussion, that they had probably identified as such, seeing as there weren't really many, indeed any, alternatives back then. Karen had managed to wangle a way of being attendant at the burial. 'I'll commend them to God. It's up to them if they want to go to him,' she'd told me.

'Or her,' I'd added.

Seeing as we were at a funeral I thought she was going straight into funeral talk but she didn't. Instead she asked me how my mum was.

'Which one?' I said, honestly. It was complicated, a bit of a moot point.

Her eyes widened and I detected behind them the slip of disapproval. 'Maureen of course,' she said. 'The one who raised you and loved you.'

My real mother, the biological one, it transpired recently was actually Celeste Strange, sister to Ted and daughter to my grandfather Septimus. But Karen was right – it was Maureen who I called 'Mum'. The rev had got to know my parents quite well over the last few months, since we discovered the remains of my long-lost grandmother, Ethel-Rose Strange.

Dad had wanted them reunited with those of his own father, Septimus Strange, who was legally, and with the full sanction of the diocese, buried in the Adder's Fork graveyard, just outside the village. It had taken more loop-jumping and reams of bureaucratic intervention, but we had managed it in the end and Ethel-Rose had been laid to rest with her husband last month in a moving service that half the town had attended. And quite rightly too, for some of them, I thought, had probably been complicit. Maybe without even knowing it. Today's committal had brought back memories. Ergo – the wine.

'Mum's fine,' I said to Karen. 'Thanks.'

'And your dad?'

'He's got the all-clear from the doctors. Needs to watch his blood pressure. But it looks like he's in rude health.'

She nodded. 'And your Auntie Babs?'

'Even ruder.'

Karen laughed. 'Yes,' she mused. 'I can imagine. I thought she might be here?'

'She's got a full day at the salon. Halloween's busy for her.'

'But that was yesterday?' Karen raised an eyebrow.

'Yeah. Halloween celebrations go on for a while these days, don't they?'

She tutted. 'I do wish people would concentrate their efforts on today. November the first is All Saints' Day. So much more wholesome than witches and ghouls. Oh sorry, I didn't mean to offend ...'

'S'okay,' I grunted vaguely. 'There's a fundraising ball going on in Lower Wigchuff tonight. The Monster Mash-Up, or something like that.'

Karen sighed. 'Popular, I suppose?'

'Yeah,' I said. 'Well, they've got a prize for the best costume: an evening with Michael Bublé.'

'Really?' said Karen with more energy this time. Her other eyebrow whizzed up to match its sister.

She was looking more interested than a woman of the cloth ought. 'Sorry, a Michael Bublé *lookalike*,' I added and watched her features sag slightly. But not enough, if you asked me. 'All the village ladies of a certain age are wetting themselves.' I managed to stop myself from adding 'literally'.

'Yes,' said Karen with a quick intake of breath. 'I can imagine. How much are tickets?'

'I think it's sold out. Sorry.'

'Oh no,' she said quickly. 'It's not for me. I have a friend who …'

'Yeah, yeah,' I said. 'Do you want a drink? I'm getting a white?'

'I'll have a cup of tea if it's on offer,' she said quite properly.

I fetched our refreshments then went off to make small talk with some of the other guests: villagers, forensic experts, eco-protestors and police, all of whom had something to do with Anne and Bartholomew. Seemed appropriate that they should come along and I think in some way they all felt that it was important to pay their respects and see the last part of their story told.

Before I could say 'More tea vicar?' Sam had trotted into the room wagging his phone at me. I wondered if that meant it was time to wind up the wake and get the decorations in.

'Put that down,' he said and pointed at my glass. He could be such a puritan at times. And a very bossy one at that.

'No,' I said. It was my habit to dig in my heels and object even if it was possibly illogical. I didn't like taking orders from members of the patriarchy. Who does? And sometimes it was important to make that point. Of course sometimes it was not. And sometimes my choice was dangerous and stupid and a little bit life-endangering. But, you know, a girl's gotta kick against the pricks. Quite often they didn't even realise they were being one.

'Sam,' I said, holding on to my glass. 'It's okay. We don't have to be stone cold sober to take the cobwebs down.'

He rolled his eyes and hissed, 'It's Monty.' Then he pointed at the phone. Sure enough there on the screen Montgomery Walker's name and number was boldly displayed.

Monty was our contact in the Occult Bureau in MI5, or possibly MI6. I wasn't sure which – I'd never been good at maths. Anyway, he ran some kind of secret department which looked into weird stuff, so of course there had to be a connection to the Witch Museum, didn't there? I had discovered that my grandfather Septimus had done work for them, but in more of a freelance capacity. And my family had been on their radar for quite a while, for varying reasons. Seriously, this year had been a TOTAL revelation. You have no idea. And Monty had been a bit of an enabler in that regard.

'So?' I said. 'Hello Monty,' scintillating conversationist, that I am.

'He wants to talk to us,' said Sam.

'No kidding,' I said, still a bit sore about the wine-ceasing instruction.

He screwed his eyes up. 'Office, now!' Then he turned on his rather smart Cuban heels and sped off in that direction. He'd dressed up for the burial in a black suit and tie, which I thought was kind of decent of him really. He looked good in them too. If he didn't then I'd have given him more of a mouthful. At the same time, it was fair to say that I was beginning to understand the curator better and cutting him a bit of slack accordingly. Whenever he was fixated on something it used up all his mental energy and didn't leave any brain space for manners and cordiality and other such trifles. I guessed whatever Monty had told him had pressed his buttons and piqued his interest. Which was all rather ominous.

With a sigh, I clip-clopped over to Vanessa. I was wearing a pair of new black heels which hadn't had an outing so far. They looked utterly breathtaking – all shiny patent leather with little straps at the sides. Though they were putting my toes through hell. When I reached the pop-up bar I eased one foot out and rubbed it while I asked our mother-and-daughter hospitality team if they could hold the fort for a mo. Which they could of course, so I hobbled around the museum for a bit till I located Sam in the office-cum-dining-room-cum-staff-room-cum-kitchen-cum-reception.

He was sitting at the long table currently laid for tea and had plonked his mobile in the middle of it.

'It's quite important,' Monty was bleating tinnily through the microscopic speaker. 'You know I wouldn't ask unless it was.'

I tucked my skirt between my legs (I'm a lady, right), got my feet on the table, then prised off the black stilettos.

'Bad luck to put new shoes on the table,' said Sam.

'Not that you believe in any of that superstitious nonsense.'

I shrugged. 'Whatever.' And chucked them on the rug. Then I directed my voice to the microphone. 'What's up, Mr Walker?'

'Hello Rosie,' he said. I could imagine him at his desk, which I had never seen, but pictured vividly whenever I heard his phone voice. In my head he was settling his elbows on racing-green leather, twirling a fountain pen in his fingers, in front of elegant bookshelves crammed with learned tomes, himself all suave suited and booted. Just like Sam was now.

'He needs a favour,' said my nearest and dearest and then made a circling gesture for me to get my feet off the table. Did I tell you he was bossy?

I continued in my refusal to bow to the patriarchy and transferred my gaze to the phone and the imagined office at MI5. 'A favour?' I repeated.

Now that was a thing. A thoroughly interesting thing.

See, I was considering delving deeper into the nature of my mother's death. My biological one. My Dad's sister, Celeste. And possibly my father's too. Whoever he was. Not the person I called 'Dad', who was my uncle. I told you it was complicated.

But I wasn't getting far and had an idea in my mind which might require the help of our friend in Intelligence. All of which meant that really, we, or at least, I, certainly should be ensuring we kept Monty sweet.

'What kind of favour?' I asked, smiling hard so you could hear it in my voice.

Despite the fact he was sitting down Sam put his hands on his hips, which meant he was a little put out. Though I wasn't sure why. Maybe he had already said no.

'A kind of "drop what you're doing favour",' Sam interjected flatly and then tutted.

'Indeed,' said Monty. 'We have a bit of a situation in a village not far from you.'

'Haven?' asked Sam.

'No. Not that village. Damebury. Some poor old chap's met his end.'

Sam's already deep frown got even deeper.

I made an 'eh?' face at the phone. 'Not being funny, Monty, but people pop their clogs all the time. That's why we've got the police and hospital and coroner's department, right?'

'Yes, yes, of course.' The sibilance in his voice made the speaker crackle. 'This one's rather different. They're saying it's natural causes. A trick-or-treat prank that got out of hand. But, well …' Monty paused. 'Some people on the course …'

'The course?' I interrupted.

'Residential writers retreat,' Sam whispered.

'Yes, that's right. Indeed,' Monty chimed in down the line, the audio balance of his voice restored to parity. 'Some of the participants believe that not to be the case.'

My turn to frown now. 'Well, they should take that up with the police then, shouldn't they?'

Monty hesitated. 'There are a few of them that believe he may have intentionally been, er, scared to death.'

'Really?' I said, surprised to hear Monty voice it like that.

'And,' he continued. 'It sounds like their theory is being given short shrift by the local constabulary who favour natural causes. A coronary.'

Yes, well with mounting paperwork and budget cuts you could see how that might be preferable.

Sam took his hands off his hips, leant forwards over the table and tapped it. 'But you're calling *us* Monty,' he said. 'Which I presume means you also have doubts that the death isn't as straightforward as the police might think.'

'No. Quite right, Sam,' he replied. 'Interestingly, I had a feeling that something like this might happen back in June. Remember Rosie, when I gave you *that* file, I said I might need a favour soon.'

That file had been full of confidential information, some portion of which had led me to discover not only my grandmother's remains, but her murderer too. As return favours went, this was therefore a hard one to refuse. 'I don't remember you saying that, but I know I owe you.'

'Splendid.' His tinny voice crackled the speaker again. 'I'll tell Tabby you'll be there in an hour.'

'Hang on!' said Sam. 'We're holding a wake here, Monts, old man.' Mr Walker's poshness appeared to have become contagious. 'We've got to take the Halloween decorations down.'

There was a pause. 'You have Halloween decorations at your wake?' Monty rasped.

I tutted loudly. 'Had them up yesterday of course! We're a witch museum. Halloween's our busiest time of year,' I said, unable to supress my sarcasm. 'And there's a tradition going on in Adder's Fork. This lot – Sam and Bronson and Septimus, when he was alive – they used to stock up on sweeties and decorate the entrance. The rest of the museum closes at five, but the lobby stays open and gets stuffed with cats, broomsticks, dry ice, cackling voices and scary witchfinders – you know the score. Visiting children go off with a handful of sweets and a quick lecture on how most women accused of witchcraft were not witches at all, but victims of injustice, scapegoating and bullying.' I winked at Sam who nodded, his face neither approving nor irritated. 'They come back year after year. Which is a miracle in itself.'

Sam sniffed at my last comment with pretend disdain. 'And we didn't have time to take the decorations down before the wake. Not that anyone minded. There's no close relatives around any more,' he said.

'Well if there aren't close relatives, can't Bronson play host?' Monty cried.

'The thing is, Monty,' I piped up, 'we've spent some time reorganising the lobby. We've got rid of the old Inquisition exhibit.'

'Stored it,' Sam added.

'And we have some panels now which talk about the link between Essex Girls and Essex Witches.'

'With a photograph of her friend, Cerise,' Sam added.

'And,' I continued, 'it's really important that we get it sorted for tomorrow because the museum's open again at ten. That doesn't leave us much time—'

'Look here,' Monty interjected. 'I'm most anxious that you go over and do some digging. Just find out about the other people on the course. See if anyone has a motive to get rid of the administrator chap who's died. As quick as you can please, Tabby is most aerated.'

'Who the hell is Tabby?' I asked, severely nonplussed.

'My dear maiden aunt,' said Monty. 'On my father's side.

She's one of the students at Ratchette Hall in Damebury. It's the Essex Writers Retreat.'

'Oh hang on,' I said. 'The Essex Writers House? I thought that had just opened in Southend? Has residencies, courses, places to stay, talks, quizzes. All sounds quite fun?'

'No,' snapped Monty. 'That's separate. Though I think they may have some relationship with Ratchette Hall, they are quite quite different. These guys in Damebury are far more upmarket – £700 and upwards for the week.'

'Blimey,' I said. 'So it's for rich people?'

'My aunt is not rich, Rosie. Just interested and able to afford it. Anyway, this is getting off point. It's quite spooked her, this business. And I'll tell you something – she has great instincts has Aunt Tabby. If she smells a rat there's probably a colony of them under the floorboards. You'd be wise to find her and see what she makes of all of this.'

I sized up the open blister on my big toe and thought about hurrying to the writers retreat on it. It wasn't particularly appealing. 'Oh Monty, can't you sort it out? I'm sure you've got cronies you could despatch to investigate this sort of thing.'

'Otherwise engaged tonight,' he said.

'Us too,' said Sam and scowled.

'And, everyone else,' Monty increased the bass in his voice, 'is up to date with favours dispensed and repaid. Apart from you, dearest Rosie.'

There was silence as we all considered the impasse. Though a thought occurred to me as I considered Monty's words.

'We'll do it,' I said, to Sam's surprise. 'But,' I added, 'I'd like another favour in return.'

'Rosie, you're a tinker, aren't you?' said Monty. 'What's that?'

I took my feet off the table and leant closer to the mic. 'I'd like to meet Big Ig.'

'Big Ig!' Monty and Sam exclaimed at the same time.

'That's right,' I added. 'Is he still alive?'

'How do you know about Big Ig?' Monty was clearly gobsmacked.

'Sam told me. Ages ago. And I've got a good head for names. Especially if they're weird like that. Ignatius, Big Ig, he was your predecessor Monty. I'm right, aren't I?'

There was no noise from his end of the line. I imagined him nodding mutely, mouth open. Possibly catching flies.

'Which means,' I continued, ignoring Sam shaking his head, 'that he was probably in office about the time Celeste died. And Araminta de Vere …' (a woman who had tried to kill me recently) '… said that she drove Celeste and her "partner", presumably my dad, into a tree. I've checked that out though. In the news report it stated that only Celeste drowned in her car. No mention of any partner. Or who he might have been.' Have I told you my life was complicated?

I waited for a response, but neither Sam nor Monty appeared inclined to make one.

'I figure Big Ig might know more on the matter,' I finished. 'More, probably, than you might locate in your files, Monty.'

Still nothing from his end of the line.

'He's not dead is he?' I added.

'No,' said Monty. 'Not yet. Retired. Enjoying golf. And peace.'

'Sort of then. Can you get me a meeting please? And we'll nip over to …' I paused. 'Where is this writers place again?'

There was a crumbling sound on the phone line. Monty consulting a map or unfolding paper. 'Damebury,' he said. 'Not more than five miles from you. It's hardly a bother.'

'Okay,' I said firmly, trying to wrap it up. 'So, is it a deal?'

Sam wrapped his arms over his chest and sucked in his mouth.

'It's a deal,' said Monty over the phone.

Sam sighed and said wearily into the microphone, 'Give us the address then.'

I got up and smiled. 'Thank you.' Then, leaving my shoes on the rug, I hobbled back into the museum to find Bronson. It would be a hard sale, but if I could persuade Vanessa and Trace to help him clear up, then I thought the caretaker would be all right with our unexpected desertion.

He would have to be.

I was going to Damebury.

I'd unpick what was happening there, then Ignatius would help unpick my own private enigma.

CHAPTER TWO

'But we're a team,' Sam was saying. 'You should have consulted me. *Before* you made the final decision. And the speed limit here is forty.'

'I know,' I said. 'I've seen the sign.'

'Observe it then,' he retorted. Sam was at his most irritating in cars. Mostly when I was driving.

'All right, all right.' I didn't hold back with my tone. 'I can't just slam on the brakes.'

'Well, ease off on the accelerator.' He leant back into the seat, his chest puffing out as he did so. It was broad and hard. I'd felt it once, when he'd climbed onto my bed. Not like that. In hospital. Both of us had been too ragged to do anything but lie there. I sighed at the thought of it.

'I don't know what you're sighing about,' he said. 'Speed limits are there for a reason.' I could feel his eyes on my cheek. I didn't want to see what his face looked like. 'And the other issue?' he said. 'The consultation. Or lack of?'

I depressed my foot lightly on the brakes to please him and said, 'Yes, all right. I know you're right. But there's such a lot that I've got to find out about my family I have to take these opportunities when they are presented. No one else is going to grab them for me. If you ever have anything happen to you like this, then you'll understand.'

He didn't say anything back. But my words seemed to touch a nerve, for he pulled away, hiding his face, and gazed through the window at the darkening landscape. I knew he was brooding. Though, at that point, I thought it was because he couldn't argue with me. That I had the upper hand with the family thing. Of course, I was wrong, but I didn't know then what I know now. Though, as Arthur Conan Doyle pointed out, it's easier to be wise after the event. Beforehand you are just simply … unwise. And like I said, this was well before it.

'Turn here,' he said a few minutes later and prodded his phone. 'You're not the only one with …' he paused, 'family …' he stopped again, selecting the right word, 'issues.'

It was one of the first clues.

'I'm not?' I framed it as a question and waited.

'You're not,' he said and pointed over the road. 'Slow down. There's the drive for Ratchette Hall.'

A small road on the right-hand side of the lane appeared in a line of trees. Their leaves waved us a welcome, showing off autumn's full palette: amber, rust, ochre, mustard. Mother Nature had a good eye for colour. She could have been a stylist.

I spied a white gate propped open by a brick. 'So what are yours? Your family issues?' I probed as I swung the car in.

The tyres crunched across tiny pebbles. A couple of them scattered and hit the bodywork. I took the speed right down and we bounced over a few potholes up to the rather grand porch. It was tall and white. A triangle of stone was held up by two thick white columns and illuminated by a large Victorian-style glass lantern.

Sam frowned. 'Not now. Another time.' Then he raised a hand to halt my 'but why?' as it formed in my mouth. 'I will say this – when you make these decisions without consulting me, sometimes, you know …' he shrugged and cast his eyes at me.

'Sometimes what?' I said.

'Sometimes, well, a few times now, you could have ended up dead.'

'Ah, yes,' I said. 'That. You're such a stickler for health and safety, Samuel Stone. Really you are.'

A hint of a smile escaped the left side of his lips and dimpled his cheek. 'Am I wrong though, Rosie Strange?'

I would have liked to have said, yes, but he wasn't.

There had been that time with the Serbian mafia and accompanying evil alchemists. Unfortunately, one of them had shot at me, which like it or not, did put that particular scenario into the 'life-threatening/possible death' category that he was talking about. But that was it, I thought, then remembered more recently a couple of villagers had drugged me, put me in a shed, doused me in petrol then attempted to set me on fire. Which possibly also embodied 'threat to kill'. Then there was that guy in the cellar with the sex trafficking … but, you know, these were details. You could get bogged down with them. 'Unlucky, that's all,' I managed.

He shook his head, tawny hair tumbling down over his ears. Needed a trim. 'And if, as Monty has suggested,' he was saying, 'there is something less than straightforward here, then we must think about our safety. That was the point I was trying to make. We need to consider things carefully, weigh up the pros and cons. Not rush into decisions.'

'We're here,' I said and got out of the car to shut him up. The bloke had a point, but he could go on a bit. 'Come on Sam.' I strode up to the entrance porch and rang the bell, then stepped back and let my eyes roam over the place. Encircled now by a flimsy mist, the house wouldn't have been out of place in a Dickens novel. Although I'm no expert on architecture, I think its build may have been Georgian. For it had large sash windows, a bundle of chimney pots on the roof and, though half of it was ivy-clad, you could still see tell-tale reddish bricks fashioned from the London Clay that had once been so popular in the area. The hall was elegant from what I could see, and large and uncluttered. Without whimsy. A good solid building with a small extension to the side. The kind of thing I might buy if I ever won the lottery.

'And this,' said Sam, catching me up, and poking a finger in my ribs. His eyes had gone all stormy again. 'This is what I'm talking about. What happened to casing the joint before making contact, eh?'

I winced. That term was so clichéd and American. 'I forgot.' I hadn't, but we could do that later. In fact, I'd insist on a tour once we were inside. The place looked rambling. It would be necessary to orientate oneself. I was guessing there were at least three reception rooms downstairs if not more. And it had another two storeys on top of that. A posh person's house. Or had been once upon a time. Lord Ratchette's I expected. Now that was a good name for a baddie. Bet he was too. My experience with lords of various manors hadn't been so good lately.

Or ever, come to think of it.

'Rosie please,' Sam said, emphasising the sibilance of my name, 'come on. Work with me here.'

I refocused on his face. 'I plan to,' I said and stroked his arm. 'Honest. I promise to consult you about everything from here on in. All right?'

He nodded, only half convinced.

'But I want to hear about your family issues sometime, yeah? You know an awful lot about mine.'

Again, he looked away, his eyes travelling past the car, over the lawn, into the trees that lined the lane. Darkness was netting them fully now but you could still see their black outlines. Above their fluttering tops the stars were beginning to come out. Hallowmas Night was upon us and a touch of frost was in the air.

Before Sam could answer, a woman in her late thirties answered the door and coughed, not to draw our attention but because she was wheezing.

'Sorry,' she said. 'Tail end of a cold.'

'Hi,' I said. 'It's Rosie and Sam. We're the investigators from the Witch Museum. Agent Walker called us in.'

The woman had fine blonde hair, held off her forehead by an Alice band, and a doll-like face which crunched into a frown of confusion. 'Agent Walker?' she said, not budging or inviting us in. 'I'm not sure I know Agent Walker …'

Before she could continue, another little figure had shuffled up to the door, an older lady who only came up to the height of the door knocker, with grey hair in a bun, navy chinos and a sweatshirt with a picture of the *Mona Lisa* on the front. With one quick movement of her hip, the newcomer, nudged the door-hogger out of the way, reached out and grabbed my hand.

'Excellent, excellent,' she said. I noted she had a very firm grip for someone of advanced years (she had to be in her seventies). 'Come, come,' she insisted and pulled me and beckoned Sam in. Then she looked up at the door-hogger. 'Oh Sophia, do get out of the way. These are the people I was telling you about. Now be a good girl and put the kettle on. They'll be wanting refreshment after their long journey. Let's go into the day room and see the others,' she said to me and winked. 'It's the cosiest.'

The Sophia-woman's mouth dropped open briefly. She hesitated for an even briefer moment, then exhaled loudly, peeved, and stepped aside so we could enter.

The hallway we found ourselves in was not as grand as the exterior might have suggested. It wasn't shabby, just functional. An elaborate chandelier hung down in the centre. Meticulously clean and gleaming, however some of the crystal parts were missing. The hall walls were a plain whitewash. Despite its charming appearance there was something in the atmosphere here that made me shudder. A vague sort of lurking feeling that was not pleasant but disturbing. I felt a flutter of anxiety, but it went as soon as it came.

The only furniture in the lobby was an occasional table with a deep mahogany finish. The place had a kind of lived-in stately home feel, which was accentuated by a quaint old-fashioned telephone that perched on the table, above which hung an antique gold-framed mirror. I checked my lipstick. All good. Across from us a rather elegant wooden staircase led to the next floors but I couldn't take in any more detail because the fierce dwarf-woman was pinching me in the back, and simultaneously directing me to a room with a wood-panelled door in the corner.

'Go, go,' she said. 'In here. That's it.'

The air pressure changed as the front door slammed shut. Our footsteps echoed across the chequerboard marble tiles. I was pleased I'd got out of my heels and into my purple cowboy boots. They had good grip and it looked rather slippery down there. Gleaming with polish. Someone had certainly looked after it well.

We entered a large room and said hello to the three people who were sitting there on an assortment of armchairs and sofas. Everything was positioned to face a well-made fire spluttering in the hearth. A brass bucket of kindling and a coal scuttle stood sentry either side. On the mantel-piece an antique sword was displayed, propped up on two mounts. It looked old. I took a step closer to inspect it. The weapon was really quite substantial, about two and a half feet long and in good condition with a distinct edge. The handle had been restored with a sturdy leather covering. At the end of that there was a sort of round bit, in the middle of which was a crucifix. Though to me, it looked upside down. Depends on which way you were looking at it, I supposed. Odd though.

'Yes,' said the spry little lady. 'Interesting isn't it? Still bites,' she said with a grin. 'Not surprised you went straight to it. You have a sense for these things, I expect. What with your occupation. My nephew's the same. That sword,' she said nodding towards it, 'was found in one of the knights' tombs. You know,' she said and jerked her head towards the door. 'At St Saviour's, down the road. There are reminders of them everywhere round here. That neat little blade is said to have been pulled from the body of a six-headed serpent in Antioch. Whoever holds it can conquer all their foes. Of course there's a price to pay – your soul.' She grinned and revealed a full set of teeth. Or possibly dentures. Maybe implants. 'Flies off straight to Satan of course,' she continued, oblivious to my dental check. 'The priest who found it wouldn't have the thing in the church. Sold it to the lord of the manor down at Wooden Ferret. The family got rid of it after he stabbed his brother in the throat. Thought it had something to do with the curse. And somehow it ended up here. Very impressive I think. You can see the workmanship. It's lasted for centuries.'

I looked at it again; it was elegant and certainly powerful. You could sense it rippling the air around it. I wondered how heavy it was and put my hand out to touch it but Tabby said, 'Later. Come, come,' and directed me and Sam to a vacant padded stool and armchair that were situated close to the fire. She settled herself in a nearby two-seater next to a silver-haired woman, who, though visibly younger than her, seemed to have half the older woman's energy. The woman stirred in her chair and blinked, like a giant tortoise coming out of hibernation.

'This is Imogen Green,' said the little lady and poked her fireside companion. Imogen manoeuvred a chubby moon face out from her oval body and sniffed the air. Bulgy eyes swivelled over us. 'She's psych thrillers.'

'Really?' I said. She did not look particularly psychologically thrilling. Still, there's none stranger than folk. Apart from me. And although I am Strange by name I am completely normal by nature. People just fail to realise this.

Imogen nodded her big bulbous head. 'It's an increasingly popular genre,' she said between yawns. 'Which means increasing readership. My work in progress is all about a woman who thinks she's woken up in someone else's body.'

Yes, I could imagine the concept appealing to her. Not everyone could be as blessed in that department as my good lady self. Though there were some basic mistakes people could make: this one's roughly cut bob looked self-inflicted. There was something very Richard the Third about the style she'd given herself.

The little woman next to her wriggled and nodded brightly and said, 'Imogen's idea is marvellous. Could be a tricky execution.' Her eyes twinkled and she slipped a wry smile. 'Which brings me to the point. Some of us think that is exactly what has happened to poor poor Graham. An execution. Of the phantom kind.'

It was all getting a bit difficult to follow. 'Sorry,' I said. 'Who is Graham?' Then I stopped. 'No hang on – first things first – who are you?'

Her smile widened. 'Me? Why, I'm Tabitha Walker of

course. Call me Tabby. Montgomery's aunt. I thought he might have briefed you? Or sent over a file of some sort. I'm sure he must have one on me, actually.' She tapped her nose. 'Used to dabble with communism, back in the day, oh yes. I'm sure they bugged me. Monty is so clever with that sort of thing. Gadgets. A bit Q. You know – the Quartermaster.' She finished tapping and winked. 'Do you like Ian Fleming? I find him rather pedestrian I'm afraid.'

I could see a resemblance to her nephew in the slightly beaky nose, but not much more than that. Monty was a tall man, broad shouldered, and his aunt was, well, neither. She peered at us over half-moon glasses with an expression that indicated immense interest in our coming response.

I was a bit dazed by her conversational quicksilver, so just tackled the last question. 'I prefer contemporary fiction.'

Imogen started. One of her eyebrows twitched. 'Do you like crime?' she asked. There was a lilt there, definitely north of the border. The border being Watford.

'Well,' I said. 'I'm on a sabbatical from Benefit Fraud, so I'm kind of dependent on it for a living. Liking it is neither here nor there. It happens. Like the proverbial brown stuff.'

'I think Imogen, I think she's referring to the genre – crime fiction,' said Tabby, then lowered her voice to a whisper. 'She's obsessed,' she said to me, even though her neighbour could hear.

Her words made Imogen smile and reveal two weird rows of little triangular teeth.

I tried not to shudder.

'Well, yes, I do like the genre,' I told the bulb-headed

one. 'Spent my early teens tearing through Agatha Christie, Margery Allingham, Josephine Tey ...'

'All women,' said the only man in the room. Apart from Sam. He was thin and bald, and wearing a jumper that would have looked better on Sarah Lund. He shook his head in weariness and rolled his eyes.

'I like James Ellroy?' I offered.

'Don't we all?' he said in a mocking tone. Or was it just because he was Scottish? Sometimes accents can play havoc with emphasis.

I decided to err on the side of caution. 'And who are you?'

'Robin Savage,' he said with a nod. 'Yes, as in Savage Books.' Then he closed his eyelids and fluttered them for a bit.

I looked at Sam who shrugged. Neither of us had heard of him.

A quick scan of Mr Savage's clothes revealed him to be a sartorial conservative with an average standard of hygiene, but I got nothing more. My senses were sluggish. I think, in retrospect, they had been numbed by the events of the summer, but at that point I just thought I was being lazy. Robin Savage looked like an ordinary middle-aged man with no distinguishing features other than an old-fashioned habit of combing hair over his bald pate. Which was noticeable because you never really saw that any more. Men these days seemed to go straight for the clippers when male pattern hair loss reared its bald pate. I didn't mind bald heads. But I preferred them auburn and flaming and attached to curators of witch museums.

'And this,' said Tabby pointing to a long Chesterfield pushed against the far wall, 'is Starla Ocean.'

She was the youngest of the three, perhaps mid-thirties, with straggly blue hair and matching eyes, wearing a velvet skirt with symbols of the zodiac embroidered on it. Not expertly either. Probably a home-made jobbie.

'Blessings,' she said. 'I hope you can help restore this place of sanctuary to harmony.'

Oh dear.

'Yes,' said Tabby. 'They will, won't you?' Without waiting for an answer, she ploughed on. 'Nicholas and Jocelyn are smoking in the garden.' She gestured out the window. 'Cullen and Laura have gone out for a walk to clear their heads. And Margot is writing upstairs in her room. She's taken the whole thing quite badly.'

'And what is the "whole thing"?' asked Sam, taking the stool next to me. He looked very business-like in that suit, borderline suave. I reckon we both did. I didn't brush up too badly after all, and despite the fact I'd changed my stilettos for the purple boots, I reckoned I could still rock my own black suit. Maybe we'd have to start wearing that sort of thing for assignments like this. Although Monty had told us that this evening's manoeuvres were strictly off-record and unassigned. Completely deniable in the event of anyone finding out our expenses were being covered.

'Graham Peacock has met with a foul end.' This from Robin, who lingered on the last word and then enlarged upon the drama with, 'An unnatural end, for sure.' He stood up and went to the windows that backed onto what I assumed was the garden. 'Tell them Tabby. Tell them what's happened.'

But it was blue-haired Starla who spoke. 'Dark forces have risen around us.' The lingering twangs of an Australian accent were evident now as she spoke. Her voice was low and rich but it quavered a little. 'I am sorry that I may have had a hand in that.' Her fingers trembled and flew to her face where they fastened on a cheek and chin. 'Yesterday,' she gulped, eyes almost pleading with me and Sam. 'In the church I chanted an incantation for renewal and regeneration. But it was about the dead ... I hope I didn't ... you know ... upset Graham ...'

Robin turned to her and then went and sat in one of several high-back chairs tucked under a wooden table at the back of the room, so his posture was more upright and rigid. 'Yes, why *did* you do that, Starla?' His eyes narrowed accusingly. 'Ah thought it odd at the time and ah think it odd now.'

Starla's voice turned bleatingly high. 'It was all about the season. Halloween is the end of one year and Hallowmas the beginning of the new. I thought it a way of registering that change. 'Tis the season in which we move towards rebirth and light.'

Robin shook his head, 'As the nights grow longer and the solstice approaches? The shortest day of the year! Ach, I dinna believe you.'

Clearly affronted, Starla got to her feet. Her heavy skirts swayed and shook as she spoke. 'It's true, I tell you.'

'Look,' said Sam, standing up and going over to calm her.

'Let's all take a breath,' he glared at Robin, 'and start at the beginning. When did this course begin? What day did you get here?'

He had said it gently to Starla but Robin rolled his eyes and replied. 'We arrived at varying times on Sunday afternoon or evening. Graham met us then showed each guest to their room for the week. We are meant to leave next Sunday but …' he trailed off and looked at the floor. 'Ah, suppose, now it'll be cut short. What with poor Graham …'

Imogen's voice rang out like a bell, a large one, like Big Ben, with a low pitch. 'The course started on Monday proper. We had a session in the morning with Laura where we talked about what we wanted to get out of the week …'

'Laura?' Sam interrupted.

Tabby piped up. 'Laura, our tutor. Her pen name is L.D. Taylor-Jacobs. Very accomplished in her genre.'

'Which is?' I enquired.

Robin huffed out a sigh and crossed his short, corduroy legs. 'Crime, mystery, etc.,' he said and did an even bigger eye-roll with an extra eyelid flutter.

'Oh right.' I took my notebook out. 'We've just arrived. Assume we know nothing.'

'That's not hard,' he muttered under his breath.

'Okay.' My fingers twitched themselves into a V. But not for victory. So I put a pen in them and began writing down the names. 'Laura = L.D. Taylor-Jacobs. Crime writer.' That figured.

'It was during the afternoon that the tone of events started to darken,' Tabby picked up. 'Laura had arranged for us to do our session in St Saviour's. It's very atmospheric.'

'The light was fading fast,' said Starla, her fingers fraying the bottom of her skirt. 'We all knew it was Halloween. But you could *feel* there was something in the air, something preternatural was stirring.'

Robin sighed. 'Blue hair, purple prose. Laura,' he went on, 'had chosen the setting on purpose of course. And it was stimulating too. Ma writing in the afternoon gave rise to a piece which referenced Arthurian legends. Very good work too.'

I scrunched my forehead. 'Why? Is that what you're writing about? King Arthur? Don't sound very crimey.'

'No,' he said tersely. 'Ah'm saying the *setting* brought the quality to the writing.'

I still didn't get it. 'But how?'

'The tombs,' he said and gestured angrily towards the door. 'The famous tombs! In the church.'

Tabby coughed and lengthened her spine. 'Ms Strange and Mr Stone may not have heard the stories,' she pointed out.

It occurred to me now that we had never actually introduced ourselves but Tabby knew our names. *She* had evidently been briefed by Monty.

'Call me Rosie,' I said and sent her a grateful grin. 'And he's just Sam.'

'Well, Rosie Strange and "Just Sam",' said Robin in something of a patronising fashion. 'You should have heard about the tombs.'

'St Saviour's,' said Sam and wiggled his index finger at him. 'Yes, yes. Of course! The pickled knights of Damebury. But I thought that story went back to the eighteenth century?'

'Clearly not,' said Robin and drummed his fingers on his kneecap.

'What's with the pickled knights?' I asked Sam. 'More attractive than onions? Or are we talking winos here?'

Then I cast a glance at Starla just in case she was going to take offence to the term and insist on calling them sobriety-impaired or something. People these days could be very touchy about the most unexpected of words.

But it was Robin who tutted, then reached into a pile of papers on the table. 'Read this,' he said and thrust a photocopied sheet into my hands. It looked like an ancient tract, headed *Curious Leaden Coffin Found in Damebury, Essex*. There were however lots of curly bits in the script that made deciphering the text quite hard.

I handed it to the expert who said, 'My, my, my. Haven't seen this for a while.'

'What's it about?' I asked.

'Ah yes,' said Sam and began. 'It refers to an incident at the church in 1779.'

'Specifically the sixteenth of October. Just in time for Halloween,' Robin chimed in the blue-haired woman's direction.

Starla caught his glance and said with pointed determination, 'As the veil between worlds grows thin.'

Robin tutted again. Both Tabby and Starla scowled.

Averting another imminent combustion Sam went on, 'Some diggers were working on the north aisle of the church, preparing a grave for an esteemed lady of the parish. As they dug deep into the ground they struck upon something hard. When they started to clear it, what emerged from the earth was an effigy of a man in stone dressed in armour. Certainly a crusader, perhaps even one of the Knights Templar. It was remarkable. About thirty inches beneath the effigy they came upon a lead coffin. Lead! Strange in itself, however it turned out to be the beginnings of a Russian Doll!'

'Do you mean a nesting Russian Doll of coffins?' I asked, thinking that was a totally brilliant idea for museum merchandise. Visiting goths would go wild for them. I filed it under 'Ways to Get Rich Quick' in my mental filing cabinet, above 'Selling the Witch Museum'.

Sam nodded. 'I do.' His eyes were sparkling and full of energy. It was weird but, just then, they made me suddenly feel sad. 'That outer layer,' he said, 'was consequently opened to reveal a further oak coffin, then a powerful seal of resinous quality.'

I sighed out my sadness unconsciously but then tried to disguise it by commenting on what Sam had said. 'Someone wanted to make sure the occupant definitely didn't get out of his tomb,' I said and tried to jazz myself up a bit by winking at Sam. 'Happens a lot. Especially with witches. Though it's usually graves with stones moved over the top. Sometimes they stick iron rivets through the thighs and ankles of the so-called witch's remains. To keep them down.'

Sam smiled at me, indulging his protégé, but Imogen shuddered and Starla gave out a little howl.

We both jumped slightly. It was easy to forget this sort of knowledge, the horror of it all, wasn't customary fare for most people.

'Yes, it's a bit hideous,' Sam acknowledged their discomfort with a glum nod. 'Sorry. Anyway, inside the next coffin was a strange liquid. I quote,' he said, looking at the sheet. '"A liquor or a pickle, somewhat resembling mushroom ketchup."'

'Ew,' I said and wrinkled my nose. 'You mean they *tasted* it?'

'So it would seem,' Sam continued. 'And here's the rub. Within the mixture there was a body.' He took a breath. 'It was perfectly preserved. The skin was white and unblemished. Leaves, lilies and herbs in the liquor were also in full bloom and showing no signs of corruption. Only the pillow, on which the corpse had lain his head, had decomposed over time and "the head unsupported, fell back".'

'Ew,' I said again. 'So what did they do after that?'

'Do?' said Robin, with indignance. 'They let the villagers gawp at it then they fastened him back in. And that was the end of that. Centuries rolled past. Then in June this year builders were excavating, this time to add a meeting room to the church. They hit on a similar tomb at the back of the church.'

'Oh yes?' Sam's eyebrows rose with interest.

'Indeed, I would have thought you might have heard about that given your supervision of something called a Witch Museum. Wouldn't this type of thing be of interest to your visitors?'

'Um,' I said out loud, remembering Monty's words. June. He had certainly heard about it. I guess he'd kept an eye on the situation to see if anything odd occurred. But nothing had. Until now.

Sam darted me a quick shush-now glance and said, 'We were involved in another case at that time.'

Robin did the eye-roll thing again, which moved me this time to react.

'Yes,' I said. 'The Bodies in the Witch Pit, although some papers called it The Murder Pit.'

Imogen's eyes widened. 'Oh I heard about that. In Adder's Fork, that's right isn't it?'

'Yes,' I said and clamped my eyes onto Robin. 'And we solved it thank you very much. So forgive us if we didn't pick up on the discovery of some ancient dead bloke's grave.'

Robin opened his mouth to speak but Tabby got in before him.

'The thing is,' she said, 'we did our workshop in the church, amongst those very same tombs and, I think, to add to the mystery of it all, Laura had us all look at *Man-Sized in Marble* by E. Nesbit. Do you know it?'

Both Sam and I shook our heads.

'Oh. It's a damn good read,' she said. 'About a young couple, very much like yourselves.'

I looked at Sam who began to colour. We weren't *that* sort of couple. Yet. One day though. Maybe. Possibly. Maybe not. Sigh.

To save his blushes, I said, 'We're partners in the museum, that's all!'

'Yes,' said Tabby, clearly unfazed or uninterested, and continued to potter on. 'Well, this couple, they find a delightful cottage in the country. But their housekeeper says she needs to leave.'

'Before Halloween,' Starla piped up and eyed Robin again. He fluttered his eyelids. It was getting annoying.

'She tells them,' continued Tabby. 'That the local church is cursed and that the marble effigies of knights entombed there come to life each year on All Saints' Eve to wreak revenge.'

'The husband is sceptical,' said Robin. 'But on Halloween he goes to the church and finds that the stone slabs on which the knights rest are empty.'

There was a creak at the French windows, then two much younger people entered the room. A whiff of tobacco floated in with them.

'When he gets back to his wife,' Starla went on, 'he finds her dead, heart attack. But in her hand she grips a cold stony finger.'

'Which,' said the young graceful man who had just stepped inside, 'is what Cullen found in Graham's this morning.' He wiped his feet on the door mat.

'Oooohhh,' I said, beginning to get why Monty had wanted us to pay a visit.

Sam had got it too. 'Life imitating art?'

'Ach!' said Robin, from his stiff wooden chair. 'Or someone's intending it appears that way. Certainly if we assume marble statues don't animate themselves on Halloween and commit murder.' Then he laughed at his suggestion. But it was thin and weedy and nobody else joined in.

'Did you tell them about my story?' The newcomer asked, and tossed his hair back. Dark and collar-length and pushed over his ears, it was kept in a kind of romantic but wild style. Slightly Byronesque. Some youngsters loved a bit of that.

And this bloke had amplified the likeness with a sexy silk shirt with a paisley pattern across it, and ripped jeans. He was clearly going for a kind of punked-up poet-fop hybrid. 'It's very good,' he said and winked at me. The accent was dead posh. Like proper posh. Upper-upper-class posh. Possibly even posher than Monty and Tabby. And he constantly sounded like he was holding back a laugh.

'What story?' I asked, wondering what else was on its way now. We'd already had King Arthur and some woman who wanted a different body.

The girl by his side rolled her eyes. 'Oh shut up Nicholas.' She sighed.

'You should read it,' said the young man, presumably Nicholas, raising an eyebrow. 'About a guy who goes off the rails once he's taken MDMA. Starts hallucinating spectres. Happened to a chum of mine.'

Sam blinked hard, then said, 'Is this relevant?'

'Only to my genius,' said Nicholas. I couldn't tell whether his face had settled into a smirk or a smug grin.

'I'm Jocelyn,' said the young woman and came over and shook my hand. I was impressed. She was the first one to do it so far. She had a shrewd look about her and an undeniable beauty. Radiant, unblemished skin, deep brown eyes and dark hair; when she took my hand her shake was firm. I liked her immediately.

'Ignore him,' she said. I detected a hint of South London in her voice. Then turned to Sam. 'No. It's not relevant. Have they told you about the police?'

'Not yet,' I said.

'Graham had a dicky heart. Very sad, but it seems like he might have been frightened by local kids. One trick-or-treat too far. Pure bad luck.'

'Didn't any of you see it?' I asked the rest, as Jocelyn went and got herself a chair from the table at the back of the room and brought it forward to sit next to Imogen and Tabby. Self-sufficient and self-motivated too, I noted.

'Goodness, no,' said Aunt Tabby. 'We all partook of some rather large whisky chasers and succumbed to bed early. It had been quite an eventful day.'

'Not as eventful as this one,' said Imogen and yawned.

At that moment the door to the hallway opened and the woman Tabby had called Sophia came in with a tray.

'Oh,' she said looking from Nicholas to Jocelyn. 'I've not made enough for you two. Would one of you mind refilling the kettle?' The wrinkles under her eyes deepened as she exhaled.

'Where's Carole?' asked Nicholas. He fidgeted in his seat. 'Can't she do it? She's the housekeeper, after all. She should keep the house and its guests – us.'

'I gave her the rest of the day off.' Sophia frowned then tried to make it into a smile. But it clearly pained her. 'She was very upset about Graham, as you can imagine. They worked here for years together.'

Jocelyn glared at Nicholas. 'Please tell me you know how to make a cup of tea, Nick?'

He sent her a puckish grin and ran his hand through his hair. 'Indeed. Call Room Service.'

Jocelyn sighed and left the room. I was surprised when Nicholas dawdled out after her, hands in pockets.

'Right. Good,' said Sophia. Despite the expensive blouse and skirt, I could tell she'd dressed in a hurry. I'm good like that. I can read people well. Or at least I used to be able to. I wasn't so sure these days. But Sophia was shedding clues left, right and centre: her cardigan was inside out and buttoned squint, and there was a ladder in her tights visible at the top of her thigh, for part of that beautiful designer skirt was tucked into her knickers. As she passed by the Chesterfield, a flushing Starla yanked the hem down, protecting Sophia's practical Marks and Sparks modesty, without her noticing a thing.

Just in time really, because she went and bent over the large table at the back of the room and dumped the tray, teapot and mugs down on it noisily. Robin took over the pouring and handing out of mugs.

'Here you go,' said Sophia and handed mine over. 'I haven't introduced myself – I'm Sophia Adams-Braithwaite. The events organiser for the Essex Writers Retreat. Came down today. As soon as I heard about Graham.'

She backed away with her own mug in her hands and settled in the chair that Jocelyn had vacated. 'Terrible,' she said and blew on her tea.

There was a pause in conversation as everybody sorted out their brews, during which time I considered the information.

When everyone resumed their places I said, 'So Graham has a heart attack and is found clutching a stone finger. Was it actually made of stone?' This detail seemed important. 'Or marble?'

'Cullen, who saw it, said it was fashioned from stone just like a statue's.'

That was good to get confirmed. The Devil, I found, was always in the detail with these things. 'And so, I'm guessing what some of you are thinking,' I continued raising my voice so they could all hear me over the clatter of teaspoons and cups. 'What you perhaps are realising is that this, therefore, uncannily echoes the short story you had to read?'

'*Man-Sized in Marble*, yes,' said Starla. 'And it was Halloween. Exactly the same time of year that the story is set.'

Before Robin could respond with any sort of cynical comeback, the door was thrown open again and a huge man and a slight woman walked through. Their gait was distinctly hurried and irregular and they both wore expressions of extreme disquiet.

'Laura, Cullen!' said Tabby. 'Whatever is the matter?

'You both look like you've seen a ghost,' Starla exclaimed, who was looking pretty limp herself.

The Laura-woman held a trembling hand out for support which Starla grabbed and then used to guide her onto the Chesterfield. She really did look very unwell. There was something about her eyes that gave her a pinched, uncertain look. She had quite a few fine lines and a redness on the cheeks that somehow suggested it was permanent.

The young man remained standing near the doorway, his bulk almost filling it, eyes glittering wildly. 'We walked to the church,' he said, his voice higher pitched than might be expected from such a hulking torso. It had a squeaking discordant sound to it: he clipped his vowels and spoke quickly, punctuating his words with pants. 'And you'll never guess what we found.' He glanced at Laura, whose face was clammy with perspiration.

She swallowed, staring straight ahead. 'I still can't believe it,' she said at last. 'It's the tombs. One of the knights has lost a finger.'

CHAPTER THREE

The hysteria and wailing brought Jocelyn and Nicholas back into the room, with more cups of tea. Once that had settled things down a bit, the gathered writers and Sophia divided into four camps: those who thought the avenging knights had killed Graham (Starla and Imogen), those who believed the trick-or-treaters had done it, either accidentally or on purpose (Jocelyn, Laura, Robin), those who were just trying to calm everyone down (Tabby and Sophia), and those who believed Cullen had done it (Nicholas).

'You found him, didn't you?' he pointed his finger in Cullen's direction. The latter had gone and perched on the arm of the Chesterfield, next to where the Laura chick was. His bulk looked dangerously heavy for the patched leather sofa.

'You could have easily stuck the finger in Graham's hand.' Nicholas's voice was heavy with icy provocation. 'Then you come back now and tell everyone it's gone from the knight's tomb. I bet it was your idea to go in there, wasn't it?'

Cullen twitched and started picking at something on his eyebrow but it was Laura who spoke. 'No Nicholas

– it was my idea to go and check the church. I wanted to go there. I was hoping to find some …' she paused and shook her head '… peace. This is my fault.' She gave way to a sob.

So this was interesting. 'Why is it your fault, Laura?' I asked.

'Because I drew their attention to the discovery of the knights' tombs. Both recent and of old. It occurred to me that Nesbit might have been inspired by this real-life event.' She put her hand across her brow and rubbed it. Her hair was highlighted with ash blonde, and she looked quite trendy for her age, which I put around the late forties. Nice red lipstick, which I approved of, was brought out by a little accent poppy brooch on her black cardigan. She had a short stretchy skirt on and leggings. Her boots were great – a dark leather with buckles at the sides, which made her look rather swashbuckling, despite the teary eyes. 'And it was I who insisted everyone read Nesbit's terrifying story. Graham included. I wanted him to take part. I don't like the separation between staff and writers.' She shrugged. 'Was a signed-up member of The Socialist Workers Party when I was at University.'

'Where was that?' Sam asked, absently.

'Leeds,' she said. 'Long time ago.'

Sam smiled, 'Not that long I'm sure.' I didn't like that smile. It was a bit too familiar. 'Did you know about his heart condition too?'

Laura's eyes grew wide and her head trembled. 'Well … we talked and I … I … what are you suggesting?'

Sophia stood up and went to Laura. 'Laura dear, it doesn't matter.' She spun round and glared at Sam. 'Staff Medical records are confidential.'

'Yes, I'm sure, they are,' I said. Data protection was a hot subject right now. But, I thought, it was possible that one of those assembled did know about the caretaker's heart condition and had, indeed, used that to their advantage. Sophia had only just arrived though, so she was out of the frame.

'The irony is,' Laura continued and clutched her arm. 'I've had a few scares in that department myself.' She looked at Sophia. 'It's all been embarrassingly public – I fainted on stage at Hay. Mortifying. Though, I have to say, being tuned in to the condition and symptoms as I feel I am now, I really didn't perceive signs of heart trouble in Graham at all.'

So that was her line, and she was sticking to it.

Imogen shook her head. 'The silent killer.' And everyone looked at her. 'Heart disease,' she explained. Tabby didn't look convinced.

'And you, you,' Nicholas was back on his feet again, pointing his thin little digit back at Cullen. 'You said you could get into the mind of a killer. That you "could really understand the impulse to kill". I think those were your words weren't they?'

Cullen grinned. 'I cannot lie. I believe I am gifted in that area.' A slow grin spread onto his cheeks.

Both myself and Tabby shuddered. There was something a little demented in Cullen's eyes. Laura took his hand, 'For heaven's sake Nicholas, Cullen is in possession of a fantastic imagination. That doesn't mean he will act on it. I have written two books from the perspective of a killer and I am most certainly not one.'

'So you say,' said Sam to a chorus of shocked gasps.

Casting doubt upon the moral stature of their leader hadn't endeared him to the group. My colleague, however, remained unfazed and stood up. 'I'm not pointing the finger, so to speak, but we'd like to speak to everyone individually.'

Robin's face was a study in contempt. 'Ay am not speaking to you! Ay said my piece to the police.' And he crossed his arms and turned away.

Starla shook her turquoise head. 'No way, no way.'

It was starting to look like we might have a mutiny on our hands but then Tabby stood up. 'I'll do it.'

And rather surprisingly, the big hulk man agreed. 'Me too.'

'Great,' said Sam.

Nicholas made a huffing noise and muttered something like 'Amateurs, ridiculous.'

So I said, 'And we'll be noting those who don't cooperate.'

Sam tapped Sophia on the shoulder. 'Is there a room available?'

'Well, er, I'm not sure …'

Then Tabby piped up. 'They're here at the request of MI5. Do you really want to be obstructing a government office?'

I thought she sent me a very brief wink.

Sophia's hands picked at a frayed thread on her cardigan. 'Well, I suppose when you put it like that,' she said. 'There's Graham's office.'

'It would be great if we could settle in there, then,' said Sam. 'So we can get to the bottom of all this.'

As he spoke, there was a creak at the door, and a slim woman appeared in the doorway. 'That's the best news I've heard all day,' she said.

'Ah, Margot,' cried Aunt Tabby. 'You look better now, dear. Come and sit down.'

She was the same age as Tabby but seemed younger on account of a more stylish dress sense: a silk pashmina wrap was draped loosely over her cashmere jumper. She wore shapely bootcut indigo jeans. Tortoiseshell glasses complemented her caramel-coloured bob, which was sleek, glossy and straight. But there was a sense of frailty about her. As she crossed the room I noticed she had a slight limp and as she bent down to sit she winced. Aware of my gaze she explained, 'Arthritis.'

Tabby leant over, once Margot had levered herself into the chair, tapped her knee and said, 'These people are Rosie and Sam from the Witch Museum. They're going to sort out what's been going on.'

'Thank you,' she said. In her hand she held a tissue which she dabbed at her left eye. 'So terribly sad. Poor Graham.'

Sophia finished her tea and stood up. 'I suppose I should start on dinner. There's quite a few of us. Any volunteers?'

Jocelyn raised her hand. 'I'll come.'

She was so helpful.

Maybe too helpful.

Perhaps there was something seething and nasty underneath all that superficial niceness.

We should approach everyone with an open mind. Like Sam said, no one was above suspicion.

There was a guzzling sound in a nearby pipe. I looked around to see where it had come from but couldn't work it out. This place was old.

Nicholas tore his scowl away from Cullen. 'Me too,' he said. 'I'll help.'

'Yes, and me,' said Starla. 'I make a mean quinoa salad.'

'Uh,' said Nicholas. 'I hope it's got gluten in it?'

I was with Nicholas on that and thought quinoa barely counted as food.

Sophia got to her feet. 'Great, thank you. I'll show these fellows the study and then meet you in the kitchen in five.'

At which point Sam clapped his hands. 'Right. Let's do it then,' he said.

I put our mugs on the wooden table and followed him out the door.

We tick-tacked across the marble floor and turned left at the entrance porch, past a door clearly indicating a cloakroom and unisex WC. I could see up ahead the entrance into what looked like a large kitchen, dining area and conservatory, but we didn't make it that far: Sophia turned right into a room that was considerably smaller than the last one we had sat in.

Graham's office contained a large impressive desk with a laptop and several folders. I went over to the window and peered into the gardens. How nice to have such a lot of land, I thought and looked up and down, noticing that this office and the WC next door appeared to be the single storey extension that had been built onto the main section of the house. Whoever had designed the add-on had done a good job of blending it in to the rest of the house.

'Make yourselves comfortable,' Sophia instructed.

Someone behind her coughed. The manager spun round startled and said, 'Oh hi,' then moved to one side and out into the corridor and disappeared in the direction of the kitchen. A small solitary figure lingered in the doorway.

'Well, you probably should start with me,' it said, and stepped into the light. Margot flicked her hair. 'I'm happy to fill in the blanks.'

It was unusual to have someone volunteer for inquisition although it did make sense: Margot had missed out on the earlier bout of hysteria and finger-pointing that the writers had entered into with such vigour.

I looked at Sam who shrugged. 'Okay,' he said. 'Take a seat.'

Margot selected a small chaise underneath the window. She wriggled about for a bit then tucked a cushion under her back, slipped her shoes off and brought her feet up.

I immediately felt like I should act like a shrink and was about to ask her what seemed to be the problem, when I remembered that we were investigating a sudden death which had upset this patient, I mean resident, quite a lot. It was therefore only right that gravity be the order of the day. Consequently, I made my mouth look neutral by forcing the ends down and bowed my head.

Sam did another shrug then took the swivel chair behind the desk. This left the leather tub chair positioned between the chaise and desk, and a hardwood stool that was also a step ladder, doubtless used to reach the tops of the very high shelves lining three of the walls. A leaded window dominated the fourth. Beside it hung a painting, oils I think, from the choppy surface. It showed Ratchette Hall at its peak, centuries ago. It was much bigger then. Part of it was clearly Tudor, though I wasn't sure that section still stood. Unless there was another wing tucked away round the back somewhere.

Sam coughed uneasily and sent me a 'What do we do now?' glance. I was becoming aware that possibly we should have worked out our plan of action before we got here. Everything had happened pretty quickly though. And to be honest we just hadn't thought it through. But here we were at the request of Monty who had asked us to come over and 'dig'. To find out about the other residents, see if anyone had a motive to stiff this Graham bloke, and investigate the possibility that dead marble carvings might be able to spring into life.

So, I thought, be logical – start at the beginning. Let the digging commence.

Sam was still looking clueless, so I asked him to get his pen out. 'Do you mind taking notes while I question Margot?'

He sent me a slip of a smile. It had relief sewn into it.

My background in Benefit Fraud meant that I'd done this sort of work before. Once I'd fixed my mind on an outcome it was fairly easy for me to structure questions so that subjects dribbled out information. Often without an awareness that they were doing so.

There was, however, something about Margot that sang 'organised' to me. Maybe it was the careful colour coordination of her outfit, the way the shades complemented her hair. The statement pashmina, that was undoubtedly expensive, the understated skirt. The crisp cut of her clothes that suited her willowy frame and were just tight enough in all the right places to show off her small but perfectly formed curves. That look would have taken years to perfect. It was impressive. I hope I looked like that whenever I got to, er, whatever age she was. Would it be impolite to ask? Yes probably.

The notion of Margot's competent management persisted and informed my first question which turned out to be, 'So when did you book this course, Margot?' Which was a surprise even to myself, though on reflection a good choice.

Her pencilled eyebrows soared. She hadn't expected that. 'Oh, months ago,' she drawled. There were hints of Finishing School or Ladies Academies woven into it. Maybe she'd been a thesp in a former life. Whatever – her voice, as Gatsby might have noted, was 'full of money'.

'When?' I asked. I was sure she'd know.

'May, I think. When the catalogue for the autumn and winter courses came out.'

I looked at Sam who noted it. 'And what attracted you to the course?'

She nodded. She *had* expected this one. 'Oh Ratchette Hall looked like a wonderful place. Elegant. Historic. Situated in picturesque grounds. So inspiring. And obviously the chance to get away from mundane everyday life … to write. What joy.' She found her handkerchief and dabbed once more at an invisible tear. An unconscious tick of distress. 'At least,' she paused, 'I imagined it would be joyful.'

Sam nodded sympathetically. 'Well, no one could have known …' he watched her face. I registered gratitude for his words in it. I think he did too.

'So,' he continued, brightening his features. 'What's your book about? Indeed, is there a work in progress at all?'

That was another good question. I hadn't thought about that. Though it was plausible that the stories they were working on might tell us a bit about the character of those writing them. Smart old Sam. He elicited a good answer too.

Margot glanced out the window. I followed her gaze and realised that the office took in the view of the side of the house and gardens. The gravel drive wound up and round the wall to a double garage at the rear. Beyond that the garden spread out, complete, I think with flower beds and lawns, though it was properly dark now. The dew had whipped up into twists of mist that currently hung over wet silvery grass. A thick jagged line of denser blackness suggested that the property was surrounded, or perhaps was cut out of, a copse. As far as I could see anyway. Things might be clearer tomorrow. See, I was already guessing that we would have to return. I couldn't see us getting through all the writers tonight, and judging from the sounds coming out of the kitchen, dinner wasn't going to be long. I considered the quinoa and sighed at the same time that Margot did. Though her exhalation was deeper felt than mine, with the touch of a moan entwined.

Her eyes came off the view, such as it was, and swivelled back to us. 'My story? Yes. It's about a lost child,' she said and picked up the amber pendant hanging from her neck.

Out of the corner of my eye I saw Sam start.

Personally, I thought that subject matter was quite common. A lot of crime writers pushed the boundaries these days. You had to be original, I guess. Sometimes that meant shocking people. And none of it, I thought, was any worse than what went on in the real world. Sam should know that, what with the Witch Museum and history and all that malarkey. I mean, you should see some of the stuff we had going on just a few centuries ago. The things people did to each other in the name of God or holiness or just to please themselves. There was a whole wall of Inquisitional torture devices which were enough to make visitors' eyes water and young men walk with a wince for at least five minutes after they'd passed them by.

'Lost kids?' I asked for clarity. 'As in dead?'

'Singular. And no not necessarily dead,' said Margot. She let go of the pendant and clasped her hands together then hooked them over her good knee. The gesture was a little coquettish and I wondered briefly how she had looked when she was younger. Charming, I'm sure.

'Abducted?' I ventured.

Sam flinched again. I couldn't work out why. Was I being indelicate?

Margot didn't notice Sam's reaction, which was a relief: we should keep her on side so the information flowed. I watched her smile thinly and brush her hair off her shoulders. 'It's an intense situation,' she said. 'Interesting. Brings out extremes. Changes people. Permanently. Don't you think?'

I thought that 'interesting' was not necessarily the word I'd use if that scenario ever unfolded in my life, and was about to answer neutrally when Margot poked her long manicured finger at the pair of us. 'Do you have children?'

Oh bloody hell, I thought, here we go again. Just because we were a man and woman hanging out together it didn't mean we were an item. Why were people so narrow? I mean this was a work situation. Plenty of men and women worked together.

Although it was entirely possible that Sam and I gave out a vibe. It had been clear, for quite a while, that we had chemistry. We just weren't sure what to do with it. It could be explosive. We didn't want to blow anything up and were reluctant to, well, talk about it. And because we hadn't talked about it over the summer months, when I had had other things on my mind which needed my attention, the whole thing had become 'unspoken'. We had consequently fallen into a routine full of stalemate and potential embarrassment, neither of us willing to make the first move. It had become the elephant in the room, on a broomstick, that followed us around wherever we went. We'd sort it though, I was sure. We just hadn't found the right time yet.

I shook my head hurriedly to dispel Margot's assumption. 'No. Our relationship's not like that. More complicated.'

Margot careered on anyway. She wasn't really interested in us, you could tell. She was more absorbed by her plot and keen to tell us about it, so we could go 'Oohhh ahhh – amazing.'

'Well,' she said, lifting her chin, 'if you don't have children then you can't possibly understand the power of that situation.' There was a whining strain to her voice, a kind of indignant condescension that I hadn't noticed before. 'It's only when you have children that you realise your vulnerability.'

Hmm, I thought, well if you make your target audience parents who've lost children then you're not going to be on to a bestseller, dear. But I didn't say anything.

Though Sam did.

'Actually,' he cleared his throat and straightened up a bit, 'I disagree.' Which kind of surprised me. 'You don't need to be a parent to appreciate what it's like to lose a child. If you ever have the misfortune to be involved with such a tragedy, no matter the relationship, it wouldn't leave you.'

That sounded like it had come from personal experience and whilst I would have liked to have pursued it, I thought we might get derailed down a 'plot line' tangent. Plus I couldn't really see where it was getting us in terms of the recent death.

Margot began saying something about legacy, which I interrupted with, 'What did you think of Graham?' Time to bring things back on target.

She stopped. For a moment I thought she was going to have a go at me, because a big nasty crease appeared in her forehead, but then she just smiled and looked pleasant again, readjusted the hem of her skirt in a straight line across her knee, and cocked her head to one side. 'Oh of course. Sorry. Graham. Yes, well he was perfectly nice. I can't see that anyone would have a reason to scare him like that. I'm convinced it is just an unfortunate case of Halloween tricks gone wrong. So sad. He seemed lovely. But after that big build-up of Laura's we were all a little nervous. That's why everyone drank so much yesterday, I think. Tension. I almost felt like we were waiting for something to happen. Do you ever get that feeling?'

I did actually, but I thought it wise not to distract her.

She was ploughing on anyway. 'You could understand why the incident, when it happened, whatever it was, might have tipped Graham over the edge. What with the heart condition. Such a silly tragic accident,' she finished with real sympathy. 'I'm so sorry.'

'Yes,' I said. 'You make a fair point. Nerves, stress. Not good for some medical conditions. Did you know Graham prior to the course?'

'Not at all,' she said, eyes widening with indignation. 'I've never been here before, have I? Why would I know him?' She began moving her arms around in a most aerated manner. 'I mean, he was an administrator. I don't mix with those kinds of people in my everyday life.'

Sam leant forward and put his arms on the desk. 'What kind of people do you mean, Margot?'

She straightened her back and fluttered a hand to her neck. 'Literary types.'

I wasn't sure if she actually meant that or had accidentally revealed her attitude to us 'below-stairs' types.

'That's why I'm here, of course.' She smiled with guile. 'I didn't know him.' Then her voice rose. 'Really, I didn't!'

Sam softened. 'We're not accusing you, Margot. We're ascertaining a foundation of facts.' He glanced at me.

I nodded. Even if he'd just made it up, I'd buy it.

But the statement seemed to upset Margot further. 'It

was an accident! The police think so too.' Her face dropped further and she let out a half sob. 'I don't know why you've come here, asking all these rude questions. You shouldn't be upsetting people like this.' The tissue popped up against her cheek again.

'No, that's fine,' said Sam. 'Thank you, Margot. Sorry, you can understand why we are having to ask these questions.'

She got herself under control again. 'I suppose so. Yes. Well, look – it's perfectly simple – I had the whisky and then retired.' Then she cackled. 'You see I am retired! And not as young as I used to be. I can't drink like I used to either. Oh you should have seen me in my heyday. I could have given you the runaround.' She winked at Sam.

Two red dots flushed on his cheeks.

I smiled at her. 'I quite believe it. But, last night, you didn't hear anything after bedtime?'

'No. Nothing. I was out for the count.' She sat back and smoothed her skirt down again. 'I did have a count once. Oh he was adorable. Quite a demon between the sheets.' She winked at Sam again, who was still burning from her previous innuendo. 'Strong, dark, allegedly Russian, though could have made the whole thing up. But we do so like our strong dark men, don't we?' she said to me.

I, for one, was not going to blush. I refused to look at Sam and asked Margot, 'Oh yes? Was Graham strong and dark?'

'Oh my goodness no. He was well into middle-age and clearly not as sturdy as he thought.'

Good point.

'But you are quite the strong man, aren't you Mr Stone?'

Margot's eyes glinted lasciviously. 'I can see your arms. Do you work out?'

'Well, that's great,' Sam said and snapped the notebook shut. 'I think we've got enough information now. Thank you, Margot. We'll let you know if we have more questions.'

She made a pouty face. 'Oh, I don't mind you probing me,' she said and batted her lashes.

Sam was trying hard not to squirm. I had to put the poor bloke out of his misery so got up and opened the door. 'You've been a great help, thank you. We do have other people we need to speak to though.'

'Fine.' She sighed, swivelled her feet to the floor and then limped out of the room, trying to conceal a very un-sexy grimace as her weight transferred onto her right leg.

When the door closed, Sam pushed his chair back. It was on wheels and glided quickly till he hit a filing cabinet behind him, which halted his trajectory. 'Good lord!' he said. 'She's a character.' Then he laughed.

'I thought you enjoyed a bit of a flirt with the oldies. I remember what you were like with Auntie Babs.'

He chuckled again and stretched in the chair then lifted his feet onto the desk. Rather naughtily in my opinion. You should treat other people's furniture as you expected them to treat yours after all. I told him to take his feet off, which annoyed him, but he did oblige. It was unusual for him to do such a thing in the first place.

'Still,' I said, 'I know she's disabled, frail and old. But she could be as likely as any of the others to have given Graham the scare of his life. If she wanted to.'

'Oh,' said Sam. 'Come on. She just doesn't look like a murderer, does she?'

I folded my arms and said, 'Hah! And what exactly does a murderer look like then?' At which point the door flew open and Cullen lumbered in.

With remarkable synchronicity we released exclamations of surprise. To my dismay I felt a blush heating the tips of my ears. For out of all of the residents, Cullen was the one who really did actually quite seriously *look like a serial killer*.

Sam might have thought so too because he began faffing around with his notebook and coughing. His hand fisted and covered his mouth like he was stifling a huge guffaw.

I stood up, greeted the newcomer, aware of a line of sweat bobbling my top lip, and invited him to sit down. Which he did, though he didn't go for the chaise that Margot had vacated but the small tub chair, further back, which he immediately dwarfed. I had a mental image of him standing up and taking the seat with him and tried not to laugh. It made the whole murderer thing a bit lighter.

I couldn't quite pinpoint why Cullen fitted the 'deranged killer' type so much. He just had that vibe. And a mono-brow. My nan, on my mum's side, always told me never to trust a man with eyebrows that met. Though she also had a lot of other weird sayings, a large quantity of which were racist, sexist, homophobic, respectful of the 'ruling class', linguistically incomprehensible or sing-songingly extracted from lost music hall performances with no discernible context. Or sense.

Even so, parking my dear nan's warning for a moment, it still had to be said, there was something about Cullen that really did set your teeth on edge. He had these incredibly large but stony eyes that jerked around the place and gave the impression of constant misdirected anger. Like, if he looked at you, you were meant to feel guilty or, er, frightened. And he was well fit, as in gym-fit, hard-muscled and pumped. He could definitely snap a neck with those hands.

All of this was topped off by a sizzling intensity, which meant he came across like the ripped love child of Charles Manson and Henry Rollins.

'You want to know how I can get inside the mind of a killer?' was his opening line.

'No,' I squeaked, swallowed, then forced myself to speak at a lower pitch. 'That's not necessary thanks.' I couldn't help myself – I pushed my chair an inch away from him. Though it was minute, a barely noticeable movement. What I really wanted to do was kick it over, grab my jacket and run out of Ratchette Hall screaming 'Get me away from that psycho.'

It's a good job I have such pronounced impulse control.

Cullen shifted his buttocks around in the tub chair. 'I've always known I was special,' he said, eyes glittering. There was a slight North Eastern twang to his voice. Newcastle maybe. 'Ever since I was young,' he went on.

Oh god, I thought, confessions? Already? Okay, well, it might wrap things up quickly. Take it away, Igor.

'You see,' he went on leaning forwards, those eyes shiny and darting about the place in short sharp moves. 'You have to be clever to be a killer. If you want to get away with it. And I'm clever.' He raised his forefinger to his cropped bonce and tapped it. 'Mind's always working, always thinking things through. Always looking at people and thinking, "Oh yeah, it could be you."'

I nodded uncertainly. This bloke was wired. If it wasn't for the fact that I had a very clear view of his eyes, which were undilated, I might have wondered about Class A consumption. Though some people just rolled like that. Overactive thyroid gland possibly. Not enough to exempt you from work. Mostly.

Sam sat forwards and put his notepad on the desktop with a thud. 'Right, sorry Cullen, do you mind if we wind back? What's your full name?'

'Sutcliffe,' he said and cast his eyes at me.

'You're joking.' My voice broke on the consonants.

'Do I look like I'm joking?' He leant forwards and shone his eyes on me.

Was that indignation in his words?

My face stiffened but I refused to blush again and girded my loins so I could hold his gaze. 'Not really,' I said.

The eyes widened. A wicked smile flashed across his face. Bloody hell, he *had* been playing with me.

Or did he just enjoy the reaction he got? Which made him what – possibly an attention-seeker? With an impish sense of mischief? But nothing more. Not really.

And a name doth not a murderer make.

If a murderer was indeed what we were looking for. At the moment I still wasn't sure that last night's shenanigans were anything more than a pile-up of coincidences. Albeit with a seriously tragic ending.

Sam pulled Cullen's attention off me, by thanking him and repeating the unfortunate surname.

'I can see what you are doing here.' Cullen began nodding. 'Establishing the facts. I've already got them though, you know. Oh yes. Fact one: there are eight of us here with two staff. Originally. Prior to the murder. Fact Two: one of them, Graham, is dead. Killed.' He was speaking quickly, bits of spit dropping out of his mouth as he emphasised particular words, namely: murder, dead, killed. 'Fact Three: he's replaced in the plot by Sophia. Fact Four: that brings the number back to ten. That's a magic number in crime. Not too many, not too few. The reader can cope with that. The reader *has* coped. Agatha Christie – *And Then There Were None*. Great book. I like to think of it as an early slasher format. You two have swung things out of kilter a bit, but we shall see, shan't we? There's a precedent: Courteney Cox and David Arquette in *Scream*, for instance.'

'Uh huh,' I said.

Cullen exercised his fingers in a jerky mechanical fashion as he spoke. It was rather disconcerting, so I focused on his face. But that was also rather disconcerting so I reached for the notepad.

'Of course, there was meant to be one other.'

'Was there?' said Sam. 'Who?'

Cullen leant forwards. 'The other tutor: Chris Devlin.' He sat back and waited for a reaction to the name.

'Who's he?' Sam asked, predictably.

The name was vaguely familiar.

'Chris Devlin?' he said with disbelief. 'He's only one of

the best-selling writers in the world! Action, crime, military, terrorism, thrillers, that sort of thing. Epic.'

'Yes, that's right,' I said, my inner eye settling on an image of a middle-aged man in a leather jacket, with aviator shades posing on a bottle-green vintage jag. Yes, he'd been in a magazine I'd glanced at lately while sitting in my Auntie Bab's hair salon. If my memory served me right he wrote about blokes with guns, running around chasing blokes with guns and getting shot by other blokes with guns or trying to shoot them. Or blow them up. Or something like that.

Cullen was nodding furiously. 'Bloody great writer. Astonishing. He's the reason why I signed up. Was meant to be delivering the course with Laura, but he had a problem – sickness. Couldn't make his flight. Can't remember.'

'Where's he coming from?' Sam asked.

'The States,' Cullen said. 'I think he lives in California now. I was really looking forward to hearing what he had to say. Don't know if he'll make it. We haven't been told. But I have a character that I think he would go wild for. A soldier with sociopathic tendencies.' He smiled at me. Slowly. 'He beheads bad guys.'

A shiver coursed down my spine. 'Nice,' I spluttered.

'So there would have been eleven people here?' Sam went on. 'But without Chris Devlin it meant there were ten.'

'Yes.' Cullen nodded again. 'And then there were nine.'

I wondered if there was anything in it, and said, 'Thanks Cullen. I'll minute this info,' and let my hair fall over my face so I didn't have to look at him for a moment.

Presumably bolstered by my approval/recording of his relevance, Cullen raised his voice. 'Then also minute this, Miss Strange—'

'Rosie,' I told him, still looking at the notepad on my knees.

'Yes, minute this, Rosie: ten strangers are summoned to Ratchette Hall, where they are forced to read a dark tale of—'

'Summoned?' I asked and looked up.

He leant forwards. My body felt a jab of adrenaline as those shark-grey eyes fixed on me. 'Yes,' he said. 'Actually no. Not specifically. Okay. Minute this then: ten strangers converge on Ratchette Hall, a dark gothic mansion in the wilds of the countryside—'

'Edwardian,' I corrected. 'Not gothic.'

'Yes,' he said, his forehead raked with irritation. 'Minute this – ten writers in the wilds of the desolate—'

'We're less than five miles from Chelmsford.' I nodded, to reassure him. 'And that's a city now, so you're not far from civilisation, Cullen, don't panic.'

His head popped up, the mouth turned down. 'I am not panicking. I'm trying to set the scene. Anyway, it doesn't matter. Once assembled, those gathered in the, er, mansion, are then forced to read a tale of—'

I opened my mouth to interject but he got in before me, 'All right, all right. We read a short story that was on the syllabus.' He rolled his eyes and settled them on Sam and shook his head. 'No imagination over there, is there?' he said.

'Oh, you'd be surprised,' my colleague replied. His mouth kinked to the side.

'Point is, the short story,' Cullen darted me a glance, 'and there is no getting away from this, point is that story strangely foreshadows the events of the evening that were to unfold. Almost as if it had been predestined.' He put his hands together. 'That means *premeditated*,' and having successfully made his point, he sat back into the tub chair.

His last word hung in the air between the three of us. It was key here, after all. Was it a series of coincidences or had this death somehow been organised with the intention to kill? Presumably this is what Monty wanted us to think about too.

I could see Sam nodding. 'Indeed,' he said. 'Who was responsible for planning the lessons, Cullen? Is it a set course?'

The young man licked his lips. 'It's Laura,' he said. 'And no, the course was bespoke. She planned it all herself.'

'I see,' I said, remembering the tutor's words in the sitting room where she had expressed her guilt. 'Yes, we should speak to her.'

'Most definitely,' Sam agreed.

Cullen seemed very satisfied with this and began to detach himself from the tub chair.

'Hang on,' I said to him. 'What happened last night? Where were you?'

He eased himself back into the leather and didn't seem at all put out by this line of questioning. 'We were together. All of us. For most of the night. Well, the evening. Had dinner, retired to the sitting room. There had been quite a bit of trick-or-treating activity earlier, around five o'clock and until dinner, but it seemed to peter out by the time we started talking around the fire.'

'Was Graham there, when that was going on?'

'In the sitting room?' He thought about the question. 'No. He excused himself and went into the study, here, to do paperwork. At least that's what he told us, if I remember rightly. But then he must have been telling the truth because Jocelyn fetched him later – the oldies had dozed off. Myself, Jocelyn and Graham helped them upstairs to their rooms. Then, I'm not sure. I was getting tired and went to bed. I think the rest of them cleared out too after that. Wanted an early night. A lot of alcohol was consumed.'

'By you?'

'By everyone,' he said. 'I didn't have as much as some. Though I did have a nightcap. Like I said we all conked out after that.'

I nodded. 'And went to bed? Separately?'

He frowned. 'Yes.'

'So you didn't hear anything?' Sam added. 'No knocking? No sounds?'

He shook his head. 'My room is on the second floor. The place is old but well insulated. I didn't hear anything last night.' He finished with a nod. 'I woke up at about six and went to get some mineral water from the kitchen. I don't trust the tap water round here. And that's when I found Mr Peacock.'

'Where was he?'

'At the bottom of the stairs. I thought he'd fallen first of all. But when I reached him I could see his face. It was ...'

he took a breath and made his squeaky voice deeper, 'a mask of fear. He looked frozen: he'd been terrified when he died. And he was gripping something in his hand. I saw it when I checked his pulse – it was a finger made of stone.'

'It is odd,' I conceded.

'And what did you do?' Sam asked.

'I went straight to the phone and called the police. Then I woke up Laura and told her what had happened. It wasn't long after that the police turned up.'

I glanced at Sam, who shrugged as if he'd got nothing else to ask.

'Well, thank you,' I said to Cullen. 'Most informative.'

'Can I go?' he said.

Sam nodded.

The young man unplugged himself from the tub chair and stood up. 'Well, good luck,' he said as he opened the door. 'My money's on Miss Scarlet with the lead piping in the drawing room.' Then he started cackling maniacally.

Sam and I looked at each other, as Cullen's cackle became a hollow guffaw. He drew breath, clutched hold of the door and spluttered out a spindly wheeze. At which point Sophia arrived to slap him on the back.

'Dear god,' she said, 'are you choking?'

'No,' he said, trying to catch his breath. 'Sometimes I surprise myself with my wit.' Then he straightened up and abruptly stopped laughing.

'Well,' said Sophia backing away from him ever so slightly; the move was as minute as mine had been earlier and very subtle, but I knew where she was coming from. 'If you'd like to go into the kitchen,' she said and gestured to the left. 'Dinner will be ready soon.'

Off lumbered Cullen. Sophia's shoulders dropped and she entered the study.

'Well, goodness me. What an interesting chap,' she said bringing her hands together and wringing them very hard. 'Will you be wanting to see anyone else just now?'

I nodded. 'We should really do everyone, but I'm not sure there will be enough time tonight.'

'Yes, yes,' she said. 'Of course you are welcome to stay for dinner?'

I thought about Starla's globular quinoa and mentally beamed the word 'no' into Sam's brain.

'Shall we?' he asked.

'I've got something in the slow cooker at home,' I told Sophia, and stepped in front of his nodding form. 'Sorry. But I think we'll have to come back tomorrow. After breakfast. Depending on how we go, I guess we might have to stay for lunch?'

She nodded, relieved, I think. 'Did you come to any conclusions?'

'No,' said Sam. 'But we've only just got going.'

'Yes.' Leaning against the wall, she bit her lip. 'I suppose so.'

I thought of all the other people we had to talk to and felt a pang of weariness. Maybe there was another way to get through them. And then it occurred to me that possibly, actually, we didn't need to talk to all of them: according to Cullen they were all together until they went to bed.

And despite what our fidgety interviewee thought about an element of premeditation, there was no solid evidence that pointed in that direction. It was all circumstance and coincidence.

Rain began to patter against the window.

Sophia sighed loud and long. 'If only it had rained last night.' And we all nodded. We knew what she meant – there would have been fewer trick-or-treaters. Maybe Graham would still be alive.

Out the window something caught my eye. A flash of whiteness skittering along the treeline. At first I wondered if it was a light. But then realised it was too dull. It was in fact a form, slightly rounded or oval and at head height, I reckoned. Maybe a barn owl or the like. I got up from the stool – my buttocks were sore – and took a couple of paces towards the window.

'Is there someone out there?' My breath steamed the pane over.

Sophia joined me. 'No, I think everyone's here?' But I think she might have glimpsed something too – there was a question in her statement.

I rubbed the glass and peered through it.

Sam had come over now and was leaning against the frame. 'One of the trick-or-treaters come back to visit the scene of the crime?' he mused.

Neither of us answered. The form flickered then became indistinct so that it looked like there was only blackness out there. And trees.

'Yes,' I said and turned to Sophia. 'Do we know who they

are? These trick-or-treaters? The ones who allegedly scared Graham?'

Sophia shook her head. 'Not as far as I'm aware. No one's told us anything. I'm not even sure they're looking.' Then she shivered as if she was in a draught and wrapped her arms around her.

'But the finger,' Sam muttered, then stopped.

I bent round to him. 'We should speak to the police tomorrow. See if they're doing anything about it. And maybe go into the village to find out if anyone knows about the trick-or-treaters? People usually have an idea about mischief-makers.'

He nodded. 'Good plan.'

I turned back to Sophia. 'Well, we'll be off.'

'Yes,' she said, continuing to hug herself tightly. She wasn't looking at me, her gaze was still fastened onto the copse in the distance. 'You know those woods over there?' she said at length. 'They're called Witch Wood. You don't think that's got anything to do with it do you?'

'What do you mean?' I asked, not getting the reference.

'Witches,' she said and swallowed. 'There's a rumour that they work in the woods and celebrate their sabbats out there.' Then she shuddered again. Visibly.

I darted a glance at Sam and waited for him to kickstart one of his 'Witches were scapegoated and bullied and probably identified as Christians' speeches. But he didn't. He took a long hard look at Sophia and returned his gaze to the woods.

Then he sighed. 'We'll talk about that tomorrow.'

It signalled the end of the conversation.

We said our goodbyes and left Ratchette Hall.

It was lit up against the night sky. On the ground floor every window was glowing. A couple of lights shone in bedrooms on the first floor, but none at the top. We heard the clatter of something hard and metallic crash against a tiled floor at the rear of the building where I guessed the kitchen must be.

Someone laughed. A woman.

The air had cooled significantly.

My eyes hadn't adjusted to night vision yet and I couldn't see anything other than the silhouette of trees in the distance beyond the car. This close to the house, the sky appeared tea-brown, slivers of the Milky Way sliding in to lighten the tinge.

In the distance an owl hooted.

'I'm surprised you didn't tackle that Sophia on her witch-prejudice,' I said to Sam.

He waited for me to unlock the car and said, 'I'm not as predictable as you think I am.'

I tried to make out his face in the darkness but could only see his jawline. Chiselled and as handsome as a statue. 'I know,' I said. 'There are occasions when you're not predictable at all.'

Something rustled in the darkness of the trees. As the doors clicked open I turned to them.

We both froze as the unmistakable howl of a wolf echoed out across the grounds.

CHAPTER FOUR

Well, perhaps not 'unmistakable'.

'Wolves haven't been around in the British Isles for two hundred and fifty years,' said Sam once we were back and safely tucked into the domestic sanctuary of Septimus's living room, above the Witch Museum, happily munching on a lamb casserole that had been in the slow cooker all day.

'Okay, so that rules that out,' I said fishing a rib bone out of my mouth. 'Something howled. It was really bestial. An animal? Or maybe someone.'

'And why would they do that?' said Sam and rearranged the tray on his lap.

'Maybe they were in pain?' I shrugged. 'Maybe they were happy. Maybe they were kind of announcing themselves?' I was surprising myself with my suggestions, although truth to be told, they were all good ones. 'Or maybe,' I concluded. 'They just wanted to scare us?'

'Like Graham Peacock,' he said. 'And why would they want to do that?'

I thought about this for a minute as I rolled a black olive stone around my mouth. 'Because they want us to go away.'

'Possibly,' he said, and laid his fork on his tray.

'Maybe just for fun? Because they can.'

He considered this. 'Depends on who is doing the scaring, doesn't it? The reason?'

'What do you mean?' I asked, watching him licking his fingers. It was a boyish appreciative gesture which made me smile with fond delight.

'Well,' he said oblivious to my burning gaze. 'If it's kids, it's usually mischief-making.'

I shook my head, partly to rid myself of a curling arousal and partly because I disagreed with that he was saying. 'Possibly that was what was going on tonight, with the thing in the bushes – if it was a person. But last night, with Graham, no. That was different. Cullen said he went up at half past ten. Graham was helping the oldies to bed. That means it was getting on for eleven when the trick-or-treaters came by. At that time it would be unusual to have children out and about. It was a school day. So if it *was* trick-or-treaters that gave Mr Peacock the fatal scare of his life, then they'd be much older.'

Sam steepled his fingers and pointed them under his chin. 'Do older kids trick-or-treat?'

I shrugged. 'Dunno. But we should find out tomorrow.'

'Where?'

'The village. The pub or at the church maybe, like we said earlier. I think we should go and look at these tombs don't you?'

'They do seem to be rather central to the matter,' Sam said. 'As does the story they studied by that writer.'

'Edith Nesbit. Yes, we should ask Laura if the requirement to read *Man-Sized in Marble* was advertised beforehand? So we know how many people were privy to the ending.'

'The stone finger in the hand is a direct echo of the story's climax,' Sam said slowly. 'Graham could have broken it off someone …'

I blinked with incredulity. 'You're not suggesting the stone knights got off their tombs and marched to Ratchette Hall with the implicit purpose of scaring the caretaker to death?'

He leaned back into armchair. 'I'm ruling nothing out. However, the laws of probability would suggest the marble digit was more likely to have been put there by a human hand.'

'Yes. The mystery writers.' I sighed. 'I didn't think Laura seemed very cooperative tonight.'

'Well, it will be easy to find out if they were asked to read up on certain texts before they arrived at the Hall,' said Sam. 'And Sophia gave me a list of everyone's details including phone numbers. So we can work through that.'

'Great,' I said. 'Why don't you text Laura now and find out?'

'Good idea,' said Sam. 'If she's obstructive then we can ask Margot and Cullen if they were asked to read the story beforehand. I think it would also be useful if we both read it. Something might jump out at us.'

'Hopefully not of the stone variety,' I said and smirked.

Sam ignored me as usual. 'I'll find a PDF online and print it.'

'Great,' I said again. 'I'll, I'll …' I petered out. I didn't actually know what I should do. I worked my spoon round my plate and gulped down the last of the casserole.

'Yes,' said Sam. 'You should think about tackling that.'

I turned and looked at him enquiringly and saw he was gesturing to a box of my grandmother's and Celeste's ornaments, sketchbooks, jewellery that I had brought down from the attic about a month ago. I had laid it down in front of the fireplace and subsequently failed to do anything else.

'Every time we sit here together you stare at it,' he went on. 'But you never touch your mother's things.' His tone wasn't accusatory. It was soft and gentle. 'Or are they Ethel-Rose's?'

'Both,' I told him.

'So why have you brought them down?' he said. 'Can't be just to look at.'

I sighed. 'I'm planning to go through them. Sort them out. Decide whether I want to keep the ornaments and jewellery. I don't think there's much of value.'

'And so?' he said. 'What's stopping you?'

I looked back at the box. A porcelain pillbox poked out of a wrap of lavender tissue paper. Beside it a question mark of pearls spread out over a silk Hermes scarf. It all looked very unthreatening: girly, lacy, fragile. 'I don't know what I might find.'

Sam didn't say anything. But he nodded. 'Would it help if I went through them first?'

'I don't know,' I said. And I really didn't.

Since I'd inherited the witch museum I'd experienced enough shocks to keep me going for a lifetime. If I didn't go through their stuff, I might body-swerve any more nasty surprises. At the same time, there were still a trillion unanswered questions involved in the story of my true past. And these worried me.

Solving the mystery of my grandmother, Ethel-Rose, and her sudden disappearance, however, had resulted in the unearthing of not only her mortal remains, but also the long-hidden secret of my true parentage. The discovery had provided closure of one sort, whilst opening up raw wounds and doors onto new mysteries. Who knew what other wells of misery and painful disclosure might lie within the contents of the box? If indeed there was anything there that was of interest at all.

Sam was being kind with his offer, but the whole issue was so loaded I just couldn't answer him. It had only been four months since everything had happened. And although I was fine at a rather shallow level and completely able to function efficiently on a day-to-day basis, I was also intelligent enough to know beneath the surface things were still in turmoil.

'Anyway,' said Sam, after my long pause. 'You decide what you want to happen and let me know. I'm here to help. I want to. Now, have you finished your casserole? I'll sort the bowls out then go up to the study. That okay?'

I nodded and handed him the tray. Fair exchange. This is how we worked things out – whoever cooked got let off clearing up. Unfortunately, we still hadn't managed to divvy up chores in the rest of the museum. Although, since the business with the Blackly Be boulder in May, we'd had so much publicity, takings at the museum were up. This meant we'd managed to sort out extra staff. Namely Vanessa, who came and did the till and Trace, her mum, who cleaned and did the books, which took that burden off of Sam. Thus we were freed up to go through the museum, systematically, working out what to do with dated exhibits and taking stock of some of the thousands of other artefacts we had in various storage rooms dotted around the place. Well, that was the theory.

Sam however, seemed to be constantly booked for talks with the various schools who now turned up on a regular basis. Lots of them wanted to know all about the Blackly Be and the 'dead head' that had ended up on it. However, as the whole affair had crossed over into my own personal domain and now involved an impending court case, we weren't really allowed to talk about it. Interest in the scandal continued to pull in punters, so to capitalise on that we were planning to update the Blackly Be exhibit, and maybe commission a film on the whole thing, which visitors could watch in a new theatre section. We had identified a bit of dead space in the Cadence Wing which we thought could be walled off and sound-proofed and thus turned into a small cinema space. We reckoned we might be able to fit in about thirty bums on seats and maybe even use it to screen films for the locals at weekends. I was up for doing midnight horror films too. Reckoned people would flock in from miles around. See, the times they were a-changing and museums, like libraries and bookshops couldn't just be single-use any more. I had plans for a café at some point too and really wanted to get an alcohol license. So, yeah, like, we were well busy.

And Sam also had at least one day off a week to devote to his PhD – *Everything You Ever Wanted to Know About Witchery in Essex but Were too Afraid to Ask*. Or something.

At times this resulted in him locking himself in the study or taking off to Cambridge for a night or two. Which was fine, as it meant he didn't drive me mad all the time and allowed me to go through certain areas of the attic and other storage areas where I had come across some of the Strange family's personal belongings. Like I said, I'd managed to bring this one box downstairs but that was as far as I'd got.

To be fair to myself, I hadn't just been sitting there staring at everything like a gormless wonder. There had been a lot of other things to attend to as well: autumn is not a resting time for gardeners. There was all this decluttering, raking, cutting back, mulching, aerating, trimming of the land around the museum. Some of the creepers needed structural support too. Bronson was getting on a bit. He couldn't do it all on his own.

Carmen had got started on chiselling some of the names of those who lost their lives to the witch hunts into these big blocks of soapstone. I thought we might have to get a stone mason to do it but she was insistent she would at least try. It would cost us less. Plus I had to sort out layers of admin regarding the burial of Bartholomew Elkes and Anne Hewghes. Not to mention that of my own grandmother, which had in turn meant that I'd really had to support my dad and my mum a bit too. Despite the fact that they weren't biologically my mum and dad. But they were in the 'upbringing' sense. In fact they were all I knew. And I loved them. And they loved me. That much was most definitely true.

Which I think was another reason why I shied away from looking at Celeste's things. I felt guilty. Guilty that I hadn't known she was my mother. Guilty that I loved my own, Maureen. Guilty that I hadn't spent much time with Celeste. Guilty that I couldn't remember the time that we had shared. Guilty that I hadn't known her. Guilty that I hadn't tried to look through her things earlier. That I had been so dismissive when people said I looked like her. That I hadn't thought about that more. Guilty.

Of course, there was nothing I could do about any of that and none of it was my fault. But that makes no difference to 'guilt'. It just sits there, like a vulture, on your shoulder pecking at you every so often when you don't expect it. Or sometimes when you do. I needed to get myself in order and shoo it away.

I shook myself out physically and got up from the sofa. Such sluggish, indulgent thoughts were no use to anyone. And pointless too. Sam was right of course: I should do something with the stuff. So, seizing this present moment of sudden motivation, I went and gathered up the box and carried it into Septimus's bedroom. There I put it on the console table near the window and had another long stare.

I removed the pillbox from the tissue paper which was dusty and a bit manky. The pillbox was edged with gold and had a looping daisy pattern pressed into it. Really it seemed quite Rococo. On the lid was a painting of a nineteenth-century woman, with finely piled dark hair. She was at leisure, with a book, sitting beneath a tree near a rambling brook. It was a pretty pastoral scene. I flipped the catch on the side and opened it. Inside, wrapped in a fine gauze, was a lock of baby hair. It was quite a shock. I hadn't expected it, and for a moment I paused to consider who the lock might have once belonged to – Dad? Celeste? Me?

I didn't want to touch it in case it made me sad and start to think weird things, so wrapped it up quickly and was about to put it back in the box, when I noticed the corner of a mustard-coloured moleskin notebook poking out. I began to pull it out and saw an intricate landscape had been doodled on the cover: rolling hills, some coloured in a dull or faded green. In the foreground a white Tipp-Ex cloud with a grey underbelly rained down large teardrops of blue ink. One in the background had lightning coming out of it and striking the ground. It made me shiver. For it reminded me of the tale my father had told me of how he became my dad.

'It was a dark and stormy night,' he had said, his eyes baggy and low. 'I didn't want to go out. The rain was lashing at the windows. The wind was up.'

'It was howling, Rosie,' added my mum. 'I had a bad feeling about that night. There was something out there in the dark. You could feel it. In a way I wasn't surprised when …' she broke off and looked at my dad, who shook his head at her in a restrained pulled-back way that he hoped I hadn't seen.

He ran a hand over his jaw. There was a slight sheen of grey stubble and sweat under his nose. 'Then I got the call from Dad. Septimus,' he clarified. 'Your grandfather. I knew there was something wrong at once. You could hear it in his voice.'

My mum had leant forward and nodded. 'Normally he was so ...' she bunched her lips together and frowned '... composed, I think is the word. He didn't get flustered by much. When Ted told me he wanted us there at once, like I said, I knew something was up. We got in the car straight away.'

'And what happened when you got there?' I had asked, holding my mum's hand so she didn't feel insecure about any of this, which was stupid really but there you go.

'Here,' said my dad, correcting me. He glanced at the museum which was winking behind me. We had been sitting in the memorial garden. 'It was here, Rosie. The museum was in disarray. You could tell as soon as we got into the car park. All the doors and windows were open, despite the rain. It looked like it was howling. Course, we went straight in and found Septimus was upstairs in his bedroom.'

'I heard you before I saw you,' said my mum and smiled and stroked my hair. 'You were so young. You can tell a new baby's cries. They're different to anything else in the whole world.'

Dad too let himself smile for a moment at the memory. 'Father had enough time to tell us he'd found you on the doorstep. On your own. There was no trace of Celeste.'

'Or my father?'

'Your father?' said Dad, then caught himself and looked away to conceal the beginnings of a burn on his cheeks. 'We didn't really know who your father was. Celeste never mentioned him to me. Or at least she was evasive whenever

I asked her. Said it was her business, no one else's. Always headstrong, my sister. Septimus only seemed to have a vague understanding of who he might be. He didn't speak highly of him. And apparently Celeste only saw him a few times. But he had been here that night while Septimus was away. Dad was pretty sure of it – extra toothbrush in the bathroom. Whoever Celeste had had in there had obviously packed in a hurry. When Septimus returned home …'

'He had been away on a case,' Mum whispered. 'But when he came back he said he went into Celeste's room. It looked like someone had been staying there with her. He expected it to be the baby's father, your father, though he was never sure. She had become secretive. It hurt him. They had always been so open with each other.'

'But he was worried,' said Dad. 'Obviously you would be – you get home and find your granddaughter on the doorstep. Without her mother. Why? How? He knew Celeste must have been in trouble. She was a live wire for sure. But she was *not* irresponsible. There is no way she would have left you alone like that. She loved you.'

The words made me swallow and bite down on an emotion I didn't want to acknowledge. 'So what happened?' I asked, wide-eyed, at the same time not wanting to know the answer. After all, I was aware of how the story ended.

'Dad had already phoned the police. And they did take it quite seriously, see.' Ted Strange swallowed. 'It was one hell of a night. There had been lots of accidents all over the county. They were coming up on the radio. "Avoid this junction here", "road closures there" because of the severe weather. It felt like all hell was breaking loose while we were driving here. Not just the gale, but the rain was pelting us. Trees were going over left, right and centre.'

Dad sent me a look that indicated this was a significant piece of information. He wanted me to digest it, so for a moment didn't speak. Then as he continued I realised his intention. 'They turned up shortly after we got there. The police.' Then he lost his words. Or maybe he just didn't want to say them. His eyes filled with water.

I couldn't look at him. It seemed intrusive, so I turned to Mum and smiled at her. But her face was drawn. The muscles around her mouth were flexing like she was struggling with an expression. I closed my eyes and let my head rest back onto the chair. The sun played on my eyelids, colouring everything brown. And then red.

After a moment Dad collected himself. He inflated his lungs and said, 'They told us that they'd found her.'

I opened my eyes and saw he had leant forwards now, putting his hands on his knees as if he were recovering from a blow and needed help sitting up. 'Her car had come off the road,' he went on, 'and ended up in the brook. Because of all the recent rain, the water level was higher than usual. She'd been unconscious when she drowned.' Then he dropped his eyes. I didn't know what was going on behind them, but I could feel shame coming off him and wondered if it was because everyone had assumed Celeste's crash was an accident. Careless driving maybe. The conditions had obviously been right. Although, now we knew, it had been an incorrect assumption. A shadow on her memory. Unjust.

But I wouldn't go into that now. There were other more pressing things to learn. So I spoke up. 'But they, the police, they didn't say anything about him?' I was going to say 'my father' but the words suddenly seemed loaded and full of blame. So I added, 'The man that was with Celeste? In her car?'

Mum shook her head. 'We didn't know if he'd been in the car. At first we wondered if it was he who chased Celeste or if he'd been responsible for her death. We just didn't know what to make of any of it. Until, lately …' Then she too hung her head like my dad had just done. They both fetched their eyes away from me to each other. It was a long low look. When their eyes met a small amount of tension seemed to go out of them. Then Mum's narrowed and she said, 'What that awful de Vere woman said … it's shocking … we didn't know for certain that Celeste was with anyone else that night in the car. Mind you, we've only got de Vere's word on the matter and god knows she and her father have lied about everything else. Ethel …' She trailed off and looked at my dad.

He bit his lip and nodded sadly, no doubt thinking about his mother. What Mum said was true. We did only have Araminta de Vere's half-crazed words. And they were not much to go on. When I was ready I'd have to go and visit that jailbird and try and squeeze some more info out of her. But when I was ready. Which wasn't when I was sitting in the memorial garden hearing the whole sorry tale pour from my parents. The cork had shot out and nothing was going to stop them get this off their chests.

I let my dad and his wife have a moment of silence, so they

could gather themselves, then I said, 'But what happened with me?'

My mum nodded then said, 'Well, it was while they were breaking the news to us, about, about what they found. About Celeste's accident. And of course, we were all stunned, shocked. It was terrible news. We forgot, for that moment, that you had fallen asleep in your granddad's bed. Then we heard a crying. And the policeman said, "Who's that?" And Septimus looked at me, and so did your dad, and we were all thinking the same thing. Was whoever did this going to come after you? You had been saved for a reason but there was too much to think through and no time and so I just said it, right then. Just popped out of me mouth. I said, "Oh that's my daughter, Rosie." And then I went to fetch you.' She tightened her grip on my hand. 'It wasn't organised. It just happened. And it worked.'

I sat back and thought through the logic of it and said, 'And that was it? You took me and nobody ever raised an eyebrow?'

Dad shook his head. 'Celeste hadn't registered your birth yet. We went to Maureen's sister, Auntie Babs, and stayed with her. Then we registered you as our own. Stayed with Babs till I could find a new job and a new home in South Essex, then we moved there with you, had new neighbours, and no one was any the wiser.'

'Apart from Septimus.'

'Of course,' said Dad. 'But he thought it was a good idea too. For a while. Then ...' he paused. 'Then later he thought it was time we ought to tell you. We didn't.'

I nodded. I had an inkling of when that might have been. There was a memory that persisted, possibly from when I was about eight years old. It was here. At the Witch Museum. I was recording something for granddad. Or was I doing something else for granddad? Moving something? I couldn't quite remember. Only that there had been a fight. Or at least cross words between Dad and Septimus. We never came back.

'Me and yer dad had been trying for a while to start a family,' said my mum and smiled at my dad. 'But hadn't been successful yet, so everyone was pleased to see you when you appeared. People just thought we'd got lucky, after all.'

'Don't talk about it any more,' I said. 'That's all I want to know.'

It was the mention of them trying for a baby that brought tears to my eyes. Not in an emotional way. You just don't like to think of your parents *in flagrante*, do you?

It was enough explanation for the time being.

Plus, I'd heard as much as I could manage. I didn't want to look at myself and wonder why I hadn't suspected any of it before. Why I had failed to pick up any hints? I mean – it was pretty massive stuff.

But now I was devoid of the energy to work out what it meant.

To my parents, about my parents. About me.

About what was wrong with me.

The sound of a cough, a purposeful announcing sort of interruption, came from the direction of the living room and took me away from that summer day of bleeding hearts and revelations.

I was grateful to him.

'So now you've brought the box in here to stare at?' said Sam. But he was smiling. In his hand he had a sheet of paper. 'I suppose it's progress of a sort.'

I turned and nodded. 'I've found a notebook.' And I waved it at him.

'That's a good start,' he said with a grin and stepped through the doorway. 'What does it say?'

'I don't know,' I said and placed it carefully back in the box. 'But I'm thinking I should try to see Araminta de Vere.'

His face dropped and his mouth opened. But then he closed it and kind of ducked, bent his face down in a manner that made me think of surrender, and made a nodding movement. 'Okay. If you really need it. I'll come too. If you'd like?' Which was supportive.

I didn't answer. I didn't know whether I wanted him to or not.

He lifted his face and we stared at each other across the room.

I think he was waiting for me to say something but I was waiting for him.

The air between us crackled.

'Well,' he said, and shook his head gently. 'Whatever. Look.' Then he held the ream of paper out. 'Here's the story: *Man-Sized in Marble*.'

I was kind of pleased for the distraction. It'd be nice to be taken out of myself and into an engaging piece of fiction.

Trundling closer to him, but not too close, I took the pages, glancing over the opening sentences: '*Although every word of this story is as true as despair, I do not expect people to believe it. Nowadays a "rational explanation" is required before belief is possible. Let me then, at once, offer the "rational explanation" which finds most favour among those who have heard the tale of my life's tragedy. It is held that we were "under a delusion" ...'*

That sounded promising. I was instantly engaged. In fact the opening chimed well with me. I had reached the point now, where I truly thought that although ninety-nine per cent of unusual phenomena had a psychological or logical explanation. There was still one per cent that didn't.

My own personal jury was out on the who, the why and the how.

I wasn't sure if I'd ever make my mind up for sure. These days those sorts of questions were plaguing me more often than they ever had before, leading me down dead ends and navigating endless roundabouts.

'Is it good?' I asked Sam, waving the story at him, just as I had the notebook minutes before. Oh yeah – I could do with several distractions right now.

'I haven't read it yet.' He smiled. His eyes had softened to a honey brown which reminded me of cartoon beavers. He was feeling gentle. 'Will do. In bed.'

Bed. Yes. I nodded and felt that my head was heavy. I was, I realised now, very, very tired. Washed out and depleted. I yawned. 'That's a good idea,' I said. 'Might do the same.'

As I turned to reach for my dressing gown, he touched my arm. 'You okay?' he murmured and moved his index finger up my forearm. 'Really?'

'I suppose. All things considering.' It was my standard

response. It made me sound like my dad. Who was not my dad.

I sighed.

He watched my face collapse. 'You look done in.' The aftershocks of the summer's earthquake still rippled through me from time to time. And sometimes I just simply didn't have the energy to keep my mask in place.

'It's been a long day,' he went on. 'What with the funeral. I hadn't thought of it but it must bring back memories of …' he stopped, realising perhaps if I hadn't already thought about it then he shouldn't be the one to flag up that dark sealed-in steamy day when we commended my grand-mother's coffin of bones and her mummified head to the sacred ground where my grandfather had lain awaiting his lost wife.

Sam swallowed, cleared his throat and made his voice jauntier. 'Well let's see – driving to Damebury when we least expected it, Graham Peacock's mysterious death, the spectre of avenging knights, a wolf in the woods. All pretty exciting and draining.'

'Yep,' I said, ready to catch on to this less exhausting thread. 'A day in the life of the Witch Museum team.'

His mouth kinked and he leant against the doorframe. '*Plus ça change, plus c'est la même chose.*'

I smiled back too. He said this on occasion. It meant 'the more things change, the more things stay the same'. And it was so very apt to describe my time of tenure at the museum.

'Let's call it a day,' he was saying. 'I've got a film back from Monty that I want to look through. I'll turn everything off.'

I thanked him and began to close the door. 'Can you turn off my head too?'

I heard him say, 'I'd like to try.'

But I knew he was just being nice. That's what he was like – a wonderful, caring individual, who was smart, handsome and wise.

He deserved much better than me: a blousy, bombastic Benefit Fraud inspector who had failed to inspect the most massive fraud at the centre of her life, the nature of her very being.

Yes, Sam Stone could do better than that indeed.

And so he should.

I squirmed out of my clothes.

Then I slipped into the bed that I had slept on that night thirty-three years ago when my grandfather laid me, so gently, down on its sheets.

When Maureen Strange picked me up and clutched me tight to her heart.

When Celeste, my mother, breathed her last bubbled breath beneath the waters of Piskey Brook.

Rain began to patter at the window stutteringly, like long-suppressed teardrops finding release.

CHAPTER FIVE

'There was certainly an eerie similarity to the state in which Mr Peacock's corpse was found,' Sam agreed. 'We should see if we can find photos of the poor man in situ.'

The countryside flanked us quietly, as we drove through the damp gloom to Damebury. It was drizzling though not cold. But the sky was unhappy and grey.

'Spot on,' I said. 'Yes, we need to speak to the police or coroner. Monty can be approached in that regard. I'll give him a call later. There are other things we also need help with. I have transcribed the list of residents, staff and lecturers that Sophia gave you. I'll email it as a follow-up to the inimitable Mr Walker once we've touched base.' I was at ease once more. All thoughts of my troubled parentage, the dubious question marks that hung over my head, my total inability to deduce the fundamental precepts on which my life was built – all of that would have to wait. I was an investigator again with a case in hand. And I was good at it. At least, I knew what to do. And how to behave. Well kind of. And I had a lot of experience I could rely on – I understood the ropes, I got results.

Sam nodded and looked out the window. 'I hope you're adjusting your speed in accordance with the slippery road surfaces. Breaking distance doubles.'

'Yes,' I said and gritted my teeth. 'All right.'

Out of the corner of my eye, I saw Sam shrug. 'Well you nearly got that detectorist back in the village.'

'Hmm,' I said. 'He shouldn't have been standing in the middle of the road.' Like a lemon and looking at the floor, I thought but didn't say.

Adder's Fork had experienced a brief influx of treasure hunters over the summer. Thankfully a new series of *Strictly* had started and, when the aforementioned booty had not given itself up at once, a lot of those who had flocked to our little corner of Essex got bored and drifted off back to the telly.

Sam didn't comment.

I continued to swerve our way round the rural lanes and byways.

The area around our destination was quite hilly and far too picturesque for a county that was meant to be flat and uninteresting, which I remarked upon to Sam. 'Shh,' he said. 'Don't tell anyone or they'll all be wanting to move here.'

Then he pointed out a sign for Butt Green and the pair of us indulged in some teenage sniggering.

'Did you hear back from Laura?' I asked, mentally ticking off the questions we'd raised yesterday but hadn't answered. See – logical mind reasserting itself. 'Who knew about her story choice? That it was specifically *Man-Sized in Marble*?'

He got his phone out and fiddled with it. 'Yes, she said that she sent the information and story details out a good three months in advance when the course had been booked up, and suggested everyone read it prior to coming down.'

'Well,' I said, 'suppose that narrows it down to the ten participants – two lecturers and eight students. No one outside of them would have known about the content. There's the housekeeper who got the day off yesterday, but I'm not sure she would have been required to read it. But we can ask.'

Sam frowned. 'Double bend or series of bends coming up. You might want to …'

'Yes, yes,' I said, 'reduce my speed.' And put my foot down on the brake quite roughly.

He lurched. 'Now, I'm assuming Chris Devlin would know of it.' Sam gripped the dashboard. 'I imagine he and Laura must have discussed the course prior to commencing.'

The roads were actually rather sharply angled. 'What?' I was quite grateful I'd slowed right down. Wow. Sam was having a positive effect on me.

'He's the other author, the one that Cullen reported didn't make it,' he explained, raising his voice as if I was deaf, not just distracted. 'I was saying that, presumably, he knew. About the text. The story.'

We passed an open field bordered by a row of young orange-leaved trees. Autumnal prettiness. I liked it. 'Uh-huh,' I said. 'Although if they were taking different parts of the course they might not have read each other's recommendations.'

'True,' said Sam. 'Devlin might have known of it anyway though. If it's a bit of a classic.'

I agreed. 'Although, he's not here is he? So nothing points to him.'

'That's correct. Oh hang on – here we are,' said Sam. 'You need to pull in. It's on your right.'

I saw the church lane open up and turned into it. 'Assuming that any aspect of Graham's death was premeditated, and it wasn't all randomly coincidental,' I added. 'Stranger things have happened at sea.'

To which he replied, 'And stranger things have happened to thee.'

Then we high-fived.

It had become a bit of a call and response thing lately. Something to defuse the tension. Because, of course, a hell of a lot of strange things had been happening to both of us of late. We'd talked about it and wondered if it was the magnetic pull of the Witch Museum or if there was something stirring up the air. Both possibilities were equally disturbing. It was another conversation that we'd have to return to when we had time. If we *ever* had any down time.

The church was perched on the top of a hill. We left the car and saw that on either side of it there were two very large houses. One, a former vicarage, the other another grand house like Ratchette Hall. The owners would have been, and possibly still remained, of some standing in the village a century ago. Both builds spoke of wealth.

St Saviour's itself looked aged in a kind of standard 'old church' way. Parts of it had uneven walls, with different, irregular stones embedded across them. Other wings were more symmetrical. And it was quite big for such a petite village. So maybe it had started off small and been added to over the years. Was it pretty? I wondered. No, not pretty but imposing, austere.

We trundled round the churchyard, with its grand tombs and weeping angels, to the west door, which was unlocked.

Inside, the atmosphere was one of rigid sternness and conventionality. The layout was that of a standard English church, designed to resemble the cross: nave down the middle, steps up to the chancel with choir to the sides, pews for the congregation set out in lines either side of the aisle facing the altar at the top. At the back there were more wooden pews. They looked slightly older, carved from darker timbers, and were mounted on a low platform. Presumably these were for the more affluent patrons – the slight elevation meant they had a good view of the church and altar.

Ironically I had been in more churches since I had become owner of the Witch Museum, or keeper, as Sam preferred to call my position, than I ever had before. These layouts were becoming familiar.

I breathed in. There was a slight whiff of damp and the smell of 'old stillness'. Despite this, I had a sense of movement: a faint mechanical whirring was definitely coming from somewhere.

As I walked down the aisle the pews caught my eye. Well, more precisely the ends of them. They were really quite something. For they had been carved painstakingly into lots and lots of different creatures: dogs with wings, monkeys that looked like old men clutching their heads in their hands like that poor lost soul in *The Scream*. Some bore strange eagles with dodo beaks and pointy wings. Others supported blubbery sea serpents with open sucking mouths.

Three-legged owls watched me as I passed under their unblinking gaze. Griffins shrieked, scaly lions and fanged gargoyles roared – all without making a single sound. They were a strange sort of guardian to have in a place of sanctity. I wondered what their purpose was.

Sam had of course told me that gargoyles were erected on the outsides of churches both to act as spouts that conveyed rainwater down from the roof and to frighten away evil spirits. But these ones were inside, set to sit at shoulder height alongside the worshippers. And the carving technique was definitely more recent than the Middle Ages. I was no expert, but the choice of the oak and some of the sculpture style reminded me of some Victorian pieces we had in the museum. Especially the strange wooden lectern that had an eagle carved into it. It too had a wide hooked nose and a man's feet. That piece dated to the 1880s. According to the notes that accompanied the artefact it had been a local carpenter's private flight of fancy. To amuse his children. These pew ends, however, could not be displayed more publicly. They were there for a reason.

I was going to ask Sam what he thought of them but he was beckoning me to one side. The speed at which his hand moved, suggested impatience. Then he said, 'Come on, stop dallying. Here's one. An effigy. No tomb though. Just the top.'

I passed under the glare of an ambiguous-looking sphinx and came to Sam's side. He had one hand on the wall. The other was on his thigh, balancing his weight as he bent into a shallow recess and squinted at the features of the prone statue lying there.

Here, then, was our great avenging medieval knight.

Looking like he was having a nap.

In a natty tunic.

He had one hand on the hilt of his sword, another on its shaft, clutching it tight. Seriously if this were a *Carry On* film there would be some serious innuendo flying about right now.

Lower down, pointy chain-mail feet rested on something that could have been a reclining dog.

His face was generic. Not like a real person. More like the impression of one: slanty eyes, straight nose. Mouth just a line, slightly curved down, a smattering of an Inspector Clouseau moustache above it.

I reached out to touch it, wondering absurdly if there might be something there – perhaps a residual energy left over from their march to Ratchette Hall?

But I felt nothing. Of course. Just cold smoothness under my fingertips.

I don't know why I had thought I might pick anything up. I guess I was thinking about my grandmother and her clairaudient abilities. But there was nothing there. Nothing that I could pick up on. Or was aware of. I didn't know if that was good or bad.

'Why has this been displayed?' asked Sam as I removed my hand. 'I thought it had been resealed and buried.'

But he had taken off to the north side of the church.

'Because,' I called over. 'It's quite beautiful.' Indeed, there was something absurdly peaceful about this sleeping knight. Still. Not moving. At peace with the world.

That is, if he hadn't got up and walked the earth on All Hallows' Eve.

'It's strange isn't it?' called Sam from the other side. 'That people had this sort of thing carved. I am wondering if it's the ancient equivalent of a photograph.'

I left the sleeping statue and walked over to him.

'There's another one here,' he said. 'This is certainly more enduring than a photograph. And more prominent. It would have been a show of status to the world. Or at least the parishioners.'

I cast my eyes to the floor as I detected a difference in the surface underfoot. I was treading on something that was a whole lot flatter than the roughly evened tiles. A tombstone. With a cross carved into it. 'Were these guys crusaders?' I asked. 'Like ...' I tried to remember where I'd seen this sort of thing before.

'Ah yes,' said Sam. 'Good thinking.'

I found the memory match and pulled it out with triumph. 'That's it. Like *Indiana Jones and the Last Crusade*. There was that old dude in the temple, with the grail. He was guarding it. He had this cross on his tunic.' I pointed at the symbol beneath my feet.

The rectangular grey stone was smooth and polished from centuries of shoes hobbling over it. Funny place to want to rest forever, I thought. But I suppose you'd always have company. At least on a Sunday.

Sam crumpled against the further wall and then straightened his face. 'Really Rosie, are all your references from children's films?'

'Yeah. And telly. And internet. And books. You?'

His laugh echoed round the whitewashed walls of the church.

'There's a cross here,' I said. 'But that bloke, the knight with the Clouseau moustache back there, he didn't have one on his tunic. Not that I could see.'

Sam turned and bent into another recess. 'No, you're right. Nor does this one here.'

'So what does that mean?' I asked catching up with him. 'They weren't holy?'

'No,' he said. 'Only that they didn't take part in the holy crusades.'

I peeped over Sam's shoulder to survey the new knight. He looked more or less like the last one. Except this one's face was a bit more eroded. You had to bend right in to see it. I didn't really like the look of him. He was darker, his eyes deeper, the mouth more pinched. And it felt like he was trying to ignore us and face the wall. This guy had both hands on his sword, gripping it firmly, like he was a heartbeat away from unsheathing it and plunging it into someone. Oh yeah, this one was definitely less *Carry On*, more *Hammer Horror.*

'So what did the knights actually do?'

'Good question,' said Sam. 'I've not had much to do with them: Knights of Christ. Religious warriors.'

'Oh god,' I said and rolled my eyes. 'Worst kind.'

Sam continued to look at the stone soldier. 'Really? Why?'

'They have faith. Faith is all about blindness. It's illogical. It demands that you overlook its flaws just so you can have it. Then when you have it, you don't let anyone budge you. However convincing their argument might be. However sympathetic you might be to them.'

Sam didn't reply. I followed his gaze and saw that he was looking at the feet. The knight's shoes were resting on a large coiled snake-like creature. 'The dog over there,' he said, 'symbolises loyalty generally. Which suggests the man may once have done something good in his life for which he was awarded recognition posthumously. Strange that this one hasn't got a similar pet.'

'So, this one was a baddie?' I thought about the sword back at Ratchette Hall, torn from the body of a six-headed serpent.

Sam shrugged. 'It all depends on your perspective really. Say "barbarians" are attacking a village and stealing their sheep, because their own community has got no food, no live stock. Knights come to the aid of the village and slay the barbarians, the other settlement's warriors. Thus they sentence the defeated community to slow and painful death by starvation. Who's the hero? The defending knight or the barbarian that tried to save their people?'

I nodded, though he couldn't see, and recited one of my grandfather's sayings. 'Perspective is a shifting sand, right?' And we looked at the statue.

'They've both got their fingers though,' Sam pointed out. And indeed they had.

I pulled back and looked over the pews again. It was so quiet. No traffic. No voices. Just the wind. As I listened I became aware of the whirring sound again. It was coming from the back of the church.

I broke off and made my way to a large jagged hole in the wall at the rear. It looked like someone had knocked through but not finished it properly. 'Ah,' I said to myself as I got closer. 'This one must be the tomb they discovered earlier in the year.'

The section had been crudely covered on the outside with a makeshift wall and tarpaulin sheets overhead that were partially transparent and thus let in the daylight. They had been fastened into place securely though and didn't flap. The space was about three metres square and looked like a bad builder's bodged extension, only half-finished. The type that would turn up on *DIY SOS*. I could see it now – the vicar despairing that the builders had done a runner. Appealing to the public to sort the chaos out.

Except this wasn't any ordinary extension. There was the beginnings of a wall, but the floor had been partially dug up. Work must have halted when the ground fell through into a previously unseen cavern. There were several lengths of blue-and-white tape cordoning the hole off, and a sign that hung down into the gap in the wall that read 'No entry. Work in progress.' Half of the strands of plasticky tape had, however, been pulled aside and thrown onto the floor so the whole 'Keep Out' vibe wasn't coming across that strongly. With that in mind I did what I do best and ignored it. Then I walked into the space and scrutinised the hole.

There was an old wooden ladder peeping out the top. I, of course, got hold of it and clambered down several rungs, onto another floor a good few feet lower than the rest of the church. It was like a cave-room, very low-ceilinged, only five feet high. I was forced to hunch over and squat. As my eyes became accustomed to the dimness, I realised that it was shaped similarly to the other recesses in the church where the other knights lay. Though this recess was obviously subterranean and, I felt, possibly older.

Dark, dank, damp, part of the wall over the tomb was glistening slightly. The air smelled of vegetation and vegetative decay with a huge dose of mustiness sprinkled in, despite the efforts of the rotating fan that was connected to an extension lead. There was a note sellotaped onto the floor in front of it: 'On no account turn this fan off.'

The blower was pointing at a tomb. That is, I assumed it was a tomb – it was rectangular and carved from heavy stone, brownish in parts. The sarcophagus had a lid, but no effigy atop it. However, as I continued to stare I realised the top had had been pushed open so that the stone coffin lid was half ajar, revealing a tantalising opening – a triangular window into the tomb.

Intrigued, I crept over and squinted into the darkness. Unable to see much, I took out my phone and shone the light into it. There was another coffin within, its lid off and nowhere to be seen. As far as I could see, the tomb was empty. Not entirely surprising, I thought, and was about to call out to Sam, when a haughty voice above me, shouted, 'Hey you! What do you think you're doing there?'

Snapping round I saw a black silhouette peering down over the edge of the hole. His voice suggested he wasn't happy about me having disregarded the 'Keep Out' sign.

'What?' I said, limply. 'I was just interested in the hole. What is it?' Pleading stupidity has never made for a great start: ignorance of the law is no excuse. I knew that. I reminded people about it.

The bending man wasn't buying it either. 'It's a very important part of the church restoration,' he snapped. As I moved towards the opening I could see light falling on grey crinkled hair crowning a high forehead and egg-shaped face. 'Very important,' he repeated, then knotted his lips into a pout. I spied a dog collar peeping over a purple jumper. 'Would you mind stepping out right away? NOW!'

I shrugged. 'Okay.' And began to ascend to the surface via the ladder. 'Sorry.'

I was halfway up when he suddenly shrieked. 'Stop!'

Which I did.

The guy's face was going a really crazy shade of red.

He gasped. 'What have you done? To the tomb? It's open! Where's the effigy?'

Then a brown boot loomed over my face. I backed down the ladder to avoid it connecting.

'I didn't do anything,' I protested as corduroy trousers and a large squidgy bottom came into view. 'I just came down to have a look. The tomb was like that.'

The ladder rattled against the muddy wall and the man jumped into the cramped space. Feet hitting the ground with a squelch, he spun round and fastened his eyes on the empty tomb. 'Oh no no no!' he cried. 'Where's the effigy?'

He half-crouched half-leapt at the sarcophagus and ran his hand over the surface. Then he looked into the crack. 'And, oh my goodness?' Twisting instantly, the vicar jabbed an angry digit straight at my chest and looked me up and down as if I was concealing something on my person. 'What … where? You Jezebel! What have you done with the body?'

CHAPTER SIX

It took a trip to the car and a thorough inspection of all possible storage areas (boot, glovebox, coffee holder, small CD case under the passenger seat) to convince Father Edgar that neither myself nor Sam had snaffled the body and coffin top.

When he finally saw the light, so to speak, we decided the police should be informed.

The local dispatch noted down the details and said they'd send someone over. But we all got the feeling we weren't going to hear the dulcet squeal of blues and twos in the immediate. Father Edgar announced they had CCTV over both doors, so whoever had taken them would be recorded on there. Then he went outside the church to make a 'private' call.

'Well, I'm glad we're off the hook,' said Sam once we were alone again.

I smirked. 'You definitely haven't got them in your pocket then?'

Sam cocked his head to one side. 'Oh don't, Rosie. He was obviously in a state of shock. And who can blame him? You wouldn't expect a desiccated cadaver and a stone effigy to be at the top of your everyday burglar's wish list.'

'Mmm. True that. Which begs the question – who has stolen it and why? Or maybe the other way round. In terms of importance. And is it the knight with the missing finger? I guess it must be. The other two looked pretty intact.'

Sam sat down on one of the pews with a carving of a Griffin spreading its eagle wings. 'Oohhh chilly,' he said and pulled his jacket tighter. 'It's so draughty here.' He moved up the pew a little. 'Well,' he unfolded his arms and pointed towards the Clouseau-esque effigy. 'You're right. He's got all his fingers. And so has the one up there.' His head rolled forwards to the northern knight and bobbed twice. 'So I guess yes, we must presume the missing digit has come from the vanished man in marble.'

'Do you think someone wants us to believe this body has gone AWOL on purpose and is now terrorising the neighbourhood?'

Sam crept up again and rubbed the rear legs of the griffin, clawed like a lion's. 'Well, I've not heard anything about marauding corpses on the radio and I imagine Monty would be down here like a shot, if there were any suggestion of such.'

I looked back at the hole at the rear of the church. 'Well deduced, Watson. But it could suggest such a thing to some people.'

'Yes, you're right. Or someone's covering their tracks.'

'Do you really think it's connected to what happened with Graham Peacock?'

Sam swivelled round and joined me in staring at the hole. 'I would think so. It's too much of a coincidence for them not to be linked, and yet we must assume nothing. My feeling is that it's likely the finger in Graham's hand came from the absent effigy.'

'Or somewhere else,' I said helpfully. 'Let's agree that the finger in Graham Peacock's hand was planted there, rather than grabbed off the Avenging Knight,' I proposed. I felt like we needed to establish a foundation of facts, as Sam had so spontaneously put it yesterday.

My friend smacked apricot lips and thought for a moment. 'It's the most obvious conclusion.'

I slipped into the pew opposite. 'But if that is the case, as Mr Sutcliffe suggested last night, that points to a strong element of premeditation.'

Sam nodded. 'We should see if Monty can run a background check on Graham, if he's not already done so. See if he has any enemies.'

'And the rest of them,' I added.

The door at the back of the church opened and we saw Father Edgar enter. His face was still screwed up with frowns. Maybe he looked like that in his natural state of repose.

I turned back to Sam. 'Although, it's got to be said – we shouldn't lose sight of the outside chance that this theft is unrelated to Mr Peacock's demise. In terms of motive anyway.'

'How do you mean?' asked Sam.

'Maybe Graham's death drew attention to the church and its effigies and attracted the eye of an opportunistic burglar.'

He shivered again. 'Ah, quite. Yes. Good point.'

'Even so, if that's the case, you've still got to wonder why this lot have been stolen? Could the body and effigy be of value?'

There was a sniff and a cough, then Father Edgar padded over. 'Collectors,' he said through pinched lips. 'Anything goes these days. If you desire to have something, however whimsical or abhorrent that might be to the many, there will always be someone who will procure it and then sell it on to you. Whether it be a human body part, a corpse, a tomb or even a still-living human being. Money has become an evil god. If you've got it and worship it, money will duly proclaim itself master. Root of all evil, if you remember, deep down with the Devil himself.'

He sounded a little preachy, but I knew that he was right about there being a market for everything. We had actually had some experience with most of the things Father Edgar had listed: body parts, skeletons, human trafficking. But not a tomb and desiccated corpse. Now I guess we could tick that one off too. Much as humanity filled me with hope, in its most depraved aspect, it terrified me utterly.

I made a noise which was half a moan coupled with a resigned grunt of agreement.

Father Edgar's beady eyes snapped onto me. They were a luminous indigo-blue. 'It's part of our battle against the encroaching darkness. I know it's unfashionable to believe in the Devil, but he is out there, securing his place in the hearts of men.'

I was surprised to hear this old-school talk, but then again if you were going to find it anywhere I supposed it was most likely in a church.

Sam stood up. 'We heard yesterday,' he leant against the pew and rubbed his arms, 'that there has been talk of devil worship and witches in the woods about Ratchette Hall.'

Father Edgar started when he heard the mention of the writers' retreat. Or maybe it was the Devil again. His eyebrows wrinkled along the top. 'Witch Wood. Yes. Now hang on a minute – have you got anything to do with poor Graham's death?' He shuffled back a couple of paces.

I cleared my throat and said, 'Yes. I mean no. I mean we have been asked to investigate the circumstances by a government agency.'

Sam shot me a questioning look. I thought the allusion to Monty might buy us a bit of credibility and to my surprise the gamble paid off.

Edgar looked at me and nodded and said sadly, 'Oh. I see, all right.'

Sam made his forehead go all frowny and asked Edgar. 'And the woods?'

'Ah yes,' he said, his shoulders deflating slightly. 'The witches.' He took a pew to the side of Sam and sat with his legs sticking into the aisle, tapping absently at the carving on the end, a deer with huge elaborate antlers. 'There has always been a dark side to Damebury,' he went on. 'The Devil has been said to run amok here.' He motioned to the aisle. 'Squirming between the legs of parishioners. People saw him mounting the altar and springing around the church from side to side.'

Now that was an image straight out of an animated horror film, I thought, and regarded Edgar's face to see if he was winding us up. He wasn't – his eyes were full of energy as he spoke, the conviction within unsettling.

I felt the coolness of the air in the old building and detected an aroma that smelled uncannily like aniseed. It was strange. The combination of sensations and the vicar's words prompted an involuntary shiver to creep across my shoulders.

'And according to folklore, on the 24th of May 1402,' Edgar went on with rehearsed detail, 'during a terrible storm, they say the Devil appeared as a grey friar and behaved very lewdly, frightening the congregation. As he danced around and exposed himself a great tempest of wind enveloped the church. Thunder and lightning descended from the heavens and destroyed the roof. The chancel was allegedly "rent and torn to pieces".'

I tried to disassociate the image of a friar flashing and wind. It was crude. It was vulgar. It was pathetically tickling me. But totally not the kind of thing that should amuse a grown woman of thirty-four. 'So what does that have to do with stone tombs?' I asked to distract myself.

Edgar looked at me and stared, seeming to forget that he'd been conversing with us at all. 'Tombs?' he said, as his eyes focused on mine. 'Stone? The missing effigy was made of wood. Not like the others.'

That made Sam stand up. 'Really?'

'Yes, it looked like stone but it was actually sculpted from ancient timbers.'

'So this one …' Sam gestured to the cavern where the knight had so recently been discovered. 'Was its finger missing?'

Edgar looked over to the cavern. 'I can't recall. There was some damage around the torso. From centuries of damp, but that was it. We have been raising funds to restore it.'

My colleague folded his arms and looked at me. 'That's interesting.'

'Interesting?' Edgar was outraged.

Sam nodded. 'Wood, however, is more portable.'

'Of course it is,' snapped Edgar. 'And bother bother bother, it could be anywhere by now.'

'Which also means,' Sam said to me, 'that the finger that the late Mr Peacock was clutching was definitely NOT from this, or the other two knights. Not if it was made of wood. The stone ones are intact. And Cullen definitely said he found a stone finger in the administrator's hand.'

'Blimey,' I said to Sam while Father Edgar tutted. 'You're right. So unless Graham habitually wandered around the house with a spare stone finger in his pocket, someone placed it there in his hand during or post mortem.'

Sam raised his head and nodded slowly, 'To suggest the E. Nesbit story.'

'And that the knights had done it,' I added.

Edgar shook his head. 'But the knight that is missing *isn't* made of stone,' he said, not following our thread.

Sam looked at me. 'But someone didn't know that. Someone who placed a stone finger in the deceased's hand.'

'They wanted people to assume it had come from a stone knight,' I confirmed, nodding, and sucked in my lip. 'Father Edgar,' I said, grinning at him, 'do many people know that the most recently discovered tomb effigy was made of wood?'

'Oh yes,' he said. 'It's been big news locally. All the parish-ioners and villagers came to see the discovery.'

I locked eyes with Sam. 'Not a local then.'

'Narrows it down,' he said. 'Quite extensively.'

CHAPTER SEVEN

'Suggest we interview the housekeeper today,' I said to Sam as we waited for someone to answer the door at Ratchette Hall.

'Why?' he said reaching inside his jacket. He was going for his notebook. He kept it in that pocket with a pen in the little one outside just under the lapel.

'Because Sophia said she'd given her the afternoon off. Which therefore means she's definitely local. We can find out if she knew that the missing knight was made of wood. Plus she might know if anyone held any grudges against Graham.'

'Ah, right,' said Sam flicking through the pages of his spiral bound. 'I believe … ah yes. Her name is Carole.'

I stepped away from the door as it opened.

'We should also ask if she read *Man-Sized in Marble*,' Sam continued rifling through his notes. 'Then proceed with tailored questioning after that's confirmed. Or not.'

Sophia's face appeared in the crack. She was paler than yesterday and the bags under her eyes were swollen. 'Oh hello,' she said. I couldn't tell if she was relieved to see us or concerned. 'The housekeeper, you say? Carole? Christmas?'

'Sorry?' I said, double-footed by the non-sequitur.

Sophia nodded to herself. 'Oh yes, of course you don't know. That's her name. Carole Christmas. Carole Blanche Christmas actually.' She grimaced. 'One presumes sadistic parents.'

Sam stifled a laugh. 'Is she full of glad tidings and good cheer? We could do with some of that.' Then he stepped across the threshold. I followed.

Sophia said, 'Mmmm,' and led us into the day room where we had met the others last night. Reclining on the sofas this time, were Jocelyn and Nicholas. Tabitha was sitting at the table in front of a laptop. Across from her Robin was reading the paper. He didn't look up when we came in.

'Thank goodness, you're here,' said Tabitha at once. 'We had an awful night. Nicholas, get Cullen and Laura. Margot. Where's Imogen?'

Nicholas shrugged. He was wearing a white silk shirt that was undone a button too far in my opinion. He shrugged and tossed his hair back. 'How should I know?' he said as if he was completely unbothered. There was strain in his forehead and tension in the shoulders which, I observed, he held a lot higher than yesterday.

Jocelyn got to her feet, flicking her long slinky hair over her shoulders. 'I'll get them. I think they're in the seminar room.'

I noted Sam's eyes flick over her slender silhouette and thought, 'She's young, she's pretty, she's vivacious, she's kind. She's exactly the kind of person he should be with. What was I thinking that he might ever want me? What a fool I've been.' Then I sighed out loud accidentally and everyone glanced my way. Including Sam.

So I cleared my voice and pretended it was a wheezy cough. We both stood aside to let the lovely Jocelyn squeeze past us, and then went and sat on the sofa.

'What's up, Tabby?' I asked the old girl, purposefully making my voice bright. It was as much for inner persuasion as external appearance.

Her silver hair was less groomed than yesterday. Strands of it were falling out all over the place. One had a hair grip dangling from it.

'Last night,' she said and clutched a cameo pendant hanging from her neck, 'we were awakened by the most terrific howling.'

Nicholas nodded to confirm her story. His complexion, I saw now, was ghastly. 'Pretty grim,' he said and swallowed. Then he looked down at the carpet and let his hair fall over his face and added, 'And pretty loud.' His voice broke slightly over the last consonant, betraying a lack of control in the breathing department. It was, I guessed, irregular because of anxiety, although the young man was trying desperately not to show it.

I suddenly realised the louche hipster role was all a camouflage. Nicholas was shaken.

I regarded him again with fresh eyes and realised he was really quite young. Perhaps no older than twenty-four. It was his instilled public-school-boy confidence that made him, at first meeting, seem older. But now that was fraying, uncertainty and inexperience were becoming more visible.

I wondered if I would be upset if I had stayed here and experienced the series of events that had played out over the last two days. I couldn't tell.

'What did it sound like?' I asked. 'Exactly?'

Robin, the bookseller, cleared his throat. 'To my mind, a banshee,' he said. The word, as he expressed it, fully announced his Scottish accent.

'A banshee?' I repeated and screwed my face up. The noun summoned up images of a strong punk chick and a man with yellow hair who had the name of a brightly coloured Australian pet bird.

Robin gulped and nodded, reading my confusion. 'The spirit of a wailing woman said to herald a death in the house,' he enlightened the gathered group. 'Nonsense of course. Superstition, folklore, etc.,' he finished. His words were sounding convincing, but his face wasn't matching them.

'But,' he went on and hauled himself to his feet. 'We talked over breakfast this morning and there's this here. Cullen pointed it out. It's from the magazine article that Laura sent us. About the discovery of the knights in the tomb.' He began to read. *The body was tolerably perfect. The flesh, except on the face and throat appeared exceedingly white and firm … The whole body conveyed the idea of a hearty youth …*' He brought it over and pointed at a line. The paper quivered as he passed it to me. '*Where the pillow supporting the head had rotted away, the head, stretching the throat back, had lacerated it and caused decay there.*'

Tabby spoke up now. 'And that's what it sounded like. A howling through damaged vocal chords.' Her fingers pattered around her own neck. Some of her dotty energy had receded. 'A kind of "ohhhhh-arghhhhh". The most terrible lamentation, I tell you.'

I wondered if it was the same thing we had heard last night as we left – the wolfish wail?

Both Nicholas and Robin nodded. They looked slightly ashamed or maybe just embarrassed. Robin went back to the table, turned the chair round and stared at me.

I realised a kind of terror was beginning in all of them.

'You all agree, do you?' said Sam, after a while.

The three nodded.

No exceptions. Not even Nicholas.

Then the door opened and Sophia trundled in with a thin middle-aged woman whose auburny hair was drawn back tightly into a ponytail. 'Carole,' she proclaimed.

A whiff of something like Dettol came into the room with her.

'All right,' said the newcomer. 'What d'you want?' Now that was a proper Essex accent.

She was scrawny around the chest and a bit wrinkled on the breastplate, so probably shouldn't have gone for the grey scoop neck top that she had on. Though it highlighted a pair of mounds that I imagined might be enticing enough for some. Too small to be falsies but with that pert perky quality that cosmetic surgeons liked to dispense. She looked after them. But not the rest. Along with the disinfectant I smelled fag smoke on her.

'Ah hello,' Sam began. 'The legendary Ms Christmas.'

He smiled.

She didn't. Her mouth tightened, revealing lots and lots of fine little lines around the top and bottom lips.

I took up the reins from my colleague. 'Did you read the

story that the writers were sent, Carole? The one about the knights?'

Her pencilled eyebrows rose up high, she'd plucked them virtually bald. 'Who are you then?'

That was fair enough – we hadn't been introduced. 'Rosie Strange. Essex Witch Museum and this is my curator Sam Stone.'

She looked us up and down, her face really quite ruddy. 'My cousin-in-law works there. Trace.'

'Oh right, yes we know Trace and Vanessa. They're great,' I said. She shook her head at me and said, 'They ain't mad.'

I paused for a moment and then Sam said, 'Indeed.'

But Carole hadn't finished. She looked round at the gathered writers and appealed to them, 'Essex Witch Museum? What's that all about, eh?' She made it sound like the punchline to a joke. A not very good one.

The others didn't really know what to do, so to avoid embarrassment or awkwardness, I snapped my fingers and said, 'And you're back in the room. Now can you answer my question please Carole? Did you read *Man-Sized in Marble*?'

'You what?' she said, and looked back at the writers as if I'd cracked another joke. Then she stuck her hand on her hip. It had a tea towel in it. 'You're 'avin' a laugh, aren't cha? Me? I'm paid to look after the place. Not run the bleedin' courses.' She sucked her mouth in so tightly it looked momentarily like a cat's bum. 'You want me readin' the stuff, you gonna have to stump up for it. Bloody cheek!'

Yes indeed, Carole Christmas was full of good cheer and glad tidings.

Sam however looked quite amused by all this. 'It didn't whet your curiosity then?'

She puckered her arse-mouth again and rolled her eyes. 'Not interested, darlin'. Now wetting my whistle – that's a different story.' Her lips stretched into a gape. The laugh that came out of them was just like machine-gun fire – har har har har har.

To emphasise her hysterical pun, Carole's bony elbow nudged Sophia hard in the ribs. The events organiser flinched then smiled weakly and said, 'Oh yes. Ha ha ha. Yes.' She took a step away from Ms Christmas and explained. 'As well as keeping this magnificent building going with Graha—' she paused, then remembered the dearly departed and changed tack. 'As well as housekeeping, Carole runs The Griffin pub in the village, where she is the assistant manager.'

I nodded. 'That can't leave you much time.'

Her face straightened into a sombre expression presumably to match the weight of responsibility her job entailed. She sniffed. 'No, that's right. Helps that I live there. Only have to commute up and down the staircase.' She smacked Sophia on the arm and laughed. Again. 'Eh?' she added. 'Ain't that right? Up and down the staircase.'

Sophia grimaced. 'Oh yes, Carole. Ha ha. Very good.'

I'd met people like Ms Christmas before, pinched sort of types who were tight with their emotions as well as their purse and disapproving of anyone who wasn't the same as them. My Uncle Del had a sister, Joyce, just like it, another bony mare who apparently did very well for herself despite an absence of any finesse and charm. Auntie Babs always said she could fall into a cesspit and would come out smelling of roses – other people's roses. Reckoned the survival instinct was very strong in old Joyce. When I met her once, at a wake after a family funeral, I saw she was ruthless enough to get what she wanted whatever the cost. She had no scruples about lying and thieving, just an absolute dedication and commitment to self-preservation and self-interest. She hadn't known I was watching as she slipped a couple of bottles of wine into her bag.

Thinking about it, I could now see that Carole Christmas had little blackcurrant eyes just like Joyce's. She also ringed them with loads and loads of brown eyeliner too.

I continued to hold Carole's curranty gaze and smiled and said, 'You were there, at The Griffin, Monday night, were you? Plenty of witnesses?'

The blackcurrants snapped onto me. The cat's arse appeared again. 'Witnesses? Yes I bleedin' do! I ain't got nothing to do with poor Graham and I don't like what you're implying.'

Sam cleared his throat. 'I'm sorry but we have to ask everyone.'

'Haven't asked me,' said Nicholas helpfully, the git.

'So what were your movements on Monday evening, Mr Blackman?' I asked.

'Same as everyone else. Sat down here then went to bed.'

'Right,' I said. 'Well, that added a great deal to what we know, thank you.'

The door opened and in trooped Jocelyn, Imogen and Starla. Cullen and Laura followed, making up a full house.

Ever the mischief-maker, Nicholas decided to add in a louder voice, 'Yes. I went to bed with Jocelyn Monday night.'

The young woman immediately sighed. 'Nicholas, you might add that we departed at our doors. And slept *separately*.'

'Worse luck,' he said and shrugged.

Starla lifted her skirts and sat down at the table. Today's outfit was tie-dyed from head to toe. She had a matching scarf wrapped round her head. 'We all retired about the same time and nobody saw anything unusual. We talked about it last night.' Her blue hair still looked unwashed and greasy.

I took this on board. 'So is there no one who stayed up?'

Everyone shook their heads. They were being more cooperative today, at least.

Sam followed up. 'And no one heard anything?'

'I think I'm right in saying,' said Tabby, the dangling hair grip swinging like an air-sock in a whirlwind, 'we all slept like logs. Not like last night.'

Starla shuddered and tapped my lap. 'The wailing, did they tell you? It was awful. We all heard it.'

Carole's ears perked up. 'Did ya? Shrieking sort of noises, was it?'

Everybody nodded.

Sophia said, 'You know something about this do you, Carole?'

'Well, they say, there's witches in them woods. Some of the regulars were talking. They've 'eard 'em. Kieron, one of my staff, said someone found decapitated animal bodies under the trees near the brook. Heads ripped clean off. The witches practice devil worship out there. All the locals know 'baht it. They say if you hear them scream then you're a goner …'

She didn't get to finish, for Sam began tutting loudly. 'Can I point out here that such hearsay is very unlikely to be true. Ridiculous, in fact. And are you talking about some old legend or suggesting this is a contemporary scenario?'

Carole looked stumped for a moment. 'Er, well what I'm saying is – it don't just happen in the past. It's happening now too.' She jerked her head at Tabby and Robin. 'And this lot says they heard 'em. Don't they?'

Bulb-headed Imogen raised her hand to Sam. 'We all heard the moaning in the woods last night. You can't deny us that.'

'Well if you are suggesting it's witches that's simply incorrect, I'm afraid.' He shook his head then got to his feet and went and stood by the fireplace so that he could see everyone. 'The witches of the past would have identified, in all likelihood, as Christians. But mostly what we're talking about, when we speak of witches of old, is a miscarriage of justice on the scale of a massacre. Born of superstitions and seeming slights.' He nodded to himself then pointed to the left. 'That was then. Now if you are talking about those who call themselves witches today, they'll most likely call themselves Wiccans. And, with regards to your woods, it is *incredibly* unlikely that they would do anything to hurt animals – they are a nature-based religion with huge respect and care for the natural world.'

'Hear, hear,' added Starla.

Sam nodded at her in acknowledgement of solidarity and carried on. 'Likewise, Wiccans wouldn't worship the Devil because he's not one of their lot. The Devil is a Christian god.'

Carole's mouth opened and she shook her face from side to side in over-exaggerated shock. 'There ain't nothink Christian about the Devil!'

'On the contrary,' Sam answered her. 'He's an entirely Christian creation with all the trimmings: his own infernal minions, the kingdom, Hell, as opposed to Heaven, adversarial status as a fallen angel. If you didn't have Christianity, then you wouldn't have the Devil.'

Starla nodded her limp blue head. 'I dig it. Always knew it too.'

Nicholas crossed his legs and said, 'What about Satanism?'

'Do you mean the Church of Satan?' said Sam. 'Yes, well, they're atheists. Don't believe in the Devil or God. In fact Anton LaVey, the founder, stated anyone who believes in such supernatural entities, is probably insane.'

Nicholas smiled thinly. 'I hear what he's saying.'

'Wiccans are different,' said Sam and inclined his head to the young man. 'There is no devil in their pantheon.'

I'd heard Sam use that word before and had to go and look it up, so I saved our gathered audience the trouble and explained, 'Pantheon – collection of all the gods in a particular religion.' Sometimes I really liked the sound of my own expert voice.

'A horned god does exist of course,' Sam continued. 'So to speak. And his horns, like depictions of the Devil, grow out his head, true. His name however is not Beelzebub or Lucifer, but Cernunnos, god of the hunt, fertility, life, creatures. And he is an old god. Predates Christianity.'

'They demonised the old gods,' Starla announced.

'I didn't know that,' Tabby muttered.

Starla drew herself up. 'But they have ways of coming down, our old gods, finding chinks in time, wriggling through that very fabric so they can communicate.' Her skirts fell down between her legs. 'With us.'

Robin tittered.

'Certainly the Gundestrup cauldron is old, yes,' Sam went on. 'Thought to date to 150 BC. There are Celtic depictions of an antlered man on the side, who many believe is Cernunnos.' Sam looked around again and said, 'There's a school of thought that suggests Christian priests worked out that natives were still secretly worshipping the old gods, like Cernunnos. But instead of banning him, they absorbed the horned one into their new religion and turned him into a villain. Cernunnos was already god of the underworld so it wasn't too much of a jump to turn him into the god of Hell. No doubt the priests hoped remaining pagans would be discouraged from worshipping a baddie. And there were associations with Baal.'

Robin cleared his throat, 'Ah yes. Baal, he of Jezebel fame,' he said, looking very pleased with himself indeed.

The name evoked images of Father Edgar and his apprehension of my good lady self in the church.

'That's right, Robin,' said Sam. 'Well done. Jezebel was the Queen of Israel. She earned her place in history when she persuaded her husband to worship Asherah, a goddess, and her consort Baal, instead of Yahweh.'

'Oh yes, so his followers weren't very happy with that were they, Sam?' Robin asked, evidently enjoying the opportunity to buddy up with the most knowledgeable person in the room and show off his own education.

Sam smiled, his mouth pulling in that familiar and adorable way to the left.

But Robin continued anyway, 'Tsk, tsk. Nae they dinnae. Yahweh was more powerful, you see.' He bowed his head, presumably to receive adulation and praise for being such a clever boy. Personally, I thought it typical that someone like him knew all about the ancient gods of other countries but nothing of those on his own shore. There was snobbery mixed into it, I was sure.

'And so Yahweh's followers,' Robin continued to explain. 'Well, they threw Jezebel out of a window and left her body to be eaten by stray dogs.'

Imogen winced. Tabby nodded like she knew the story too.

'Indeed, thank you Robin,' Sam went on. 'And of course we know that the victors write history, so Jezebel, the defeated, became associated with false prophets and lots of other generally frowned-upon female qualities: seduction, manipulation, heresy, etc.'

Witch qualities, I thought to myself but didn't say out loud.

Starla sighed. 'I always had an idea that the story behind Jezebel was something like that: she was guilty only of worshipping her goddess. Should have known.'

'And Baal,' Sam added. 'Which generally meant "The Lord". You see, there were lots of different Baals: Bal, Bel, Bael or Balder in Northern Europe, often associated with Beltaine, or May Day; Baal-Gad, the goat god, who shares qualities with Pan; Baal-zebub, the Lord of the Flies.'

'Ew,' said Jocelyn. 'Gross. Fancy being a god of them.'

Sam laughed. 'Ah, well his name also stood for Conductor of Souls – flies were thought to be the common forms taken by souls in search of rebirth. He was also meant to be the Prince of Devils, as in had command *over* devils. He was able to exorcise them. Eventually of course he just became associated with the Devil, all nuance was lost. Then he was given horns and associated with Cernunnos, who in turn becomes associated with the witches' god, as depicted in the Goya paintings.'

I saw Nicholas yawn.

'Interestingly,' Sam went on, oblivious to the fact he was losing some of his audience, 'in 1335 a French woman called Catherine Delort was burned for signing a pact with "the demon Berit", who appeared in the shape of a purplish flame. Berith was a Canaanite lawgiving deity. Her confession featured a man with black skin and eyes of burning coals who was dressed in an animal hide. He transformed at one point into a huge goat then revealed himself to be Lord of the Sabbat, the Devil. Then she ate babies.'

'Of course,' I said.

'Baby-eating features a lot in continental witch trials,' Sam said casually. 'Although she did confess to all of this, one must remember it was under horrendous torture.'

Starla shook her head, not in a particularly negative way. It was more like an expression of wonder. 'How do you know all this?'

Sam shrugged. 'Just do. Occupational hazard. Witch Museum.'

I noticed Imogen, Laura and Jocelyn's eyes were also as wide as saucers. The others gathered seemed to have been knocked into stunned silence apart from Robin who was sitting up proudly with a smug smile on his chops.

I forgot that stuff like this was news to some people. I'd already heard this theory from Sam and kind of agreed with it, as it was a bit like what happened with the witches: like the horned god, they had morphed from innocent to depraved over time. Human beings just seemed to soak up hangovers from the past and inherited moralities without questioning them or looking at them closely. Well, maybe I should just speak for myself, for that's precisely what I had been doing, until I inherited the Witch Museum and then everything had become debatable. And I mean everything. Nothing was fixed any more. There was no permanence.

'They say there's an old ruined temple round here somewhere,' said Carole softly. 'Pagan.' Then she sort of juddered and appeared to wake herself up from a trance. 'But the heads,' she whinnied. During Sam's little speech, she had gone and taken a chair next to Robin and was sitting there wringing the tea towel. 'What about the heads? The decapitated animals. That's not natural or normal is it?'

'Like I said,' said Sam. 'Wiccans respect nature. Even if they are performing rituals in the woods, it's extremely unlikely that they would do anything to harm the habitat or the creatures who live in it. They worship nature. They nurture it.'

I decided to chuck my penny's worth in. 'I'll bet your local animal decapitation problem might have more to do with hunting and trophies,' I said. 'Antlers and taxidermy are very in vogue right now. Just skim *Elle Decoration*.'

'Mmm,' said Jocelyn. 'Or *Living Etc*.'

'Or *Ideal Home*,' agreed Imogen.

I nodded. 'Yes. It means the desecration is more likely to have been carried out by your fine upstanding members of the establishment. Or entrepreneurial types with air guns and contacts in the world of interior decoration. Rather than witches or Wiccans.'

'There's nothing fine about killing animals like that,' said Starla.

'I was being sarcastic about them being fine,' I told her. 'I just meant – you know, that nastiness is unfairly associated with witches but it's actually the hunters who are responsible. And hunters are more likely to be wealthy. The wealthy are more likely to have power and influence – ergo establishment.'

'Bravo,' said Tabby.

Nicholas made a noise that sounded like a car tyre letting out air. 'Well, well, well.' He started clapping slowly. 'Aren't you just the cutest little class warrior? What about farmers and the pests that spoil their crops? Some people have a perfect right to hunt.'

I looked over and saw him wobble slightly. For the first time it occurred to me that he might be drunk. 'I'm saying hunters are more likely to have a large disposable income. A decent shotgun can put you back a grand.' It was amazing what you learnt, hanging around the Seven Stars.

'That's not unaffordable,' Nicholas persisted.

'I'll tell you what,' I said, feeling that I might lose control of myself if this little contretemps didn't end soon, 'I'll ask about that at the food bank, next time I'm passing.' Which, thankfully seemed to do the trick. 'Anyway,' I went on, 'I'll bet common ownership of the folklore, means common ownership of that land. That's what usually happens. And farmers tend to sort out their own farms and leave public places to the council.' Not that I'd had much experience of farmers back in Leytonstone Benefit Fraud. 'So this might be a rogue hunter. Or someone from another part of the county.'

Nicholas continued to pout. 'I'm just saying that wealth doesn't always breed corruption. And hunting is, should be, considered a sport. Keeps a lot of people in jobs.'

'Shut up Nicholas,' said Jocelyn.

Now he was beginning to flush. 'I'm just trying to get my point across,' he yelled.

I stood up. 'Yes, well, over the centuries rich powerful men have had quite a good track record in that department, thanks.'

Starla joined in and wagged a finger. 'Check your privilege,' she said, then faced me. 'He's the heir to the Blackman fortune. As in the condiments. Those orange chilli sauces that are really quite nice.'

'Too hot for me,' said Imogen out of nowhere. 'I preferred the original stuff.'

'Mustards,' confirmed Tabby. 'The wholegrain variety is exceptional.'

'My great great grandfather's wondrous offering,' Nicholas

said and bowed. 'Colonel Blackman may have been an ass but he was an inventive one at least.'

'Colonel Mustard,' said Starla and nodded sagely. 'That's what they used to call him.'

That figured. Cluedo characters were popping up all around me. It made me feel like I was in some kind of dream.

Colonel Nicholas Mustard sighed loudly and rubbed his forehead with a knuckle. I could feel my anger receding. Thank god.

Nobody spoke for a minute then Carole got up and began walking across the floor to the French windows, her face still puckered in different places. The action defused the tension in the room. We all watched as she blew on a pane of glass and dabbed it with the tea towel. 'They say if you hear a howling in the woods then next you hear the bell.'

Again, nobody spoke. I think half of us didn't know what she meant and the other half were worried about setting off another argument.

'The bell,' she said again. 'That means somethink don't it? You should know,' she continued and waved the tea towel round the room. 'You're the bleedin' writers. "For whom the bells tolls ..." or summat.'

It was Robin who got in with the quote first, 'Never send to know for whom the bells tolls; it tolls for thee.' He was doing well this afternoon.

'What does it mean?' asked Jocelyn.

'Didn't you do it at school?' This from Nicholas who sent her an accompanying smirk.

God he was irritating. Or was that how he made an impression? Left his mark on the people around him so as not to be forgotten? How terribly insecure.

Jocelyn shook her head – she was so patient – as Tabby piped up. 'Well, John Donne was referring to funeral bells. Wasn't he suggesting that with each bell that tolled we were closer to the grave. And that at some point the funerary bell would indeed toll for us?'

'It's about death,' said Carole annoyed. 'That story. If you hear the groans from the witches you're going to be a goner.' She pointed her scrawny finger around the gathered crowd. 'So if you all heard it, well, Death will be coming this way for sure.' Then she let go another high-pitched machine-gun cackle. I don't think she was being serious, but no one responded with glee.

'The banshee,' said Robin, his voice grave. 'It also presages death. I told you.' He turned to where I was sitting. 'Didn't I? Earlier? It sounded just like a banshee to me.'

I didn't know what to say.

Cullen swallowed noisily.

The quietness in the room made us all self-conscious.

Then Nicholas clapped his hands suddenly. 'Right, that's it,' he said. 'I'm off.' And jumped to his feet. 'This isn't fun any more. I'm getting a shitty feeling about this place and it's not just the god-awful catering. The situation is getting worse. And I, for one, am not going to stay here and get picked off like poor Graham. I'll be back to London on the next train and I suggest the rest of you do the same.'

'Oh Nicky,' said Jocelyn, but she didn't move to stop him.

Then Imogen nodded and creaked her way upright. 'For once I think I'm in agreement with the idiot.'

Nicholas narrowed his eyes, but then Robin pushed off from the table. 'Me too,' he said. 'Ah better pack up now. It's a long journey back to the Highlands.'

Even Laura started to nod. 'Perhaps it's wise to abandon the course. I know we've been doing our best, but let's face it, we're all quite unnerved. These are not the optimum conditions for creative writing. It might be wise to cancel.'

'I don't think we are in a position to offer refunds, I'm afraid,' said Sophia as softly as she could.

But everyone heard it.

'Fine,' said Nicholas and waved his hand at her in a gesture of limp dismissal.

The others made murmuring noises.

'Suits me,' said Carole. 'I've already been paid for the month.'

'Outrageous,' Starla exploded. 'As you know, I run a mental health clinic for cats, and have had to shell out for replacement carers to come in and help my partner out. This is most distressing.'

Robin started walking towards Sophia gesticulating wildly 'Ah really cannae see what your problem would be. These are exceptional circumstances – death and banshees for god's sake?'

'Not forgetting it could well be murder,' Starla wailed, her voice rising in desperation.

'OMG,' a strange voice bellowed from the doorway. 'This sounds awesome!'

Everyone stopped what they were doing and turned to locate its owner.

We had been so caught up in the drama unfolding in the middle of the day room that none of us had noticed the shadow at the door. Though now we could see him clearly, it seemed odd that he had managed to evade our notice for so long.

At first sight I thought it might be some tragic rocker from an early eighties stadium band – all curly black hair, shades, leather jacket and leathery tan.

'Hi,' he said and beamed us a grin that must have cost a few hundred bucks at least. 'You simply cannot be committed writers if you're turning this kind of experience down. Not in my books.' He grinned. 'Literally.' Then he took off his shades and winked.

'Good Christ,' said Cullen. And lumbered towards the man with his hand out. 'It's Chris bloody Devlin.'

CHAPTER EIGHT

The appearance of Chris (bloody) Devlin apparently changed everything.

Of course I had heard the name before: his books had huge marketing spends behind them – you saw posters on train platforms, sides of buses. I remembered I had even seen one on the telly once. But it was a bit rubbish and just had a woman walking into a room and then turning round really quickly and gasping. I recalled thinking if that was the best bit of the book then I wouldn't be queuing up at midnight the night before it was released. I think it did well anyway because he was on loads of chat shows, sprawling over sofas in his puffed-up leather jacket, trying to sound manly and louche at the same time. Reckoned he was a bit of a ladies' man too. You could just tell. Oozed self-assurance. Not the public-school type but the kind of sureness that was born from being told you were brilliant by hundreds of thousands of fans, a hundred thousand times, and assured of your place at the top of your tree which in this case was represented by the many branches of the action/crime/thriller bestseller lists in both the UK and

USA. Oh yes, indeed. A lot of people thought a lot of Chris Devlin, including Chris Devlin.

He walked in a kind of swaggery way – Tom Cruise meets Liam Gallagher. And no one moved like that naturally. He must have spent weeks in front of a full-length mirror practising it.

And then there was the money thing. It hit you in the face. The quality of the jacket, the Rolex on the wrist, the chunky gold choker, the US designer jeans – they all shouted, 'I'm loaded, baby'.

Nice work if you can get it. And quite clearly Cullen, Robin, Margot, Starla and Tabby really wanted to. Fawning was the word that came to mind as their faces changed when recognition kicked in. Even Jocelyn and Laura came over a bit blushy.

Sophia took the lead, 'Oh Chris! How wonderful,' and went and greeted him, holding out her hand, then colouring vividly when Devlin went in for the cheek kiss and bear hug. Lots of introductions and handshaking. Some of the ladies broke into a sweat.

Only Imogen and Nicholas seemed relatively unmoved. I wasn't sure if anything, anyone or any substance had any physical effect on the former, whilst the latter was struggling to keep his 'I don't give a flying one' face in place.

As the other writers grinned and giggled over the newcomer, Imogen inched over to us. 'Do you want me to tell you about Monday night?' she asked out of the side of her mouth.

I shrugged. 'I'm guessing you're going to say you went to bed and didn't hear anything?'

She nodded. 'Yes I am. And to save you some work – the others all said the same. I asked them all. Individually.'

Sam and I regarded her for a minute, then he said, 'Thanks. It does help.'

I wondered if this was a particularly professional thing to do – let one of the suspects do some of the investigating? But then Imogen was probably right. And anyway – we weren't the police. We were here at the behest of Monty. If we found evidence that should be turned over to the police then we certainly would. I for one, wasn't exactly over the moon about being here, when we had things to do back at the museum. Especially as we weren't being paid for it, just merely repaying a favour.

'Which makes me more than certain it is foul play,' Imogen said suddenly. 'No witnesses. Not sure why Graham was the victim, though. Doesn't seem to make sense. You talk to Carole and she'll tell you he didn't have an enemy in the world. Perhaps there may be something in his background? I didn't know him for long, but he seemed extremely personable. Though you never can tell, can you?'

Sam nodded. 'We have a friend in Intelligence who may be able to look into Mr Peacock's background. But I'm beginning to think you're right, Imogen. There are certain indicators that suggest malice aforethought.'

Over by the doorway people were dispersing.

Sophia turned to Imogen and called, 'We're going to go into the kitchen to have lunch. Chris wants to get to know the students. Then he's happy to run a workshop later.' She stopped and watched Imogen rise. Nicholas hopped off the arm of the Chesterfield and sighed like he had nothing better to do. As an afterthought Sophia asked, 'Rosie and Sam – do you want to join us?'

Sam looked at me. 'Could do? Get to know them a bit better?'

'What have we got lined up for today?' I wondered out loud, reading through my mental To-Do list. 'Phone Monty, check the woods, walk back to the church, ask around the village about trick-or-treaters and witch legends.'

'Yeah,' said Sam. 'Not much.'

I thought he was being sarcastic, but he turned to Sophia. 'We'd be delighted to join you, thanks.'

In the event, however, we weren't able to enjoy more than a bite of quiche, as the phone rang and Sophia informed us the police were at the church and required our presence pronto.

She suggested we come for breakfast tomorrow instead. We accepted. I was feeling exhausted already and wanted to go home and check in on the Witch Museum. And there was an old lady in the village who died last Christmas Day. A relative from America had contacted us with a view to selling some of the witchy paraphernalia that he had found in her house. I'd promised to phone him this week. Apparently, she had quite a few stuffed cats. Sam wondered if some of them might be mummified. It was once an old British custom to keep them in your cottage walls to ward off bad spirits and apparently prevalent in Adder's Fork. I thought it was a bit grim and nasty but Sam said as far as blood sacrifices went this was quite tame. I left that one alone and thought about

Hecate and how she would simply not have put up with that at all. Wasn't sure if she'd take to the mummies either. We'd have to see.

Anyway, we said our goodbyes and trudged down the drive and up the road to the church where we'd left the car. We had wanted to see how long it took to get from there to Ratchette Hall.

It was a weaving, writhing route that periodically gave out to spectacular views over the countryside. Little cottages and large, more stately houses punctuated the wayside. Some of the chimneys were smoking. I turned up the collar of my jacket and stuffed my hands in my pockets. Should have brought gloves.

As we walked, my eyes wandered over the heath. Little patches of yellow Dwarf Gorse, at the end of their seasonal bloom, bobbed in the hedgerow. In the valley beyond, dark pines rustled. Closer to the road, clusters of leaves were turning to rust. Loosened from their branches they were swept up and tossed about by the bitter north-easterly wind. I watched a little cyclone of them spiral and chase each other at the side of the pavement and suddenly imagined them as little playful imps: all different colours – lemon-peel, copper, chestnut brown – and different sizes – star-shaped, oval, petalled, but moving in a similar way, almost as if they had a collective purpose. That kind of thinking could have got you hanged in the past and quite often did. I thought of Ursula Cadence and her alleged familiars: Tittey, Jack, Piggin and Tiffin. Two cats, a toad and a little white lamb. There was something rather pathetic, or childlike, about the way the pamphlet recorded her listing them. I remember detecting a doleful yearning there, as if Ursula did crave these pets, perhaps for company and how Sam had told me about another 'witch', Elizabeth Chandler. Elizabeth had been so poor and reviled and lonely that she gave names to two wooden sticks: Beelzebub and Truillibub. One she used to help her walk. The other stirred her cooking pot. Matthew Hopkins, the demented self-appointed Witchfinder General, decided that because the old lady talked to them they were demonic. Of course, Elizabeth denied this, but she was poor and friendless so got hanged anyway.

Beelzebub. I ran my tongue over the word. That was the second time I had heard the name today. Associated with the Devil. Lord of the Flies. Probably not the best name for an old woman to choose. Though to be sure, a girl should really be able to call her sticks what the heck she liked.

Of course, Sam had told me on the way over here, Damebury had its own witches. Had to really. There was a reason why Essex had at one point been called Witch County. This lot were Joan Smythe, Widow Stokes, Susan Spilman and a man too – John Smythe. Which was unusual. I wondered what he'd done. We hadn't got into the nitty gritty of that yet or found out if they had been executed for their crimes. No doubt that would come.

I was guessing it was to them the howling in the woods was attributed. Witches were the habitual scapegoat for anything that went wrong or got weird – they were usually poor, ergo powerless, commonly at the bottom of the social scale and more often than not uneducated and put-upon.

When I looked up at St Saviour's I noted there were woodlands around it. No doubt more 'devilish witchery' was nestled about there.

In the past, back in Leytonstone, whenever I had thought of Essex, my mind had conjured images of the seaside and new estates, modern semis with integrated garages and little greens for all the kids to play out on. However, since Adder's Fork had beckoned, my perceptions had undergone quite a change. Now I couldn't look across the fields and copses without wondering about the events that they had seen, the stories they knew and the secrets that they kept. Sometimes I could hear the county groan. Sometimes, I heard it breathe. And sometimes, very occasionally, the land of Essex spoke to me. But not often. And, of course, it might just be my inner voice. But I was opening my mind to the idea.

When we reached the church we found Father Edgar bent over by the hole with a mug of tea in his hands. Hearing our footfalls he at once straightened up and greeted us.

'They're here,' he shouted into the cavern below.

I didn't realise he had company and looked down into the hole, just as Sue Scrub's face filled it. 'I'm starting to think you two and hocus pocus,' she said, and rolled her eyes, 'go firmly hand in hand.'

'Occupational hazard, Sue,' I said with a grin.

We'd met Sergeant Scrub during the incident at the Witch Pit. Although she hadn't warmed to us at first, by the end of the caper, she had thawed considerably. In fact, I might go as far as to say that she'd even been sweet. She didn't look sweet now. She looked decidedly put out and irritated.

To be honest I wasn't surprised: I would have thought that church thefts might have been beneath her pay scale.

She must have read my mind, as she reached out for the ladder and began to climb. 'Edgar's my brother-in-law,' she explained. Ah, well that explained why this Yorkshire lass had ended up in Essex, then. 'It's a strange one,' she went on as she reached the top and lurched over to get a footing on the ground. 'Edgar said you think the missing items have something to do with a recent death at Ratchette Hall.' It wasn't a question but a demand for a full explanation at once.

Edgar swilled the tea in his mug. 'You insinuated that, didn't you?'

'Well,' I said. 'It might not.'

'But it also might,' Sam finished. 'It's a stunning coincidence if you consider the circumstances surrounding Mr Peacock's death. One must keep an open mind.'

'Unambiguous and as helpful as ever,' Sue muttered under her breath. 'Now do me a favour ...' she said and held out a hand.

After some considerable heaving we got her up out of the excavation/extension and into the church.

She straightened out the same raincoat that she had worn during the summer. At the time I thought her overdressed. Now it was quite peaky I was thinking maybe she should have put on more layers.

While she brushed the dirt off her hands, she sort of sighed and said, 'Look, I'm going to ask you this once and get it over and done with – have you two nicked the body?'

Sam and I did some energetic and emphatic head-shaking. 'The effigy on top?' she continued.

More vigorous denials.

'Good,' she breathed and slipped her hands into her pockets. 'Thought it unlikely, but I have to ask these things.'

'Yep,' I said.

'We know,' added Sam.

'Father Edgar says there's CCTV footage.'

'We were advised to put up cameras over the doors that we still use, when we discovered the new tomb.' Edgar cleared his throat. 'So we've run through the tapes. It's puzzling. I'm the last person out of the church last night. And the body and effigy were certainly there when I left. Then no one goes in until you two turn up, this morning.'

'How curious,' said Sam.

'That's a word you could use,' said Scrub. 'I could suggest several others but I'm in a church and wasn't brought up with a potty mouth.'

I couldn't think of what to say, so went and sat down at a pew with the griffin carved into the end and stared at the mythical creature. It was definitely draughty in here. I supposed it was an old building. But even so you'd have thought they'd have sorted it out – some poor mugs had to sit here for over an hour on Sundays. I pulled up my boots and zipped my jacket shut.

'So,' said Scrub coming over to join me. 'How the heck can this effigy theft be linked to Graham Peacock? The way I heard it, sounded like natural causes.'

I watched her slip along the pew in front and button

up her trench coat. 'Mmm, they might have had a helping hand,' I said. 'So to speak. How long have you got?'

When we had finally finished explaining the ins and outs of the whole palaver – the E. Nesbit story, the timing of Halloween, the detached stone finger found in Graham's hand – Scrub and I sat there scratching our chins. Sam and Father Edgar came over and sat down next to me.

'So,' Sue said at last. 'I suppose I'd better take a closer look at Graham Peacock's background.'

Sam and I nodded. That would be one less thing to ask of Monty.

'Any chance you could let us know what comes up?' Sam added.

But it was the vicar who replied. 'Oh yes, well if they're linked you'll have to, won't you, Sue?'

You could tell that grated on her, but she tried to conceal it with a smile that wrinkled her nose and pronounced her teeth, which reminded me of a squirrel about to chow down on a nut. 'If you keep me informed about what you find out at the Hall. Deal?'

We nodded, but Father Edgar said, 'Deal,' and put his fisted hand into the centre of our little grouping. Weirdly, Sam and Sue joined him, so I kind of had to as well. When I put my hand there we all fist-bumped each other and Sam and Sue said, 'Agreed,' too.

It was a bit of a cringe.

As I withdrew, trying to supress a shudder, I inspected Father Edgar more closely. He was a very different type of minister to our Karen, who was short, trendy, young(ish) and female. In many ways he was the polar opposite: tall, dress sense out of last century, old, male. In fact, there was something very Professor Plum about old Edgar, which included a faint odour of mothballs and orchids.

Cluedo again. I wondered if my subconscious was trying to tell me something. That game was about deduction. Perhaps I should spend some time thinking a bit more about the people on the course and who might be eliminated. Which, at the moment, was only Carole Christmas: I was pretty sure she was not faking it when she denied reading *Man-Sized in Marble* and requested payment should that be required. I shivered as I recalled her cackling laugh. It sounded like a murder of crows sighting carrion.

But that was her out of the picture anyway.

Not much elimination.

This was not a particularly impressive analysis.

One had to think about motive, yet that was very unclear. One of the policemen who I had met earlier in the year (and snogged and very nice he was too, thank you very much) had told me that the two main reasons for murder were sex and money in some form or another. It didn't sound like Graham Peacock was loaded, if he had to work and live at Ratchette Hall, but you never knew.

'Can you get access to his bank accounts?' I asked Sergeant Scrub.

She just raised her eyebrows in a don't-you-tell-me-how-to-do-my-job style which reminded me of just how terrifying she could be when she wanted. So I decided this was the time to make our exit and go and worry the locals.

The sky was darker outside and swirling.

But Sam didn't want to go for cover. He touched my arm and said, 'You want to have a quick look at those woods?'

The clouds above were touching their grey underbellies to the ground. Certainly they appeared full and swollen with moisture. 'Quickly then,' I said. 'Looks like rain.'

We crossed the churchyard and found a path that ran alongside a cluster of trees. Hurrying along we reached a gap that opened onto a beautiful view down the hillside and onto the south of the county. Well, it would have been a beautiful view if we had been able to see it, for at that moment the heavens opened and dumped a mother lode of rain.

We spun on our heels and legged it back towards the church.

I made it there first. It was locked. Scrub and Edgar had gone, the latter taking no chances with the security of the two remaining knights. When I turned round to check where Sam was, an empty churchyard spread out before me. The wind picked my hair up and lashed it against my face. The rain was hard now, coming at me almost horizontally.

I blinked into the landscape. Where was he?

I called his name but if he replied it was lost in the wind.

Sheltering my eyes with my hand I tried to look more closely.

It was no good. The whole place had darkened.

All I could see were the trees waving back and forth amongst the jagged tombstones that stood still at odd angles over the yard.

I began to move forwards, searching for him. When I reached the middle of the yard I finally spotted him under a bushy yew. He was squatting over a grave, hunched and rather little-looking. As I drew closer I noticed a dark streak running over his cheek. His head was bleeding.

'Sam! Sam! Are you okay?' His features had frozen, the eyes were vacant, unfocused, gazing into the mid-distance. 'What's happened?' I yelled against the wind.

He didn't answer at first, then when I shouted again, he looked at me and pointed unsteadily to the headstone.

'Look,' he said eventually, his hair, picked up by the squall, blew all around. 'I slipped on the grass and cracked my head. But look, look at the name.'

He touched his forehead where the skin had split.

I hurriedly got out a hanky and started dabbing at the cut.

He swatted me off and grabbed my hand and held it. 'Rosie, look at the name.'

At last I turned and looked at the old lichen-clad headstone sinking crookedly into the earth. Sam had obviously pulled some of the moss away from the inscription for there were clear patches where the lettering was clear. I read: 'In ever loving memory of Samuel Stone. Son and brother. May his memory be eternal.'

Ooh, that was a surprise.

I sat back on my heels. 'Freaky,' I said.

'No,' he said, still rigid, but urgent. 'The birth date. It's the same as mine. To the day, only a hundred years earlier.'

'Oh yeah!' I said and turned back to him. 'So what? Strange coincidence.'

But he looked aghast and shook his head. I waited for him to say something.

'He didn't.'

So I tried to get him up and said, 'Yes, I see.'

The rain was soaking us. I could feel my mascara sliding over my cheeks.

Now standing, I continued to try and heave him to his feet.

He resisted. 'And,' he said, jabbing crazily at the tombstone, 'this person, Sam Stone, dies *next year*.'

I let go of his hand and shook my head. 'No,' I said firmly. 'This Sam Stone died ninety-nine years *ago*. Now, come on! You're soaking. If we stay out here any longer, we'll catch our death of colds and pop off this mortal coil much sooner than either of us anticipate.' God I sounded like my mother. Who wasn't my mother. But this was no time to go into that.

Sam didn't move. He just sat there and said, 'It made me fall, so I would take notice.' He put his fingers to the fresh wound. 'It's a warning.'

This wasn't like Sam at all. I could only think that the knock on the head had concussed him.

In the end I grabbed hold of his arms and dragged him to his feet, and once I had managed that, took his hand and pushed and pulled him towards the church.

The old building sheltered us somewhat from the rain.

'You okay?' I asked, as we got round the side, and the thousand-yard stare seemed to recede.

He shrugged but said nothing.

It was only a short walk from here to the car park so I got

to it quickly, frogmarching him round the outside walls of St Saviour's over to where the car was parked.

Once in it, I examined his head. He'd broken the skin but I didn't think he'd need stitches. I had a first aid kit in the glove compartment, so fished out an anaesthetic wipe, cleaned the wound and stuck a plaster over it.

'There,' I said, admiring my handiwork. 'You look like a proper little soldier.'

But he didn't laugh.

As we pulled out of the church car park, trundling down the lane, he gestured up ahead. 'Look, there's The Griffin. Can we stop and have a drink?'

Still pale and strangely quiet, I thought a brandy was in order. Something was needed to put the colour back into his cheeks. And anyway, there was a good logistical reason for the stop-off: we had planned to ask the locals about trick-or-treating customs in Damebury. This pub was as good a place as any to tick that off our list.

I pulled in past a tall pub sign that depicted a mythical griffin dancing on the top, just like the one at the end of the pew. We parked round the back in the car park.

It was a well-maintained building, whitewashed and wattled with red tiles on sloping roofs and a look of the eighteenth century. There were a couple of outbuildings dotted around the yard – one looked like a modest function room, the other a store room for the pub.

The windows of The Griffin were proper old-looking and panelled, the frames painted a violet-grey. We entered via a side door painted to match the windows.

Inside, the décor was pleasant – wooden floorboards and refurbished armchairs which wouldn't look amiss in a pub uptown. The surviving fireplaces were very old indeed, much earlier than the outside might suggest. Two were brick and iron but another was wider. The hood jutted out, sheltering a large chimney.

While Sam went and found a table I ordered the drinks.

The chap who served me was polite. Young with a bit of a bent nose and cropped black hair, he wore a badge which read 'Keiron'. His demeanour was friendly too so I fired out some questions without sugar-coating any of them.

'We're just staying at Ratchette Hall,' I lied. Sort of. 'Thus the brandy. It's not been the same since Graham died.'

'Oh yes,' said Kieron, squirting the diet coke into a glass. 'Heard about that. Wasn't he frightened to death or something?'

I nodded. 'Trick-or-treaters. You know many kids or teenagers round here that might do something like that?'

'Well.' Kieron paused for a moment and looked out the window. 'Oh yeah, course. We've got our fair share of young people here – good and bad. There's a couple who might be up for pranking. It's trendy now isn't it?'

'What do you mean?' I said, leaning on the bar and giving him a nice wide smile.

'You know – they film themselves and put it on YouTube to get followers.' He shook his head. 'My nephew – he's only ten, but reckons he's going to make a living out of it when he grows up. Vlogging, I think they call it. I dunno.' He shrugged in a kind of 'young people today' manner. Even though he was barely out of school.

'Is that so? Crazy,' I said and sipped the coke. 'I suppose it's better than wanting to be a reality TV star.'

He turned his back on me and went to the optics. 'It's a phase, isn't it?' he said over his shoulder. 'There's a couple of kids round here, Ben and Stevie, who have a channel. Prank Anthem TV. They do practical jokes. Harmless mostly. But the naughtier the better. It's how they rebel, I suppose.'

'Like what?' I asked.

He put the shot on the counter. 'Like filming themselves eating scotch bonnet chillies raw,' he said and made a face.

'Raw?'

'Yeah,' Kieron laughed.

At least they weren't the double strength ones straight out of my dad's allotment. 'Painful.'

'Got a lot of views. And likes. They keep going on about "monetising" it. Reckon they can get sponsorship and ads if they get enough views.'

'Right,' I said. 'And that's what they're after? Do you think they could have pranked Graham? For likes?'

He shrugged. 'I don't know. They wouldn't set out to hurt anyone. They're not like that.'

'What's the point of it all?' I asked.

'A bit of a thrill. There's nothing much for them to do, you see.'

I looked around. The place was rural but not remote. 'What about Chelmsford? That's not far.'

He put both hands on the counter. 'It's tough getting back. Cab fares are steep if you haven't got money.'

I gestured around the pub. 'They can't hang out here?' It seemed quite nice.

'No chance,' he said. 'Ben wouldn't do it. And his mates wouldn't fancy it either. They're nineteen/twenty but some of their girlfriends are seventeen so can't drink in here.'

I laughed disbelievingly. 'Don't the kids of today do fake ID then?'

He laughed back and shook his head. 'Ben would never let them. It's his mum's pub. She's tough, Carole. You do not want to cross her.'

'Carole Christmas?' I wondered out loud. 'I thought she was the assistant manager.'

'Well, she's like a manager really. We have an area manager that supervises across several pubs. Cost-cutting.'

'Right,' I said and picked up the drinks. 'Yes, well I can imagine Ben would not want to incur his mother's wrath. Might put a dampener on things.'

Keiron picked up a glass and began to rub it with a towel. 'I know they been hanging outside lately. Some of the youngsters go down to the common with cider. When it's not raining, like today.'

I stopped and leant my elbow on the wood. 'Really?'

'We've all been young once,' he said with a wink. Then someone else waved a note and he went off to serve.

I thought I might hover for a bit but whoever was putting their round in was making it a big one. Anyway, Kieron had delivered some useful information. We'd definitely have to check out Ben Christmas and his mate Stevie. I rummaged in my hand bag for a notebook or phone and noticed it felt a bit light. After further investigation I realised my mobile wasn't there. It wasn't in my pockets either. Damn! It must have fallen out when I was helping Sam up by the other Sam's grave. I'd have to go and look for it.

I took the drinks over to not dead Sam, who was sitting at the table staring out of the window.

I gave him his drink. He didn't even say thank you.

'Sam, I've not got my phone. I think it might have fallen out in the churchyard.'

He raised his head wearily. 'Do you want me to go and look for it?'

'No, no, you have your drink. I won't be a sec.'

And I stepped into the twilight.

CHAPTER NINE

I didn't know where the time had gone. It felt like we'd only been here five minutes but already the day was disappearing. Night was coming out, spreading its wings.

As I approached the church, silhouetted against the thunderous sky, a solitary bat flew erratically out of the bell tower and headed off against the wind into the trees beyond the churchyard.

Bats in the belfry, I thought and wondered if that was the first time I had ever seen a bat in such an edifice. Or rather, pop out of it. I'd always thought that was a metaphor for something, but couldn't remember what.

It took me till I reached the church gate to pluck out the notion that it meant mad or odd or chaotic, which was apt considering the day we'd had, Sam's schizophrenic mood swings and the whole marching knights malarkey. Dead ones. No, not dead ones: stone knights. And one wooden one.

The graveyard was full of movement as I struggled to find Samuel Stone's headstone in the swirl. Rain was coming down thicker now, which meant I had to put my handbag on my head to protect my hair. Still there was no one about so I didn't mind looking like I had multiple bats in my own personal belfry.

I tried to retrace my steps – I had been halfway across the graveyard when I realised Sam had disappeared. I reached the point and, turning round, thought I saw the whip of a shadow a few yards behind me, but it must have been a trick of the fading light and the scudding storm clouds as, of course, there was no one there.

A couple of graves over I saw the headstone with its half-scraped lichen, leaning into the air as if it were going to topple over at any moment.

Though I wasn't happy about it, I got down on my knees, removed my bag from my head and began scrabbling amongst the overgrown weeds and stones. It did cross my mind that I might look rather strange, clawing at a grave with my bare hands. But a girl has to do what a girl has to do when her phone is at stake, and I was sure it had to be here somewhere.

I had just bent my nail on the grave marker and was cursing my head off loudly when something changed in the light around me and I became aware of a darkening close by. I put it down to the clouds drawing together and continued rummaging until a little rectangular light came on about head height.

When I looked up at it I saw my phone momentarily suspended in mid-air. The sight made me blink and then suddenly I was visited by a series of unconnected images – whistling wind, fluttering feathers, shadow.

It took a moment more for me to realise there was a shape behind the mobile. And it was saying something.

'I said, is this yours?'

My eyes lifted to take in the figure who was holding it and who, weirdly, seemed like they'd appeared out of nowhere. Or possibly from the ground.

Working my way up I clocked black boots, like cowboy boots, but the type that only came up to the ankle; black jeans; a black silky shirt that was open, despite the elements, and revealing a cluster of dark hairs; a long slate greatcoat, unbuttoned, which looked ex-military, but not our military, more soviet in style; raven hair, white face, cleanshaven, black eyes. Good eyebrows. Well defined.

A goth.

Of course.

We were in a cemetery after all.

I tried to look gainly, as opposed to un-so and nodded, feeling a stream of water run down the side of my face and off my chin. The gale and rain were blasting bits of leaf into my eyes so I had to squint as I got to my knees and then stood up.

'Yes,' I shouted at the guy, unsure if the words had been caught up and tossed away by the streaming air.

There were raindrops all over the dark man's coat, glistening like little crystals, but his hair, which was loose and shoulder-length, seemed not wet, but only to shine as if there was some internal luminescence in it.

'Thanks,' I yelled.

He had unfolded himself into an upright position too. Taller than me by quite some, he smiled and held out my phone.

'It was over there,' he said, pointing beyond the grave-stone. His voice was steady and made it through the elements clearly though he did not raise it.

'Thanks,' I said again and reached for it.

A bird swooped over our heads and made an angry chirping noise.

As he handed the mobile over, our fingers touched. His were cool.

Something buzzed in the exchange, maybe my phone, and again I was visited by a strange sensation which evoked images, like a filmic montage, and which played across my internal mind-screen: a starting pistol, a brigade of pounding muddy feet, a wolf shaking raindrops from its mane, the crack of a whip on stone, a caw of crows alighting on an elm, one single drop of water falling in a cavern, old wine that tasted thick and rich and heady, oily perfume, frankincense.

My fingertips prickled with an intense jab of electricity and I dropped the phone again.

'Let me,' he said and, quick as lightning, scooped it up. In one sweeping, looping motion he appeared right by my side.

My face must have betrayed my inner confusion at the physical sensation and weird data stream I'd just experienced, because he said, 'What? Did you feel it?'

But before I could explain, a strong gust picked up again and started lashing my hair against my cheeks, so hard it was quite painful. I was happy to thank him properly but there was no way I was going to stand out here and do it.

'Over there,' I barked and pointed to the timber porch

which was the only sheltered spot I could see and we both ran over to it.

Once inside, we stood leaning against opposite walls. Although I was panting, he didn't seem to be at all out of breath.

'Dorcus,' he announced.

This bewildered me for a moment so that I wondered if, what with the coat and all, he was foreign. There was certainly something exotic in the shape of his eyes, an almond sweep bordered by dark dewy lashes, that was not unattractive.

He laughed. 'Dorcus Beval. It's my name.'

'Oh,' I said. 'I thought—'

'Yeah,' he said.

The air around us calmed and became very still.

'What's that then?' I said between breaths, so as to make conversation, though it came out a bit pouty. 'Welsh?'

His next laugh sounded like an exploding canon. So strong and hearty. As he threw his head back to give it utterance, exposing his white flawless neck, something animal stirred within me. A sudden unbidden image of sitting astride him, naked, staring down at his wide chest, flashed across my brain.

Sex. Blimey, I hadn't had any for ages. I felt my blood pressure rise.

'Welsh?' he said to himself, as if trying it out on his person. His eyes were glinting now, with a stomach-curdling energy – amusement and interest perhaps. 'Something like that,' he said, and pushed his hair back so I could see his face properly.

Was it just me or had he been inching closer?

He was, I noticed, broad-shouldered although that could have been the coat. Certainly, he wasn't a thin man. Well-built and lithe. Pale though. His cheeks had no colour at all, like all the blood had been leached from them. It didn't detract from his overall appeal, which I was beginning to succumb to despite myself. I didn't usually get turned on by graveyards and churches but there was a first time for everything.

'Here,' he said and offered the phone to me, holding it by its end so I might be able to avoid physical contact. Which was sweet considering he didn't know what had just happened.

I took it and put it in my jeans pocket. 'Thanks.' Then I realised that he must have seen me on my knees, scraping at the grave. That was most definitely not a good look. And even though I hadn't had my handbag on my head, heat started to circulate in my cheek area. 'I was looking for it. Er, down there.'

'I figured,' he said with a grin, that creased his face and made his eyebrows rise.

Wow. Great cheekbones, I thought, and the smile lingered.

'Right,' I said. 'Well, thanks very much.'

'You're lucky it didn't get wet,' he said and looked out the doorway into the writhing cemetery. The smile had grown smaller but his eyes remained crinkled at the sides. Those crows feet, I reckoned, put him a few years older than me. But not many. He could have been thirty-six, maybe thirty-eight.

'Well, thanks,' I said again, suddenly reluctant to get back to the pub.

He pushed off the wall and took a step towards me. I felt the power of his frame approach and swallowed. 'What's your name?' he asked.

The wind was getting in through the cracks in the roof and starting to scream.

'Rosie,' I told him. 'Rosie Strange.'

A dozen leaves blew in onto the flagstones between us.

'Are you local, Rosie?' he asked stepping on a cluster of them, the colour of dried blood.

I looked up into the dark pupils of his eyes and saw that they were twinkling with little pools of light, like moonbeams or reflections of disco lights. I had no idea where that was coming from, as although it was dry in here, it was also still dark.

'Oh no. I'm in Adder's Fork. Just visiting Damebury for a bit,' I told him. 'Are you? I mean, are you local?'

'Same as you,' he said. 'Visiting. Popped back to collect some things I left here a while ago.'

'Oh right,' I said at a loss to continue the conversation.

And then he stared at me, and smiled again, though there was curiosity arching his eyebrows as if he wanted me to say something else. But I was suddenly self-conscious and couldn't think of anything witty to say, so shrugged and went, 'Right, well. Hope to see you soon.' Which sounded stupid.

I thought about putting my bag back on my head, but was conscious of his gaze, and anyway there was no point now – I was pretty soaked through. Just hoped my mascara had held.

As I ran into the storm I heard him whisper into the wind, 'Me too, Strange one, me too.'

Back in The Griffin, I decided not to share my peculiar encounter with the attractive stranger with Sam. Although his mood had lifted and he looked pleased when I returned to my seat and made concerning noises about my soggy state, I could tell he wasn't back to normal.

'Come on,' I said, when I'd gulped down a large measure of diet coke, wishing I'd gone for something a bit stronger. 'What's up? This isn't like you.'

He cupped the glass in the crook of his hand and shuddered. 'Someone walked over my grave.'

I wasn't sure if he was joking or not and thought about saying something like – yeah it was me – but guessed that given his melancholy air and potential freaked-out concussion that probably wasn't the best course of action. So instead I settled for, 'Ha ha ha'. And left it up to him to steer the conversation.

He stared at his glass, as if the answer to some unspoken question was in there waiting to be found.

It was odd. Another oddness, upon all the other oddities that were accumulating today.

'That tombstone,' I ventured after the lapse of more than a minute, which is a long time if there's just two of you. 'If this is what it's all about, you've got to realise it's just a coincidence. You'd be telling me the same thing, were I to suddenly develop an attack of the heebie-jeebies.'

More silence.

'Is there any such thing as coincidence?' he said eventually.

I was going to answer that when I met him he had told me that often you might assume things were connected when all you'd done is concentrate on a certain matter. And because your attention was on that, you ended up attaching meaning to anything that happened which might have any relevance, real or not, to that particular sphere or subject.

But he looked up with purpose and fixed his eyes on me. They were turning from amber to pine-cone brown, and rather disloyally I found myself thinking of Dorcus's deep black eyes and how they had slanted upwards and gleamed. That would not do, I told myself and redirected my gaze to his.

With the short back and floppy fringe, the cut of his hair, and the plaster on his head, he suddenly put me in mind of a wounded soldier from the First World War. Then I thought of the inscription on the gravestone and shook the notion out of my head. Silly.

'I've had a few moments lately,' Sam said with an uncharacteristic indolence.

Now this was interesting. I'd had a few too, though I wasn't sure if they were the same kind. Mine ranged from spasms of lust to feelings of utter dejection. Always the extremes with me.

But this wasn't about me, was it. 'Go on,' I said.

'I've been ...' he stopped and took a slug of his drink, '... I've been feeling out of sorts.' I thought about feeling things. Body parts mostly. Then mentally slapped myself and refocused. Gawd, what was I like? One man shows me a bit of attention in a wet and windy graveyard and I can't stop thinking about him. Ridiculous. Especially as I was sitting with another man who really did dominate my every waking hour. And my sleeping ones too.

Get a grip on yourself, Rosie Strange, I thought. Because no one's going to do it for you. More's the pity.

So, I coughed and shook out my shoulders, put my hands together on the table and gave Sam my full attention. 'Okay,' I said. 'Fire away.'

'I wasn't sure whether or not to tell you. It's been playing on my mind for a bit.'

Oh god, I thought. What now? I really couldn't handle any more major revelations. I was still getting over the seismic rumblings of summer.

He threw the rest of the brandy down his neck. 'I got the tape from the Seven Stars stake-out.'

'Oh yes?' I said. Phew. This was better. Something that didn't really relate to family or relationships or any touchy-feely sexy stuff.

Mmm – sexy stuff.

'Do you remember what was on there?' he asked.

'What?' I said.

His voice changed. The rhythm accelerated. 'Are you with me, Rosie?'

'Yes, yes. Sorry. The tape.'

'Do you remember?' he asked again.

I refocused my attention more firmly. Oh yeah, I could bring to mind that stake-out pretty easily. It was when lots of crazy stuff had been going down in Adder's Fork. The peasants were revolting and someone had to step in to sort things – cue yours truly.

We had set up cameras by the road outside the local pub to see if any paranormal phenomena might occur. Now, usually I wasn't what you'd call a believer in such things, but, after a while spent with Sam, you changed. Anyway, we liked to claim our motto was 'open mind and healthy scepticism'.

At some point, that night, when I'd crossed the road from Sam's camp to my friend Cerise, I had been trailed by what looked to be a sentient dust cloud.

I know.

When I had glanced at it, that's just what I'd seen – a dust cloud that appeared to be taking shape, holding itself together. Sam and my friend Cerise, however, were convinced they'd seen some*one*.

The film footage hadn't been conclusive. As in most of our night-time stake-outs, the focus of the camera often shifted. This was mainly because of flickering lights and such. On this particular occasion, the street lights had gone out and the quality of the footage had been affected by clouds crossing the moon. It had distorted the image. But what I thought we had got was the footage of a weird dust cloud.

I summed all of this up, by saying, 'Yes I remember.'

'You know I sent it off to be cleaned up by the lab?' This was a specialist agency that Monty had access to. They worked on film and managed to extract workable images.

'Er, you probably told me ...'

'Well, I've had it back.'

I was starting to feel uncomfortable myself. 'Uh huh, uh huh,' I said. 'And?'

He took a long ominous breath in then looked at me and said, 'I think there's a ghost on it.'

CHAPTER TEN

The thing with Sam saying something like that, meant it was different to anyone else saying something like that.

When I had first met him, obviously in the context of the Witch Museum, I had assumed that he was a bit of a nut. Well, you would, wouldn't you? What with the job and where he lived. You know, most normal people didn't live in a ramshackle old building with the look of a skull and spend their lives researching witches in Essex. So I reckon I could have been forgiven for assuming that he was one of those crazy believers, off with the fairies so to speak. It didn't take me long, however, to realise the man was a sceptic. A sceptic who hoped there was more to life, more to the universe and all that. But just hoped. I didn't know why he hoped but I knew he did. However, he was a rationalist. In fact he had told me quite early on that he was something called an empiricist too. This meant he drew conclusions on the basis of physical evidence, observation and experimentation. Which basically means – it's got to be seen/heard/felt then recorded and analysed and agreed upon. Yeah – empiricism, right? So it works for things like black holes and gravity, but ghosts? Anyway, it's a good word to use if ever someone thinks you're thick. Being a blondish blingish chick from Essex with more than a bit of natural bounce in the chest area and a nice rounded accent too, that kind of attitude came at me from snooty people all over the place. Believe it or not there are people who make judgements based on their first few seconds of meeting you. I know. As if I would do anything like that. But a good way to punch them on that nose, down which they are looking, is to trot out a few choice words from your vocabulary pocket. Empiricist is one of them. Nuance works on occasion. Pareidolia is not bad either. Sometimes it shocks them so much their mouths drop open and if you happen to have a clutch of peanuts in your hand a lot of fun can be had by trying to throw one in. You have to get your aim right though.

Anyway, my point is Sam didn't say things like that lightly. Usually he explored every avenue and sought other explanations.

So, this being quite a bombshell, it did not take us long to leg it out of the pub, back to the Witch Museum and up into the study area, where Sam had a desk with several pieces of recording equipment and monitors.

I spent the whole journey back saying, 'Are you sure?'

While Sam responded with, 'It's the closest thing I've seen so far.'

'Is that a yes then?'

'It's the closest thing I've seen so far.'

And then, 'Are you sure?'

So round and round we went, with Sam periodically

punctuating the repetitive cycle with instructions to 'Slow down', 'Keep your eyes on the road', 'Bend!' and the usual passenger-seat driving he was so well loved for.

So when we got into the study and pulled up the chairs, I was, it might be true to say, in a state of high expectation. In fact I think I might have had my own mouth open when he played the clip.

And I hate to say it, but what I saw was definitely a bit of a let-down. Whoever had edited the footage had cut together a nice little sequence that worked from both angles.

Half of it was supplied from Sam's all-singing all-dancing relatively new camera that he had acquired from Monty and which Monty had acquired from some unknown benevolent 'patron'. It was extremely sensitive, even in virtually no light. He kept going on about it and boasting about his massive pixels (who didn't like a guy with massive pixels, eh?). Plus, even better than that apparently, it had some kind of extra filter that also allowed it to capture extra infrared detail in the dark. So that footage looked pretty cool, especially as there was quite a lot of light from the moon that night. Then, on the other hand, there was the stuff from the run-of-the-mill night vision camera that had been positioned by the hedge where Cerise and I kept watch. This film had a strong green tinge and was a little on the dodgy side.

So the sequence opened with me, caught on good quality footage, faffing around with Sam and the other woman who was helping us in the stake-out, Chloe Brown from the Forensic Archaeology department at Litchenfield University. Once I had procured a bottle of prosecco off of them, 'Film

Rosie' spun round and sauntered across the road, looking hot, I thought, in shorts and cowboy boots, and also giving the impression that she didn't have a care in the world. There was something a little bit Daisy Duke, I thought now, about my hair in the summer. It looked quite good, a little longer than I usually liked it, but I remembered I'd recently had a Brazilian (on my head hair) and it had taken out a lot of the frizz. Not bad, I thought, and noted that that combination of shorts, tee and boots was great. The boots were particularly fetching and kind of 'relaxed looking'. They had been scuffed up earlier in the year during a fight with a ruthless human trafficker, but that had just made them look more 'worn in'. On reflection, I thought that was now preferable to spankingly new. I made a mental note to self and got back to watching 'Film Me' sashay in the road.

Halfway over however, I saw myself stop and peer at something on the ground. The shot from the night vision camera was not particularly good at this point. Though the moon was coming through the clouds and there were some pockets of light, my figure seemed to merge with the hedge behind which Chloe and Sam were hidden. It was difficult to make out the difference between vegetation and living flesh, and I've never thought that before.

The footage cut to Mr Massive Pixel's camera. We watched Film Me turn in Sam's direction and raise a hand, as if to wave. But then I paused, the hand hung limply in the air. My head turned away. At that point clouds must have eclipsed the moon, because the light seemed to vanish and everything got very dark indeed.

'See here,' said Sam, and pressed pause. 'You're looking at this.' He moved his finger to the screen, where I could just make out a kind of shadowy oval blob, darker and denser than the rest of the air. He pressed play and we watched as it seemed to move within itself, although externally stayed stationary.

'That summer though,' I said, and Sam hit pause again, 'there were loads of crazy things going on. Remember – we had the dead birds, the possibility of poisonous gas which might have been released when that grave was opened. And the sky kept doing strange things the week we did the stake-out. There was that weird orange dust and those red clouds that they said had been caused by a storm in Arabia or forest fires in Spain or something.'

'But so localised?' said Sam and stared at the screen. 'To an area of a couple of metres? My friend at the University thinks not.' He pressed play again.

Film Me looked startled and opened her mouth. Sam hit stop again and said, 'Look. You say something, but your breath vaporises.'

I shrugged. 'So?'

'It was summer,' he said. 'The temperature that night was twenty-three degrees Celsius. I've checked. That can't happen.'

We both ogled the screen as he pressed play and the dark cloud thing appeared to form a point out of what might be judged as its shoulder area. Film Me turned to peer at Cerise's hide-out.

Sam took his finger to the screen and circled the area of the dark cloud – a thin line of similar density had flowed out. 'You follow where it looks like its pointing. It's directing you. Then, look, you put your hands over your ears. Can you remember why?'

I saw Film Me shake her head and did the same. 'Not clearly. I have the notion there was a blast of static noise or something. I told you this over the summer.'

'I know,' he said. 'But I'm also aware that back in spring when we were hurtling round the country looking for the remains of Ursula Cadence, we had that moment in the car. Do you remember? It was when that gangster, that thug—'

'Bogović?'

'Yes him – the guy who worked for Countess Barbary, when he had stolen Ursula's bones? Do you remember? The Countess had them—'

'And she was about to do some kind of upside-down weird ritual with her nutty alchemist mates.'

'An inversion ritual. Yes. But my point is, when we were in the car, on the way to Hades Hall, we got that call. It was also like a blast of static. It came out of the speakers in the car. We both heard it. At first it sounded like "Harry". But then afterwards we thought it might have been "hurry". Which makes a difference.'

'But didn't we decide we'd picked up a taxi broadcast?' I asked.

'We didn't draw a firm conclusion,' he said slowly. 'But we spoke about it after that night in La Fleur. Remember, when you saw the girl?'

I nodded. Of course I remembered her. She had been a terrible sight – sores around her mouth, thin and ill. I would never forget it.

He smiled fractionally. 'She directed you over to the cellar, the one next to La Fleur, just at that crucial moment. What a coincidence eh? Just when there was a power cut and alarms on the cellar failed where they were keeping those poor women. She alerted you. And yet she was so similar to the depictions of the Foundling girl who had been kept in La Fleur all those centuries ago. A girl who had been tied up and tortured to death. Plus it is worth noting that she, the girl you said you saw, she never showed up on any footage.'

I stammered, 'She, um, she was too far away ...'

Sam's voice was become emphatic, almost aggressive. 'And yet you described her as flitting. The very same word you used to describe this manifestation here.' He pointed to the shimmery darkness on the screen.

'Yes,' I said. 'But ...' I didn't know what to object to. He was right. I just didn't like where he was going with it.

He lowered his voice so it was more gentle. 'All these coincidences are piling up, Rosie. I think it's time to talk about them.'

'Well,' I said. 'From a purely statistical point of view, these events could be considered to be random. Not meaningfully related.'

'Is that so?' he said and pouted.

'What about our motto – "open mind, healthy scepticism?"'

'Yes, that's right. And an open mind doesn't mean knee-jerking into denial.' Sam folded his hands on his lap and rubbed the middle knuckle on his right hand.

He hit play again. 'Is it possible?' his eyes swung back to the screen. 'That this is a non-human entity interacting with you?'

Film Me looked at the floor, then over to Film Friend Cerise, who was gesticulating wildly. Film Me looked back at the gas cloud. It was dissipating. Now I could see only slender ribbons of transparent darkness hanging in the air. The camera angles swapped and Film Me jogged towards Cerise.

Sam stopped the recording. 'And that's the point, Rosie,' he said, a bit like a teacher. 'These things, they are always interacting with *you*.'

I wasn't sure if he was accusing me of something. 'Which means what?'

'I don't know? I'm going to send this to Monty's science guys. See what they make of it.'

I'd never heard of them before but guessed they were in the secret Ministry.

I didn't say anything, but stared at the screen for a minute until Sam said, 'What if you're a conduit?'

'You mean like an aqueduct?' I asked not unfacetiously.

He sighed. 'If you want to put it like that.'

I thought of Roman Britain.

Then Sam said, 'What if you are like a magnet that attracts these … phenomena or whatever they are?'

This kind of talk began to alarm me. 'There's got to be another explanation. What about being a sceptic Sam?'

He smiled easily at last. 'Well that was much easier before I met you.'

I tried to smile but I was feeling queasy.

'Well, some would say, it doesn't matter what you believe. It's all about the evidence.'

'Empirical evidence,' I said glumly for want of anything better.

We both sat in our chairs and looked at the screen.

'That's the thing that truly terrifies me,' said Sam. 'That this here is empirical evidence.'

'But of what?' I said nervously.

He shrugged. 'The whole darn gamut. If we've got a ghost, then that means it's evidence of the afterlife, the soul – a whole raft of belief systems become validated and compounded.'

'Oh god,' I said. 'That sounds like big league stuff.'

'I know,' he said and nodded quietly. 'We have to be responsible about what we now do.'

After a moment more, I shook my head and said, 'No. It's ridiculous. I'm not buying it. There's got to be a logical explanation for this.'

'Of course there's an explanation for it,' said Sam. 'It just might not be logical.'

His closing thoughts on the matter did not help me on my way to sleep that night I have to admit. In fact, after tossing and turning for a good hour, I decided to get up and do some stuff. I put a load of washing on downstairs. Then I phoned Monty. I thought he wouldn't answer, but he picked it up on the ninth ring.

He sounded jaunty, as always. Didn't matter what time of day or night it was, Mr Walker was always daisy-fresh.

'Rosie,' he whispered. 'Is this urgent?'

'No,' I said frankly. 'Do you want me to phone back?'

'No,' he said. 'But you know what you're like.'

That was indeed a fair comment. I did tend to call Monty whenever I felt my life was in danger.

'What's up then?' he asked. 'I've got a couple of minutes. But I'm out on an observation. Interesting case,' he added. 'Melting frogs.'

I ignored the last piece of information which would just unleash more questions and right now I had a couple of them on the go, and truly, madly, deeply that was so so enough to be going on with. 'I was going to ask you if you could do some kind of Military Intelligence background check on everyone at Ratchette Hall.'

'Mmm,' he said. 'Text me their names, I haven't got a pen to hand. But use your OTHER phone. The one I gave you.'

'Okay, okay,' I said.

'And don't show anyone else.'

'All right, I won't.'

'How's it going anyway?' he asked.

'Good,' I lied. 'Just need to do a bit more investigation. One of the bodies has gone walkabout from the church.'

'Oh yes?' said Monty.

'Not literally,' I added.

'I guessed,' he said but didn't laugh.

I sighed. 'After the conversation I've just had with Sam I can't take any chances.'

'How so?' Monty's voice now included another tone suggestive of mild curiosity.

'He's got some footage back from the lab and it's completely freaked him out. He thinks there might be evidence of a ghost on it. You should have a look at it when he sends it to your "science guys—"'

'I've already seen it,' he said at once. 'Tell him not to bother sending copies. We are putting it through some extensive testing and close analysis …'

'What? But he hasn't sent it back yet—'

Monty's voice went quiet. 'I have a man at the lab, Rosie,' he said. 'Sam doesn't realise he's not looking at the master. We have that under close wraps right now. And don't tell him either. We haven't tampered. We just needed to ensure we had the original.'

Of course he did. I wasn't surprised. British Intelligence. They had men everywhere.

'And how is Sam coping with the conclusion he appears to be drawing?'

'Mmm,' I said.

'Well, I suppose he would be like that,' Monty said inexplicably.

Interesting, I thought. 'What are you talking about?'

Monty paused. 'How much do you know about Sam's background?' he asked. 'Has he told you yet?'

I was shocked by the statement and retorted, 'What do you mean?'

'His family,' said Monty. 'What happened to them.'

'His family?' I repeated. 'Well, I know his mum and dad live in the States. There's a sister in Ibiza, amazingly. That's about it. Why? What happened to them?'

A voice in the background said, 'Sir,' then another female, further back, started to swear.

Monty's voice became more clipped. 'Sorry Rosie,' he said. 'I've got to go.'

Then he hung up.

Leaving me very much in the dark.

CHAPTER ELEVEN

'It was shimmering, like a figure on a rack stretched with pain and tortured. And yet dark. Shimmering, shimmering, shimmering darkly. Like they had got off the rack and were the other way round and floating, hovering. Like an angel. Yes, yes – an archangel! Oh my god! An archangel, like Michael, returning from above to herald the apocalypse, the end of times, to sound the trumpet, complete the prophecy and dispense apocryphal everlasting justice. It was there, it was commotioning and the commotion bellowed "I am coming for you, *for you all*."' Chris Devlin took a breath. 'Then suddenly it just vanished, like that.' He snapped his fingers, narrowed his eyes and nodded at us.

I prodded the assortment of twigs and leaves on the floor and looked into the sloping forestry at the edge of the Hall grounds.

'Couldn't it simply have walked off?' asked Sam after a bit. He was standing by Devlin looking at the area where a phantom had allegedly been sighted last night.

'No,' said Devlin sounding really put out. 'It wasn't like that. It was MAGNIFICENT. It was crazy.' He looked at his shoes, which evidently agreed with him, nodded again, then looked up and added, 'It was awesome.'

Now I was listening to him in the flesh I realised his voice had an East Coast curl to it, though I had always thought he was British. He looked American, with the tan and stiff jeans and that.

'You know, this is really fantastic,' Devlin continued, his voice rising to match his enthusiasm. 'I love it. I couldn't have asked for a better residency. I can use this. We all can. You know, the fear was exhilarating. Honest to goddam god, I experienced such a totally, like, evocative response.' He glanced at me and looked back at Sam. 'It made me hard.'

Monty had once told me that when you were an investigator there was no such thing as 'too much information'. But I think Chris Devlin had just proved him wrong.

'Oh,' said Margot, breathily. 'Chris, I feel you.'

She wished, I thought, then told myself off. Older women were just as entitled to weird sexual peccadillos as younger ones. And though Mr Devlin did nothing to float my boat I could see his wealth, power and success might enhance his nautical buoyancy in certain female eyes. Or male ones. Though Devlin seemed so straight he was almost a parody. Which meant there were always possibilities there.

For me, personally, the Lovejoy mullet was a massive turn-off. And my radar might be a little wonky at the moment but that man had 'stadium rock fan' coming off him in heavily amplified waves. I bet he liked Bon Jovi.

'I mean,' Margot recovered herself, 'I know what you mean, Chris.'

Cullen, the final member of our expedition, who had shadowed Devlin the whole time and was now staring at him with his mouth open, said, 'Commotioning – is that a word?'

The famous author looked at his fanboy with an expression of pity then slapped him on the back. 'Cullen, my man, you want success, you gotta play outside the rules. Embrace the maverick within. Think, watch, observe. Ask questions. Communicate freely. Let your spirit flow.'

Cullen nodded, suitably chastised. I felt a bit sorry for him, despite the whole creepy serial killer vibe: I bet Devlin had a whole host of proofreaders who regularly cleaned up his freely flowing spirit. Mind you they were probably used to that sort of thing over there – a lot of their top brass tended to 'misspeak' and make 'misstatements' these days.

'So,' said Sam, swivelling back to face Devlin. 'This commotioning then – when did it actually take place?'

'I couldn't sleep.' Chris rubbed his chin and strutted over towards me to join in my peering duties. 'Jetlag,' he explained as he swaggered. 'After midnight, for sure.'

'About two, I'd say,' Margot confirmed. 'I'm a light sleeper.'

'Did you hear it?' Sam asked Cullen.

He looked like he wanted to nod, to join in, but he shook his head and said sadly, 'No. But I would have liked to.'

'So it was a thin shimmer?' Sam was noting it down.

Devlin stared into the woods and blinked. 'Oh yeah – a shimmering, er, shimerescence.'

I glanced at him out the side of my eyes. I'd never heard that one before.

Margot piped up, 'I thought it had horns.'

'I can't say I saw horns, because I was thinking angels,' Devlin said and didn't elaborate.

'I was thinking horns,' said Margot, letting her eyes swivel over the minor bulge in Devlin's jeans. Oh yeah, Margot, I bet you were, I thought but didn't miss-say. 'After your talk about witches and the Devil,' Margot continued to explain to Sam in a tone of voice that seemed to suggest all this was his fault. 'Your story about the Canine-ass.'

'Cernunnos,' Sam corrected.

Margot bit her lip. 'Yes. But, at the same time, my eyes, you know, they're not as good as they used to be ...' She shook her head with regret.

'And it made a noise?' Sam continued. He looked dubious, which was a marked change from his attitude last night. But nonetheless welcome, as far as I was concerned. I liked Sam more that way. That was the norm. Deviations from it worried me. Personally, I couldn't really understand why the footage had wired him so. I remained unconvinced. Though perhaps combined with the grave episode and a bang on the head ...

Then there was also Monty's hint dropped with a clang last night that there was something else going on with my dear friend. Something disturbing that involved his family.

But it would all have to wait because Chris Devlin was bellowing out a noise hybrid that sounded like both a chimpanzee taking fright and the kind of grunts the best-selling author probably made when he was having shouty sex.

'Like that,' he finished and puffed out his chest with pride, nodding at Cullen for confirmation.

For the first time since I'd met him the young man looked afraid. 'Er …' he said.

Margot touched her hair. Her voice broke as she muttered, 'Oh yes, Chris.'

Ew.

I picked up a stick and tried to dislodge some mud from my boots. This soggy environment wasn't any good for embroidered leather. There was already a damp patch on my right toe that was turning the purple into more of an aubergine shade.

Sam cleared his throat. 'Right. It made some kind of noise. Possibly a "commotioning/trumpet/bellow/scream/grunt". And then disappeared?'

Chris nodded. 'I was the only one to see it with my bare eyes. And yes.' He clicked his fingers once more. 'It went, oh yeah, it went in the flash of a blink.'

Gawd, I thought, his editors must really look forward to getting his drafts in.

I glanced up and saw Sam was also now watching the woods.

Despite the fact it was morning, the day was overcast and the darkness of the trees foreboding. The forest was thick with ferns and boulders or fallen logs. I could see mulch on the floor, leaves that had fallen off in last night's storm, and not been cleared away or absorbed yet. There was still a smattering of green leaves holding on. And a couple of dashes of colour too – bushes with purple berries, a couple of patches of pinky-mauve and yellow flowers that were still out and hadn't yet realised it was November. A thin blue flower bobbed its head deeper in. As I took my eyes off a thick bush with dark frothy leaves growing out of the roots of an old oak, a grey squirrel popped its head out. Sensing eyes upon it, it froze, beheld the scene, then ran up the trunk into the branches above.

And who could blame it?

'But you can't say for sure that it didn't go in there? Into the woods?' asked Sam. For a second I thought he was referring to our little furry friend. Then I remembered it was an angel. Or possibly a devil. Or a devilish archangel. Of course.

Devlin also looked into the wood. 'Not to my knowledge,' he said. Which didn't really seem like an appropriate answer to me.

Sam let it go.

I went back to my boots. The mud had come off the heel now. Looked much better like that.

'So I'm getting the distinct impression,' Sam continued with his probing, drawing my attention from the other current loves of my life, 'that it wasn't necessarily, er, witchlike? Or what you might come to think of as witchlike?'

'No,' said Devlin, speaking for the three of them. 'Carole had something to say about the Devil and a bell, but I'm not sure it was a bell I heard. More like the death calls of a carrion demon, a discharge of fury from the Devil's hell-hounds, the raspy bellow of Lucifer himself.'

We all stared at him.

I tossed my stick into the wood. Margot jumped.

'Sorry,' I said and noticed that she was shivering. 'How about we go inside? Then we can warm up with coffee.' I held Sam's eyes. 'And have a chat with Carole.'

The rest of the group returned to the Seminar Room at the front of the house, where Laura was apparently holding a character-building workshop. As if they needed more in these trying circumstances.

Sam and I decided to look for Carole. I was pleased to see my colleague's mood had picked up a fair bit since last night. He hadn't mentioned the 'ghost' again and I hadn't told him about my conversation with Monty. Of course, I was completely intrigued by what the agent had said, but realised if it was a big subject that affected Sam quite fundamentally then I would have to move slowly. Certainly, as gently as he moved with me and my family's myriad secrets.

Carole Christmas, full of joy and benevolence, was in the kitchen clearing up whilst whistling to the tune of 'Who Let the Dogs Out'.

'Oh 'ello,' she said and sniffed and stopped whistling. 'They said you'd be coming. Ain't got no food. They ate it all. Don't hold back this lot. Not when other people are making it. But there's no lunch to be had. They're all going down the pub. We reserved the snug. I'm off there meself in a couple of hours. Then I'll be back to sort dinner.'

'It's okay, thanks,' I told her. 'We haven't come to eat. Chris Devlin was telling us there was another incident in the night. And that you had something to say on it?'

Her face dropped into classic indignation mode, her shoulders hunched. She thumped a wooden spoon on the counter. 'I had nothink to do with it. Nothink.'

'No,' said Sam. 'We're not saying that you did.'

'Someone's having a laugh,' she said and looked at us with

accusation in her eyes. Which was a bit rich really, as Sam and I must be the only ones here who definitely could not have got up to any of these jinks, high or low.

Sam cleared his throat. 'Chris said you mentioned something to do with the Devil and a bell? Another rumour perhaps?'

A sigh leaked out of Carole's thin mouth. The air seemed to go out of her momentarily so that she leant on the counter and said, 'I didn't say it was the Devil. I ain't stupid. I said it sounded a bit like the story. You know – from the church.'

'Carole, remember we're not from here.' I added, 'We work with Trace at the museum. Now, we've heard the one about the Devil and storm.'

For clarity, Sam expanded. 'The roof came off. Edgar, the vicar, told us there was another incident where the Devil, made manifest, ran between a parishioner's legs. A friar if I remember correctly?'

I waited for Carole to come out with some crap pub joke humour but she didn't. She looked worried. 'There was a bell. He dropped it because we got Bell Hill Wood. It's still there – the hole it left. They call it the Bell Crater.'

'Interesting,' said Sam. 'I'll check it out.'

Just then Sophia bustled in. 'The group are going to walk into the village for lunch and a session at The Griffin. Chris wondered if you wanted to join them?'

I looked at Sam who shook his head. 'I think my time is better spent researching the legend.'

But at the thought of the pub an opportunity presented itself to me. 'Is your son, Ben, in?'

Carole's eyebrows furrowed. 'I think so. Why?'

'I want to ask him about his YouTube channel. That okay?'

She nodded without enthusiasm. 'If you can find him, you can do what you like with him.'

I turned back to Sophia. 'I'm in.'

Stand on the highest point of Essex and you can see the world. Or that's how it must have felt for centuries before photographers and then the media allowed us a window into exotic climes us Britons barely knew existed.

I don't think you could help but be impressed by the majestic sweep of the hills and mounds that led the eye into the distant ridge. I was back atop the highest point of Damebury, looking at the view that I'd been unable to appreciate yesterday in the rain.

In the distance purple clouds brushed low over tawny heaths. As I watched, the cloudbank broke and a singular golden beam shone a brief spotlight over this little patch of England. For a brief moment, the scene looked utterly glorious, and I thought it no wonder that the people of Damebury should choose to inter their dead here, as they had for centuries in the nearby churchyard. Their dearly departed would be as close to heaven as possible, and should be very happy with the ever-changing view.

'Oh mighty Apollo, Isis, sun goddess,' said a voice beside me. Starla was stretching her arms skywards, curls of blue hair caught by the wind flowed and danced like party streamers. 'Come to us, warm our skin. Give us your blessing now.'

A bird hooted in a nearby hedgerow.

Nicholas made a tutting noise and continued to walk alongside Chris and Cullen on to the path by the churchyard.

As speedily as they had parted, the clouds closed ranks and blocked the sun out once more.

'Och, now. Give it up. Let's be quick,' said Robin, who was at the front of our group, having taken upon himself the mantel of guide. 'To the pub! Before the rain comes back.'

Starla brought her arms down to her sides. Her brows had a thick crease between them.

Jocelyn shrugged at me. 'Each to their own. I'm looking forward to this workshop. It's one of the reasons I came onto the course. Devlin's a very successful writer.'

I nodded. The wind blew onto my face. In it I could feel dampness. Robin was right – we should rev up a bit, for grey spray was darkening the horizon. Down the hill the breeze brushed the grass and rippled it, like the hairs on the back of a great sleeping beast.

I fell into step with Jocelyn and Tabby. Monty's auntie was the oldest in our walking group, as Imogen, Laura and Margot had opted out and were getting a lift to The Griffin. Couldn't blame them really. It was a hilly walk. But it was certainly the prettier way.

We hurried along the path by the graveyard. Overhead the trees' skinny arms held each other, creating a skeletal arbour, a passage to the graves and their underworld below.

We scuttled past the churchyard. A couple of our party sent glances over to the church. I thought about meeting Dorcus. More precisely the way he looked when he laughed:

the spritely dancing of his eyes, the hard line of his jaw, the certainty and confidence of his gaze and sparking intimacy that existed for that brief moment before I left him. I did really hope I'd bump into him again.

I had no time, however, to linger on Dorcus because Starla had caught up with me, and was edging between Jocelyn and Tabby.

'Poor Graham,' she said.

Tabby and Jocelyn squinted at the church. Mr Peacock would forever be associated with those strange tombs now. Unless we were able to unpick what exactly was going on. But it was quite messy.

I thought over it – Graham had died on Monday night. We had arrived on Tuesday and talked to some of the writers. Wednesday we had gone straight to the church and discovered the theft of body and effigy. Then we learnt the residents of the Hall had heard banshees during the night. Carol had talked about witches in the wood. Then last night there was the 'commotioning' and Devil calls or something. I couldn't work out exactly what Chris meant by his descriptions, but the point was – strange stuff was still going on. Despite the fact that Graham was dead.

Which, basically, meant if it had all been designed to scare Graham to death then the objective had been achieved. One had to wonder why therefore the 'haunting' or scaring continued.

Who else was being targeted?

I had no answers at that moment but, in the past, once I'd let such questions marinate in my brain fridge then answers would eventually pop up. We just needed to dig as Monty instructed we should.

We reached the pub as the others arrived in the car. The men had already gone in so I stood back and let Imogen and Laura go through the front door, while Margot brought up the rear. Cullen to my surprise showed great gentlemanliness and held the door open for us to pass through. Once Margot had limped ahead, Cullen closed it and followed us in.

Our little group snaked alongside the bar heading towards the snug at the end. We passed a couple of older men leaning against it, nursing half-filled pint glasses. One with tufty white hair and a zip-up cardigan with leather patches turned and surveyed us and said, 'Hello ladies!' with a smile and a leer.

The other, who had thinning brown hair that was silver at the sides and who was wearing a navy jacket, followed his friend's gaze and then smiled and said, 'You back again?'

But nobody said anything.

I squinted and tried a smile.

But the guy in the navy, who had more than a couple of empty pint glasses on the bar next to him, shrugged and went, 'All right then. Suit yourself.'

Cullen nodded at them and they almost smiled back, but we hastened on, weaving between the tables and chairs, and entered a room through a large archway. A thick red rope across the front bore a 'Reserved' sign.

It was cosy within: a brick fireplace already had a fire on the go. There was a window to the rear of the snug, fairly high up the wall, which overlooked the back and the car park. The sky through it was the colour of dirty ice stippled with oil – the rain had broken. It was misty out there.

Three tables had been pulled together into the middle of the room so that they formed one big square with enough space for four people on each side. With only eleven of us it was quite relaxed and roomy.

As we arranged ourselves a young waitress who was cheery, but clearly busy, handed out the menus and asked if five minutes would be enough to choose lunch. We all agreed it would be and spent some time scanning them.

When we'd ordered, Chris Devlin took to his feet and threw back his shoulders.

'Welcome my lords and ladies,' he announced with a deep bow. 'May you now have the pleasure of Chris Devlin's Greatest Fears workshop.' Then he flashed his super-bright gleaming teeth.

Margot began clapping and the others fell into line.

I wondered how often the writer referred to himself in the third person. In my book that was kind of odd. Though Devlin seemed very comfortable with the idea.

'Right,' he continued. 'Now I realise you've been writing stories, some of which I've heard, some of which the best-selling author hasn't managed to read because of flight delay etcetera etcetera.' He stuck out his little finger and waved his hand around. 'He pinky-promises to get on to that soon. But now we must hear something from those who haven't read them out yet. Then after that we'll commence the workshop – which is all about fear. How to perceive it, how to convey it, how to harness your own feelings in that process: to be aware of your fear, my fear and fear itself, right?'

Nicholas rolled his eyes.

'Fear – oh yeah, baby,' Devlin continued. 'Don't for one minute assume that this is going to be an easy ride,' he went on, eyeing each of us one by one. 'I want you all making notes. Get a pen if you haven't got one. Here's some produced by my publishers for the latest book.' He produced a small silver pot full of biros and put them on the table in front of him. They had a slogan printed down the length: 'Don't go out – *on your own!*'

As they were passed around, I thought now might be a good time to duck out and pop upstairs to see Christmas Junior.

'Come on,' said Devlin. 'Let's start with you Jocelyn.'

The young woman pulled a sheaf of notes out of her bag. 'Actually,' she said. 'This story is perfect for the session really. It's about a woman whose greatest fear is reality.'

'Oh yeah,' said Devlin with approval and punched the air. 'That's what I like. Rock on, Joanne.' He gleamed at her.

Jocelyn ignored the misnomer and began to read, rather surprisingly, in an American accent. 'I could tell you a thing or two 'bout my soon-to-be-ex-husband,' she cooed like a Southern Belle. 'And not much of it would be pretty.' Then she winked at Starla, on my right, who started.

Tabby, who was on the other side of the blue-haired one, chuckled at her reaction. Blimey Jocelyn was good. I was tempted to stay.

'Saying that,' she went on, immersing herself in the

character of the narrator. 'Even I had to admit, as I looked out the window this morning, ole Ron was starting to develop great taste in broads. His latest flame was a knockout.' Jocelyn sent a lazy smile over her clearly rapt audience. 'Which was about time.'

Nope, I couldn't be pulled into this. As enjoyable as it might be to sit in a chair with a glass of diet coke and listen to people telling me bedtime stories, I had some serious sleuthing to do.

Muttering to Margot about needing the loo I exited discreetly from the nook.

I passed the fraught waitress and asked her how I could get up to the private apartment so I could see Ben Christmas. I made it sound like I had a message from his mum. She knew about Carole's work up at Ratchette Hall, so it all sounded plausible enough for her to direct me to the back of the pub where a door led into a short hallway and a set of stairs carried me up to the first floor.

The front door to the flat was open, but I did knock.

I waited a decent amount of time, but there was no answer so I pushed it and popped my head through. 'Hello?'

Still nothing though, other than a shuffling somewhere within which indicated a human presence or maybe massive rats. Preferably the former. With that in mind I stepped rather cautiously over the threshold into a narrow passageway. It was old up here. The floor was uneven, the floorboards squeaking as I trod on them and sloping slightly downwards to the right. Overhead, low beams signified another level of accommodation on top of this. In between the beams, plaster was painted white. The place looked clean and tidy, but I thought, could probably do with an update.

At the end of the passage I pushed the door open and saw a young man nodding to music on his earphones. A quiet tinny rattle came out of them. He was sitting at a table in an open-plan kitchen-diner, fumbling around with a toolbox and screwdrivers and reams and reams of fairy lights, some of which he was taking apart. Christmas decorations I supposed.

'Oh hello!' I said. 'I'm Rosie Strange.'

The boy immediately jumped. His upper torso receded back into the chair, lips forming a terse o-shape.

I laughed involuntarily then added, 'Sorry. I didn't mean to surprise you. The door was open. I did call out but you couldn't have heard.'

The lips closed then formed a tight flat line. He pulled an earphone off one ear and brushed back a fuzz of gingery hair. I wasn't sure how old he was – his skin was kind of soft-looking and he had roundish eyes, which made him look young and innocent. But his build, concealed behind a fake Dolce and 'Gabana' t-shirt, was sturdy and there was a smattering of bumfluff on his chin. He could be anything between seventeen to twenty-five, I reckoned.

'I'm Rosie Strange,' I repeated, while he removed the second earphone. 'I'm doing some investigating up at Ratchette Hall,' I added. 'Carole said I might be able to have a few words with you. That okay?'

Now he completely removed the headset and put it on the table. 'Carole?' he said and tensed. 'What about?'

I tried to look friendly and smiled. 'There have been quite a few strange happenings at Ratchette Hall, as I'm sure you're aware?'

His eyes dropped to the small parts scattered across the table top, which he began to clear away. 'Yep, heard about that.'

'The barman downstairs ...' I tried to remember his name but failed. 'He told me that you like to film pranks. You've got a YouTube channel, I understand. Have you been pranking during the night? Filming them outside Ratchette Hall?'

A smirk suckered in his cheek. 'In the night? Er, that wouldn't make for good footage, would it?' His tone was laced with smug sarcasm. 'Filming in the dark is pointless.'

I made a big thing of nodding and considering this. 'You should try night vision cameras or thermal imaging. I've used both. The image contrast isn't spectacular but you can see what's going on.'

Gratifyingly stunned by this information, Ben screwed his eyes up and paid me closer attention. 'What do you do again?'

'I'm an investigator. Did you do any trick-or-treating on Halloween?'

He laughed at me. 'How old do I look?'

I wanted to say that I wasn't sure but thought that might rile him so changed tack.

'Where were you last night, please?' I got straight in so there was no chance for prevarication and alibi building.

For a second, he floundered. Then he shook his head and said, 'At work.'

'Doing what?'

'I'm a specialist cleaner,' he said with disdain.

'What kind of specialist?' I asked and wondered if he was one of those crime scene cleaners? If that was the case then it might be worth keeping a very close eye on Mr Ben Christmas's movements.

But he said, 'Animals.' Which was disappointing. As long as he was telling the truth, that is.

'Can you prove it?' I asked, trying to be casual, which was a struggle as it wasn't really that kind of question.

And in response Ben's eyes popped. 'Prove it? Why? Why do I need to prove it?'

I narrowed mine and leant towards him. 'I see. Does that mean you can't?'

Ben bent forwards, across his nose and about the fleshy parts of his cheeks, a sunburn-red was spreading. Indignation, I thought and watched him reach into the back pocket of his jeans and produce a leather wallet. Curling his bottom lip he pulled out an ID card and laid it on the table in front of him.

I couldn't see the writing. There was a logo made from a bent tree and a paw print, beneath which was a photograph that very clearly matched the man in front of me. 'My ID card swipes me in and out,' he said.

Bugger. I thought I was on to something for a moment. 'So you didn't have anything to do with Graham Peacock's death?'

Now the attitude vanished. Ben shook his head quickly. 'It wasn't me. I was at work that night too. I can prove it. When you swipe your card through the stiles, they keep a record, for timesheets. I'm sure you can contact my employers if you need to.'

This time, his eyes were wide. There was no bullshit going on.

I believed him.

Without anything left to ask him about, I turned and made for the door. 'Okay, well thanks. I might be back with some questions,' I said. 'So don't leave town.'

It occurred to me that Ben hadn't asked me for my ID which meant he might have mistaken me for police. Now that was certainly something I could put to my advantage if I needed to at a later date.

Downstairs the pub had filled up a bit. I slipped round the bar, surprised to see Cullen talking to the two old men there. I smiled at them as I passed. When Cullen saw me, he made a point of stopping and saying, 'Instructions to the gents. You haven't seen the men's toilets have you?'

I said, 'Oh no, sorry,' and continued to the snug, but cast a last glance at the bar before I entered: he was still with them.

My salad had arrived while I'd been upstairs, so I slipped along the table next to Starla and tucked in.

The mood in the snug had sombred.

Robin was talking about his partner back home and how he had once grabbed a drink from his bedside table and glugged down about '100 millilitres of water and a live moth' which flapped around in the back of his throat till he managed to cough it up and then free it from the room.

'Greatest fears,' whispered Starla. 'Robin is afraid of moths crawling into crevices.' She gave a little smile. 'Very Freudian.'

I shuddered and shovelled in another mouthful of feathery salad leaves.

'You missed my story,' Starla went on in low tones. 'It's got Persephone in it.' She nodded at my salad. 'You know – pomegranate seeds.'

I forked one and popped it in my mouth. 'What about them?'

'The myth,' she said. 'The abduction of Persephone by Hades, the god of the underworld. I suppose, thinking about him now, he's probably a bit like that Cernunnos Sam was talking about. The horned one.'

'What's this got to do with my salad?' I asked, though Laura was frowning at us for talking.

'I'm getting to it. Surprised you don't know, Rosie. Weren't you taught Greek myths at school?'

I wrinkled my nose. 'Can't remember. There's all sorts of stuff I can't recall from back then.' I pulled my chair in so that Cullen could squeeze round the back to his seat.

I watched him slide into his chair. He had an air of satisfaction about him. Must certainly have been a rewarding session in the lavatory.

'The story has got supernatural tones, you know,' Starla went on. 'And it's entirely sexist, of course.'

I snorted. 'Quelle surprise.'

Laura glared at us.

Robin flapped his arms like a chicken and started

whinnying. His eyelids were doing that fluttering thing again. 'Be gone, thou Terrorfly,' he proclaimed.

Then everybody gave him a round of applause and started talking, which gave Starla the time to fill me in properly.

'Well,' she brought her head down to mine. I could smell lasagne on her breath. There were red stains in the corners of her mouth. 'Hades bursts through a cleft in the earth and grabs beautiful Persephone, taking her down to the underworld to be his bride. When her mother, Demeter, finds out she searches all over the earth for her vanished daughter, with Hecate's torches lighting her way.'

A mental image of our museum cat walking on her hind legs and carrying torches in each paw caused me to smile. Honestly, I wouldn't put it past that one.

'Demeter was so upset that she forbade the earth to produce anything. So, the world was plunged into despair and nothing grew. Prompted by the cries of the hungry people Hades was forced to return Persephone. However, the dark god tricked her, giving her some pomegranate seeds to eat. Because she had eaten six seeds Hades told her she would spend six months of the year down there, in the earthy tomb of the afterlife. And that, of course, is when we have winter.'

I nodded and bit down on a seed. This one was bitter. Outside the grey was lightening.

'My story,' continued Starla, 'is about a woman whose husband develops photophobia and can't bear light. She spends six months outside with her children having a normal life then six months in the dark with him. In her dark world she finds herself becoming cold, deadened and stone-hearted, longing to feel sunshine and joy again, to feel wonder. She weeps.'

That's me, I thought and an internal voice said, 'Since summer passed I have been low in the underworld, becoming dead and cold like Persephone. When will I be able to feel joy again?' Then I caught myself and thought blimey, where the heck did that come from? These writers and their purpling prose were clearly contagious.

Chris Devlin was calling my name, '... joining us. What's your greatest fear then, Rosie?'

I pushed my plate across the table and folded my arms. 'It's already happened.'

He smiled, then frowned. 'What is it?'

'I'm not telling you,' I said.

Nicholas tutted and threw the remains of a shot down his throat, adding the empty to several on the table.

Devlin could tell from the look on my face that I wasn't going to budge because he turned to the young nutter up the end of the row and said, 'Yours then, Cullen? Be a gentleman and share.'

All heads turned and looked upon Mr Sutcliffe with interest.

'Nothing much frightens me,' he said to Devlin's dismay. 'Except,' he went on, 'I spent the first three years of my life in Australia. I know,' he said to Nicholas's raised eyebrows, 'no accent. But it did leave me with something more than a healthy respect for snakes.' He shuddered. 'I can't bear them.'

Over the other side of the table, Laura began nodding. 'Me too,' she said. 'I can't even watch them on television.'

'I read your story about the man with a phobia about them,' said Jocelyn. 'It was great.'

Laura nodded, pleased. 'Thank you. Yes, in a cathartic way, I did enjoy writing *The Eden Tree*.'

'So,' said Chris. 'You put your fear into it, didn't you?'

L.D. Taylor-Jacobs nodded. 'That's right. Thank you for your endorsement Chris. It sold well.'

'It's a really scary story,' said Jocelyn. 'I read in your Author's Note you used your own phobia of snakes to ramp up the tension. And all that stuff about snakes, serpents and Satan …'

Laura couldn't help but smile. 'Yes, well the symbolism was too good to omit – snakes are often identified with evil, chaos, the underworld.'

'And here we are back with the Devil again,' I said from my corner.

Everyone turned to me and waited, but just then Imogen let out a rather awful moan, which was rather uncharacteristic, what with her being seemingly devoid of emotion.

She shuddered in agreement. 'Not sure I would be able to read that. I'm not fond of snakes either.'

Nicholas looked up, engaged at last, and grinned. 'Well I guess none of you have heard the news about the local zoo?' he said. 'One of their Royal Pythons is missing.'

CHAPTER TWELVE

Nicholas's announcement had, as I imagined he intended, a radical effect on all of us gathered there. We collectively started. Starla and I, sitting next to each other, both went, 'Oh,' and synchronised a sudden intake of breath.

Cullen visibly blanched. I thought for a moment he was going to gag.

'Nicholas, you'd better be joking,' Laura thundered.

The fop giggled, looking suddenly like a little imp, with red skin and mischief in his heart. 'Not at all,' he said with reckless bravado.

Laura's sense of humour had evidently evaporated because she muttered, 'Twat,' and then pouted at him.

Colonel Mustard however had blunted his faculties somewhat and continued, oblivious to the change of mood in the snug. Or more likely he was just enjoying the stir. He hicced then held up his phone. 'BBC news alert. Came up this morning.'

Jocelyn grabbed it off him, scrutinised the screen then nodded glumly. 'He's right. Posted this morning.'

At which point Devlin clapped his hands. 'Excellent. We

can all use that. Right I want you three to sum up the way you are feeling in three adverbs or adjectives.'

Laura side-eyed Nicholas. 'Heightened. Punchy. Violent.'

Imogen cocked her head to one side. 'Uneasy, er, wanton, physical.'

Devlin grimaced, took his gaze off her and pointed to Cullen. 'And you, my man – three words?'

Cullen crossed his arms and muttered, 'Very pissed off.'

Everyone laughed and tittered. Except Devlin, who sighed.

Then Jocelyn piped up. 'A lot of people are frightened of the unknown. What they imagine is the supernatural.'

'Good,' said Devlin and gleamed at her.

'Graham was,' said Nicholas. 'You could tell the way he reacted to your recital in the church.' He turned to Starla. His words were laced with mocking accusation. 'It's almost as if you knew exactly what you were doing Ms Ocean – frightening him. And you didn't leave it at the church either, did you? You carried on till his heart gave out.'

'Oh Nicholas, shut up.' This time it was Tabby who voiced what the others were thinking. 'You can't think Starla's hopeless mumbling had anything to do with Graham's death.'

Starla wasn't sure whether to be grateful or offended.

Tabby continued to tut. 'Such hocus pocus can't raise the dead. Or else we'd all be at it. There'd be a "Necromancers R Us" in every soulless retail park.'

'But what I'm saying,' he carried on, a pronounced slur to his words. 'Is that Starla's "hocus pocus", for all its worth, might not have raised the dead. But it did send Graham closer to the grave. Her incantation *increased* his sense of fear.

And thus, like it or not, contributed to his heart attack. How do we know that Starla didn't do that on purpose?' He looked around the table and shrugged. 'We don't. None of us know anything about each other.'

'Me?' said Starla, now definitely outraged. 'But why would I want to cause Graham's death?'

Nicholas scoffed. 'Perhaps you knew him before coming here? Maybe you flirted with him and he turned you down? Maybe you wanted revenge for that!'

'That's certainly a motive.' This from Cullen. 'Sex and scorn are often stimuli.' As Nicholas's fiery gaze clapped onto him he shut his mouth.

But it was too late – young Cullen had raised his head above the parapet and now was going to pay the price.

'Oh yes, well you know all about motives don't you Cullen. Because you can get "inside the mind of a killer",' Nicholas said and tapped his own head, aggressively. 'You total utter psycho.'

'Nicholas, shut up,' said Jocelyn for probably the thirteenth time that day.

'We're all writing crime,' said Cullen. A note of pleading had crept into his voice. 'We can all imagine what that's like.'

He looked like he was going to remain quiet, rather sensibly, but then Nicholas said, 'Yes, but you do it with so much conviction.'

At that point Cullen's eyes darkened. His mouth formed into a snarl. While the muscles in his cheeks flexed he said, slowly with measured deliberation, 'And you're always so angry. Can I remind you what Laura told us: "Murder is an extension of anger."'

I'd never heard that before. It was an interesting comment though, and a previous experience would certainly bear that theory out.

There was a crack on the table as Nicholas whipped round and faced the female crime writer, knocking over a glass on the table in his haste. Jocelyn started dabbing at the spilled wine.

'Indeed,' he said. 'And there you have it. Our criminal mastermind. Yet no one's pointing the finger at Laura are they? But she knew Graham was here. She has admitted she spoke to him on the phone, that she talked about her ideas. Certainly, she introduced the story to him.'

Chris stood up and began waving his hands in front of Nicholas. 'Sir, I admire your passion but you have made your point. Please let others speak.'

But Nicholas didn't care. 'And let's not forget – the famous *Eden Tree.*' He held up his phone and stabbed at the screen while he swayed. 'Ah here we have it. "L.D. Taylor-Jacobs has murder in her heart – the best criminal mind published of late. *The Eden Tree* is a testament to the cunning and brutality of contemporary life",' he said as if he were quoting a review. 'You wrote that Mr Devlin.'

Chris's eyebrows remained unmoved (Botox probably) but his mouth dropped open.

'So I believe you, Mr Devlin, superstar crime writer, you must be regarding Laura with no small amount of suspicion too,' Nicholas went on. 'Yet, you're just as bad, aren't you? How many people have you both murdered? In fiction. Allegedly.'

'Okay,' said Laura. She bent her head towards the table and put her hands on it, like a judge calling the courtroom to order. 'Enough. We still don't know what the coroner has to say about Graham's unfortunate accident. But I think I can speak for the group when I say we've had our fill of your theories now, thank you Master Mustard.'

'Methinks the man doth protest too much,' said Imogen eyeing Nicholas with disdain.

Devlin also got to his feet. 'Let's call it a day, folks. I, for one, am going to have a pint.' He squeezed round the table. As he lurched through the arch he called over his shoulder. 'If anyone wants to chat informally, you're welcome to join me.'

'Ooh,' said Margot, clutching the pendant at her neck. 'I think I could do with something stronger after that.' She sent Nicholas a rueful glance.

Laura sighed. 'The rest of you can have some free time to write. I'm heading back to the Hall.'

The atmosphere in the snug wasn't exactly conducive to delicate questioning, so in the end I joined Laura and Imogen on their return walk to the Hall.

As we left the pub we saw Jocelyn ahead of us, pulling Nicholas up the road.

'Sorry,' she yelled from the other side. 'He's drunk. I'm going to take him to the tea rooms to sober him up.'

We watched Nicholas stumble across the pavement and round the corner out of view.

'That woman is a saint,' said Laura.

I nodded. 'No doubt about it, Nicholas is a wild card.'

Laura grunted.

'The thing is,' said Imogen, who was in between us. 'I think he's right about Cullen. There is something, er, unusual about his character. The way he stares at you. And he seems to pop up in the shadows, lurking, just when I think I'm on my own.'

I thought back to earlier. Why had he been talking to those men at the bar? Was it really for directions?

Though hadn't one of them said, when we walked into The Griffin. 'You back again?' Yet, everyone on the course had promised they'd never been here before. Apart from Laura.

I looked at her fiddling with her satchel, closing the lock on the front. She was personable, fairly erudite, sharp, seemingly successful. Was it possible she was behind all the trouble at Ratchette Hall? Certainly, she'd been the catalyst with her choice of story and venue, that much was true. But the killer?

And although there was something off about Cullen I couldn't really see, right now, why someone like him might have anything to do with the mild-mannered caretaker of the Essex Writers Retreat.

'But why would Cullen be involved with Graham?' I said out loud, as we walked.

Imogen raised her bulb-head to me. 'I wouldn't put it past that boy to do something like that as an experiment. To see if he could scare someone to death, then write about it. He's very hungry for a traditional publishing deal. Desperate for validation.'

'Really?' I said. Seemed a bit far-fetched.

'Well,' Imogen continued, 'I was thinking about it yesterday afternoon. He was the one who found him, which means he could easily have placed the finger in Graham's hand. To make it look like the story and throw off any suspicion. It's an interesting proposition.'

I nodded. 'He did find Graham, you're right.' I mused silently – would someone really murder another human being for a book deal? Especially when, if you were found out, the stakes were so high – you'd probably go away for a long, long time. No. That was too deranged. But then again – Cullen. 'It's something to think about,' I concluded.

Laura slung her bag over her shoulder. 'I'm not sure. Think about the one stirring up everything, pointing the finger at others. Nicholas certainly likes a bit of drama.'

'Huh,' said Imogen and raised her big face to where he had disappeared with Jocelyn. 'That boy is an arsehole.'

I don't know why, but it amused me heartily to hear that pop out of Imogen's mouth.

I started to snigger, but before I knew it, my mouth had opened and turned into a laugh which then became rather an enormous guffaw that shook my chest and made me gasp for breath. The other two had to stop walking as I leant my back against the tall garden wall of a row of cottages. Imogen had begun to giggle too. As she did her face became brighter, and for a moment I saw her eyes flicker with uncharacteristic mischief.

The laughter, being one of the more pleasant infections of the human condition, sprang from Imogen to Laura and soon the three of us were standing there huffing and puffing until someone banged on the cottage window and made a hand and finger gesture that symbolised he wasn't keen on us loitering in front of his home.

I finally managed to get myself under control and we were able to calm down a bit and recommence our walk.

'Oh ho,' said Laura in a wheezy, sing-songy way. 'He's not that bad, Imogen, though I appreciate your candour. He's just young.'

'And scared,' I added.

Laura looked at me with eyebrows raised. 'You have amazing depths of insight for ...' then she stopped herself.

My humour immediately evaporated. 'For what? An Essex Girl?'

She dropped her eyes and said, 'Of course not. I was going to say, "for a Benefit Fraud inspector" but I realised how many assumptions I was making.'

I grunted and began walking faster in semi-abandoned fury.

They both increased their speed.

'You are bright,' said Imogen. 'Laura's right. Did you go to University?'

God why did everyone equate intelligence with academia. 'Actually I did,' I told them with triumph. 'But I dropped out.'

'Why was that?' asked Laura.

'Because it wasn't what I expected. There wasn't much teaching. It didn't really satisfy me. I thought it would be better than that.'

'What did you read?' asked Imogen.

'English and Psychology,' I said.

'Ah,' said Imogen as if she was solving a conundrum. 'Thus the vocab.'

'No,' I said. 'It is possible to be working class and articulate you know—'

Laura cut me off. 'I did my MA in English.' She seemed keen to avoid any further outburst. 'Actually, I was thinking about it earlier. Our "arsehole", Nicholas, reminds me of someone I studied with. An old boyfriend. He was young, handsome and passionate too,' she said wistfully. 'Though he was nowhere near as vicious as Nick. Only with himself. So sad,' she said and looked away.

Imogen grunted. We were approaching the top of the hill. 'Where was that Laura? Would you recommend it?'

'Leeds,' she said. 'But it was back in the nineties, so I doubt any of the tutors would still be there. Anyway, if I were you, Imogen, I'd think about doing a Creative Writing MA. But be careful about which one you choose. They all look at different aspects.'

And they went off on that tangent till we turned into the drive. As we neared the house my car drove past me, sounding the horn as it went by. Sam was in the driving seat. Bloody cheek!

When he got out he took a box of equipment and put it on the roof. 'Just popped home for supplies,' he said and ducked down to fetch a smaller crate.

'In my car!' I was outraged.

'Indeed. How else was I meant to get there? Walk?'

'But you're not insured.'

'Oh yes,' he said. 'Didn't I tell you? I am. Monty sorted it out. You can drive mine too if you like. He thought flexibility would help.'

'Nice of you both to tell me,' I said and made further disparaging remarks about Sam's car, rust and the Flintstones.

'Hello,' said Laura when she and Imogen had caught up with us. 'What's all that then?'

'Some surveillance equipment,' I explained.

Sam grinned. 'We'll see if we can film some of your night-time pests.'

As it turned out however, Sophia was not immediately thrilled by the prospect of installing cameras on the Grade II listed property. In fact she told us to leave it with her and she'd make a few phone calls.

Sam, however, sent me a wink and followed her into the study. I took my cue and joined them, closing the door after me.

'To be fair,' he said to the events manager, 'if you'd like us to get to the bottom of things I would suggest that Rosie and I spend tomorrow here and monitor the equipment in the evening.'

Sophia looked surprised by this suggestion.

'We can play it by ear,' I added. 'But this sort of method-ology has had a tendency to shed light on things.'

Sophia took this on board. 'Well, let me see what I can do. Why don't you come back in the morning, as I suggested. I'll let Carole know that you'll be joining us.'

Sam surrendered. 'Okay.'

We would miss out on anything that happened this evening, which I thought was rather short-sighted of Sophia. But she didn't look like she was going to budge so we said our goodbyes and made for the museum.

It was a good time for us to take stock.

CHAPTER THIRTEEN

Back at the ranch we decided to look over some of the equipment. Sam's feeling was that we should throw everything at tomorrow's proposed stake-out, should we be allowed to go ahead with it.

Bronson came in halfway through and asked us how things were going, which Sam summed up neatly and cleanly, then apprised us of what he had learnt about the Devil and the Bell legend. Which wasn't much really and went along the same lines as all previous mentions of Himself Downstairs: during a storm, with the church unguarded, the Devil materialised as a great black form and decided to steal the largest church bell. He was on his way down the hill, making for his underworld kingdom, when his horns were spotted by the priest who shouted out 'Stop, in the name of God!' The Devil, in fear, then dived into the ground, leaving the bell. His speedy departure created a crater which could still be found today.

Bronson had been nodding all the way through this and added rather ominously, 'Yes, that's right. And they say that when he wants to return you can sometimes hear his bell ring.'

I tapped Sam on the arm. 'Could that be what Chris Devlin heard last night?'

He smiled. 'You mean, what someone wanted Chris Devlin to think he heard last night.'

'Yes, that's right,' I added, glad his stretching credulity didn't lend itself to belief that the Devil rang bells. Then a thought struck me. 'Do you remember when you were talking about Cernunnos and Baal, the other day?'

Sam paused and nodded.

'There's a lot of devil mythology raising its little horned head in this village. And, remember how Carole mentioned that there was a pagan temple somewhere. You don't think Bell Hill is Baal Hill, do you? Baal was a pagan god wasn't he? Consort to Jezebel ...'

Sam nodded. 'He was a pagan god, yes, but consort to Asherah, the goddess of fertility and the sea. Baal was also the god of fertility, and of wind, rain, lightning, seasons.'

'Well maybe his crater is the entrance to his underground temple.'

He stroked his chin. 'That's an interesting theory, Rosie. I'd like to explore it, I think. But after we've sorted out Ratchette Hall. I'm not sure that any of them had heard about Baal before I mentioned him. They didn't appear to.'

I cast my mind over that episode. 'Robin did,' I said.

'Mm, yes. I forgot about that. He did, you're right.'

'Is it a stretch to imagine he's got a hand in the "haunting of Ratchette Hall"?'

Sam sat back and thought about it. 'Open minds,' he said,

'should not be shut to possibilities, however unlikely they may appear.'

So I took it further. 'The vicar called me a Jezebel. He would have known the story about her – it's biblical isn't it?'

But Sam laughed. 'Murdering vicars indeed!'

It kind of irked me. 'But Sam, he has access to the tombs, the knights. We've only got his word for it he was the last one to lock up.'

But then Bronson put down his bucket with an announcing clang. 'Right,' he said. 'I'm off to the Stars for a pint. You want to join me?'

Well, actually that did sound great, I thought, but Sam jumped in. 'Thank you, Bronson, but we might have a late one tomorrow night so should be fresh for it, right Rosie?'

'Yeah,' I agreed with reluctance.

But then Bronson sent me a sympathetic nod which made me feel suddenly rebellious. 'Oh come on Sam,' I said. 'I don't fancy cooking. Let's have dinner there.'

To which he surprisingly agreed.

We settled in to a table by the inglenook fireplace complete with its well-polished horse brasses and blazing fire. The Seven Stars was a nice old inn that looked well average on the outside but inside was old and traditional, with low wattle ceilings and beams across them.

There weren't that many people in the pub now that the detectorists had moved on and the treasure seekers had pretty much given up all hope of finding the Howlet Hoard, which to be fair, had not been sighted for centuries. Apart from a little urn of coins that were found back in the summer. But that was a whole other story.

Bronson went off to 'say hello' to Bob Acton. The old farmer was standing at the bar talking to Nicky from the village shop, who was wearing a biker jacket with lots of studs, and his pitchfork, Woody. That was Bob's pitchfork, not Nicky's you understand. Nicky was far too style-conscious to consider such an accessory, unless it turned up in *Country Life*'s 'This season's must-haves'. Which, come to think of it, was also not beyond the realms of possibility.

I gave up calculating the odds on that and perused the menu, plumping for sausage and mash – I'd had salad earlier so it cancelled out the calories – which I ordered, along with Sam's preferred dish, from Lisa, the new landlady. The previous landlord had beaten a rather hasty retreat after the last Wicker Man-ish episode in the car park, with some developers and a rather large boulder. The latter of which I was hoping might be relocated to our museum Garden of Remembrance once the Museum of London had finished with it.

Having sorted dinner, I returned to our table where Sam was poring over his notepad.

Wanting a bit of attention, I coughed. Then when that didn't work I came straight out with, 'So then Sam – what's going on do you reckon? Could it be the unquiet dead who've got those writers' knick-knacks in a twist. Or is it this Cernunnos/Baal bloke that's making Devlin hard?'

Sam looked up, cringed, then laughed and dropped his pen onto the table. A good sign – his attention was mine for a minute or two.

'Yes indeed,' he said, crinkling those eyes of his. 'That *was* a rather startling comment, I have to admit. I think the poor man was trying not to sound emasculated whilst at the same time admitting to being unnerved.'

'Poor man?' I scoffed. 'The guy is loaded. And personally, I think he was showing off his virility,' I said and then winced. 'To some men of a certain age that kind of thing matters.'

Sam pushed his hair back. 'And some women.'

I frowned. 'Like who?'

'I was thinking about Margot.'

'Oh yeah,' I said. 'You been doing a lot of that?'

'Rosie!' he said and sighed. Then his lips pulled into a smile. 'There are various older women I think about, but Margot isn't one of them.'

I didn't know what to make of that and didn't want to go there, so funnelled back to Devlin in order to head off further discussion on that particularly thorny subject. 'So do you think what Chris was saying was genuine? Or was he putting it all on? Sometimes it's difficult to tell with that accent. It makes him sound phoney.'

Sam let himself be led back down the conversational path to the events of this morning, though I had a sense he knew exactly what I was doing. 'He had the signs of being thoroughly shaken. But I was of the opinion, at the time, that his conviction was real.'

'He believed that he'd seen something that was, er, unnatural?'

'Or supernatural, to his mind.' Sam wrinkled his nose (adorably). 'The strange, unearthly "commotioning".'

I smirked, but Sam flexed his brows. 'He's no different in that to most of us. Our minds are open to it.'

I wasn't sure about that one. People weren't born open-minded – parental attitudes transferred over pretty early on. Some however developed the state, and others, like me, had open-mindedness thrust upon them. Because if you didn't have an open mind re some of the stuff that went on around the Witch Museum you'd either have to go and live in a sanitised bubble, like that kid in America, or board the express train to Nutsville. And that place rarely ran returns.

'Witches on broomsticks, old gods, restless spirits,' he went on. 'They fulfil a role – to give humankind hope that it's not living in a vacuum,' he said, voice deepening. 'Hope that there are things out there we don't understand, that are beyond our current understanding. Greater beings, gods, they suggest to us creatures caught in chaos, that there is order somewhere within.' He waved his hand about the pub, which although I have to admit had at points resembled something of an Alcoholics Hieronymus painting, actually looked fairly subdued tonight.

I loved listening to him when he was on one like this. Funnily enough it had bored me at the beginning. Now I could see these were moments when the spirit within him stirred. It animated his face and body. It made him happy. I liked it when he was happy.

'What about you?' I ventured, curious and keen to keep him in this mode, so I could look at him easily. 'Do you believe it? Or want to?'

He scrunched his forehead and cocked his head to one side and gave me a funny look.

'Well?' I said and realised I was leaning on my elbow, cupping my chin in my hand, gazing at him like a love-sick teenager. Pathetic. I immediately shifted focus to the table top, picked up my cider and necked a quarter of the glass.

Sam watched me, mirrored my move and took a sip of his own drink, then sat back into his chair. 'I think I'm with Carole on this one. Someone is trying to wind them up.'

'Okay,' I said with a grin. Internally I was relieved, what with all his metaphysical wobbliness of late. 'No friars in the ferns then, or banshees in the birch trees, as entertaining as that sounds?'

'Hmmm.' He tapped his chin. 'The exploitation of super-stitions and folkloric belief in order to manipulate people psychologically has been going on for centuries. We know that superstitions and superstitious belief flourish in an atmosphere of insecurity and tension.'

'That sounds exactly like what's been created at Ratchette Hall,' I said, trying to pick up the thread and stop looking at the outline of his well-worked shoulders. 'Insecurity and tension.'

'Indeed. And that situation, in which emotions are already running high, can generate behaviour which runs contrary to rational thought.'

'Uh huh,' I said. I hadn't really been going for this when I asked the question. But now I realised it presented too good an opportunity to miss re the ghost on tape. I still wasn't sure if he had been genuine or if, in some way, he was trying to test me. The notion that Sam, man of open mind and healthy scepticism, was buying into the idea that we had discovered empirical evidence of a supernatural phenomenon, ran contrary to my experience of him thus far. But then Monty had chucked the 'Sam family history' bomb into the whole equation, which spannered everything anyway.

'I mean, think about our good friend Cecil Williamson from the Museum of Witchcraft and Magic, God rest his soul,' he was instructing as I came round from my thought cycle, resolved to get a question in. 'Cecil Williamson?' he repeated when I failed to respond.

I scrunched my eyebrows together and summoned up a mental image of a man in tweed, round glasses and a slight Scottish accent, into folklore and magic in a very 'Sam' style. Possibly, possibly, possibly even more knowledgeable, if you could imagine that. 'I thought his name was Benedict,' I said eventually when I'd retrieved the full picture from my mental filing cabinet. 'The curator of the Museum in Boscastle?'

Sam squinted through his own thoughts and then shook his head. 'No, he's the current curator. Remember the founder? Cecil Williamson? Old guy. Well, he was old when he died.'

Ah yes, I recalled the audio of Mr Williamson that I had listened to on a CD. He had been describing how he'd located the bones of the 'witch' Ursula Cadence. 'That's right. I remember him now. Posher, than Benedict, very magical.'

Sam smiled at me. His eyes twinkled. I swallowed and felt something, not wind, move in my stomach, which emboldened me to take another glug of cider and leave my hand closer to his when I put the glass down.

Unfortunately my niggly, pithy inner voice took that opportunity to whisper into my head. 'Don't be ridiculous. That boy deserves better, remember? Someone less, less ...' I could hear it struggling for the word and simultaneously I saw an image of the museum, tattered and bruised, after a particularly nasty storm we had once suffered. 'Someone not so weather-beaten,' my inner voice concluded.

'That's right,' said Sam, like he'd listened in on this process. 'Cecil.'

'So what about him?' I replied, having turned myself grumpy.

Sam evidently had no clue of any inner turmoil in the woman sitting opposite him and went on with his story regardless. 'Do you recall when we were returning from Boscastle? I told you about the "Witches' Ritual" that occurred in the Second World War in Ashdown Forest? The "Cone of Power".'

'Here we go,' I thought. 'More lectures.' But I rummaged through my mental drawers again, to please him. Eventually I recalled the conversation in which this reference had occurred. Originally it was framed within another larger chat about my family's connection to the MI5 and MI6 occult bureaux. It had blown my mind at the time. Now it just made me go, 'Oh yeah.'

'That's right,' Sam said, again with uncanny (possibly telepathic) accuracy. 'Operation Mistletoe. Witches or possibly Canadian Airmen, met in Ashdown Forest and conducted a ritual to repel Hitler's advances across the channel. So when word got back to Hitler, who was very superstitious, it worried him thoroughly.'

'Oh right,' I said. 'Thus, manipulation.' Might as well try and follow what he was talking about, I supposed.

Sam's eyes were whirring again. 'In fact some of this business at Ratchette Hall reminds me of an episode that happened in Italy in the 1920s.'

He was waiting for me to urge him on.

'Do tell.'

'Well,' he said and gave a chest wiggle. 'According to Captain Jasper Maskelyne, who had been a stage magician prior to the war, a group of soldiers were acting as an advance patrol and created a device which was more or less a gigantic scarecrow. It was twelve feet high and able to stagger forward under its own power. They rigged it so that as it moved, it emitted flashes. Great electric-blue sparks jumped from it and as it reeled down the streets it made several loud bangs. The inhabitants of the villages literally took to their heels, swearing that the Devil was marching ahead of the invading English.' He went on. 'The knock-on effect was that, as they fled, the villagers completely congested the roads and snared the retreating German troops. So the army was able to go in and take them.'

'Ha,' I said, trying to sound engaged. 'I suppose you could say the Devil himself, as a concept, is a fantastic way of manipulating people.'

'One of the originals,' he added. 'Sin and you'll spend an eternity roasting in the flames of hell. If you don't fancy that then you have to follow the rules.'

I nodded. 'Which brings us again to the Damebury shenanigans.'

'Yes, through rather a circuitous route. Of course, the residents in question aren't peasants. This time they are educated. But they are also story-makers. Architects of the imagination.'

'Oh.' I suddenly got his point. 'And someone or something is trying to exploit their superstitions and imaginations?'

'To the death, in one case,' he agreed.

A log in the fire spluttered.

'Any idea who?' I asked.

'Not really. I think it will be good to spend a day there tomorrow, then execute a surveillance operation in the evening.'

'From where?'

'Oh.' He grinned. 'I thought we could cuddle up in the study. It's quite cosy in there.'

I darted a glance at him. He looked absurdly genuine. Or was he taking the mickey? While I watched him he dropped his hand on the table next to mine. His little finger crept out and rubbed against my thumb.

Had he gone mad?

I nodded, feeling the need to breathe in deeply but not wanting to show that he had effected such a physical change in me. Did he realise what he was doing or was it an absent-minded gesture? 'You're rubbing your finger on mine,' I said eventually, always one for subtlety.

'I know,' he said.

A ball of orangey pleasure seemed to diffuse my body from the abdomen up. And yet I couldn't take the intensity of the moment so looked at the floor and swallowed noisily.

But I left my hand exactly where it was.

'Rosie,' he said, in his gentle voice. 'I know you've been through a lot and I feel like I've given you the space you've needed,' he said as I felt the heat rise to my cheeks.

Oh my god.

'But sometimes,' he tendered, 'I do wonder if you're pulling away from me?'

'Pulling away?' I said and looked up, despite the redness in my cheeks.

Someone burped by our table, which prompted us both to withdraw our hands with speed.

Bronson sat down heavily in the free chair. 'I'll be pulling away soon, if you don't get another one in. Sam, it's your round, ain't it?'

'Oh yes.' Sam got to his feet with a little reluctance. 'Rosie, another?'

'Yes please,' I said with such enthusiasm I hope he realised I was really talking about something else.

Then he was off, leaving me to gurn at Bronson.

'Your timing sucks a big one sometimes, B,' I said and glowered.

'Oh, not going well in Damebury is it?' He took off his sou'wester and hung it on the chair. 'It's a funny old place Damebury. Full of secrets and mysteries. Very old, you know. They used to say there were tunnels from the church to that pub. Whatchermacallit – The Lion?'

That pricked up my ears. 'The Griffin?'

'Yes, that's it,' he said and smoothed his moustache. 'Smugglers were it? Or priest holes or somesuch. I can't remember what.'

I was still irritated so said, 'Try,' with a lot of emphasis on the 't'.

Bronson stroked his moustache again, shifted his buttocks on the seat and said, 'Ah yes, let me see, that's right.' Then he shook his head and said, 'Yes, I don't know anything.'

I gritted both sets of teeth and buttocks. If anyone had squeezed me right then, I think my head would have blown off. 'Tunnels,' I said eventually. 'You said there might have been tunnels between the church and The Griffin.'

'Oh yes, that's right,' he said.

'Go on.'

'You're right: I did say that.'

I was thinking now that he was teasing me on purpose. 'Oh come on, Bronson, you always do this and inevitably you always end up knowing more than you let on. Tunnels in Damebury. Enter it into your mental database and let it knock around for a bit.'

He tried looking slightly perplexed but I had a feeling he was putting it on. I crossed my arms and continued with the glowering theme.

'You wouldn't have said it if you didn't know more. Tunnels between the church and the pub.'

'Tunnels?' said Sam, appearing behind him with three pint glasses. Bronson took his, then Sam came and handed mine over. Our fingers touched as I took the glass, and suddenly I felt bashful again.

'Unfortunately,' Sam parked himself in the opposite chair, 'you'll find rumours of tunnels in every old village. Many of them might well have been true, once upon a time. Sadly they're so old it's likely most of them have fallen in. Could even be untraceable. There's legends about them here too. Remember Rosie? When we first discussed the Howlet Hoard. There were stories of tunnels leading from this pub to the Manor House?'

'Oh yes,' I said, keen to re-engage. 'When they were digging, did they ever find anything?'

Sam opened his mouth, then closed it. Bronson blinked hard and looked at the floor.

'I don't know how to answer that,' Sam said eventually.

I was going to ask why, but before the question popped out of my mouth I understood the reason for his caution. There had been excavations of course: they had uncovered two skeletons from the seventeenth century. And then when they transferred their efforts to the manor gardens, they recovered the headless remains of my grandmother.

It had been a discovery that opened a Pandora's box for me. And the surviving Strange family.

Despite myself I found my thoughts wandering once more to my lost mother, Celeste. This woman who had birthed me then been caught up in something that had killed her.

What had she been like really? I thought at length. And who was with her in the car?

Then I remembered the notebook I had discovered underneath the trinket box.

I must make an effort to read it, I thought, as the waiter brought the dishes to our table.

But as I picked up my knife and fork I was visited by the sudden understanding of my own limitations. It was unlikely I'd go anywhere near it soon.

It would be too intimate. Intrusive. Potentially stomach-churning or frightening.

And now I had no appetite.

I sighed out loud and looked around the table. Oh dear, Sam's words had had an impact on both himself and Bronson.

For none of us were tucking in with gusto.

My long-lost mother's memory was quieting them too.

And although the table was laid for three, it felt like there were four of us there.

CHAPTER FOURTEEN

'Well, I'm sure you'll be delighted to hear that we had no disruptions last night whatsoever,' Sophia announced proudly when we arrived at the Hall. 'So we had no need of the cameras after all.'

She was leading me into the breakfast room. 'Your colleague is just running through the footage from the free-standing camera,' she informed me.

We'd arrived in separate cars today, mainly because I needed to put a conditioning treatment on my hair and Sam didn't want to hang around.

'I allowed your colleague to erect his tripod in the Orangery window,' Sophia said as she bustled me across the polished marble floor. 'Somehow I doubt he'll find anything there. He's in the study, so if you could call him for breakfast we'll see you round the table in two minutes please.'

I was quite surprised to hear that nothing had happened overnight. I had had a hunch that the activity might escalate. But no, it appeared this was not the case. I was wrong. It didn't bode well for any of my other intuitions.

I knocked on the door and went straight in. Sam was bent

over the desk looking at some black-and-white footage. He had headphones on, so I tapped him on the shoulder.

He jumped, then smiled and pushed the headphones back over his hair so that half of it was flat and the other half sticking up. 'Ah, there you are.'

'Sophia wants me to bring you into breakfast,' I informed him.

He nodded. 'Yes okay. But there's something on here I want to show you.'

'She said there were no shenanigans last night.'

'Not that anyone noticed,' he said. 'But the camera picks up things that the human eye can miss.'

'Show me after,' I said. 'I don't want to keep her waiting. We need her to cooperate so the others continue to too.'

He took my point and left the headphones on the laptop.

I thought we'd be the last seated round the breakfast table, but there were still two spaces left. Tabby had gone to get her glasses and Cullen had not yet surfaced. Nicholas began moaning about having to wait so Robin suggested we started anyway, which we did, and the subject of last night's lack of incidence was entered into playfully.

Everyone seemed genuinely relieved, although I kept my eyes peeled. But jokes popped lightly back and forth across the table, which was bigger than the one we had back at the Witch Museum and covered with a gleaming white linen tablecloth. Unlike the Witch Museum, all the crockery and cutlery matched. There were several servers full of eggs, bacon, sausages, tomatoes, mushrooms and beans which were kept warm on cordless silver hot trays.

The kitchen diner was large and spacious, but still cosy. To one end was the kitchen and at the other French windows, which opened onto a small patio and the gardens. It had skylights which kept it bright and cheerful and a radio in the background which was playing popular classical music.

I had a couple of slices of toast and marmalade and coffee, which was remarkable given that I felt like I'd been consuming a good 3,000 calories a day lately – it being autumn and all that. One needed a good coat of fat to keep your bones warm and I had been no stranger to the lamb stew, lasagne, wine and the odd cream cake. I wasn't going to waste away if I refused the Cumberland sausies.

Tabby joined us and heaped a large plate full of bacon and tomatoes, and as she did, expressed concern that Cullen was missing out on the hot food.

Unusually satisfied and to avoid succumbing to eating more just because it was there, I volunteered to go and rouse him.

Nicholas made a crude comment about that.

This time Imogen told him to shut up. Jocelyn thanked her. Nicholas shrugged and scooped out everything that was left in the bacon server. Starla began instructing him on karma. Devlin said he'd written a book about the subject. Laura said she'd liked that one very much. Sam said it sounded inter-esting and asked Devlin what the title was. Sophia gave me instructions on which room Cullen was staying in and how to get to the second floor. Robin thanked me for going and said his knees were playing up.

I was actually quite happy to get out for a bit on my own. I quite fancied having a poke around in the rest of the house.

The carpet was seagrass throughout the top two floors, which was a good choice: hard-wearing but aesthetically pleasing. If I ever got the money to refurb the living quarters of the museum properly, I would definitely go for something similar. The walls had a fresh chalky white slapped across them and lots of pictures along various literature-related themes: a profile of Virginia Woolf, a painting of a female hand holding a pen, which on closer inspection was made up of the repetition of the words 'Dare to be free'. There were of course several photographs of writers caught in the act of creation, captioned so there'd be no mistaking their identity and place in the canon: Hemingway on his typewriter in the open air in front of a ridge of low-lying mountains, Sylvia Plath sprawled across a sun-lounger looking intense and pissed off, Susan Sontag grinning over a manuscript, fag in hand, George Orwell, also smoking, his cigarette about to ash all over his typewriter, Hunter S. Thompson glaring at the camera in front of a spear and an enormous hi-fi speaker. Next to him was a picture of Ian Fleming looking exceedingly louche and debonair and pointing off-screen. Cleverly, his finger directed the viewer to a communal bathroom, separate shower and loo which ran off the landing. Although it also seemed that most of the rooms had small en suites with showers and toilets. Well, most of them that had been left open for Madam Noseypants here. Or rather, Mademoiselle Investigator I thought, and heard at the same time my inner voice take on pronounced Clouseau overtones. In fact, as I peeked around ze various rooms, I did feel like I vaz missing a magnifying glass.

There wasn't too much to report though. Generally the bedrooms were furnished simply, and were clean. The decoration was modern and minimal – there were a couple of photos of the knights in situ at the church, some ceramic vases, clocks – the furniture old and distinct. It was a good combination.

There just remained an airing cupboard full of towels and sheets, and a tall closet with ironing boards, irons, light bulbs and linen. Beside those was a kind of nook, which had a desk, with a lamp and a window with a view into the gardens. Nice work if you could get it or afford to pay for it. What happened to those that couldn't, I wondered. Probably too busy working for a living to sit down and put pen to paper. Or finger to keyboard. And probably unable to fork out £700 to get expert feedback from published writers. Wasn't fair really was it? Perhaps I should open up a desk at the Witch Museum for writers to come and use? No fee, maybe just a couple of hours on the till as payment in kind. Yes, that'd be an idea, I'd have to think on it more, I thought, as I bounced up the next staircase to the second floor.

This landing was smaller with fewer rooms coming off it. I could see there was one opposite, a large double, that had its door open and looked like it hadn't been used. Lovely views in there, and quite a nice bathroom too. But I really shouldn't linger, I had spent too long snooping and now should go and wake up the psycho.

Room 12 was on my right. Its door was closed so I knocked on it.

I thought about having a peek into Room 11, the door of which was ajar a couple of inches, but then worried my absence might seem over-long so knocked on Cullen's door with renewed vigour. 'Cullen? You awake?'

Still no answer.

I waited for what I deemed a reasonable amount of time, then shouted, 'Breakfast's up! You'll miss all the bacon. Nicholas is being a fat pig and eating it all.'

When I was sure nothing was stirring in the room, I tried the door knob. Maybe he'd gone out for an early morning walk or run? He looked the type. If I ascertained that he wasn't here then I could go back to the table having fulfilled my duty.

I pushed the door open.

The silence inside the room was different.

Eerie.

Stagnant.

I took a deep breath as I noted the bed. The lump in it. The face at the top. The lack of movement there.

There was an awful pallor to the skin which reminded me of spilt candlewax.

Then, for one brief shocking moment, my heart also stopped.

The funny thing was, when I thought about it afterwards, there was absolutely no way I could have known in advance. And yet as soon as I saw Cullen lying there prone, his face rigid, his arms crossed across his chest, his eyes closed, I had this swift understanding, like a visitation, a kind of great plopping sensation that seemed to drop over my mind, which left me with the utterly indisputable knowledge that in the form on the bed, all life had been extinguished.

Completely obliterated.

The spirit that had once animated this fresh corpse had departed.

I was struck by the sheer *emptiness* of everything: the room, its sound, the human within.

It was so strange. But so natural. But so unnatural.

I can't explain. I should just tell you what happened next. Yet I can't say in great detail because the recall isn't entirely there.

I can remember the first moments, that I've described above, but the next minutes are not so easy to grab on to.

I think I felt the neck. But like I said, I already knew he was dead. I just had to go through the motions like I'd seen people do on telly. You have no other framework to reference this kind of thing, do you? Unless you're a paramedic or you've been in a situation like this before.

I hadn't.

So I felt for a pulse.

Beneath the tips of my fingers Cullen's throat was cool. That was so weird. When you touch another human being you notice the softness of their skin, perhaps the contours, the colour. Unless asked to comment on it, you never notice the temperature. Not normally. But to feel cold skin, lifeless skin – it's a shocker.

What was even more awful than the temperature and absence of pulse, was what I saw when I took my fingers away: two red dots with some bruising around them, right on the side of his neck.

The sight made me step away immediately.

And look around the room.

Maybe it wasn't as empty as I had first thought.

Could those possibly be the punctures of a snake bite?

Jesus.

That thought was all that was required to send me spinning on my heels, toppling towards the door, half stumbling, half falling down the stairs till I got into the breakfast room.

As soon as I entered, I closed the door and put my arm across it.

'Don't go out there anyone,' I commanded. 'Sam, call the police. Quick! Now!'

CHAPTER FIFTEEN

'Well, this is quite a mess you've left me. I suppose you'll be expecting me to clean it up and then polish it for you as usual?'

Scrub was in her regular high spirits.

Sam was kind of jumpy.

I was frazzled and very tired.

Everything had happened very quickly after I'd made my announcement in the breakfast room.

I pulled out Sophia and Sam and told them about Cullen. I also informed them of what I'd seen on the side of his neck.

Sam called 999.

Sophia went into some kind of weird trance state, so we stuffed her in the study and told her not let anyone out of the breakfast room. Then on Sam's instigation we went upstairs to see if I'd closed the bedroom door or not.

I knew exactly what he was thinking – if it was a snake that had left those fang marks then it could still be here. Or worse – somewhere else in the Hall.

But what if it wasn't a snake? The puncture wounds looked rather wide apart, after all. Well spread.

An unbidden image of the bat in the cemetery flapped across my mind prompting an astonishing left-field response: what if the fangs had not injected venom into Cullen's pale neck, but sucked something out? Something red and liquid?

'Oh god,' I muttered quietly as my mind started hurtling to conclusions so speedily that Ms Ennis-Hill would be proud. What if, just what if, it thought, leaping from one conclusion to another with irrepressible energy, what if there was a VAMPIRE on the loose? What if, what if, it thought, vaulting from the puncture wounds on Cullen's neck to the howling in Witch Wood with ease, what if it wasn't a wolf or a witch or a hunter out there aprowling? What if it wasn't trick-or-treaters who were frightening people about the Hall? What if it wasn't a low-bellied reptile that had slithered into the bedroom to feast upon writerly blood?

I'd seen *Nosferatu* – I knew the buggers could be ugly. Maybe the sight of such a monster shocked Graham's heart into arrhythmia, terror squeezing it so hard it shuddered out its last beat?

No, no, no! I was letting my errant imagination run away with itself and a whole raft of wrong-footed conclusions. It was a snake of course. An everyday unextraordinary escaped serpent from the local zoo.

Gulp.

Just a run-of-the-mill, slithering, common Royal Python.

Oh my god oh my god oh my god oh my god there was an escaped snake on the loose, I screamed silently, as I followed Sam.

So WHY THEN WAS I GOING BACK UPSTAIRS?

Putting myself in the line of BITING?

Had I completely lost it?

No, I hadn't, I told myself, regulating my breathing and oxygenating my blood.

I was doing it because, despite all my flaws, and I know I've got some, notwithstanding excellent taste in hair and cowboy boots, I was actually an honourable person and wanted to show off a bit, but mainly safeguard the writers downstairs.

Except for Nicholas. I'd be quite happy if he got done in by the opportunist adder or whatever species it was. Python maybe – no flies on me.

Though, actually thinking about it, snakes were probably repelled by blue blood.

Anyway, point is, despite my own nutball mentalism, I was trying to be gallant. I was trying to be *nice*.

'Oh god,' I said (again), as we mounted the first set of stairs and a fresh thought occurred to me. 'I hope Cullen didn't see it coming. He's terrified of snakes. He said so in the Greatest Fears workshop yesterday. Down the pub.'

'Sh!' whispered Sam. 'Don't think about it now. Grab that walking stick,' he ordered, pointing at one leaning against the door outside of what I guessed must be Margot's room.

'Why?' I said, frowning hard.

'In case we need to hit it.'

Oh crikey – I'd never been much good at hockey and that had been with a hard, round thing that someone hit your way and warned you about. An elastic invertebrate with an open mouth, sharp fangs, and an ability to climb and hide was going to be a more dastardly foe than the Leytonstone Under 15s. I wasn't sure if I was ready for it yet, but I picked up the stick anyway and followed Sam up the stairs, our speed slowing, the sounds our footsteps made muffled by the seagrass, our breathing less heavy, conspicuously more controlled.

When we reached the top of the stairs we both sighed with relief. For the door was firmly closed. I must have shut it on the way out.

Thank god we didn't have to go in there, I thought. But then Sam put his hand on the door knob.

'What are you doing?' I whispered in alarm.

'Clues,' he said and began to turn.

'No,' I said and whipped his hand off it. 'We don't need clues. The Adder had him.'

'Python,' he said, but dropped his hand, thankfully. 'Can they cover that much distance?'

That, more or less, had also been the question that Scrub posed when she arrived.

Once her team had got there we were immediately ordered out whilst the area was secured.

By 'area' I mean Hall. So we were indefinitely contained in The Griffin whilst another police team and forensics combed the Hall for escaped reptiles or other beasts.

Carole, who was not happy about any of this if you can imagine that, had been forced to let Scrub commandeer the small office downstairs in the pub, which is where we were gathered now.

'I mean, it's a snake,' Scrub said again and shook her head. 'They haven't got legs, have they?'

'They are crepuscular – awake at dawn and dusk – but spend most of the day sleeping in their hides,' said Sam, holding up his phone. He had already checked it out on Wikipedia. 'So, if that's the case, it would have had to be extremely agile. Colchester Zoo is about eighteen miles away, as the crow flies and flying covers a lot more ground more quickly than any amount of slithering can. The news came over the airwaves yesterday morning. Which means if the snake is only active at dusk, it would have had to move at about nine miles per hour to get all the way here, avoiding main roads, where it could be sighted, traffic, horses, farm machinery, Ophidiophobes, etc.' Before Scrub and I could ask, he replied, 'People with a fear of snakes. Sometimes it's referred to as herpetophobia. But that's incorrect and means a fear of reptiles or amphibians.'

Scrub tutted and rolled her eyes. 'Yes, well that would just be sloppy of me to mix those two phobias up, wouldn't it? I do however, get your drift, Samuel.' She cupped her rounded chin. 'That python would have had to have bloody good map-reading skills too.'

'They don't, do they?' I said, still a little hung-over from last night's session at The Stars.

Sam and Scrub ignored me.

My colleague gestured to the panelled wall, beyond which, a good mile away, lay Ratchette Hall. 'So the python must have been brought here?'

'To kill Cullen?'

Scrub sniffed, 'If indeed his death was caused by a snake at all?'

'You think it might be something else?' I shuddered. 'A spider?'

'Or something in human form,' Scrub grunted.

'Oh bloody hell,' I spluttered, my worst fears realising. 'A vampire! I thought that too, but worried to say it in case I looked crazy.'

Scrub cocked her head and said, 'You all right, chuck?' then turned to Sam. 'In shock mibbe?'

He shrugged. 'She seemed okay this morning.'

'Delayed reaction?'

'Hang on,' I interrupted. 'You just said that Cullen's death might have been caused by something "in human form" …?'

'Yes,' she said. 'As in a human.'

Sam nodded and sat down. 'Another writer? Murder?'

'We'll have to see what Kitty, the medical examiner says. Graham Peacock was a cardiac arrest. Confirmed. But that doesn't necessarily mean that, if it was somehow induced, the "assailant" won't face charges. Homicide by heart attack is rare, but not unknown.'

She straightened her slacks and swung left a little bit on the office chair. 'I'll be very interested in what Kitty makes of Mr Sutcliffe. But while I'm waiting for her to have a look I want to know exactly what you know. And fast. Go out there and start typing me a timescale. You can talk to the others but don't tell them what you're doing. I want to know what happened from the moment you got here. And why exactly you were called in.'

'What are you going to do?' I asked stupidly.

'I'm getting one of my people to phone the zoo.'

'And then there were eight,' said Nicholas. Two tables had been pushed together to accommodate all the residents from Ratchette Hall. Sophia was up one end on her phone. Carole was behind the bar restocking and swearing about the fact her pub was being used as makeshift waiting room.

Sam looked at the table and counted them loudly. 'Yep,' he said. 'There's eight of you.'

'And that is relevant how?' I said, perhaps a little unsympathetically considering the circumstances.

'Be nice,' I told myself and remembered that they knew Cullen better than we had. They'd spent days and nights with him. Got to know him. In fact Laura, up the far end of the table looked very red-eyed. Tabby was on one side of her stroking her palm, Devlin on the other was restless and wired. Margot, Starla and Imogen all had a kind of stony gloss to their eyes. I wondered if it was shock.

Jocelyn hadn't looked up. Her eyes were resting on the coffee cup in front of her. They all had one and there was a cafetière in the middle of the table with milk and sugar and a spare cup. I went and grabbed it and poured some coffee in. Black and unsugared, like a slap round the face. It was just what I needed.

'There were ten of us staying at Ratchette Hall on Sunday,' Nicholas spoke steadily, which surprised me. 'Monday evening we ate and drank lots of whisky and wine. Graham died in the night and then there were nine. Nine little Ratchette writers staying up late, one got bitten and then there were eight.' His voice trembled but he kept going. 'It's an Agatha Christie story with a very unpleasant title. I'm sure you've heard it. Recently it was dramatised on the BBC as *Then There Were None*.'

'Yes,' I said. 'Cullen had the same thoughts. He mentioned that story on Tuesday.'

Nicholas's eyes widened. 'Did he? Well, let's hope we don't run foul of the rhyme: One little writer left all alone; he went and hanged himself and then there were none.'

Jocelyn slapped him hard on the arm, then apologised. 'Don't Nicky, please. We're upset enough as it is.'

'Well,' he said and pulled his arm away. 'It's true. Someone's going through us.'

Tabby turned her head from Laura and pursed her lips, 'Nicholas! Please, this isn't helping. We're all in states of distress. Poor Cullen. It's tragic. Don't make this about you.'

I thought that was well said and assumed the subject was going to be dropped but Devlin stood up. 'Then I came along and made it up to nine again. And Sophia came down too. So actually dear Nick, the numbers are going up. Rosie and Sam add to us too.'

Nicholas rolled his eyes.

'You were really horrible to him too, weren't you?' Jocelyn said ruefully. 'Here, yesterday.'

'And now he's dead,' said Imogen like a judge passing sentence.

A heavy silence dropped on the table like a stone, flattening all conversation.

Eventually Robin fluttered his eyelids and said, 'We should let the police do their work and not jump to conclusions.'

Murmurs of agreement rippled round the table.

'Okay then,' said Devlin. 'I don't want to appear crass ...'

As if he could ever appear crass, I thought.

'... but we're here and we're on a course. Let's do a writing exercise. It'll take our minds off it.'

The reaction was sluggish. No one had any enthusiasm, but they all started reaching for their bags and notebooks.

'You can join us,' he said to Sam and me.

But Sam's phone had started ringing. He walked away towards the front door to answer it in privacy.

'We've got some work to do,' I told Devlin thinking I would rather stick needles in my eyes. Then I remembered I was trying to be nice. 'But you go ahead.' I sent him one of my own toothy smiles. 'We'd love to hear what you've written later, though.' Which wasn't true but I thought they'd probably forget.

Amazingly this seemed to animate them.

I followed Sam to the door. He was calling over his shoulder, 'It's Monty. Ask Scrub if we have permission to leave for a bit?'

Luckily Scrub didn't care where we went as long as we presented ourselves back at the office 'soon', however long that was, to share our timescale and what we'd gleaned so far. So we went and established ourselves in a tea room down the road and sketched out the timeline. Monty phoned back after Sam texted him. The agent had the intelligence reports back on the Ratchette residents.

'Right,' he said. We had him on loud speaker. 'You're in a secure environment yes?'

I looked around the café. There were a couple of waitresses hovering round a gaggle of young mums with newborns and toddlers. They were all very preoccupied. On the next table an old man hunched over tea in a bone china cup and crumpets with what looked like honey on them. 'Yes,' I confirmed, then bent lower to the speaker and whispered, 'There's just a mum and toddler group ...'

'Mums and toddlers?' Monty blasted so that phone crackled.

'Correct,' said Sam, as a plastic bowl in the act of emptying its baked beans, sailed through the air and hit the wall next to the old guy. 'They've got their hands full. I don't think they'll be paying any attention to us.'

But Monty's grunt sounded unconvinced so I added, 'And just one old man here but he's got a hearing aid in.'

'A hearing aid?' asked Monty in a tone that meant it wasn't a question. 'You mean something to make him hear better? Where are you both?'

'Kitty's Tea Rooms,' said Sam quietly into the speaker. 'I don't think anyone will be able to hear the detail. Not all of it.'

Monty muttered something under his breath which may or may not have been a swear word. 'For goodness sake, you two. I am really going to have to give you some training.' He took a deep breath in. 'Phone me when you are in an environment where no one can overhear you. That's funda-mental to a *secure* position. And take something to make notes with. I am not repeating myself.'

We phoned back from a shady, and thus private, fairly secluded, plausibly ill-used track with no mums and toddlers or old men with hearing aids, which led into a wooded section of Damebury Common.

Chastened by Monty's reproachful tone we even went so far as to heap a couple of fallen branches and dead leaves over the roof. Sam assured me he would get the car cleaned and valeted, though he always said that and never did. I went with the camouflage effort anyway.

The whole thing reminded me of another time we had done something like this, outside a certain Hades Hall. Now *that* had been a crazy old night. Spectacularly so. Please god we weren't going to get involved with anything similar when we kept vigil at the writers retreat. If we were still going to do that, now that there was the whole kind of further unexpected death thing to consider.

Death again. I sighed. It seemed to be all around me lately. From the first moment, when I had discovered the museum had been left to me after my grandfather's death, right up to this moment with Cullen's. With some odd 'worse than death' scenarios peppered in for good measure which reminded me of the unholy ritual that we had disrupted in that chapel in Hades Hall. If I closed my eyes I could recall the temperature of the night air, the scent of cypress pines on the wind. My mind roved over the inverted cross erected behind those chapel's doors, the gleaming bowl at its foot, waiting to collect some unknown bodily fluid, cruelly rendered, from some fresh victim.

I shuddered.

Although I had a sense that there was darkness afoot, metaphorical darkness, I had no notion of organised nastiness, of the kind we had encountered in the proprietor of Hades Hall, Countess Elizabeth Barbary, and her circle of cronies and desperado alchemists. Though there was certainly, and now very evidently, danger in the air here, it was a subtle undertone that I detected around the Hall, possibly scented in the sweat of the disquieted residents, the raw discharge of chemicals from frightened armpits, dried adrenaline perhaps. Whatever way you explained it, I knew that I was picking up on fear. Yet it was a niggling feeling. Not the breathtaking, blade-like danger and hateful antagonism I picked up during the Barbary incident.

'I think that will do,' Sam said touching my arm as I piled another heap of dead leaves on the boot. I had forgotten what I was doing and covered it with a good three inches of mouldy brown leaf detritus.

'Sorry,' I muttered.

Sam managed a quick smile. 'It's your car. Let's be organised – do you want to take notes or shall I?'

I thought about that and said, 'I will,' and got into the passenger seat. Sam passed me his laptop. I settled it onto my knees and switched it on.

As Sam was dialling Monty's number I said, 'Do you think in a few years' time we might actually have a clue about what we're doing?'

He put the phone to his ear, looked straight ahead out the windscreen at the trees around us and said, 'No. I don't think so.'

Which was, at least, honest.

When Monty connected, Sam put the call on speaker. He reassured the agent that we were indeed in the middle of nowhere in what was now a specially camouflaged car.

I dutifully fired up Word.

Down the other end of the line Monty went into tutorial mode. 'I suggest you draw up some kind of document and take notes as I relay the information.'

'Already on it,' I said, inserting a table into the document. I was going to be efficient and thorough. Monty would make an agent of me yet. It was becoming a more attractive career possibility than benefit fraud. The hours were much more flexible and I didn't have to sit opposite Charlie and his stupid ties.

'Destroy after use, of course. Okay,' said Monty in a voice that demanded attention. 'I'm not wasting any time with an executive summary. We know where we are and what's happened. So here we go. Regarding Graham Peacock, he is astonishingly unremarkable. And I use that adjective because you wait to hear about the rest. Now, if we look for the usual motivating factors pertaining to Peacock's demise, I'm afraid there are scant pickings. Mr Peacock had been the adminis-trator and caretaker of Ratchette Hall for eleven years. Before that he was a teacher in Birmingham. Glowing reference when he left. Doesn't seem to have had a problem with anyone that we are aware of. Never married. One long-term affair with a fellow teacher who was Canadian and returned home to live with her ailing parents when the relationship ended. It was amicable. They remain in touch. After that Mr Peacock seems to have been quite content with his books and his job. No extended family, although he had one nephew whom he was fond of. Only appears to have had a few thousand in savings. Nothing to kill for I'd say. His nephew is well established as a businessman in Manchester with a family. So, as you can see, in terms of motive, like I said, there is not much to go on. Though of course there are limits to what one can ever find out about anyone.'

Sam nodded ferociously. My fingers tap tap tapped away at the keyboard recording the information.

'The residents then, I will go through in alphabetical order,' he continued barely drawing breath. 'Surname first. Got that Rosie?'

I nodded then said, 'Yes,' when I remembered he couldn't see me.

'Okay then, numero uno: Blackman Nicholas.'

The mere mention of his name had me sighing. The evident weariness was loud enough to be audible to Monty down the line.

'Ah, yes,' he responded. 'I can imagine he might be a handful. I gather Nicholas is going through a rebellious stage. He's had a bit of a journey lately. Father is the heir to the Blackman Mustard empire. The business will be passed down to Nicholas as the first-born son, when Mr Blackman senior retires. The family is quite traditional that way. Nicholas, however, is not making noises about going into business. Ergo – he's enrolled on the course and has aspirations to write. Graduated last year from Durham University. Classics. Got a third. Family not happy. Were expecting a first, but they are aware that he's not exactly on the rails at the moment. Like I said Rafe Blackman is rather hoping he'll grow out of it.'

'Hmm,' I said and grunted. I thought that might take a while. 'Well his dad's being very tolerant and understanding.'

'Perhaps tolerant, perhaps guilty: Mrs Jocasta Blackman, his mother, died in a shooting accident four years ago,' Monty continued. 'Blew her brains out. Nothing suspicious as far as we are aware, although …'

My ears pricked. 'What?'

'Although Rafe Blackman married his secretary six months later. Two weeks after they returned from their honeymoon the new Mrs Blackman gave birth to a very healthy baby girl called Maisie. Maisie Blackman now has a new one-year-old brother.'

Ah, I thought, that could well explain some of Nicholas's surly behaviour. 'And no foul play?'

'None of which we are aware of. Although the police report is not what you'd call "thorough". Mr Blackman had a lot of influential friends who were inclined to keep him out of the spotlight and move things on quickly for the grieving father and son.'

'Very quickly indeed,' said Sam.

'The young Blackman however, appears to have no connections to Peacock as far as we can ascertain, until he got here. Though Mr Blackman senior currently resides in Chigwell, which is in Essex, and thirty miles from Damebury.'

He let that settle in for a moment then promptly went on. 'Second: Chris Devlin. Well you can wiki him. It's all there.

Bestseller, etc. I haven't made a great effort because you said he wasn't present when Mr Peacock died. Also he's living in the US and the agencies over there haven't responded with what we'd call "great zeal".'

I wrote down, 'Devlin. No zeal.' Then typed in 'Imogen Green' because Monty was already detailing the sixty-eight-year-old. 'Unextraordinary career in Customs and Excise,' he was saying. 'Was married in '67 to a co-worker, Terrence Green, later divorced. One daughter, in her forties with two children. They live in Bristol not far from Imogen herself. Who as far as I'm aware lives a quiet but comfortable life. She's a member of a bridge club and regularly attends the WI on Wednesdays.'

'A party animal, then,' I said deadpan.

'Well you may say that, Rosie dear. But all of us in this conversation are aware that appearances can be deceiving and indeed Mrs Green was born Imogen Zoppé.'

Sam's head popped up. 'Not Zoppé as in *the* Zoppé family?' he asked in amazement.

'Indeed,' said Monty.

'Well I never!' said Sam.

'Who are the Zoppé family when they're at home?' I asked.

'Oh they're never at home, dear gal,' chuckled Monty.

'Travelling circus folk,' Sam explained.

'Imogen's father was a strongman,' Monty detailed. '"Samson the Iron Hercules". Did all sorts of interesting things with cannonballs and metal bars.'

'Ohhh-er!' I said and winked at Sam but he wasn't looking.

'Her mother,' Monty continued, 'was a Mabel Dare,

Queen of the Amazons. Strapping woman. Stunning to look at, a trapeze artist of great athleticism, who sadly ended her days in a wheelchair after a fall.'

'Wow,' I said, stuck for anything else to say. 'Who'd've thunk?'

'Who'd have thought indeed?' said Monty. 'Beneath the most conventional of exteriors lurks many a colourful past, I can tell you.'

'Yep,' I said. 'I can confirm that,' defaulting, as was my habit these days, to Mum and Dad. 'They'd have worked hard to conceal that.' I spoke my thoughts out loud. 'I mean Imogen would have had to have worked hard ...'

Sam murmured an agreement. 'Perhaps why she chose a path of superficial conformity.'

Monty snorted. 'Certainly worth bearing in mind as you move through your investigation. But on the surface no connection to anyone at Ratchette Hall,' he went on. 'Neither does Margot Lovelock. Who lives in a village in Hertfordshire with her husband, a former pharmacist, who has two adult children. Actually, he is her second husband. Her first was rather wealthy. Aristo. Society wedding with all the bells and whistles. Aunty Tabby might remember it if you jog her memory: there was some scandal, what with Margot being a commoner. At the time she was known as Goti, a successful glamour model. The sixties were very much her heyday. But she got respectable, donned an apron, became a model housewife and dutifully produced an heir for Peregrine, the husband. Unfortunately said heir died in his twenties and the marriage pretty much went downhill from that point on.

There was a minor scandal over the divorce but by that time it was the nineties and only aristocracy batted an eyelid at that sort of thing, and I think Margot felt she was well off out of it. And well off. She had a good divorce lawyer.'

'Cancer?' I asked, referring to the son.

'Eh?' said Monty.

'The heir. How did he die if he was young?'

'Accident?' Sam suggested.

The ruffle of pages crinkled down the line then Monty said, 'According to the Leeds Coroner's report it was suicide. He'd been very depressed after the breakup of a relationship.'

'Oh dear,' I said. 'Poor Margot. What a waste.'

'Now here's an interesting one,' said Monty as if the others had been as dull as ditch water, 'Starla Ocean. She runs some kind of clinic for cats.'

'Mental Health,' Sam added. His face betrayed no emotion.

Monty paused. 'Yes,' he sounded doubtful. 'I wasn't sure if Peggy, the researcher, was having me on. Okay then, well the Starla and Catnip Mental Health Clinic for Feline Distress has been established for three years now. And it is flourishing.'

'There's a lot of depressed pussies out there,' said Sam and looked at me.

I wasn't sure if he was making a point, thought it unlikely, but had a quick glower anyway on the off-chance.

'Indeed,' said Monty. His voice cut out for a second so we didn't actually hear the last consonant sounded properly.

'Is that what's interesting?' I asked. 'You said she was interesting.'

'Oh no,' he said. 'You see she was born in Brisbane Australia as plain Helen Boddle, but came over here sixteen years ago.'

'Not enough depressed Aussie cats,' I muttered to Sam.

He nodded sagely, 'It's all that sunshine and surf.'

'The "lucky country", I think they call it,' I added. I'd once had a boyfriend who didn't stop going on about how friggin' brilliant Australia was. 'God's lucky country,' he kept telling me again and again and again.

'Well,' said Monty. 'Ms Ocean got involved with an animal rights group and went down for her part in a kidnap plot.'

Sam and I looked at each other, jaws having just crashed onto the car floor.

'Good lord!' said Sam. 'You could not make it up, could you? Starla Ocean and "kidnap plot". Two things I would not expect to be mentioned in the same sentence.'

'Who did she kidnap?' I asked.

'The owner of a farm that bred rabbits for a research laboratory,' Monty's disembodied voice went on. 'Served twelve months in the end. Underwent some kind of epiphany in prison. Came out, changed her name to Starla Ocean, started working for the "Dove UK project", a peace movement. That was where she met her partner, Catnip Saggins, formerly Tracey. They've been together for seven years now.'

I shook my head. All these people so seemingly ordinary. What strange creatures human beings were.

'Next: Tabitha Montgomery. Need I say more?' Monty's voice was firm.

I wrote her name down while her nephew banged on about vouching for her impeccable character, good sense, noble attitude and award for being a good egg or something. In the end I typed 'Above suspicion blah blah blah. Never so much as missed a television license payment blah blah blah. It's all on Monty if she turns out a wrong 'un blah blah blah.'

'So next there's Robin Savage,' the agent continued, having ordered Tabby off the suspects list, if there was ever going to be one drawn up.

'Well, Robin at least has got to be straightforward,' I said summoning up the Scotsman's Scandi-knit jumper, cord trousers and thinning hair.

'Indeed,' Monty went on. 'Runs his uncle's business, Savage Books. Will inherit it when the elder Savage shuffles off his mortal coil. Robin Savage was educated at Ballen Heights, a private academy. Father was hoping he'd go into insurance like he had, but Robin had other ideas, erring towards books, arts and literature. He married in 1985. Two children, a girl and a boy, Janet and John.'

'Janet and John?' Sam asked. 'I'm surprised he had such a sense of humour.'

'Family names,' Monty sniffed. 'It happens.'

'He mentioned a partner in the pub,' I tendered. 'I had the impression it was a man.'

'Yes,' Monty answered with speed. 'Robin left his wife ten years ago for Ray, who he lives with now. It's all very amicable.'

'Is it really?' Sam sounded sceptical.

'Apparently so. Mrs Savage is remarried too. All of them

get on. Ray and Robin were guests at her second wedding. But, moving on, Robin has nothing in common with Graham Peacock, apart from an interest in books. Ditto Cullen Sutcliffe.'

'Actually Monty,' I said, remembering that we hadn't yet mentioned the events of the morning. 'Cullen does share a quality with Graham Peacock, I'm afraid. As of this morning he's also dead.'

'By Jove!' Monty exploded. 'What the hell's happening down there? And you didn't think to mention this because?'

'I thought it might have come up on your "tom toms",' I said, but my voice was weak. 'You always seem so well informed.'

'Clearly not today. You'll have to bring me up to speed now,' he insisted.

Once we'd managed to relay everything we knew about the situation (which wasn't a huge amount), he said, 'Well I never. I had my eye on him. Thought he was a potential suspect actually.'

'I think we all did,' said Sam.

'Interesting. Well, here's the lowdown: parents are civil servants, his sister is a personal trainer. Sutcliffe graduated with a chemistry degree from the City University in London but was working as a pastry chef in an Eastbourne delicatessen, where his parents live. My sources tell me he was particularly skilled in the fondant icing department. Although, he had been applying to the army for a while. There had been issues with eczema. And his psych evaluation.'

'No kidding,' I muttered under my breath.

'His uncle was in the army, but left it in the nineties to become a soldier of fortune. Got up to some rather nasty antics in Sierra Leone. But apparently Cullen adores him.'

'Or used to,' Sam said.

'Quite,' Monty agreed. 'There was, however, an accusation of assault two years ago, outside a pub in Eastbourne but the charges were dropped. It appears to have been an alcohol-fuelled disagreement over a spilt pint.'

'Yeah, I've had some of those,' I said.

Sam raised his eyebrows but Monty was already moving on.

'So, to the Course Leader – Laura Daphne Taylor-Jacobs. She started off life as plain old Laura Taylor. Again, you can wiki her but I'd say the most extraordinary thing about dear LD is the number of books she's managed to churn out: twenty-two so far. Very prolific. Not as productive as Mr Devlin to be fair, but acclaimed, and has also won prizes. Apart from that her life has been unextraordinary – degree in English from the University of Essex so has had links to your area. Did some inconsequential jobs, then a few years later took a masters from Leeds. Graduated with Distinction. Went into publishing. Has been with her husband, Jacob John Jacobs the journalist, for twenty-five years. Married him sixteen years ago and had a daughter a perfectly respectable year later. Eloise, apparently.'

'Sounds like the title for a book,' said Sam. 'Eloise apparently.' He looked at me and nodded at the same time, expecting a compliment.

I thought it was more likely to be a pretentious eighties

song from a group of young men with loads of make-up and crimped hair, so ignored him and asked Monty, 'Jacob John Jacobs. He's quite famous isn't he? I think I've seen him on some of those Sunday morning talk shows. He has views. On lots of things.'

Monty's nasal twang came out as he said, 'Ye-es. But he's a left-wing liberal and isn't particularly controversial. Though consider everything.'

Sam and I muttered that we would.

'Mrs Taylor-Jacobs did, however, deliver a course at Ratchette Hall a couple of years ago – *Crime: Plots and Patience* – which would indicate she and Graham were acquainted. I don't think they have met since, but you could ask.'

So Laura knew Graham. Actually, I think I kind of had that impression already. It didn't feel like it was too much of a surprise, but perhaps we should tackle her about it.

'Is that everyone?' I asked. I was starting to feel a bit cramped in the car, balancing the laptop on my knees.

'Just Jocelyn Vincent,' Monty said. 'Young and bright. Achieved a first in Business from Oxford. Her mother is Liberian, father from Dorset. Mum runs a cosmetic line, called IQ. Dad has his own aluminium window manufac-turing company. Jocelyn works in IT for Sony. But she's shown promise and is rising up through the ranks very quickly.'

None of this came as a surprise to me. I'd pegged Jocelyn as 'one to watch'.

'Anything weird or unsettling about her?' I asked, and shot Sam a look. I'd noticed the way, he'd lingered on her figure when we arrived. And although I was thinking that I possibly wasn't the best woman in the world for my curator at the moment, I wasn't going to set myself up with any competition. Jocelyn was pretty, intelligent and nice. There had to be something dodgy in that.

'Mmm,' said Monty. We heard more rustling. 'There was an episode at school, once. She hit a boy over the head with a brick and then ran away.'

'A violent nature!' I exclaimed loudly. Sam blinked twice. He was as shocked as me.

'Well,' said Monty. 'Says here she was nine at the time and the boy had, according to eye-witness accounts, been harassing her for a kiss.'

'Still,' I said, trying to watch Sam out of the corner of my eye. 'That's pretty outrageous. What a mentalist.'

Sam narrowed his eyes and sent me an odd look: low eyebrows and mouth pulled to the right this time. Definitely not a smile going on there. He looked at his phone and angled it diagonally towards his mouth. 'Does that conclude our list of suspects?' he asked Monty.

'Yes, I suppose you should be thinking along those lines. I take it we haven't heard any more about cause of death?' Monty asked.

I remembered Scrub's mention of Kitty, the medical examiner. 'Graham Peacock, the medical examiner reported, was a cardiac arrest. But she also said something about "homicide by heart attack" being rare but not unheard of.'

'Really?' said Monty. 'Well do keep me informed of the outcome.'

'So that's it?' Sam asked. 'There isn't anyone else is there?'

'No,' said Monty. 'That's the sum of it.'

I finished typing and saved the document. 'Well,' I said, shutting the laptop. 'We'll keep an eye on developments of course. Cullen Sutcliffe might also have died of fright. If he wasn't poisoned by the snake bite. Or maybe it was a double whammy – fright and poison? Hang on does anyone know if Royal Pythons are poisonous?'

There was silence down the other end of the line for a moment. Then Sam started stabbing his phone with his forefinger. 'I'll check.'

Monty coughed. 'The chances of being scared to death are quite low if you don't have a heart condition or disease.' Down the line something beeped. Possibly another laptop. 'Completely depends on your heart functionality. As we know, Graham had a weakness there.' He shuffled his papers. 'Cullen, however, according to the records, had no such issues. He was young. He was healthy and fit. Apart from the eczema. He exercised regularly. The odds of him, in particular, being scared to death are remote.'

'But he said he was scared of snakes, Monty,' I ventured. 'Publicly, in the company of all the others at The Griffin.'

'When was this?' Monty asked.

I thought about it then realised it had been less than twenty-four hours ago. 'Yesterday!' I said. 'That can't be a coincidence – Cullen announces his weakness, then we hear there's an escaped snake on the loose, and then he turns up dead. That's his greatest fear. Come on, Monty.'

Monty continued. 'Yes, I hear what you're saying, Rosie.

But in terms of shock – Cullen's body, unlike Graham's, would, in all likelihood, be able to deal with the output of adrenaline, even if he did experience intense fear for a short while.'

'So then it was the actual snake bite that killed him,' I concluded.

To which Sam replied, 'Ah, Royal Ball Pythons. That is indeed the species that escaped from the zoo. And these, it says here, are neither poisonous nor venomous. In fact they're recommended as snake "starter" pets.'

'Ew,' I shuddered. 'Freaky.'

'Not poisonous,' he said again and looked at me.

'So,' said Monty. 'We'll have to find out what the medical examiner says. If he has been poisoned, and if it was by a snake, then we can conclude it wasn't the Royal Ball Python. Another species must have been purposefully introduced with the sole intention of biting him.'

'Blimey,' I said. 'So it's looking like two murders, then?'

Monty sniffed, 'You should most certainly bear it in mind.'

'Is that a yes or no?' I demanded, stupidly.

Sam put his hand on my arm. 'You know as well as I do that we can't be so reductive. There is no way you can take a case of this complexity and reduce it to one thing or the other. If you do that, you boil away all sense, and then you don't come to understand the "how" or the "why". Come on, that's what we're about now – nuance, correct? Feel it.'

He was absolutely right of course, to remind me of this, but I didn't tell him that. Instead I did a pouty kind of pose and tossed my hair back.

Monty came in anyway at that point and said, 'I have to terminate this call. I'm aware you haven't delivered your background research into the templar aspects, but Sam you can mail me.'

'Templar aspects?' I said. But Monty had already gone.

'The knights,' Sam said. 'I presume he wants to hear about what we've learnt. Did you tell him about the missing bod ... oh no,' he said suddenly, catching something in the rear-view mirror. 'Dearie me,' he said. Then to my amazement, he leant towards me. 'Rosie, kiss me. Kiss me now.'

Oh my god.

For a moment I couldn't breathe. I was too overwhelmed by the words that had just popped out of his mouth. You just couldn't tell with some blokes could you?

I could feel the heat rushing to my cheeks. 'Well this wasn't exactly what I had in mind but ...'

He reached over and put his hand behind my head. 'Now! Quick!'

It wasn't the right time. It wasn't the right place. But how could I ignore such a desperate plea.

My mouth twitched and puckered on his. Awkwardly at first, then as the sensation of his fleshy lips pressed into mine a gorgeous tremor passed through them, down my body, to my feet then up again. I was so surprised by it that I let out a little gasp.

'Oh Sam,' I said breathily and closed my eyes, waiting to feel his tongue wiggle through my pearly whites and onto mine.

But it didn't.

In fact his lips stayed shut and didn't move much.

I opened one eye and saw that his were open too.

Which wasn't very romantic.

And was, to be honest, a bit bloody odd!

Yet I wasn't about to look a gift horse in the mouth. I was going to get my lips round it and snog it. Without coming up for air, I got hold of the loose fabric at the front of his shirt and pulled him closer to me.

He made an 'oof' noise and I felt resistance pull at the cotton in my hand just as a hard rap sounded on the window.

I started, broke off minimally, regretted it then immediately tried to get back in there.

But the knocker, whoever the hell it was, persisted, the raps coming hard and fast with four very firm knocks.

I sucked down a gulp of air and shouted over, 'Sod off.'

Sam completely leant back and turned round. 'Oh dear,' he said with artificial animation and wound the window down.

There was a black jacket-clad torso right outside. A black jacket-clad torso in an additional padded vest. With a walkie talkie and a blue badge which read 'Police'.

Brilliant.

I leant forwards and watched as said torso bent double and a chunky-looking man in a peaked cap leant into the car. He had an astonishingly tidy ginger beard and very blue eyes which immediately clapped on to us and narrowed.

Instead of 'What's all this going on here then?' he simply stated, 'Damebury Parish Council has a zero-tolerance policy towards any incidence of dogging.'

'Dogging?' I spluttered.

'We haven't even got a dog,' said Sam with indignance.

Bless him.

A lift in one corner of his mouth was the only hint of amusement in Tidy Beard's delivery. 'I see you have made an attempt to conceal the vehicle but I'm afraid we do checks on this area regularly, it being popular with the local dogging community.'

'We're not dogging!' I announced with emphasis on the last word.

'We were snogging,' said Sam. 'Up Lovers Lane.'

He sounded so old-fashioned that I started to laugh.

And it seemed infectious too because Sam immediately juddered and snorted.

'You may find this a laughing matter,' said PC Tidy Beard. 'But used condoms can present a formidable threat to local wildlife.'

'Ew. That's disgusting,' I said, the passion that had been aroused just moments since wilting very fast indeed.

'Your number plate has been noted,' the constable went on. 'Now if you'd like to move on, we'll say no more.'

If that was the offer, we were up for taking it. Sam put his foot on the accelerator.

We were out of there faster than you could say 'indecent exposure'.

CHAPTER SIXTEEN

'Hmm,' Scrub grunted when we located her. She had still not moved from the tiny office in The Griffin. 'Someone told me the Wurzels had arrived.'

'Wurzels?' Sam asked, as he slung his bag on the floor and parked his nice fit derriere on a filing cabinet resting against the wall.

She eyed us cautiously. 'Apparently you just turned up in a vehicle resembling a very small combine harvester.'

There was nowhere to sit so I moved a paper waste bin aside and got onto the floor. 'In our line of work we sometimes have to be inventive when it comes to covert operations.' Oh I liked that, it made me sound very agency indeed.

Scrub, as usual, wasn't impressed. 'Is that what you call it these days?' she said with a cheeky grin.

I was assuming this was merely her dry humour in play here. It was doubtful, with her eyes and ears on the situation at Ratchette Hall, that she would have been informed about the 'dogging' incident on Damebury Common. But, anyway, I didn't think the policeman would have bothered to ring it in. After all, we had not been required to submit our names and had been super speedy complying with Tidy Beard's instructions and legging it out of there as quickly as we possibly could.

Not that we had anything to do with dogging, an activity that I'd had to explain to my colleague and which had caused him to go pink around the ears and then vehemently deny attempting any such behaviour with me. He also went to great lengths to apologise for the earlier kiss, telling me he'd sighted the officer in the mirror and thought he might be put off from approaching the car if we looked like 'a young couple enjoying themselves on Lovers Lane'. Honestly, the way he spoke sometimes – it was like keeping company with the 1950s. Needless to say, the rest of the journey back to the pub had ranged from awkward to hyper-conscious of each other, then when we remembered we hadn't taken any of the 'camouflage' off we had a bit of a giggle. Despite the fact we had attracted quite a few glances on our way back from our 'covert operation', I was pleased that the greenery had diffused the tension between us.

Personally however, I was experiencing a mild form of post-traumatic stress via some uncomfortable flashbacks to my 'Oh Sam' moment. This meant that every so often, I was overtaken with an unbearable urge to cringe. Physically.

Whilst I was sitting on the upturned waste paper basket I experienced another one, which shook itself from my stomach to my chin and made me murmur, 'Weurgh.'

'You all right?' asked Scrub, swinging round on her chair to survey me from above.

Sam eyed me carefully.

'Yeah,' I lied. 'Just thinking about snakes.'

Trouser snakes.

'For god's sake,' my inner voice chided me.

'Indeed,' Scrub said and stuck out her legs. I focused on her trousers instead, which were navy blue and wide-legged. Officer worker uniform. They had a bit of stretch in them, but looked quite unbreathable to me. I'd say there was a high mix of polyester in that weave. You could tell from the shine. I preferred something a bit airier. Maybe that's why Scrub got grumpy a lot: sweaty groins were no one's idea of fun. I would suggest a mix that was heavier on the cotton. At some point in the future. When she wasn't scowling at me.

'There have been developments,' she said. 'Which I am prepared to share with you, if you can tell me what you know about the residents. My officers have taken down statements from each of them but we would appreciate your input,' which in Scrub-speak meant 'prepare for interrogation'.

Both Sam and I grunted agreements – all resistance was futile anyway.

'Good,' she said. 'Right, well first things first. The ME.'

'Who?' said Sam.

Scrub sighed. 'Kitty.' Even I knew that one.

'Medical examiner,' I reiterated. It was like he'd never seen *Silent Witness*.

'Oh right, yes?'

The sergeant crossed her hands across her stomach and leant back. 'The medical examiner, Kitty Wakeman – have you met her?'

I thought back to the time in the Seven Stars pub when we had been introduced to three forensic officers. One was Chloe Brown, who now volunteered at the Witch Museum from time to time. The other two I couldn't remember.

Sam shrugged. 'Should we? Did she work on the Witch Pit?'

Scrub shook her head. 'No, I think she was in Madeira then. Anyway, Kitty says, on first inspection, she doesn't think the puncture marks come from a snake bite.'

'Really?' I said. 'It looked like that.'

'No,' she shook her head. 'Not unless it's a snake with uneven fangs and a very wide smile.'

'What else has that wide a bite mark?' Sam asked and scratched his scalp above his ear.

'A small vampire?' I said and then wished I hadn't.

I got a look off Sue, who rolled her eyes and said, 'She's inclined to believe it's a human being.'

'What?' I said. 'One with fangs?'

The sergeant gave me another one of her glares. 'With a hypodermic.'

Ah right, I thought. That figured. There was a little part of me however that kind of liked the idea of a vampire.

'Ohhhh,' I said, after a few seconds of rumination. 'So he was *injected* with poison?'

'Kitty's not confirming anything officially until we get the toxicology back from the lab, but she surmised that a sedative was most likely to have been used to overpower someone of Mr Sutcliffe's size. Possibly this was followed up by a lethal injection.'

'Wow,' said Sam. 'But there *was* an escaped python reported on the BBC, wasn't there?'

Scrub nodded. 'Oh yes. We've been in touch with the zoo. The missing python is back in its quarters. The director thinks she must have found a way out of her cage. Possibly went exploring, but then finding the environment hostile or confusing, decided to call it a day and bugger off back home.'

I leant against the wall and pushed myself up into standing position. All this talk of escaping snakes made me feel vulnerable down there. 'I guess it sounds more feasible than slithering all the way over here, biting Cullen and then, mission accomplished, returning home.'

'Agreed,' said the sergeant. 'Although losing snakes isn't brilliant PR. You can see why they might want to play that down.'

Sam seemed to have been thinking this over for a while. 'Would a python really be able to go out of its environment then find its way back?'

But my mind was running along different lines. 'A lethal injection means poison, right?' I said quietly. 'Laura wrote a story about poison and snakes. It was a fantastically plotted and devious murder apparently.' Nobody was listening. '*The Eden Tree.*'

'Never underestimate the coldblooded brain,' said Scrub. 'Did you hear about that octopus in New Zealand?'

'Octopuses aren't reptiles,' I said. Although I didn't know how I knew this.

Once again Scrub failed to register my comment and carried on addressing her comments to Sam, who was proving a receptive audience. 'They reckoned he climbed to the top of his tank when someone left the lid open, went down the side and travelled across the floor of the aquarium then squeezed into a fifty-metre-long drainpipe which led into the ocean.'

'And freedom,' Sam added. 'I do remember that. They are very intelligent creatures. An octopus typically has nine brains. And possibly the Kraken legend is based on the beast. It's a legendary sea monster of giant size sighted off the coast of Norway and Greenland.' He smiled at me and continued. 'Destructive and sometimes cunning. Can we say the same of snakes?'

I sighed. 'Well, I reckon all of them, tentacles or not, are unlikely to have picked up a syringe and stuck it in Cullen's neck.'

'Indeed,' said Sam. Scrub nodded too.

There was something else still bugging me though, 'But the snake went missing yesterday. On the same day that the workshop, "Chris Devlin's 'Greatest Fears'" had been scheduled to take place. Again, there is a discussion of fears, which ups the ante. But we know now, that the snake was already missing. However, if someone wanted to scare Cullen, they knew his anxiety would be heightened if he'd already been talking about his greatest fear.'

Scrub sat up straight and took a notebook off the desk. 'It would definitely suggest research and planning. Who told you that the snake was missing?'

I thought back to the workshop. Oh yes, of course. 'Nicholas Blackman,' I told her. 'He announced it to everyone at the same time.'

Picking up a biro, she sighed. 'Come on then. Let's start with him. What's he like?'

'Total sod,' I told her.

'You'll have to do better than that,' she said.

I gestured to Sam for his laptop, got back on the floor, now we were pretty sure no snakes had been involved. 'Okay,' I said. 'There was a possibility his mother was murdered. Guns.'

When we later emerged from the office, it was with Scrub's blessing that we should spend a night at Ratchette Hall and covertly record any happenings. We were good with covert stuff after all.

Apparently, the sergeant's decision carried more weight than any objections Sophia and the Write Retreat directors might have. Scrub even declared she'd inform the events organiser herself. I couldn't see that being a very fluid nor easy conversation and was very glad I wasn't going to witness it. But then Scrub could be persuasive and she was grateful for our information and the timeline.

The Hall, we learnt, was open again and receiving visitors, having been given the all-clear by 'Fang Control' or whatever department was responsible for making sure there were zero snakes in the vicinity.

Apparently a group of writers, Laura, Jocelyn, Robin, Margot and Imogen, had gone for a walk. Starla and Tabby had returned to the Hall. We had passed Chris Devlin and Nicholas on the way out of The Griffin. It would be fair to say they appeared to have been taking advantage of the day-long lock-in and were talking very loudly in a manner that was quite raucous indeed. They had invited us over for a drink and an arm wrestle, but we informed them we had a report to file, as tempting as a test of strength might sound, and promised to see them at dinner. This gave us a couple of hours to creep around the house and set up cameras.

In the event, dinner turned out to be a rather subdued affair, back in the breakfast room/kitchen again. I suppose it was to be expected given the circumstances. Sophia and Starla had lit lots of candles. Some were aromatherapeutic, allegedly designed to lift our spirits. The air was filled with the cosy nurturing smells of sandalwood, nutmeg and then one vegetarian and one beef cottage pie.

Chris toasted absent friends, and a fair few bottles of wine were imbibed. I had a couple of glasses myself despite Sam's admonishing looks. Starla lamented the fact that none of them were able to leave 'this temple of death'. Scrub had told them they needed to be on hand for a while.

Laura agreed with Starla.

Margot said the circumstances were awful but she was getting a lot out of the course and brushed her elbow against Devlin's.

Nicholas agreed with Margot, for once. Tabby muttered something about making a silk purse out of a sow's ear, then Imogen announced there were people outside who were knocking on the window.

Nicholas and Jocelyn went to check but there was nobody there.

Tabby tactfully moved Imogen's half-empty wine glass away and suggested she have an early night.

Robin got to his feet and staggered after them, announcing, 'Ah'm gonna go with them too. Upshtairs.' There was a distinct slur to his voice so nobody dissented.

Everyone else then decided to retire to the day room for after-dinner drinks, so Sam and I made a big thing about 'leaving' and withdrew to the study, which was to be our HQ for the night.

The set-up in there was unlike other stake-outs I'd done. Largely because the house was so big and the grounds so sprawling Sam had digitally linked the cameras to laptops which he told me we had to constantly monitor.

There was no talk of dogging or snogging, just a clinical explanation of which camera was focused where, and instructions, as I'd come to expect, to note down anything that was usual or unusual. Sam said he'd kip for the first part of the evening so I could sleep in the latter half.

I watched him try to make himself comfortable on the chaise longue. He was quite tall though and his long legs sprawled over the end. I pulled the leather chair over and lifted his feet onto it. We hadn't brought sleeping bags so he had to make do with the woolly fleece that was draped over the armchair. In the end though he must have managed to get some Zs in because he started snoring lightly.

I amused myself watching him for a while then monitored the screens for a bit, noting down when everyone went to bed. Then I got bored and decided to go and help myself to a very small shot of whisky. Sam was zonko so wouldn't notice. Plus, I had a bit of a taste for it after the wine. I told myself I would only have one, which considering the amount my friend Cerise and I put away on a girls' night out, was pretty minimal so I didn't think it'd be a problem.

After several excursions, worrying that Sam might notice my absence, I located the scotch in the bar in the sitting room. It was contained within a bloody expensive-looking Bohemian crystal decanter, which I hadn't noticed before. There was a collection of shot glasses on one of the shelves so I helped myself and looked out the window into the garden as I sipped my drink, which made me feel like I wasn't slacking.

When I'd finished, I returned to the study, took up position behind the desk and sat with my head in my hands watching the screens.

There were four in total. One was pointing at the stairs in the hallway. Anybody going upstairs, out of the door or between the day room, kitchen, study where we were, sitting room or seminar room would be picked up. They'd also have to be very thin and very cunning to avoid being filmed if they were to exit via the front door.

Another camera pointed at the landing upstairs where the bedrooms were, but we'd had to be careful with that because of privacy laws and new data collection policies or something that sounded like it had been invented by a bureaucrat who was frightened of being sued by someone, anyone. So this camera took in the landing and a few of the bedroom doors. Personally, if it was me and there was a killer on the loose, which it was looking increasingly likely that there could be, I would be prepared to give up a bit of privacy. But Sophia was emphatic that we could only direct the lens towards the carpet. Ours is not to reason why blah di blah.

There was one camera on top of the porch outside and another on the roof of the orangery. This meant that most places were covered, though of course there were black spots.

The thing was, nothing was happening. So the views were pretty uninteresting. Occasionally the trees on the perimeter of the grounds trembled and swayed. The moon was out so you could see the tops of them. The house became quiet and still.

Sam's breathing got deeper. There was REM activity going on under his lids – I could see them moving and flickering.

It made my own eyes feel tired and, I don't know whether it was because seeing someone else in the land of nod makes you sleepy, but really quickly, I started to yawn.

I leant back into the chair and tasted the sour fuzz of the whisky on my tongue. Just for a second I closed my eyes so I could concentrate on identifying the area which tingled the most.

It wasn't the tip. No, that felt okay.

Nor was it the left side of my tongue.

It wasn't the bit down the front on the right.

It wasn't the bit down the back where your wisdom teeth used to be.

It wasn't the bit behind the canines.

It wasn't …

'Rosie! Rosie! Wake up! For god's sake! You had one job …'

I was being shaken out of a big reddy-pink cave which looked very much like a mouth.

'Oh crap,' I said, trying to prise open my eyes. 'Sorry Sam. I think I just bored myself to sleep.'

'Just?!' he said. 'Just? Look at the damn clock Rosie.'

I didn't because I was having trouble trying to shirk off the cloak of doziness. I was so tired, so tired. Even the touch of Sam's hand on my shoulder did nothing to energise me, which was particularly unusual. I could usually cope with a quantity of spirits (both drink or other – if they existed). Plus, I was no stranger to Buttery Nipples. So, yeah, it was odd I felt so sluggish.

When I did finally manage to open my eyes I realised my head had been face down on one of the laptops. My cheek had the imprint of the keys across it. Sam, I saw, was beside me, hoicking his jacket on over his shoulders.

'Up there on the right-hand screen. Just in the corner,' he was saying, pointing to the laptop which I hadn't drooled all over. 'It's mostly off camera but I saw a movement.'

As I rubbed my eyes we both heard a noise outside. One long note, thin and tinny. Or maybe it was a long way away. There was an echoey quality to it which did something to the air – made it quicken and sharpen.

Sam froze.

He had been doing up the zip on his coat but stopped and turned his face to the window.

I too stopped mid-rub and held my breath.

'Come on,' he said and darted towards the door. 'It's right outside.'

I struggled up, my limbs still irritatingly heavy, and grabbed my jacket.

Once I started to increase my pace I found movement became easier, so I broke into a jog and followed Sam out into the hall. In his haste he was fumbling with the locks on the front door. I helped by drawing back the heavy bolt at the top.

Once opened, Sam legged it, running round the corner of the house and disappearing into the night.

I sped after him.

The screen he had indicated in the study was one that connected to the camera on the orangery roof, which meant that whatever had moved there, and possibly made the horn noise, had been in the south-west corner of the garden where the trees bordered the woods. It was the same spot where Devlin had indicated the 'commotioning' was coming from yesterday morning.

Visibility however was pretty bad. The garden was wreathed in mist. As I rounded the corner of the house I heard the sound come again. Louder now, I thought it more like a bell than a horn.

Sam was running diagonally across the lawn, presumably to its source. As he did, the ringing seemed to increase the volume. The mist claimed him, and then, strangely all at once the noise stopped. I paused for a moment to catch my breath then heard an 'ugh' in the corner and swiftly made for it.

As I got closer I realised the noise had come from within the trees. Sam must have gone into them. It looked exceedingly dark in there. The trunks, sturdy and black, stood like dark wooden crusaders. For a second, I hesitated.

I thought about running back to the house for help but then realised that would take too long, so after a moment in which I urged myself to be 'bold', I too entered Witch Wood.

Oh god – Witch Wood where the decapitated animals lay. Witch Wood from whence the commotioning came. Witch Wood where the witches danced.

Witch Wood.

Dried foliage and twigs split and rustled underfoot as I tramped into the darkness.

It was pitch black. My eyes hadn't adjusted to night vision.

Ahead I could just make out a rift in the trees where weak moonlight was coming down. I did a quick calculation and concluded that whoever or whatever had made that noise, was probably in the same situation as me light-wise. They'd be stumbling around for ages in the blackness. So it was likely they too would head for that small glade to navigate themselves. Well, it was as good a guess as any.

I orientated myself in that direction and now no longer running, because of all the obstacles on the forest floor, began to pick my way over fallen trunks, bushes and bracken.

'Rosie!' It was Sam, low down somewhere. Hiding maybe? 'He's up there.'

'Who? What? Sam, where are you?' I moved towards his voice and located him on the floor by a lump of rotten wood. 'What are you doing down there? Did you trip?'

'No. I nearly had them but they must have doubled back and hit me on the head. They've gone down there. Towards the stream.' A dark limb pointed into the thickness of the trees. 'Go after them. I'll follow you. They dropped something. It clanged. I heard it. It's here somewhere. Must find it.'

That didn't sound like a good idea at all to me. 'Hang on. But you've been whacked on the head? I can't leave you here if you're injured. Let me help,' I began to bend down but an arm stopped me.

Sam's voice was hoarse but commanding. 'No, I'll be fine. YOU mustn't let them get away, Rosie! Go! Now!'

Something loud cracked: wood, a large chunk of it, was splintering somewhere in the trees.

'Quick!' said Sam again.

And so I went – hopping over the logs and undergrowth, moving deeper into the loops of mist twisting about trunks, weaving into hollows, circumventing branches, treading over twigs and leaves, brushing bushes.

The air was moist and damp and smelt of dank vegetation and night and mystery.

Another wood-like object snapped loudly in the dark, like a warning.

I reduced my pace as the trees became dense and put out hands to feel my way through to the noise. My fingers touched crumbling leaves, withered petals, shrivelled berries, ridged bark, soft moss, something fleshy that might have been a fungus growing out the side of a dead tree, pale like a ghost.

Another tight clap echoed across the wood. Whoever made it was approaching the clearing, for the sound ricocheted off nearby tree trunks.

I could feel a change in the air, as if it was loaded with energy. My fingers and tongue started to tingle.

There was a loud thud as something heavy like a large branch fell to the forest floor.

Whoever was up ahead was strong and big. How else were

they snapping their way through the woods? It made me wonder if I would be able to take them on?

I paused and swallowed. In other circumstances, maybe. But I wasn't used to being in this kind of environment. The concrete jungle was my preferred habitat. There it was usually illuminated, even if only by a dull synthetic orange glow. But things rarely fell. Rigorous health and safety checks put paid to that sort of thing.

This was rather different.

And thus daunting.

The ground was sloping quite a lot now as I descended deeper, deeper into the trees. Several times I slipped on the mud and skidded, only avoiding falling into it completely by wind-milling till I hit a nearby trunk or low hanging branch, whereby I would steady myself. It was inelegant and stupid-looking and I was very glad no one else was here.

Apart from my prey.

I went on.

I hunted.

Gradually I lost my bearings.

At one point I stumbled into a hollow.

I strengthened my resolve to apprehend the someone or something lurking in the wood ahead. If I could get to the moonlit glade I could tell them to give themselves up, bring them back to the house, then Sam and I could unmask the prowler, sort this mess out, satisfy Monty and we could toddle back to the Witch Museum and maybe do some frolicking.

There was another snap and then a great and strange blast of air which seemed to resound through the whole wood.

Woah, I thought, that was weird.

The loudness made me pause, breathe in and duck down.

It came again – a kind of crackling that roared like a sudden gale, as if someone had just opened the door on a furnace.

As it continued, it seemed as if the noise was saturating the entire woods, encompassing everything around me so I couldn't tell if it was up ahead or to my right or behind me.

Disorientated I swung round, becoming aware that my heart had started beating hard. Possibly it was all this impromptu exercise, along with a massive bung of adrenaline wrought from alarm.

'Who's there?' I called out.

I took another step into the trees, now sweating all over.

The blast began to diminish: someone was 'shutting the furnace door'.

For a moment there was quiet and stillness in the wooded glade. I stopped and felt my ears twitch, like mini radars, searching for noise, clues, direction.

But the forest was holding its breath.

I experienced the sudden sensation that I was being watched and became keenly aware of my solitude.

A pang of nausea swooshed through my stomach.

That prompted a rush of caution and I began to have second thoughts about continuing my hunt. In fact I was seriously thinking about giving up when there was a sudden and energetic rustling in amongst the dry leaves.

Although it sounded like it was emanating from the bracken by my side, it also seemed to come in stereo from a place further down the incline. Or maybe that's where it originated. I just couldn't tell so stumbled lightlessly downhill until something hard cracked against my forehead. A branch, I think, for it went with the forward motion of my body for a moment as it stretched, then, when the plant fibres were extended as far as they could go, the wood pinged back. It was such a sharp return it toppled me over.

On my way down I threw my hands out hoping to grab on to something to steady myself. But only air slipped between my fingers.

Gravity won.

The next thing I knew I was sprawled before a weird bush. More precisely I was lying on the dirt, my chin resting on a large moss-covered branch. I hadn't lost consciousness, I knew that. But everything had happened so fast that I couldn't work out for a minute how I had ended up in this strange prostrate position. I could not give it any further thought because a splashing had started up. No, not a splashing as such, more like the sound of running water diverting round an obstacle.

I pulled myself up onto all fours and tried to sight my target, but my eyes were going in and out of focus. My chin brushed against splinters of wood. It took a gargantuan effort to zoom in on the stream five to ten metres away. The moon must have broken through the clouds because the further bank looked like a silvery shore.

For a moment it resembled a thoroughly pastoral, almost romantic, scene – the gurgling brook, the sylvan trees beside it, the steep bank, fauna bathed in a shiny wash, fairy-tale twee. Then suddenly there was a movement within, like a piece of the scenery had detached itself and was beginning to move forward, wading through the stream.

Although I couldn't see in great detail, I had the sense of a gleaming coat, the coarse hair on it, sleek and sinewy flanks. There was a snort and a puff, and the air was filled with steamy mist, which smelled of goat and hoary freshness.

I narrowed my eyes and saw, glistening in the moonlight, the back of a huge creature emerge from the stream: regal, immense and awe-inspiring. It stopped and straightened, then lengthened its spine. Water dripped off the hindquarters.

The beast shook its shoulders, sending drops flying off in all directions. Then, as I watched, its head rose and stretched. Atop it I saw a set of spikey antlers glittering like a crown.

It was such a heart-stopping scene that I could do nothing but gasp.

And it was then that I felt it stir within me, as if I had breathed in something in this air that had made me hyper-aware. Something that had pushed a button and heightened my senses in response to the entity in the water. For its presence was remarkable, demanding both attention and respect.

The beast bellowed, loud and clear. It began to stalk a couple of paces up the other side of the muddy bank. Cloven-hoofed feet struck at the earth and, just then, the notion of devotion became very real in my mind.

In fact, the thought of the thing, standing just a few paces away, cowed me.

Physically.

I bowed my head, conscious I was in the presence of a

creature that I could feel with more than my five human senses, conscious that I was in the presence of *power*.

Then came a weak high-pitched whimper nearby: feral, though puny, as if its maker was surrendering, acknowledging a mightier beast.

I took a breath and then heard the noise start again, weaker and yet still raw, pure mammal.

It was a good few seconds before I realised that the creature making the whinnying noise, well, it was me.

On the other side of the bank the stag halted.

Its spine arched, the head rose up, the forelegs, which now looked like arms, pushed off from the ground. The beast's back flattened and it moved the bulk of its weight to the rear quarters. Then, effortlessly as if it had been accustomed to doing so a thousand times over, the thing reared up on its hind legs.

I could swear that it towered over everything. Its physicality, topped by those antlers dwarfed everything around it for I believe it stood at twelve or thirteen feet tall. Its muscles rippled with strength and energy.

The head and horns dipped, then rose up again sharply to the moon and delivered the most unearthly howl. Or maybe it is more accurate to describe it as a roar, a ferocious response to my call.

It was the howl of a hunter who had missed its prey.

And slowly the antler crown began to turn.

Towards me.

I could not for all my will stand before this being that radiated such power.

I could not ...

Then I was not there within the forest, supine on the floor, but standing in a dark dripping cavern, deep in some sacred subterranean hollow. There was an altar and on the altar sat a male form. I don't know what he looked like, for the air was tingling, filled with black fluttering things and tiny spheres that glowed and darted about the weatherworn sepulchre.

The feeling came over me that I was sitting in the stalls of a theatre, waiting for the curtain to go up so I could watch some amazing spectacle. I felt no fear, only a sense of the ancient, and something infinitely lovely nearby.

Again my senses were strung high.

Then I felt it: a tickle as he touched my ear and whispered. Although the words went in, they were silent. But I saw in them an energy made visible, light, and this energy transmitted images of connection, of heritage, history, bloodlines, togetherness, duty, love. And *all* of this was magic. And I became conscious of a strange emotion: a kind of realisation of knowledge and the harmony that came with it. Then his hand left me and, released from this silent transmission, my head dropped.

'Come out. Take my hand.' My chin hit the log sharply, and flinching, was raised up again, so I could see the antler god, still turning, there on the other side of the bank.

My fearless interlude now over, horror seized me.

My internal organs contracted with terror and I vomited down on the sodden earth.

A hoof slipped and clopped on a stone and made a scraping noise as it steadied itself again.

This time when I looked up I squealed.

The eyes of a man-beast locked on to my face.

'Come out of the undergrowth. Here, take my hand.'

The words leapt over each other, alien, loud, strange. I wasn't sure if I was hearing them with my ears or if they were inside my head.

'Rosie Strange. Are you okay?'

There was a face stretching before me, shining and white. The eyes were reflecting dazzling orbs of light that made you blink and shut the moon out.

I'd seen them somewhere before. 'Wah,' I said, barely able to control my tongue. 'Wah. God. Antler man.'

Strong hands pulled me up.

'It's Dorcus,' the face said bobbing up and down like a balloon. It looked up to my temple. 'Oh god. Is that blood?'

'Grod. Tree-ping. Hand-head,' I blurted – though gawd knows why. All my words were getting mixed up.

'Blood,' said the balloon face and licked its sharpened teeth. 'Look,' he said and spun me round. 'I can't explain this now but you need to run.'

'Snakeling drip drop beer tray.'

'Now,' he yelled, then an animal screamed. I heard a kerfuffle of sounds and leaves and murmurs like the forest was transforming itself into human form, and was visited by the sudden sense that something was after me!

I took up Dorcus's warning and fled. Never had I run like that before.

Back through the wood.

Wailing and screaming.

Screaming and wailing.

On my lips words were coming out. The same ones over and over again.

As I reached the edges of the forest, my half-fried mind processed them:

I was chanting something about being touched.

Touched by the hand of a god.

CHAPTER SEVENTEEN

Sam later explained, when he came to collect me from hospital, I had more likely been touched by the hand of a plod. Specifically, PC Lambert, who had been sitting in a patrol car outside the Hall minding his business whilst puzzling out a sudoku game, when he had become alert to a disturbance in the porch.

On further investigation he ascertained two residents appeared to be chasing each other round the side of the house. Radioing said activity through to Operation Control he left his vehicle to inspect the premises. The residents appeared to have been in such a hurry that they had left the front door open. PC Lambert duly ensured said premises were secure and not vulnerable to intruders. Once satisfied that there was no further activity of the criminal variety taking place in Ratchette Hall, he proceeded to search the grounds and gardens.

At 0500 hours our fearless duty officer discovered a man sitting by the edge of the property where the woods began. Later identified as Samuel Stone (Caucasian IC1) this person of interest was, at that moment, in what can only be described as a state of high agitation. He was holding a hand bell, which, unprovoked, he demonstrated to PC Lambert. Unfortunately, the noise then caused some breach of the peace and Mr Stone was advised to desist immediately or face consequences. Luckily no further residents of Ratchette Hall, who PC Lambert had been charged with observing, were wakened by him.

After several exclamations and incoherent expressions of frustration, one of which involved offensive language, Samuel Stone then explained that his partner, Rosie Strange, was currently in pursuit of an intruder suspected of ringing aforementioned bell.

At this, PC Lambert, realising said incident may well require the filling-in of much paperwork, namely a report for his higher-ranking, rigorous and often displeased Sergeant (Scrub), immediately began to search for his notebook. After recording the time of the incident, he then requested details from Mr Stone as to why he came to be sitting on the grass at this hour.

Stone, however, grew increasingly hostile, indicating not only that he may have incurred an injury to his person but that his partner, Ms Strange, being in the woods for quite some time and in pursuit of the unknown bell-ringer, may have put herself in the path of danger and may perhaps require assistance. Stone was, however, unable to identify exactly how long she had been absent despite several questions and different approaches and also was unable to give a description of said bell-ringer.

Having not yet connected the unknown fleeing bell-ringer

with the assault, PC Lambert was at a loss to understand why Mr Stone was expecting him to enter the woods and proceeded to question him with some rigour regarding the consumption of alcohol and/or recreational drugs.

Receiving denials, which also bore signs of increased aggression, Stone got to his feet and began to grab at PC Lambert's arm, demanding the officer enter the wood and seek out Ms Strange.

Worried that the current situation might escalate into mindless violence, PC Lambert began to caution Mr Stone with a view to arrest, whereupon, with much uproar (which most definitely constituted elements pertaining to a breach of the peace) Ms Strange emerged from the wood. Being covered in a muddy solution from head to toe, with hair and face in varying states of disarray, Ms Strange was clearly exhibiting symptoms of recreational drug use.

PC Lambert promptly restrained Ms Strange and applied handcuffs. Whereupon Ms Strange appeared to lose consciousness. PC Lambert immediately radioed for backup and, noting a cut to Ms Strange's forehead and grazes on her chin, the ambulance service.

'But,' I said to Sam when he had finally stopped doing his Old Bill impression, 'Did he go in? Into the woods? Did he see the man? Dorcus?'

'No,' he shook his head. 'Not then. Who is this guy?'

'Oh I'll tell you later. But there was an animal-stag-god thing in there. Did they search it?'

'Er what?'

'Doesn't matter. Did they enter the woods?'

'They did when the backup arrived. The light was coming at that point, but it had started to rain and I'm not sure they found anything.'

I considered this and the strange coil of events that had brought me to my spot in Outpatients.

'I'm not surprised,' I said.

'No?' said Sam. He was sitting on a chair next to me, waiting for the nurse to sign me out.

'That's right,' I said. 'Because it's not a person whose been doing this.'

Sam's eyebrows peaked a couple of inches above the top lids. 'It's not?'

'No,' I said and shook my head, which ached rather a lot. 'It's Cernunnos. Possibly accompanied by a vampire called Dorcus.' And then in a very quick and thoroughly overexcited fashion, I explained what had happened, finishing with my visit, to what I had surprised myself by calling, the 'sacred cave of knowledge.' I also detailed the giant 'man-stag' and mentioned Dorcus sending me back to safety. He was a good vampire.

'Ah,' said Sam when I had finished.

His composure was completely odd. I couldn't believe that he wasn't jumping up and down, clapping his hands and trilling about proof of a world beyond this, a world we didn't fully comprehend or know, and the triumph of supernature.

'Sam,' I said and took his sleeve and shook his arm up and down. 'This is amazing news. Why aren't you punching the air and phoning Monty? This changes everything. This is better than your ghost, right?'

For a second he drew back and looked at me. A cloud of uncertainty passed over him. Then he mastered himself, cleared his throat and adjusted his sleeves. 'Right, yes. Now, listen. I've got to tell you something.'

His face was grave. I looked deeper into his eyes to see if he was masking another emotion, something perhaps that he couldn't contain. But they were a practical corduroy colour – no whirring flicks of granite or amber in them. No light from another realm that played upon the irises. No excitement.

I puffed out a sigh. 'What?'

'Look,' he said and turned towards me, his knee knocking mine. I was too deflated to even feel a spark of electricity from the brief physical contact. 'Everything's all right,' he said in a soft tone. 'And the doctor says you're fine now, so don't worry, but there's a possibility, quite a high one, she thinks, and I do too, that you may have brushed or fallen into belladonna. Didn't the doctor tell you that?'

'She was going on about some bird called Trophy Donna who liked peery herbs or something. I zoned out.'

'Atropa belladonna is a perennial herbaceous plant.'

'Okay,' I said flatly.

'Deadly nightshade,' he said firmly.

Images of the plant, cut into stems and arranged in a bouquet back at the museum flashed over my mind. 'Deadly nightshade? Oh shit.' Yes, I'd heard of that before.

Sam nodded slowly. 'Indeed.'

'Oh god,' I said. I knew it could be fatal. It was deceptive: the petals looked like tiny bells and were an attractive brownish purple. Their pointed leaves were a lovely pale green and ribbed so that if you were tactile you might be inclined to run your thumb back and forth across them, as I had nearly done once.

Town dwellers might be caught off guard if they picked them in September. But, then again, it wasn't summer. 'But it's autumn,' I said to Sam.

'Yes,' he said and nodded. 'Some varieties continue to bloom until mid-December. And it has been a mild autumn this year.'

Then I remembered peering into the wood after Devlin had seen the angel commotioning. Had I seen purple heads in there?

'But,' I thought out loud, 'wouldn't Graham have got them off the property? As they were dangerous. Wouldn't someone have taken charge and done that?'

He shrugged. 'There are quite a lot in there. Witch Wood isn't the responsibility of Ratchette Hall. The police searched it this morning. There are definitely a variety of shrubs growing. Many have been trampled on but some have grown high.'

'Wow,' I said. 'So when I fell ...'

He nodded. 'You probably touched them. The poison can be absorbed through the fingers if you're not wearing gloves. Or through eating the berries.'

Oh blimey, yes, Chloe the forensic archaeologist had told us about that back when we got the 'flower bomb'.

'Well, at least I didn't do that,' I said. 'Eat them, I mean.'

'Not you, no,' he said.

We lapsed into silence as I thought back to that moment

in the cave. I could remember it so well: the knowledge, the feeling of it. 'It felt so important,' I said and shook my head. 'So real ...' My mind returned to the giant-sized man-stag, an image which prompted a weary sigh. 'I thought it was a god. The horns, the great proportions ... and then Dorcus ...' I stopped myself from saying any more. It all seemed ridiculous now.

'I'm afraid hallucinations and delirium are all part and parcel of aconite or atropine poisoning, Rosie dear.' Sam looked down at his feet then said. 'Lilliputian hallucinations are not uncommon, according to the doctor.'

I looked up at him. 'What's that?'

'When things can appear smaller or larger than they actually are.'

I nodded. 'That sounds like Alice in Wonderland syndrome.'

'It's similar.'

'Blimey. I thought that sounded crazy when Dr Roberts first told me about it.' I shook my head in dismay. 'So I probably just saw a deer, but because I was tripping, my brain amplified it?' And maybe Dorcus wasn't even there. I had allowed myself to linger a little longer on him over the past day than perhaps I should have done. Though *someone* had pulled me up. Or maybe I pulled myself up. The whole thing was getting foggy and blurred.

'Something like that.' Sam patted my shoulder. 'There are other symptoms too – headache, rash, flushes, dry mouth and throat, slurred speech ...'

I tried to think back. Mmmm, all of those were possible.

He continued. 'Nausea, confusion and,' he fidgeted in his seat, 'coma.'

I nodded, remembering back in summer when we'd received that particular bouquet. 'Death, I thought, sometimes, too.'

'It's such a good job,' he said, 'that you threw up when you did.'

'How did you know you that I threw up?' I said. I had tastefully omitted that particular detail in my description.

'Oh Rosie,' he said. 'You were covered in a veritable pot-pourri of aromas when you emerged from the grips of the forest. And you had some down your front. I spotted sweetcorn from the salad at dinner. Anyway, you gave PC Lambert quite a fright.'

'Did I?' I said and giggled inappropriately.

'Oh yes.' Sam extended his hand and ruffled the hair on the back of my head. 'The words "Stig of the Dump" were used.'

'Oh,' I said, feeling less amused. It was not the most flattering of comparisons.

'The doctor reckoned it could have been a lot worse, if you hadn't "expelled the toxins".'

For a moment he looked so pale and stricken that I put my hand on his arm and said, 'Well at least I'm all right now. Don't look so worried – I'm not going to die.'

'No,' he said and cast his woody eyes onto mine. 'But Imogen and Robin might.'

I gasped and retracted my arm. 'What? No. What's happened?'

'Atropine poisoning. Same as you.'

'Why? How?'

He shook his head. 'Several members of the household awoke when the police backup arrived last night, or rather, this morning. But others didn't. Myself and PC Lambert informed Sophia of what was going on and she told the residents. After that some of them went back to bed again. I stayed to give my statement to the police and go through the tapes with them. Then,' he shrugged, 'when I thought I'd got everything sorted, I had a kip.'

I nodded. That was cool. I didn't mind.

'I knew you were at the hospital and being checked, so …'

'It's okay,' I said again. He looked guilty for sure. 'No worries.'

'Well, they started breakfast apparently. Everyone was quite bleary-eyed and tired anyway, but Tabitha and Jocelyn worried when Imogen and Robin didn't come down for breakfast. They were usually so prompt.'

'Oh my god,' I said, remembering their behaviour last night at the dinner table. 'I thought they were a bit pissed at dinner, but it was the poison taking hold.'

'I'm afraid so,' said Sam.

'How on earth did you work out it was atropine poisoning?'

Sam winced. 'Imogen had picked a bunch of flowers on her walk yesterday. She had some in a vase and some spread over her desk: ferns, pennyroyal, soapwort, daisies, late blooming belladonna. And one withering strand of wolfsbane. That's aconite and atropine poison in one double whammy. She must have been called to dinner halfway through arranging them.'

'At least, that stopped her handling them any further,' I added.

'Yes.' Sam shook his head. 'But their symptoms are quite severe, which may suggest they consumed berries too. We just don't know.'

'That's awful,' I said. 'You would have thought Imogen might have known about that plant and its qualities. From her, er, background.'

Sam frowned. 'I don't think being descended from circus folk automatically qualifies you as a botanist.'

'No,' I said and looked at my hands as if they might be stained with aconite juice. 'I guess not.'

'Robin had been out walking with Imogen and several of the group. He must have helped her pick them.'

'Wow,' I said again. 'How unfortunate. Any chance of foul play?'

'Possibly. If they were directed to pick the flowers by someone else, who did in fact know what they were and what the effects would be.'

Sam tapped his fingers on the side of the chair. 'The police are looking into the *Atropa belladonna* bushes. It does seem that there are rather a lot of them. We're considering the possibility that some may have been planted there specifically for this purpose.'

I frowned. That was a dark and nasty thought. If that had occurred then the pair had been cruelly manipulated. 'But who would do that?'

Sam shook his head. 'We don't know when they came back yesterday afternoon. The police weren't surveying the place at that point. Scrub muttered something about "cuts". But apparently Sophia and Carole got back to the house first so they could start preparing dinner. The walking group broke up. They drifted back in their pairs, or one by one. Nobody noticed when Robin and Imogen entered the house, and of course no one is admitting to having walked with them. The only ones who are in the clear are Nicholas and Devlin who had alibis from the pub.'

The funny feeling was back in my stomach again. It amplified the darkness there and sent a jolt of bile up into my mouth. I swallowed the bitterness and said in a low voice, 'And then there were six.' And four dead or incapacitated: Imogen and Robin, Cullen and Graham. Three writers and one member of staff. It was strange. What was the connection, if there was one at all? And why had Graham been the first? Graham the mild-mannered janitor, who nobody seemed to mind.

'Monty's so not going to be pleased about this. Since we've arrived the whole situation has got worse, not better,' Sam grumbled. 'Which reminds me, we need to find out if you can leave now. Monty's coming to have a look at the bell. If we're lucky it will have fingerprints on it.'

'Or claw prints,' I said, joking. Well half-joking, maybe.

Sam just tutted and said, 'Oh Rosie.'

CHAPTER EIGHTEEN

When the doctor arrived, over-rushed and frantic but trying her absolute best to appear calm, she gave me the all-clear, told Sam to keep an eye on me and to come back if I started to develop any worrying symptoms.

That was good enough for us.

We got back to the museum. I climbed up into Septimus's bedroom and took a nap.

I think I was out for a couple of hours. When I woke up I felt okay considering the poisoning and the fact I had been up all night. Then I remembered I hadn't been up all night: after that whisky I'd fallen asleep on the job. Literally. In fact I must have got at least three or four hours in. Then, after my trip on the dark fantastic, I'd been conked out at the hospital too. So actually, I'd had more sleep over the past twenty-four hours than I usually did.

If there were any more kinky edges to my senses they were totally sorted out by the new power shower I'd had installed in the bathroom. There was nothing like a good cleansing blast to blow away the cobwebs and residual side-effects of goth flower poison. And it gave me some time to think and process.

Afterwards I was left with a mild headache and a feeling that my tongue had been lightly singed. I decided some paracetamol would sort that out and bring me up to 100 per cent, so went downstairs to get a glass of milk and line my stomach.

In the office/dining room, however, I found Monty and Sam deep in conversation and knew immediately from their expressions, which were dark and clouded, that they had been talking about something serious.

The agent was standing up, but leaning against one of the filing cabinets. This particular one had a stuffed barn owl and palmistry hand, amongst other items, displayed on the top. Monty had his hands in his pockets and despite the well-tailored formal suit, smart shiny shoes and immaculate shirt, was doing a good impression of looking leisured and languorous. He always had that look, like nothing ever freaked him. But, I suppose, with all the strangeness he encountered through his job, ordinary murder and whatnot were quite unexceptional.

Sam was sitting on the table opposite, a little hunched over. The afternoon sun filtered through the round stained-glass window, shining onto the curve of his back, making a little patch of red there.

'Hello,' said Monty, when he noticed me hovering in the doorway. He pushed off from the filing cabinet, removed his hands from his pockets and straightened up, ever the gent. 'How lovely to see you looking so radiant my dear.' Then he treated me to a wide grin that showed his perfect teeth. 'When Sam told me what happened last night, I really did not think you'd appear as glowing. But, dear gal, you have most certainly bounced back remarkably well.'

He was regularly this charming and well-mannered, happy to use flattery as a means to an end. But he was definitely one of the good ones.

'Thanks,' I said and went and took a seat. Usually I'd be mortified to be seen without my make-up and my bang-on-trend wardrobe. But today, I simply couldn't be bothered. And Monty said I looked all right, so …

'How are you feeling?' asked Sam and sprang off the table. As he cantered round to my side I saw he had lines across his forehead. I wasn't sure if they were due to my appearance or if they still lingered from whatever conversation he had been having with our friend.

I told him I was okay.

He offered me a cup of tea and I accepted and asked what they'd been talking about.

Monty produced a square plastic bag from behind the stuffed owl and waggled it. The object within clanged. 'Sam's brought me up to speed with developments at Ratchette Hall. I'm so sorry to have got you involved in all this. One can never anticipate these things. What first appeared to be a case of purely allaying fears has turned into something more …' he looked up into the stained glass for inspiration, '… more sinister. But,' he continued, placing the bag square on the table. It made a muffled clanking noise. 'We're hoping that this bell may yield prints that go some way to solving our little mystery.'

'Uh huh,' I said and pulled the teapot over and lifted the

lid. Everything inside looked treacly brown and very well stewed. I pushed it over to Sam. 'It's not a *little* mystery is it? Not really?' I had been thinking about this in the shower. 'Two dead – Graham Peacock and Cullen Sutcliffe – and two in hospital who may not survive. It's turning into a massacre.'

Monty looked at the floor then glanced up again at Sam. 'Just to give you a bit of a heads-up, Rosie – I've already relayed this to Sam – we know that Mr Sutcliffe was murdered. The toxicology results indicate sedatives and an excess of potassium chloride.'

Sam finally took the hint with the teapot and picked it up and went into the kitchen. 'I'm putting the kettle on.' Then, before he disappeared through the arch he paused and explained, 'Potassium is naturally occurring in the body, but in excess it can cause cardiac arrest.'

Monty ambled over to the table and pulled a chair out. It squeaked on the parquet as he sat down, lifted his trousers then crossed his legs. 'We think that the sedatives were injected into the neck.'

It was more or less what the ME had suggested via Scrub. 'And they left what looked like fang marks? So we'd think it was from the escaped snake?'

Monty smiled. 'From a very odd snake, but yes, that's an option we can't yet rule out. Another implement may have been used to make the puncture wounds larger, more noticeable.'

Sam returned with three fresh mugs and a steaming teapot.

I bit my lip and tried to concentrate. 'So, whoever found Cullen would see the marks and assume it was a snake. As we'd almost been set up to expect that, or certainly prepared for it, with the news about the escaped python and all the phobias about snakes and serpents in the Greatest Fears workshop.' I shook my head. It didn't add up. 'But whoever injected him would have to know that there would be tests done. That the game would be up. So why go to all that effort to make it look like a bite?'

'For show? At that very moment of discovery,' suggested Monty.

'But why?' I wondered out loud. 'The illusion that the snake did it has lasted no more than a day. The murderer can't be very bright.'

'Unless they had another reason? The idea of snakes in the nest at Ratchette Hall would no doubt considerably increase stress and anxiety among the remaining occupants. We know, because of the nature of the course, that they all have fertile imaginations. Aunt Tabby's is terrific,' Monty said and popped out a proud smile. 'But anyway, Rosie. Here's a point you should know: the average IQ of the serial killer is, well, average.'

Blimey, I thought, a serial killer. Is that what we're looking at? But I didn't voice it. Instead I said, 'Is it?' It wasn't the case on TV. The famous ones like Hannibal Lecter, Dexter Morgan and Kevin Spacey's John Doe were all seemingly intelligent, able to elude the police and sustain their dastardly plans for ages, hatching elaborate and cunning plots.

Monty leant forward towards the table. His head dipped into a pool of amber light from the window, which gave his skin a lovely tone. 'There's a study that's been done which puts the mean, the average, at around ninety-four. The average citizen of the British Isles hovers at around one hundred.'

'Is that so?' I said then whistled and wondered what mine would be.

Monty shook his golden head. A little beam of light caught on his forehead and shined. It was where his black glossy hair was starting to thin. Didn't look bad on him though. I quite liked it. 'It's a misconception to think serial killers are all young, white, male and intelligent. They're not.'

I nodded. That was a point to take on board.

'In many cases,' he went on and pinned me with those fossil-grey eyes that sometimes let me glimpse within profound and quick-witted acumen. 'Murder often comes hand-in-hand with passion. And both passion and anger are not rational. Passion and anger make mistakes.'

I mulled it over and came up with another possibility. 'Or the killer doesn't care about being found out. Or they think they've been so careful they won't be caught.'

'Sounds about right,' said Sam, who had now pulled up another chair next to me. 'Don't arrogance and murder go hand in hand too?'

'Not generally in crimes of passion,' Monty told him.

'But this isn't one, is it?' I said, trying to figure out some sort of logic myself.

'Don't assume it not to be the case.' Monty wagged a finger at me.

'Okay,' I said, summing up. 'Well, there's definitely strange stuff going on at Ratchette Hall. It's not just the murders, but the noises in the garden, by the woods. We know someone was out there last night.' I glimpsed my goat-footed god darting between the trees and Dorcus with his elastic face. Man, what a trip aconite was.

I shook the images from my head. Best not to be distracted again.

'One must assume that these sound effects are there to capitalise on the superstitions that we've learnt are connected to the woods – the Devil, god of the witches, the walkabout knights – and so freak the writers out. Sam, you said this kind of thing happened all the time in the war, didn't you?'

Monty raised his eyebrows at my colleague and bent his head towards him.

'Well,' said Sam, as if protesting. 'It's true. You know that, Monts. Belief in UFOs, satanism – you can't dodge the fact that your department has been involved. There was that nasty stuff in Northern …'

Monty's eyes flashed with warning.

Sam paused and then ventured tentatively, 'All executed to manipulate people. No doubt for the greater good, but come on – you can't deny it's been going on for decades. Centuries even. And it's much easier to manipulate in an atmosphere of insecurity and tension.'

Monty shrugged and avoided answering. 'Tabby has agreed there is a sense of besiegement and fear among the residents.'

Sam laid the pot of tea on a cork coaster on the table. 'And staff,' he added.

'Yes,' I agreed. 'And it's been increased this morning with the discovery of Imogen and Robin. I have a hunch that's all part of the plot. Someone directed them to pick the flowers.'

'Could have. Could also be an accident.' Monty nodded. 'Though think about the former and work out who that might be.'

'I think,' Sam piped up, 'from our recent experience the "who" usually comes when you've worked out the "why"?'

'Yes,' I said, thinking aloud. 'And talking about "the why" … there's something that's been bugging me since Sam told me about Imogen and Robin. You know – one of the victims is clearly the odd one out. All of them have been participants on the course – apart from Graham. We've been looking for links from them to him. But what if his death was actually the accident?'

Sam stopped pouring the tea and put the pot on the table. 'You mean he was mistaken for someone else?'

'Something like that,' I said.

Monty stood up. 'Keep thinking along those lines. That's good work. Now, I'm afraid I can't stay for another cuppa – I promised to look in on Tabs while I was here. I have an early Christmas present for her which I think she'll quite like.' He tapped his nose. 'Acquired it on the hush-hush. Aunt Tabby has taken a keen interest in self-defence.'

I stood up abruptly. 'Well good. We might need it,' I said. 'And I'll follow you. We've got to set up for tonight anyway.'

'Not a stake-out?' Monty asked. 'There'll be police outside, of that you can be sure.'

'Rosie,' said Sam and came and touched me on the shoulder. 'I'm not convinced that you're up to it?'

'Yes,' I said and made my voice firm. 'I am. I've got a

feeling that things may come to a head tonight.' Then as I was going through the door, I called, 'Sam you clear up and bring more tapes. I'm just going to pack, and of course I must get my clothes on.'

As I ducked round the wall I heard one of them say, 'Well truly, isn't *that* a shame.'

But I wasn't sure who.

CHAPTER NINETEEN

We reached Ratchette Hall about forty-five minutes after Monty, which was pretty good going and only achieved because I had agreed not to straighten my hair. I had negotiated with my curator and brought my straighteners with me instead. So now they were packed in my pull-along suitcase with my sleeping bag and pillow and vanity case and make-up and toiletries and toothbrush and small free-standing mirror with magnifier on one side and faux fur throw. All of which I stowed discreetly in the study, after several trips to and from the car. A girl has priorities you know.

Once I had set up my equipment, I went off to find Sam and was told by a burly looking officer positioned outside the seminar room that he had joined Detective Brown and Sergeant Scrub inside. When I asked to be admitted I was denied, which then provoked some rather loud argy-bargy until Sue Scrub stuck her head out and asked, 'What's all this going on here then?' and gave me access.

I hadn't been inside this room before.

It was another pleasant space with a lovely peaceful vibe.

Or the potential to have such a feel to it, if it hadn't instead been filled with people who were rather prickly and wired.

Large Georgian windows looked out over the front lawns. It wasn't very nice out there. Rain had broken again, and the wind was whipping it up and smashing it against the windows.

Desks and PCs were positioned at one end of the seminar room. Down the other an interactive whiteboard and rows of chairs. Sam was in one of them, but he'd turned it round so he could face Chris Devlin, who was standing, leaning against the wall between the windows. For the first time since I'd met him, the best-selling writer seemed to be exhibiting symptoms of anxiety: his hands kept straying to the toggle on his aviator jacket, which he played with when he wasn't pulling the longer hair at the back of his curly mullet. Plus he was flushed. Very.

There was another man, in plain clothes, who I didn't recognise, sitting on one of the desks, eyeing Devlin with a face that might as well have had 'suspicious' tattooed on the forehead. He was lanky and very dark-skinned, maybe with sub-Saharan roots. When I entered with Sergeant Scrub, he cast his gaze at me. It was so fierce and scorching that for a moment I wondered if I had any unpaid parking tickets that he knew about. He just had *that look*. He could see through you into your guilt.

Scrub introduced me and said, 'This is Constable Bobby Brown.' Then looked with meaning at Devlin and said, 'One of the best.'

'Oh,' I said and grinned at the stranger. 'Bobby Brown. Cool. Like the make-up?'

Constable Brown looked at me and without smiling said, 'No.' He swivelled back to Devlin, crossed his arms, and then, as if he had nothing better to do, carried on glaring at him.

'Now where was I?' Scrub asked.

Brown pushed off and walked over to the author. He stopped just a foot from where Devlin was leaning and proceeded to inspect the writer's face whilst answering his boss's question. 'You were suggesting Mr Devlin take the opportunity to clear up any misunderstandings that might have taken place regarding his statements so far.'

Wind squeaked through a crack in the windows and stirred the long curtains either side.

Scrub nodded and pulled one of the chairs next to Sam up closer to where Devlin stood. Now he was hemmed in on all sides by the detective and sergeant.

It might sound quite odd but seriously, if you could have felt the energy in Bobby's gaze you would not want to be the hypotenuse to that triangle.

In his chair, Sam squirmed, I think, out of empathy.

I tried not to make a sound and went and sat next to him.

Despite the fact that the skin on his nose and above his lip was glistening, Devlin was trying desperately to put on a poker face.

It wasn't working.

I knew it, Sam knew it. And if we knew it, Scrub and Constable Brown definitely knew it too.

'I told you,' Devlin bleated. 'I don't know what you're talking about.'

Constable Brown clicked his tongue and slowly shook his head back and forth.

Scrub crossed her legs and said, 'So you say Mr Devlin. So you say.' She sat back and crossed her arms to match, then she eyeballed him, almost as fiercely as Officer Brown and said, 'Or should we call you, Mr Cumberpot?'

On our chairs, a fitting audience, Sam and I gasped.

'What?' I said. 'You mean he's not Chris Devlin?' I swung round to Sam. 'Do you know what – I thought he was a bit low in the old IQ department. And the stuff he came out with when he was describing the "angel" thing – it was dreadful. Not a decent writer by any means.'

The imposter sniffed and let go a little groan.

'Oh he's Chris Devlin, all right,' said Scrub. 'But he entered the country on a passport registered to Rodney Cumberpot.'

'Oooh,' I said, and whispered to Sam. 'Yeah, I can see why he might want a pen name.'

The man, who was not an imposter but actually the writer Chris Devlin, however, was looking even more spiky. 'My friends used to call me Rod, actually,' he said, and with a defiant toss of his hair, turned his gaze on me. 'Ramrod.'

I sucked in the giggle that was threatening to explode out of my mouth. Of course he was 'Ramrod'. Of course he was.

'Can you explain then, Ramrod,' Scrub demanded through tight crinkly lips. I think she was finding it all ridiculous too. 'Can you explain how you entered the country on Saturday but failed to turn up to the course residence until Wednesday? We understand from Sophia Adams-Braithwaite that you reported your flight was delayed. And yet Los

Angeles International has confirmed that Flight VS 0090 arrived at Heathrow on Saturday on time.'

At that moment the door opened and in trotted Monty. He clocked the look on the writer's face, which bore much in common with rabbits unaccustomed to headlights. 'Has he confessed yet?' he asked the coppers.

Bobby Brown shook his head, but kept his eyes glued onto Devlin's. ''Fraid not, Agent Walker. We're going to have to work him harder.'

The concept of Officer Brown working him harder appeared to be more than Devlin could bear. 'Okay, okay,' he said and put his hands up. 'I was with a woman.' He gave a little headshake, and sneaked a congratulatory smile, thus confirming his virility to all those there. 'Oh yeah and what a woman, she is.' God, that man could over-write.

'Oh yeah?' Scrub sighed. 'Name?'

'Oh, I can't tell you that,' said Devlin. He stuck his chin up high and out in a display of noble defiance.

'Fine,' responded Scrub. 'Bobby, arrest him for obstruction, will you?'

Constable Brown took a half step closer and cleared his voice. 'Rodney Cumberpot, I am arresting—'

'Clarkeson. Angela Clarkeson,' Devlin volunteered immediately. 'That's Clarkeson with an "e". C.L.A.R.K.E.S.O.N.'

Boy, was he a gentleman.

'Forty-five Farthing Lane, Sidcup,' he sang, canary-like.

That figured. Sidcup was on the way from the airport if you flew into Heathrow. It wouldn't present much of a detour.

'I would appreciate it if you exercised discretion,' Ramrod went on, recovering his composure. 'My wife wouldn't be very happy if she found out I'd seen Angela.' He turned to Constable Brown and winked. 'She's an old flame.' But his voice had lost all the cocky bravado that we had become accustomed to.

Constable Brown continued his most excellent glaring without a single blink. He was amazing.

Scrub took out a notebook and flipped it open. 'And this Angela Clarkeson will be able to confirm your whereabouts on the nights in question, will she? Or else I'm afraid you have a great deal of explaining to do.'

I didn't hear Devlin's answer because a neuron had flared in my memory zone. 'That morning, we were in the garden,' I whispered to Sam. 'Devlin said he had angels on his mind, remember? Angels – Angela?'

Sam nodded. 'He could be telling the truth,' he said. 'But if he was in the country, he's back in the frame for Graham Peacock's murder.'

'Oh yeah,' I said. 'Unless this Angela alibis him.'

A head popped between our shoulders. It was accompanied by a sharp citrusy aftershave that smelled both expansive and expensive.

'Listen chaps,' Monty whispered. 'I'm afraid I have to be off. Tabby seems fine. I've given her the Christmas present, which should keep her safe and sound, but I'd like you to watch out for her tonight, all right? She's not as young as she used to be. I'll be expecting you to ensure her safety.'

'Aren't the police going to be around?' asked Sam. His Adam's apple bobbed up and down. Possibly he was as daunted as me at the responsibility.

'Yes, but you two are going to be *inside* the building, aren't you?'

We looked at each other. Sam mouthed 'study'.

I nodded. 'Yep.' Wherever I lay my vanity case that's my home.

'Jolly good. I'll leave her in your capable hands, then. Do give me a tinkle tomorrow with any updates.'

Despite all external signs to the contrary Monty really could be quite an Essex geezer sometimes. Always countering favour for favour. Not that I would ever get involved in such behaviour, of course.

Which made me think of Big Ig and then immediately gave me another idea. 'Monty, I will most definitely look after Tabby tonight. You can guarantee my utmost vigilance.' I took a breath. 'If you get me an appointment with Araminta de Vere.' Despite evidence to the contrary I hadn't forgotten about my biological mum.

Both Sam and Monty blinked hard and stared at me.

'Please? She knows more about Celeste than she's letting on.' I shrugged. 'I'm thinking, what with the whole thing about her being in prison for trying to burn me alive, she might not be inclined to accept a visit from me. But if *you* make the appointment, Monty, and pull a few strings in that way that you do so very well ...?'

Monty's features became taut across the top half of his face, betraying a frisson of irritation. But it was visible for only a fraction of a second before the good-natured and pleasant façade was pulled up again. 'I applaud the seamless segue from my aunt's wellbeing into your jaunty request,' he said with a smile that was probably not natural.

I fluttered my lashes and also smiled in a way that was not natural. Yet these kind of gestures are a language of their own. One that Monty was fluent in. 'And, Mr W, can you do me another favour please? Take the whisky decanter for testing too? Last night's shot was, by rights, far too strong. It flattened me more quickly than a trio of Buttery Nipples. And seriously,' I said out the side of my mouth, 'I know how to handle my Buttery Nipples.'

Monty's eyes widened. 'The mind boggles,' he murmured.

'Never backwards with coming forwards,' Sam whispered under his breath. 'But she's got a point.'

'Come on then Ms Strange,' said Monty, jerking his head towards the door. 'You'd better show me which decanter you're talking about.'

Which was good timing because Bobby was doing some high-octane glowering while Scrub turned the screws on Cumberpot.

Sam and I followed the agent out. I didn't want to stay in the seminar room anyway – I don't enjoy seeing grown men cry.

CHAPTER TWENTY

It was late. Almost midnight. Sam and I were trying hard to remain alert despite the dim lights and quiet house.

My colleague had taken up position behind the desk, where I had so magnificently failed to stay awake last night.

I was on the chaise. To start with I had got into my sleeping bag, but it proved so cosy that I climbed out of it for fear I'd doze off early again. Instead I'd pulled the fleece over and kept watch on the garden out of the window.

It wasn't particularly nice out there. Dark inky clouds obscured the moon. The evening had been a wet one, and inconsistent, with sporadic showers and a limp drizzle. The lawn looked very moist and the line of trees that edged the garden seemed blacker than before.

Both Sam and I had remarked that we felt it unlikely the bell-ringer would return tonight, particularly as he, or she, had no bell. And it was very soggy underfoot. And there were two panda cars in the drive.

At the same time, we were aware that tonight was the last night of the course. If the murderer was going to strike again this would also be their last chance.

Scrub hadn't yet decided whether or not she wanted the residents to continue their stay 'in town'. As that might require their transferral en masse to the Premier Inn in Chelmsford and a large accommodation bill, I thought it was probably unlikely.

So I had eschewed wine at dinner and instead made a cafetière of strong coffee, which we were topping up from an electric kettle lent discreetly by Sophia.

I was necking the dregs from my third cup when Sam said, completely out of the blue, 'Why do you want to see Araminta de Vere?'

I pulled my face away from the window and stared at him. Over the tops of the monitors, his big dark eyes put me in mind of a hound. 'Why? What do you mean "Why"? Why shouldn't I?'

Sam shrugged and sat back into the leather chair, but his eyes were still keen. 'Er, most people prefer not to see their attackers. That woman did try to kill you.'

I rested my coffee on the window sill and folded the curtain back so that there was no light leaking out. 'I know she tried to kill me, Sam,' I said. 'I was there at the time.'

He continued to stare, without any blinking, like he'd just had some training from Bobby Brown.

I sighed. 'I want to see her because I think she knows who my father is.'

Sam held my gaze. 'You know who your father is.'

I shook my head. 'Not like that. My biological father.'

He opened his mouth, looked about to speak, closed it, then opened it again. 'But don't you think there's a good reason you don't know about him? I mean where has he been all these years?'

My turn to shake my head. 'His absence doesn't necessarily suggest disinterest. Mum and Dad said that Celeste didn't tell them about her boyfriend. Perhaps there was a good reason for all the secrecy. And Araminta de Vere, when she was dragging me across the lawn ...' I said, casually, '... she said that night she chased Celeste, she was in the car with "her partner". Araminta kept saying "they". "*They* lost control of the car", "*they* skidded off the road", "*they* hit the tree". Not to mention her insistence that "*they* didn't go in the brook" when she was present. There's a lot there that I need to understand.'

'But the police report said that only Celeste was found.'

I rolled my eyes and waved my hand. 'Tsk, tsk. Come on, Sam. You've met Monty. You know how some information can be "forgotten" in reports. And this was decades ago when people were careless and easily bribed. Have you not seen *Life on Mars*?'

He breathed out heavily. 'But you were drugged.'

'So?'

'You might have remembered it incorrectly.'

'Exactly,' I said. 'Which is one of the reasons I need to see her. Go over it again.'

'But she might not tell you the truth. She hasn't for years. What reason has she got?'

'None,' I agreed. 'You're right. But it's not going to stop me trying.'

Sam rubbed his forehead then sat forwards and switched

his gaze to the monitors. 'Why do you need to find him?' he asked eventually.

I thought about it. 'Because I feel obligated to.'

'To him?'

I shook my head. 'No. The gods. Last night they told me to.'

'Oh dear.' He jerked his chair even closer to the desk and put his elbows on it. 'Perhaps you should have a sleep. You're still not better are you?'

His assumption bothered me. 'I am,' I said so you could hear the petulance. 'I was thinking – even if my vision last night wasn't real – it still came out of me. Out of my head. So what I saw, last night, the god. It's a part of me that's trying to tell me something. And the more I think about it the more I feel I should try to find out who my real dad is. It might help me unearth what happened to my mother. Celeste,' I explained, in case he was in any doubt.

'But what if you *do* find him?' he persisted. 'Have you thought about what that will mean?'

'Well,' I said. 'If I find him, I'll have to say hello won't I?'

Sam sighed and sent me a weak smile. 'But,' he said gravely, 'he might be dead.'

'He might be alive.'

'He might be alive and not want to say hello back. He might have a nice life with a new wife …'

I was getting fed up with this. 'Look, Sam, why are you trying to put me off?'

'I just care about you, Rosie. Very dee—'

'Shh,' I cut him off and sat up.

Sam winced. 'I was just about to tell you how I—'

'Sam, shut up,' I whispered and put my finger to my lips for emphasis. 'I just heard something.'

For a moment he looked very annoyed. Then he said, 'Oh,' and held his hands up. 'Where?'

I pointed to the office ceiling. 'Sounded like someone on the roof.'

'The roof?' Sam spluttered, then froze, as we heard a rapid scattering sound, lots of little knocks which came in quick succession, like gravel being kicked about up there. 'But that's the bedrooms isn't it?'

Sometimes I was surprised by his lack of observation. 'This is a single-storey extension, Sam. Hadn't you noticed?'

'Oh.' His eyes darted to the monitors. 'Hang on. Look here – movement on the first-floor landing.'

I swivelled my legs off the chaise longue and was about to say, 'I'll go,' when we were both alerted to the sound of tapping. Although it could have been on the outside of the building it reverberated down the internal wall of the office.

'Where is that coming from?' Sam asked, then before I could answer said, 'I'm going outside to find out. You take the landing.'

I nodded and wrapped the fur fleece around my shoulders. As he buttoned up his coat I said, 'Be careful though Sam. Right?'

He grinned. 'You too.'

I watched him leave, hearing the quiet click of the latch on the front door, and had a quick peek at the monitors. Sam was right, there was something dark and curious moving about the first-floor landing. That particular camera lens was not sensitive so all I could see was a cloud-like shape crawling or writhing on the floor upstairs. Although I wasn't immediately spooked, I did find my feet were reluctant to tip-toe out the door.

They obeyed me though and within seconds I was at the foot of the stairs. I draped the fleece on the bottom post and slunk into the shadows, shifting the weight of my foot to the first step.

As I lifted myself onto the second I thought I heard a snuffle. Something animalistic, like the breath of a beast, above me on the landing.

My heartbeat, which was already faster than average resting rate, started to accelerate.

Upstairs there was another noise. Something that I can only describe as a faltering cry, a fragile moan, as if a creature not of this world was lamenting its inevitable demise.

No, I thought, what a silly notion. There will be, as usual, a rational explanation to all this. Maybe it's the pipes. I forced myself up on the third step, then the fourth, then the fifth.

By the time I had got to the turn on the stairs I knew it absolutely was not, no way José, the pipes. For the simpering was now accompanied by a deeper wail, and I thought I heard another person whisper, muffled and from further away, 'Oh my love, let me in.'

This is bloody ridiculous, I thought. We're in the middle of Essex, not out on the wily windy moor. This was more likely to be a boy-racer trying for a bunk-up than Cathy haunting her Heathcliff.

Not that it was likely to be a ghost at all.

Because ghosts didn't exist.

Although …

Sam, himself, was having doubts.

'Shut up, Rosie,' I told myself, almost on the landing. This was no time for close contemplation of life after death and the consequent existential implications that may or may not come with that.

As I got to the top of the stairs I glimpsed something bedraggled and black, oozing up the side of a door, scratching its dark nails at the wood. It was a bizarre and surreal sight, which got even stranger: for the thing heard my tread on a floorboard. Although I halted immediately and held my breath to make no more sound, it became aware of my presence.

I flinched as I saw in the darkness, the awful thing rotate its head, neck dangling before me. My lips let go of a scream.

Just at that moment the door, which the thing had been scratching at, flew wide open. Light flooded the landing.

'Rosie,' said the silhouette framed in the doorway.

I recognised the voice.

Laura!

Thank god it was just her.

'What on earth,' she said, looking down on the ground. 'But what on earth is Margot doing on the floor?'

I clocked the 'spectre' and realised that Laura was right. In the light from her room, a rather dazed Margot was half crawling, half sitting, now blinking at the ceiling.

'I heard something …' she said. 'Tap, tap … I … where am I? Have I been sleepwalking again?'

At once relieved, though still uncertain of what was going on, I let the air come out of my lungs.

'Oh dear,' said Laura. 'Let's get her back into bed.' And she knelt down and folded the old lady up in her arms.

I went and got under Margot's other shoulder, then we both heaved her up. 'No,' I said, and stopped her. 'Do your bedroom and Margot's both overlook the office and cloakroom downstairs?'

'I think so, yes.' Laura nodded.

'Right then,' I said. 'Let's get you downstairs into the day room.' It was the safest place now, I thought, being at the back of the house. 'There may have been someone up there, outside your windows. Sam's gone to investigate.'

'Oh,' said Laura, startled. 'I thought I heard a voice. Some knocking. I wasn't sure if I was dreaming or not. Do you think we should wake the others?'

I thought briefly about Tabby, but then decided that she'd be safer up here on the other side of the house. 'Let's leave it for now.'

'But, what if …?' Laura began.

'No,' I said. 'We should get her some water and check her over. Let's try to get her downstairs.'

We had been in the day room for just a minute when Margot came to.

Laura was standing by the fireplace in front of the sword on the mantelpiece. I had propped Margot on the Chesterfield and was sitting at her feet arranging a blanket across her knees.

'What a thing,' Margot said, her voice clearly very shaky. 'What a scare. I am quite unnerved. Rosie, dear, fetch us a whisky,' she said, then turned to Laura. 'I know you don't like it dear, but think of it as medicinal now. We all need one.'

Laura murmured assent, then a voice at the door said, 'Best bloody idea anyone's had all day.'

It was Nicholas in a pair of silk pyjamas. Jocelyn was trailing behind him, yawning in a onesie with rabbits printed over it. She looked cute. 'I'm in,' she said.

'Get five for all of us,' drawled Margot.

'You'd better make it six,' said Tabby, who appeared behind Jocelyn and went straight over to sit next to Margot on the sofa. 'What's happening? What's all the commotion outside?'

'Outside?' I said, surprised that there was something more dramatic going on elsewhere.

'Yes,' said Tabby. 'Voices. Lights. I think the police are here.'

'Oh,' I said, and thought about going to help, but Margot called out, 'Quick Rosie, we need to calm the child,' and nodded her head at Laura. So I turned back to the corner bar and saw the whisky in the bottle, not the decanter, which I remembered I had given to Monty to test.

'I'm okay, thank you,' said Laura. 'I don't like it.'

Then the reason why I had asked Monty to test it came back to me and nearly knocked me over.

A massive lightbulb switched on inside my head.

The whisky.

I knew it.

My tolerance to Buttery Nipples was real and strong. I knew that too. Why had I even doubted myself?

'Hurry, Rosie,' said Margot again, and with one mighty internal clunk the penny finally dropped.

'Good grief,' I said, as I looked at the bottle and slapped my forehead. 'It's been staring me in the face the whole time.'

'What has?' asked Tabby, as I turned round to face her.

'So obvious,' I said. 'But then you don't always think these things through, do you? And we're so conditioned by society. Plus, you know my insight thing – it's been kind of muted. Since the summer.'

Tabby's face was blank.

'What's she talking about?' Nicholas said in a low voice to Jocelyn who replied in a loud whisper, 'Not a clue.'

Another shade drifted through the door, a satin kimono with a fuzzy blue cloud perched at the top. 'Why is everyone up? What's all the noise about?' Starla floated over to a chair by the table.

Nicholas and Jocelyn shrugged.

'Not sure. I was hoping she'd dish out that delicious whisky,' said Nicholas.

I laughed simultaneously whirling round and facing him. 'You know, I did wonder if it was you who might be at the bottom of all this,' I said to the silk-clad fop.

'Me?' he said. 'Why on earth …?'

'Because you're so vile,' I explained. 'And tried to point the finger at everyone else. At The Griffin that afternoon when you were doing your nut about Cullen and Laura—' I stopped as Nicholas's face took on a proud and twisted grin.

'You were making such a fuss I thought perhaps you were just trying to take the heat off. I mean, if anyone was going to play a cruel trick, for a laugh, you fitted the profile.'

Nicholas's eyes widened. His jaw dropped as he gave in to full-flowing indignation. I had him on the hoof so carried on. 'But then, on Wednesday, you were clearly very unnerved.'

Now Nicholas snapped his mouth shut, wrinkled his nose and puffed out his chest. 'Was not indeed!'

Jocelyn tapped his arm. 'There, there, Nicky,' she said.

'Ah yes. The lovely Jocelyn,' I said, and turned my gaze on her. 'Even considered you. You seemed too good to be true. Helpful, intelligent, talented, confident in your abilities. Practically perfect in every way. Which means, unless you're Mary Poppins, there's murk beneath the surface.'

Jocelyn didn't bat an eyelid. 'I thought it might be Cullen,' she said, her voice calm and even.

'Me too,' I nodded. 'But then he ended up a victim himself. You might wonder why that would be, mightn't you Margot? Frail little Margot.'

The kimono was strutting into the middle of the room. Starla put her hands on her hips. She had no make-up on and looked better for it if I'm honest. 'Can someone tell me what is going on?' she pouted.

'But then it was you, Starla Ocean,' I held a hand up to halt her progress, 'who really stoked up the tensions in the church, that first day on Halloween, by reciting a chant to raise the dead. On Halloween! Now that really was interesting timing, wasn't it? After all, everyone knows anxiety is not what the doctor might order for a patient with a heart condition. Did you, Starla Ocean, hold a grudge against Graham? Was there a reason behind your provocative recital?'

'I thought it would add to the atmosphere,' Starla whimpered.

'Oh, it most certainly did that,' I said, feeling a bit of a cow as I trotted the comment out. But I had my reasons. 'Didn't it?'

'It was spontaneous,' she bleated again.

I watched her flush. The pink skin looked wrong against the blue hair.

'Is this a show?' said a voice at the door. Devlin entered the fray, wrapping a shiny dressing gown around his middle.

'Possibly,' said Nicholas. 'The woman is certainly making a spectacle of herself.'

'Ah, Mr Devlin, always late to the party,' I said. 'Do join us. Shame you couldn't on Sunday, despite being in the country since the day before.'

Margot snapped her head to him. 'You were?' she asked.

Devlin swallowed and focused his attentions on pulling a chair out from the table and sitting on it. He lifted the fabric of his pjs and resettled them. 'Bit of a misunderstanding,' he said, keeping his gaze somewhere on his knees.

'I don't believe it!' Nicholas grumbled. 'I really am going to demand a refund for this.'

'But,' I continued, now fully channelling Monsieur Poirot. 'Why would a best-selling novelist wish harm on a harmless mild-mannered janitor?'

'I wouldn't,' said Devlin, and crossed his pyjama-clad legs.

'No,' I agreed, hoping that Sam was going to get in here soon and back me up. 'Why would *any* of you wish to see Graham Peacock dead?'

A general muttering of dissent filled the room. Lots of 'Not me's.

'Quite,' I said. 'Because, my dear writers, Graham Peacock was not the intended victim. He was collateral damage. The murderer had not, in fact, factored him into the plan.'

The door opened again and Sophia came in rubbing her eyes. 'Why is everyone up?'

'Shhh,' said Jocelyn and Nicholas, which kind of surprised me. But I realised, as I opened my mouth, I had everyone enthralled.

Starla straightened herself up and moved to the sofa. 'Come on then? How did you work that out?'

'Well might you ask Starla. Well might you ask,' I said wagging a finger at her and wondering again where the hell Sam was. I had a distinct feeling that I was going to need backup imminently. 'Because,' I couldn't delay my announcement much longer. 'Because Graham did not drink the whisky, did he?'

Devlin shrugged. 'I wouldn't know.'

Sophia, who had remained near the door said, 'He wasn't a spirits man. And he had to be careful about drinking.'

'Right,' I said, nodding. 'I've been thinking about that since yesterday night, when I sneaked a shot from the decanter. I know my limits and one shot never touches the sides when I'm in Leytonstone.' I turned round and addressed my next comments to Laura. 'But all of you had some of that whisky on Halloween and all of you conked out.' I turned back to Sophia. 'Apart from Graham, who cleared up like a dutiful administrator should, and being the last one up, opened the door and,' I set my eyes on Tabby, '... experienced a scene so very frightful it scared him to death.'

Tabby was alert – her eyes followed me as I began to move away from the cabinet.

'A fright,' I continued, 'intended for someone else altogether. I expect, when I get the results back from testing the whisky decanter, there will be evidence of sedatives laced into the liquor. With the same chemical composition, I'd wager, as the variety injected into Cullen.'

Starla and Tabby gasped.

Laura shook her head. 'I don't like whisky. I didn't have any but I also "conked out" as you put it.' She sent a glance to Tabby who confirmed it.

'Laura doesn't like it, that's true,' she said. Then, she let out a breath, as a neurone flared a memory, and put her hand to her mouth. 'Oh my. Though you did have one, Laura! I put it in your hot chocolate. Couldn't find the brandy.'

'But,' I said and inched my way towards the middle of the room, 'if Tabby hadn't dosed you accidentally, you, the only non-whisky drinker here, would have been the one to open the door upon the frightful sight. And you, like Graham, have a heart condition.'

Laura's hand went to her throat. 'But who would want to ...?'

'Yes, who would want to knock off Cullen too?' I said to

the room. 'Someone who was worried their cover story was about to be blown.' I moved to the table and perched on the edge, ready to spring off if necessary. 'Like Graham, why would anyone want Cullen dead?'

Nobody volunteered an answer.

So I told them. 'Because Cullen, I think, was on to the killer. He said he could get into the mind of one but I don't think that was what he did. I think he wanted to impress you, Chris. He was a great fan. I recall you advised him to "think, watch, observe. Ask questions. Communicate freely." Unfortunately for Cullen he did just that. Certainly, he began asking questions. A few too many in The Griffin. You see – when a group of us from Ratchette Hall walked into the pub on Wednesday afternoon for your workshop Chris, a man at the bar recognised one of our party. One of them commented, "You back again?" I saw Cullen talking to them later. Only today did it occur to me, that he might have been trying to find out who they recognised. Who was "back again". For none of you admitted to having been here before.'

'Apart from me,' said Laura.

I nodded. 'Apart from you. L.D. Taylor-Jacobs, author of *The Eden Tree*, in which a skilled young woman tires of her lover and poisons him, doing her best to make it look like a snake. That sound familiar to you?'

Jocelyn put her hand to her mouth and darted a look at Laura. 'Of course! It just didn't occur ...'

I continued. 'Part of me wondered if you had taken Cullen as a lover. Physically, after all, he was a rather fine specimen.'

Laura cringed. She was either a fantastic actress or I was barking up the wrong tree with that one. 'Several people here have admitted to reading that book,' she said.

'Nevertheless,' I went on, nearing the denouement. 'It seems now that is exactly what Cullen's murder was contrived to resemble. Interesting, don't you think?

'I don't have single ownership on that idea.' Laura's eyes blazed.

I left her to it and moved on. 'For a while I considered Imogen,' I said, aware that things were becoming clearer to me only now as I spoke. Still, who would spot a few white lies intended to draw the suspect out? And if I was right, who would care? 'You see, Imogen ...' I continued with a flourish to the ceiling and the bedroom where she had slept, '... Imogen had been one of our party that entered the pub together. But obviously the events of today have ruled her out. I'm not sure why she has been dispensed with like this. Perhaps she and Robin represent collateral damage. Perhaps they had also begun to suspect.'

'Suspect who?' Laura asked backing into a corner by the fireplace and leaning against the wall.

'Yes, Laura,' I said and took a step towards her. 'I hate to tell you, but I'm afraid that all of this is down to you—'

I couldn't finish my sentence, for a strange, low and fiendish growl was coming up from the direction of the sofa. Before you could say 'hip replacement', it was accompanied by a loud click and, one of the three women sitting there leapt to the mantelpiece and snatched the sword from its holder.

I had never seen Margot move so fast. It was crazy. She had always appeared so fragile. And yet here she was expertly wielding the medieval sword, and aiming it at Laura, who was edging herself away from the threat and pressing up against the wall.

Margot's eyes burnt blackly, like hot roiling tar, full of violent intent. 'Silly ickle girl,' she muttered through gritted teeth.

'Oh my god,' said Jocelyn. 'Margot's gone mad.'

But Margot heard the words and flipped her eyes over to the girl, relaxing ever so slightly and pulling back from the cowering author. 'Oh I've been mad for a long time now,' she said and laughed with a fierce bitterness that made Starla shudder and move away.

Not too mad, I thought, quite clever really: her limp had completely vanished. However, all evidence of calm intelligence was singularly absent. There was a looseness about the older woman which signalled some kind of depravity to me, a feeling of disregard and desperation.

I didn't know how old or how sharp that sword was, but it could undoubtedly inflict some amount of damage if it was forced into flesh. Margot might be in her seventies and petite, but like I said, there was a vigour about her now which, presently unleashed, could only lend force to whatever she did. Anger is an incredible energy and it was absolutely animating Margot.

Was anyone else going to intervene?

A quick glance told me that they were either too stunned or too confused to do anything at all.

I sighed inwardly, gave up on the idea of backup and took a step towards the sword-wielding aggressor. It was my fault after all – I had provoked the whole thing. 'Now listen Margot, I'm not sure how you managed to organise all the theatrics, I'm assuming you had an accomplice on the outside.' As I said that I realised how weird it sounded. 'But,' I went on regardless, 'you did what you set out to do – you gave Laura a good old scare.'

Margot's eyes flamed and she lifted the sword and rested its point on Laura's right breast. 'Didn't kill her though, did I? She's still here in front of me living and breathing, which is more than can be said for some.'

I took another step and held my hands up in classic surrender mode showing, as if there was any need to, that I was unarmed. 'Look, Margot, there's no point trying to get at Laura now. The police are outside. No doubt with your accomplice. You're surrounded,' I said, but my words really lacked conviction. I breathed in and put my shoulders back and made my voice deeper. 'Give it up Margot. Give me the sword. There's not a chance you're going to be able to get away now.'

The old girl rolled her eyes and spun round to me, dropping the sword to the floor, using it to lean on for a moment. 'Get away? You silly ickle girl. I don't want to get away. I want justice. I've been waiting years for this.'

I thought Laura might take the opportunity to hop out of harm's way but she didn't. Her eyes were opening wide, her mouth dropping down too. 'Oh my god,' she said. 'Silly ickle girl.' She copied the older woman's diction, running her tongue over the words, feeling them out, testing them. 'Silly ickle girl,' she said again, as Margot pivoted round to face her.

A light had come on in Laura's eyes. 'Silly ickle Billy!' she exclaimed. 'You!' she jabbed an index finger at Margot, eyes drawn wide. Her other hand went to her breast where the sword had been. 'You're Billy's mum.'

'*Was* Billy's mum,' Margot spat. With two hands she hauled the blade up and rested it on Laura's throat so that, with one deft move, it might easily cut into it. 'Till you killed him.'

My brain was whizzing through what I'd learned from Laura over the last week, till I picked up the conversation we'd had outside The Griffin that afternoon. 'The poet!' I said. 'The one who reminded you of Nicholas?'

'That's right,' said Laura and raised her hands in a surrendering gesture.

'He's nothing like that twat,' Margot spat.

I could see Nicholas's eyebrows lurching right up into his hairline. Yes, I hadn't expected her to use that description either. Even if it was quite accurate. Though now was not the time, etc. Right now, I needed to calm things down, distract Margot with sensitivity so that I could inch behind her and wrestle that sword out of harm's way. I couldn't work out why Laura wasn't doing it herself. Maybe she was frightened she'd injure herself or Margot would simply slice her.

'But Margot,' I said, recalling Monty's report. 'The coroner concluded it was suicide.' An appeal to good sense might work, if there was any vestige of such operating inside her head.

'Suicide?' she laughed, but again it was a cruel rancorous sound. 'Laura Taylor might as well have handed him the razor blades herself.'

'I did no such thing,' cried Laura.

'You killed him,' said Margot and moved the sword up to her neck. 'You broke his heart. You stopped it beating, just as I intended to stop yours. I'm sorry Graham got in the way. But that's what happens in life – innocents get in the way all the time. Just like my Billy did. He got in the way of your ambition and no one was going to stop Laura Taylor going places, were they?'

'But Billy,' Laura began, taking down a lungful of air. 'Look, I didn't realise he cared so much,' she said. 'I thought it was just a bit of a fling. And I was already engaged to Jacob.'

'Oh yes, the celebrated Jacob John Jacobs. Rich and handsome and happy to give you a leg up for a leg-over. Of course you'd get rid of Billy if someone like that came along. See Laura, I've watched your career with loathsome interest,' Margot said and nudged the sword forward so that Laura whimpered. 'Always watching and waiting, looking for a chance to make you pay for your crime. Then, when you fainted at Hay and announced the heart condition – anything for a bit of publicity eh? Well, it gave me an idea and I started to plan. When this course came up with you on it …'

A trickle of blood was running down Laura's neck. The

sword had pierced the flesh. I heard a murmur of shock pass over those by the door. Margot was going in for the kill.

'Very clever,' I said. 'Well done Margot, you have most certainly succeeded in scaring Laura and, I think, several more. But now, it's time to give it up. Think about the consequences of your own actions and face them.'

Her rattling laugh echoed against the wall again. 'Not yet. She hasn't paid enough. I want her to face fear. Real fear. God knows I have. The worst fear a mother can have made real: to lose a child by their own hand.'

The sword pressed into Laura's thin neck. If it reached the subcutaneous layers of tissue that would be bad. I really should be thinking about getting it off her now before any permanent damage was done. Perhaps I should try and 'relate' to the perp, as the Americans say. Yes, Margot was talking about loss. Well I knew that. I knew it now. I touched the soft spot inside my heart and felt it. Yes, it was there – authentic pain. I felt it again and winced. 'Oh Margot, I know pain, I know what it feels like to lose a mother.'

And yet this raw confession had no effect on my perp. I thought about adding, 'I lost a mother I never knew,' but the mere notion of those words surprised me with the ferocity of feeling they unleashed inside: a lump clogged my throat and I became keenly aware I might lose focus. I left it unsaid.

'Mothers are love,' I ventured instead. 'The loss is just as bad. My mother was killed,' I said hoping this unique revelation might at least surprise her.

But then Nicholas piped up, 'Mine too. Fucking awful.'

'Oh yes,' sighed Starla. 'Devastating. It's why I moved over here.'

Unfortunately, these confessions irked Margot even more.

'It's not the same!' she yelled. Her immaculate persona had vanished, now without make-up her face was sallow, coloured only by florid cheeks. Spittle edged her lips as she shouted, 'That's the natural order of things – losing a parent. The young must mourn the old. A child! Losing a child. It is the most devastating of misfortunes.'

I thought briefly of Celeste and the mystery man, who could be my father, and wondered if he had felt like he had lost me. Had he made any attempt to see me or find out if I had survived? No, I thought, don't go there now.

'No, no, no,' Margot echoed my inner monologue, her tone becoming more shrill.

I banished thoughts of that unknown figure and returned to the urgency of the situation. But, as I did, Margot paused, and, as if she were breaking off to explain a point like a teacher, she brought the sword down for a second and leant on it. 'No, indeed,' she tutted as she turned to Nicholas and Starla. 'You don't understand. You can't know. You're too young. It's different.'

With the blade out of Laura's vicinity I could see the opportunity to tackle Margot and looked meaningfully at Laura, trying to draw her attention. If she acted now, one quick and hard push would send the old girl tumbling.

But Laura was transfixed. I flapped a hand and only succeeded in attracting Margot, who clocked my signal to Laura and spun round to face her with such sprightliness and verve, I was taken aback. Her eyes blackened so that they became dark voids which fixed onto their prey once more. Brutal resolve stiffened her features.

'Billy was special!' she spat. 'He could have been someone. Someone better than you, with your stupid crime novels. Entertainment is all well and good but you might as well have been a minstrel for all the impact you've had on the world.' She heaved the sword up with both hands and rested it on Laura's other shoulder, beside her neck. I swallowed. My throat had gone dry.

'Billy was a deep thinker,' Margot went on. 'He had points to make. But he was sensitive, my poor darling. Delicate. Your callous words were the sword to his heart.' She took another shuffle closer, so that the point of the sword moved over onto the edge of Laura's collarbone.

I watched in increasing discomfort as the blade broke Laura's pale skin and a little bobble of scarlet appeared. The poor woman bleated.

A crackle of startled cries broke out from the residents behind me as a scarlet ribbon unfurled and curled down Laura's front.

'Your time's up,' Margot sneered. 'Kneel down,' she said, and for a moment I thought I heard not one voice but two. The other a deeper timbre, resonant and full of electrical reverb.

To my dismay, Laura complied. Her knees cracked as she bent onto them and held her head up.

Oh my god, that pose was ominous.

The scene was starting to look really worrying. Where were the friggin' police when you needed them?

'Now,' intoned Margot, 'is the time to repent of your sins.' The acoustics in the room had somehow changed. Her words were echoing and ricocheting around the room. Like they would in a church or a cave. 'Time to pay for taking my boy. A life for a life.'

Laura began to full-on sob.

Margot smiled and I heard a dark demonic howl begin to issue from her. It sounded too full and bassy to come from such a small frame but there was no one else laughing here. 'Poor dear William lost his head for a moment,' she crowed. 'So it's only right that you now lose yours.' And with that, she summoned her energy, arched her back and raised the sword to Laura's neck, measuring up for the strike.

I breathed out loudly. 'Come on Margot, put it down. This is ridiculous.'

'Oh, you don't think I'll do it, do you?' She sniggered and, oh my god, began to swing back the sword, gathering momentum to chop through Laura's slender neck. 'So funny,' she grinned, her voice high and staticky, 'how nobody thinks old ladies are any threat at all.'

'Oh I wouldn't say that,' said a voice to my side, and instantly the air was filled with a strange buzzing noise.

A wiry metal contraption leapt across the room and fastened onto Margot's back. The woman bolted upright immediately, dropping the sword from her hands.

Laura shrieked as it hit the floor and broke into two pieces.

Margot's body shuddered and jerked as if she were doing some crazy victory dance.

It was such a strange sight that it took me a couple of seconds to realise what was going on. But by then Tabby had tasered Margot to the ground.

CHAPTER TWENTY-ONE

The next few moments were filled with panicked activity. The noise, the instant neutralisation of the sword-wielding loon, and the wail that went up from Laura, all contrived to unloose the gathered spectators from their paralysis, and bodies flew about all over the day room with remarkable speed.

Nicholas went for Tabby who seemed to be enjoying her nephew's early Christmas present a little too much. He prised the stun gun off her and laid it on the carpet several feet away and out of Tabby's grasp.

I jumped over to Margot's prone and dazed form. Barbs from the gun were still stuck onto her black pyjamas so I turned her over and pulled them out. Jocelyn helped me roll her on her side and put her into recovery position. She seemed to be breathing fine but her eyes were still an inky black, as if her pupils had dilated to fill the sockets.

Starla had plucked a phone from her kimono pocket and was shouting into it requesting an ambulance, police and, for some unknown reason, a fire engine.

Devlin had raced across to Laura and was cradling her in his arms. 'It's over now Laurs,' he was saying. 'All over now.'

'Chris,' I called. 'How's her neck? Do we need to staunch the wound?'

Gently he tilted her head and checked it. 'Not deep, but I'll use my robe chord. I think she's in shock. Better hurry up with that ambulance.'

I instructed Sophia to get water and the first aid kit on the double.

'How did she do it?' said a voice from the sofa. Tabby had gone and sat back down on it, assuming her taser duties were now over.

'I'm not sure,' I said. 'But we'll find out.'

At which point in the festivities, Sam finally appeared in the doorway with a policeman sporting a familiar tidy beard, and a young man in cuffs. The latter was wearing a suspicious black tracksuit with a hoody. Rather weirdly, perched on top of that were a pair of sequinned reindeer antlers. They looked completely anomalous, the kind of frivolity you saw stupid people wear to stupid council Christmas parties.

The expressions on their faces suggested that in terms of abnormal scenarios none of them had been prepared for this slasher pyjama party gone bad.

The three paused by the entrance, whereupon Tidy Beard looked from Laura and Margot to me, then shook his head. 'Strewth,' he said and turned to Sam. 'Can't you two just stick to dogging?'

Luckily, he didn't wait for an answer and instead piped up to ask if an ambulance had been called, which Starla confirmed very promptly.

Tidy Beard's shoulders relaxed very slightly. I expect he was relieved he wasn't going to have to sift through this mess on his own.

Sam started to ask what (the hell) had happened, when the young man in cuffs began shouting, 'It was her, there on the floor.'

In the absence of a free pointing-finger, he executed a soft headbutt in Margot's direction. 'She paid me. She was the one. Said it was a prank. All of it. I just thought that would be good for the channel. Didn't know nothing about anyone getting done in.'

I looked over at him more closely. The antler pattern was weirdly familiar. Oh blimey I thought, he couldn't possibly be my goat-foot god. Shame began to heat my cheeks.

Sam, who was holding the boy by the scruff of his hoody, shook him. 'I found him tapping on the window of Laura's room,' he said. 'This, would you believe it, is Ben Christmas.'

'Eh?' I shook my head. 'No,' I said. 'Actually I don't. Ben's got red hair. I met him.'

The boy in the hoody laughed. 'Oh you're the one Stevie spoke to, are you? Up at the flat?'

I threw my mind back to the interview I'd conducted in the living quarters above The Griffin. 'He said he was Ben …' Actually, now I thought about it, he hadn't said his name at all. I had just assumed that he was Ben because he was a teenager and was in Carol's flat, chilling out and looking like he was at home.

'That was Stevie,' Real Ben said. 'I was out buying

batteries. I was well pissed with him when I found out though. Thought he might blow the whole thing.'

'Blow the whole thing?' I repeated wondering about a bomb.

'Yeah, he said he showed you his zoo staff ID.'

That's right. He had needed to prove his alibi. If I remembered rightly the card bore a picture of a tree and, oh dear, a paw-print. There was a possibility of a giraffe in there too. It hadn't seemed important at the time.

Nicholas, who had lost his regular sneer and was watching everything with languid regard, spoke up. 'Don't tell me – he had something to do with the missing snake.'

'That's right,' said Ben. 'Stevie borrowed it overnight and tipped off the radio. But,' he glanced at the policeman who was too busy eying up the taser on the floor and scratching his head, 'it never left the bleedin' zoo. He put it in an empty tank in the Reptile House. Mrs Lovelock said she didn't need it, after all.'

The police officer gave up trying to work out what had happened and went to check on Laura, who was the most noticeably damaged person in the room.

'So we never had a snake here at all,' Nicholas concluded.

Jocelyn looked up at him and said, 'I didn't think we did really.'

Then suddenly, on the floor, Margot started to convulse.

There was the sound of feet and more bustle in the hallway then Sam shouted, 'Quick! In here.'

In the blink of an eye the room was filled with green-clad paramedics, a couple more policemen and two very fit but slightly bewildered firemen.

Which was all good really because I was feeling dog tired.
Now was the time to hand over responsibility.
Just for a moment I closed my eyes.

CHAPTER TWENTY-TWO

Turns out it's not advisable to stay up all night, increase your heart rate and engage in stressful situations when you're recovering from a cocktail of atropine and aconite. Who'd have thought?

So I spent my second night in a row in Litchenfield Hospital. The nurse there luckily recognised me, which prevented my name being taken down as Margot Lovelock. Unfortunately, the moment I shut my eyes just for a fleeting second, I had passed out. Which meant, faced with two unconscious women at the hospital, when medical staff needed to sort out who was who, they allotted the sword-waving to the sturdier candidate.

Once the nurse had corrected that misidentification I was put on a ward and Margot was secured in a private room patrolled by her own policeman/minder till she came round again.

'Yes,' said Sergeant Scrub, while we waited in her Citroën in the car park of The Griffin. 'My wife is fond of the phrase, "What a tangled web we weave when first we practise to deceive." I think it applies perfectly well to this particular situation.' Though, it might have applied just as purposefully to most of the cases we'd chalked up so far. 'My wife,' she said as an aside, 'is Edgar's sister.'

I recognised the name then placed it underneath a mental snap-shot of the Professor Plum vicar from St Saviour's. 'Ah right,' I said.

'Well,' said Sam. 'Your wife's quite right. I'd have never worked it out myself. It's a good job that Rosie here,' he leant over and tapped my knee, 'has an expert eye regarding Buttery Nipples.'

Sergeant Scrub nodded. 'I'd never heard of them before,' she said. 'But me and Bobby had a go down the social club last night and, you're right, Rosie – they won't fell you. Bit of a buzz. Very tasty mind. I'll be getting the ingredients in for Christmas.'

I nodded with approval. 'Exactly. I knew that whisky shouldn't have knocked me out like it did. That's why I thought Monty should have a look. Dozing off after one shot is uncharacteristic behaviour.'

Sam grinned. 'Not just a pretty face.'

'Never,' I said, and felt sparks kindle in my abdomen. To avoid displaying my pleasure overtly I took my eyes off him and leaned towards Scrub. My hair fell forward over my cheeks. 'So, Sue, are we correct in assuming Margot hired Stevie and Ben to dress up as the knights and make those noises in the garden?'

Scrub undid her safety belt and hefted herself round in the driving seat to face me. 'That's what they've said. Ben did most of it as Stevie had to work. But they're both jointly responsible. According to them, they thought it would present "wicked content" for their YouTube channel and attract more "subscribers". They filmed it, of course, so we've got plenty of evidence.'

'Interesting,' said Sam and also edged forwards. He was sitting directly behind Scrub and aimed his words at her ear. 'So the whole caper was Margot's idea? Hatched when they met at St Saviour's?'

Scrub tried to turn even further round to Sam but got her knee stuck between the gear stick and the handbrake so gave up and looked at me. 'Yep,' she said. 'Well crafty. She changed her instructions halfway through the week when she learned about the devil legends and this Cernunnos bloke you've been talking about. Got Ben and Stevie to ditch the knight costumes in favour of black, and reindeer horns.'

Sam darted a glance at me. I knew what he was thinking – this explained my 'gods theory'.

I still hadn't come to a definite conclusion about that. I might well have been hallucinating but I did feel there was something in it. Call it intuition or a hunch.

'It's bizarre, isn't it?' I said. 'That we actually influenced the case? Without even realising what we were doing.'

'Indeed,' said Sam. 'We must take note and in future be sure to exercise more caution.'

'Well.' Scrub shrugged. 'I wouldn't dwell on it too much. Margot Lovelock was out for revenge. She was going to use whatever she could get her hands on, and she wasn't going to let anything get in her way. Nor anyone. Not Graham

Peacock, Cullen Sutcliffe. Not Imogen Green nor Robin Savage.'

Sam sighed and shook his head.

Yep, it was quite a wreck Margot had left in her wake.

Although Robin was still in a coma, Imogen had regained consciousness and confirmed that it was indeed Mrs Lovelock who had led them into the woods in search of flowers to make a bouquet for the house, ostensibly 'to cheer everyone up'.

Making excuses for an inability to bend, due to her much-promoted (non) gammy leg she had instructed Imogen and Robin to help her with the beautiful purple-berried stems, and what Imogen described as the 'pretty mauve poppies' that she also noted seemed to be growing in an odd position – in the middle of the path. Sam and I agreed the 'pretty poppies' sounded like wolfsbane, one of the UK's most deadly plants. How it had come to be in full bloom and in the middle of a pathway was something I expected Scrub would unravel at some point.

But Imogen had more news to tell: poor Robin had fallen headfirst into the clump of flowers. Had Margot pushed him? Imogen wasn't sure. She hadn't seen. Robin had been by her side and Margot behind her, so maybe. And the motive for that, Imogen was asked? She herself had spoken to Robin about the men at the bar of The Griffin and their comment about someone being back again. Cullen overheard the conversation and informed them he also had some interesting news on that matter. He never actually told them. But the police had interviewed Jack Reynolds, who was one of the regulars. A farmer with a barn conversion on Airbnb, which he had rented to Margot in the summer. This was what Cullen was going to share, but somehow Margot must have got a whiff of it and put a stop to that.

'And Cullen, for clarity …' said Sam, knocking me out of my thought cycle, '… he was definitely poisoned?'

'Oh yes.' Scrub nodded from the front seat. 'The odds are Margot had intended to use it on Laura, if she hadn't popped her clogs after the knight-scaring episode. However, she perceived Mr Sutcliffe to represent more of an immediate problem. The lad had a high level of midazolam in his blood. It's a common medication used for anaesthesia, sedation. Despite his bulk, the dose could have killed him on its own. But Mrs Lovelock apparently was taking no chances: she added in some potassium cyanide for good measure.'

'Good gracious!' said Sam. 'Where did she get that from?'

But I got there first. 'Her husband is or was a pharmacist.' I looked at Scrub. Monty had mentioned it in his report.

The Sergeant shook her head. 'He is, but I'm not sure she could have got it from him either. There are strict rules about these sorts of things today. It's possible that she might have acquired it from the Dark Web. Or someone with access to it.'

'Stevie and Ben Christmas?' I asked but Scrub made a 'pfft' noise with her mouth.

'Hardly,' she said. 'The words "piss-up" and "brewery" have been used to describe their entrepreneurial ventures.' We heard the crackle of gravel and Scrub looked towards the corner of the building. 'Or more appropriately, a piss-up in a pub.'

I followed her gaze and saw a sleek black Mercedes pull into the car park. A figure in a slate-grey suit was at the wheel.

'That your man?' asked Scrub.

The driver hopped out, opened the rear door and Monty emerged from the car with more grace than I could ever muster. He stretched and wriggled his shoulders then grinned at Scrub's rather bashed-up Citroën.

'It surely is,' said Sam and clapped his hands. 'Excellent! I can't wait.'

The beer cellar of The Griffin was exactly what you'd imagine: low-ceilinged and grubby, full of pipes and fridges making rattling sounds and lots and lots of piled up barrels and crates in different shapes and sizes. Sam and Monty had to stoop as we all trooped into the main part where the beer barrels were kept. I breathed in the smell of stale beer and damp.

There were eight of us down here: myself, Sam, Sergeant Scrub, Monty and two of his young cronies in fantastically unobtrusive white shirts and ties with uniform 'nondescript' blond haircuts. They were the same height too, so the only noticeable differentiation were the suits which were contrasting shades of grey. Detective Bobby Brown arrived minutes after Monty and emerged from his car hand-cuffed to the young man who had appeared in the hoody on that Saturday night at Ratchette Hall.

He had been positively identified as Carole's son, Ben Christmas.

'So,' said Scrub, asserting herself over the other men present. 'First things first. Where's the body from the tomb and the effigy?'

Ben yanked his cuffed hand (and Bobby Brown's). 'Over

here,' he said trailing his custodian. 'The wooden knight thing's propped against the wall. It's got the *Star Wars* duvet cover over it.' He turned to Bobby and said, 'For disguise.'

'And has it got a missing finger?' Bobby asked. He spoke very carefully, pronouncing each consonant.

'Sort of,' said Ben. 'We chipped it off like she said. But we didn't know which hand she wanted so we did both. Didn't give them to her. She must have come up with her own stone finger. We didn't know that it was wood till we moved it. It looked stone to me. But she must have thought it was and got a stone finger from somewhere else. She's the one what put it in Mr Peacock's hand after he'd carked it. Then the next day, she phoned us up and we told her how we done both hands. And she goes mad, says it's not the story and shouts we got to "hide the darn thing". But we didn't know if she meant the statue what's on top or the body what's underneath in the tomb. So we took the lot.'

'But how?' asked Monty then explained. 'It's not as heavy as marble but it's still got some weight.'

'Same as barrels,' Ben shrugged. 'We used the beer trolley. Was a bit hard with the height, but, well, you'll see.'

Bobby looked down at Ben and stared. 'So where's the body from the coffin?' he demanded.

Ben pointed with his free hand to the furthest wall. 'In the Unlikely freezer.'

'Unlikely?' Monty asked.

'All the stuff that don't get used that often. Most of the food is stored upstairs with the fresh stuff in the kitchen or the store out back. This has got tripe and tongue, faggots, some eels and that. You know – old stuff. No one ever comes down to it.' He began to weave between the towering barrels and then dodged round a wall into a passage out of sight.

Everyone made to follow, Sam and I included, but Scrub shook her head and said, 'You two wait here.'

Then the rest of them went off to view the 'Unlikely' freezer, leaving Sam and me on our tod.

He was fidgeting, hopping about on one foot then the other. 'Excited?' he said.

I shrugged. 'Well, it will be interesting to see what it's like.'

'I can hardly contain myself.' He grinned. 'Such a strange twist to come out of it all. An actual real secret tomb.'

'So they say,' I said, feeling more cautious. 'We'll see. Ben Christmas is known for pulling pranks. I wouldn't be surprised if this is another one.'

'But what's he got to gain by that?' Sam asked, hope lighting his eyes. I couldn't see them properly now, but I was guessing that if I got closer to him, they'd be whirring with amber.

'Mmm, yes you're right,' I said. 'He'd lose the goodwill of the constabulary.'

'Indeed,' Sam agreed. 'But it does seem plausible, don't you think? There are other subterranean tombs around the church. It would explain how Ben and Stevie managed to get the body and effigy out of the church with no one seeing them …'

There was a loud sniff and the sound of footsteps on the flagstones and Scrub's gang returned to barrel central.

'You couldn't make it up,' she said, shaking her head. 'He's only gone and hid the body in his mum's second freezer. It's down there in all that offal, with some frozen peas and carrots.' She shook her head. 'I tell you one thing – I'm crossing this one off my pub grub Top Ten.'

Monty followed close behind. I couldn't hear everything that he was saying but it sounded like he was giving brusque instructions to one of the suits. As he got closer I heard the words 'archaeologist', 'museum' and 'Procedure Four'. Then the dark grey suit, who had been on the receiving end, nodded silently and slipped away up the passageway whence we had come.

Monty caught my eye and grimaced. 'I doubt our good lady Christmas will be particularly happy, but we'll have to secure the premises for a while.'

'Don't worry,' said Scrub. 'She's a proper ray of sunshine. Make sure you tell her in person. Now,' she said and turned to Ben. 'Let's see this so-called tunnel. You say you found the entrance last year?'

Ben grunted an affirmation and shuffled round, causing Sam and me to stand aside and let him through. Once past, he ducked round a stack of barrels, with PC Brown in tow, then stuck his head out indicating we should follow him. 'Took us ages to get down to the other side, but we done it.'

When we caught up with him we found, stacked against the furthest cellar wall, more crates of varying colours and brands, full of bottles in different sizes.

Ben jerked his head at them. 'Mum always reckons she's going to recycle but she never does. Some of them are well old. Me and Stevie were looking for some to make a bottle bomb ...' he stopped and gulped at Scrub and PC Brown and hastily broke off, 'Not like that kind of bomb. It don't matter. Point is, when we were going through these, we found the door. It's behind this,' he said and pointed to the nearest stack of crates. Monty's remaining man, Sam and Scrub collectively moved them out of the way. As they did, the outline of a stubby wooden door emerged. You'd be forgiven for missing it, as it had been painted over several times and now almost completely melted into the wall. The only signs of its shape were the dislodged paint chips and flakes, where Ben and Stevie had hacked.

Ben pulled at the wooden knob and we saw the door lurch open. 'It was bricked up here. But we knocked them in.'

'Where are the bricks now?' asked Monty, then turned to Sam. 'Might be useful for dating.'

'Some round there,' he said indicating to the crates. 'Some in here.' He tried to point, but simply yanked PC Brown's hand about a bit. 'Oh, can I have these off?' he whined and pointed to the handcuffs. Scrub nodded and Bobby Brown released him.

'And can I use a phone?' Ben asked. 'For the torch? It's all right, there's no signal down here.'

Scrub grunted again and nodded to Officer Brown who handed Ben's mobile over. The rest of us also decided illumination might be a good idea so got our own phones out and turned the torches on.

'I'll go in first,' said Bobby and disappeared through the doorway.

'There's a bit of a difference in the floor level,' Ben called.

We heard a 'hoof' and then a request for instructions to the light source. Ben told him to hang on then vanished through the entrance too.

A dull light came on inside. Through the tiny doorway we could see a mud-brown, interior. It appeared to be glistening.

PC Brown shouted 'clear' and the rest of us, intrigued, began to squeeze through the opening.

Behind the wall another cellar opened up. Its floor was about three feet lower than the one we were in so we had to jump down from the doorway. And this one was from another age. Dark and round with not much head height, none of us could stand up. The ground was made of dirt and uneven.

Nor was it as large as the one we had been in. Maybe only five feet by six, the size of a small box room. And with seven of us in there it was all very intimate.

Ben waited for us to straighten up and adjust to our surroundings then said, 'We scooped out the mud because we could see the top of this.' He moved some light cardboard boxes to one side to reveal an arched entry giving on to a dark, yawning passage. 'There had always been rumours of tunnels in the pub but we had it in our heads that it was from the fireplaces. That's where all the oldies said it was. But when we come and saw this, we knew it was the one what all the stories was about.'

Dull illumination was provided by a string of battery-operated fairy lights in the shape of butterflies, which was really at odds with the antiquity of the place. Now I recalled

– that's what Stevie had been playing with when I found him upstairs at The Griffin.

Ben caught me looking and said, 'We couldn't fink of how to light it. We didn't want to run electricity in or someone might have sussed it. Anyway,' he said and turned round to face the other direction. 'Here's where the tunnel begins. It was jammed just there but we got all the stone and rubble out and knocked through. Looked like someone had blocked the passageway on purpose. They didn't want no one going in.'

'How do you know?' asked Monty.

'There was writing on some of the stones and some drawings. Stars, and pentagrams, like the witches, old stuff.'

Sam gasped audibly. 'Well I never. Where are these stones now?'

'Oh sorry,' said Ben. 'We smuggled them out then took them down the tip.'

Sam's face dropped but he didn't say anything.

'Sorry,' Ben said again, 'You know. My mum – if she found out.'

Nuff said, I thought.

Monty instructed 'Note that,' to light-grey-suited man.

Then Ben aimed his phone into the void and he and Bobby entered the darkness.

I had to admit that I was feeling a little claustrophobic. But at the same time curiosity was doing a good job of overpowering fluttering fears and reservations.

Sam entered the tunnel, which was very narrow and perhaps only five feet high, requiring we all bent our heads.

It sloped downwards. The floor glistened and flickered. There was damp there. You could smell it in the earthy atmosphere too.

Stapled to old wooden beams overhead, strings of twinkling fairy lights guided us down deeper into the earth. We're going to Never-Never Land I thought.

Artificial light from mobile phones cast an irregular pale blue glow as we passed tiny stones and gems pressed into the walls. Other sections were just plain earth, more fabricated from stone slabs.

So strange, I thought as we trod on.

PC Brown shuffled up ahead and presently another light source was turned on.

I heard Monty cry, 'Good bloody grief.'

As if underlying the drama, his words echoed.

It was extremely unusual for him to swear, but when I came out of the tunnel into the new chamber I could see exactly why he had. For we had emerged into an underground cave, possibly about fifteen feet high, and wider, much wider than the tunnel, maybe twenty-five feet across. I couldn't really tell, the light wasn't strong enough. The ceiling curved and fractured. Great stalactites were suspended from it. Liquid, maybe water, seeped slowly off them, creating a soundscape of tricklings and drips.

Ben and Stevie had tried to make the place safer by sticking iron poles up in various places.

'Scaffolding,' said Ben. 'Nicked it from some place on the Essex Road.'

I thought Scrub might say something, but she too was

completely mesmerised by this circular opening, this subterranean cave.

'Amazing,' said Sam. 'Are those tombs?' He pointed to two stone rectangles behind us.

'Yeah,' said Ben and shrugged. 'They got bones in too. There's another one over there,' he said and pointed into the dimness, 'and one behind the altar.'

'Altar?' snapped Monty and looked over.

'There,' said Ben and directed the beam on his phone a couple of metres to my right where I saw a larger slab of stone.

'That's what we call it,' said Ben, again. 'It looks like an altar don't it? And it's got symbols on. Like those on the stones we chucked.'

'Yes it does,' I said walking slowly towards it. 'Sam, this is like what I saw in my dream. You know,' I said, hearing my voice crack, 'with the gods.'

I thought he was going to come over and stare at it with me. But he didn't. For Ben was saying, 'We found some clothes there. Old ones. Boots. Like army clothes. A duvet too. But they've gone now.'

'Gone?' Monty's clipped tones pierced the thinning air. 'You mean someone else was here?'

Ben shrugged. 'Dunno. Stevie said it wasn't him what took them. But he lies a lot. Probably put them up on eBay. Vintage stuff's worth a bob or two, innit.'

'Note that,' Monty instructed his minion. 'Speak to Stevie to confirm. Get a description of the clothes.'

'Anyway – there's two tunnels here.' Ben's voice hit the

walls and came back again. 'That one down there, we think comes out in Bell Hill Wood.'

Baal Hill Wood, I thought. An underground temple. Carole had mentioned there was a legend …

'We didn't get far into it.' Ben's voice dropped out as if he'd turned round. 'But this one goes up to the church.'

I could hear shoes shuffling off to one side and Ben saying, 'Yeah – St Saviour's. Comes out underneath the griffin. The one on the end of the pew. That's what marks it. Not X marks the spot, but the wooden griffin.'

Sam tutted. 'Of course it does. It was very draughty there, now I recall.'

But I didn't answer. I wasn't following them. I was too transfixed by the slab of stone. The carvings roughly hewn into it resembled a spiral and a crescent moon. And as I peered at them, my mind cast back to the strange vision I had experienced under the influence of aconite, the man sitting on an altar very much like this, whispering in my ear. Dorcus in the wood.

I had seen this place in my dream, hadn't I? Or did I just think that now, because certain elements were similar? But there had been the altar and a man. And the man had dropped words into my ear. Fractured words, like a riddle. Something like a brain-teaser, a puzzle.

In my head I caught sight of the antlered man turning his red eyes on me just over there on the bank. I could hear the water in the brook.

'Come out of the underworld. Take my hand.'

And then I was back in the dream with the dripping noise

and his words and trickle of water and the darkness, Dorcus's face flashing, the fairy lights flickering and the—

'Rosie!' said Sam and shook me. I opened my eyes and realised we were upstairs in the snug at The Griffin. 'Are you all right?' his voice had large quantities of concern woven into its texture. 'You haven't said a word since we came up from the caves. Though it's quite understandable. Totally amazing wasn't it?'

I blinked and focused on my surroundings – the fireplace, the window. 'Eh? How did I get up here?' I said. I was sitting at a table next to Sam, with Monty and the dark-suited minion.

Scrub, Ben and Bobby Brown had disappeared.

'Oh dear.' Monty tapped the table with a pen. 'It's not unlikely that you may experience flashbacks from time to time. It does happen to some people. I'd like Harry here to come and take some notes from you once all this has settled down. Such poisonings are not common these days.'

I was still frowning, trying to work out how I had lost that time.

Monty carried on and turned to Sam. 'So, do we believe Mr Christmas's story about the tunnel opening in St Saviour's?'

'What did he say?' I asked, having missed that particular section of the tunnel system. Or at least having no memory of it.

Monty grimaced. Such inelegant expressions rarely passed over his face. But he kept his eyes light. 'When he and Stephen followed the tunnel up, it came out underneath the raised pews. Took them quite a while to get the lid open but when they crawled through it they found Margot Lovelock watching them. What was it he said, Harry?'

Grey Suit fished out a notebook and read. '"The light was blinding", sir.'

'Go on,' said Monty.

'"There was that old woman there. She said, 'My god you nearly scared me to death, you rascals. Come out of the underworld. Take my hand.'"'

I'd heard that too. The echoes and acoustics must have played havoc with my ears. And there was me thinking it a message from above.

'That's right,' said Monty. 'Turns out, our villain had come down to do a reccy before the course. And presumably commenced her plotting,' he finished.

'Margot promised not to tell anyone what the boys had discovered as long as they helped her,' said Sam. 'She told them they were perfect for something she had in mind: "a bit of a joke". She didn't know about their YouTube channel of course. Didn't realise it was exactly the right line to take.'

'Of course,' Monty continued, 'Ben denies any involvement with the various poisonings. Though he does admit to "pranking" Graham Peacock, which Stevie denies. Ben said he dressed up as a knight. But he thought he had just scared him, as required, then ran away. Said he didn't see Peacock fall. Though we've only got his word for that. We'll see what your friend, Sergeant Scrub makes of their plea.'

'Mmm,' I said. 'That will be interesting I suppose. She's a tough cookie.'

'Aren't we all,' said Monty, with a wink right at me. He could look very saucy when he wanted to. 'Right, Harry,' he said, turning to Grey Suit. 'Get the boys from Department Eight down on the trot and put this place on lockdown. Lots of potentials in the offing, I suspect,' he added. I could tell from Sam's face he had no idea what Monty was on about either.

The agent fixed his flinty dazzlers on us. 'I'm assured I can expect confidentiality from my dear colleagues at the Witch Museum?'

'About what?' I said, and gave him a wink.

But Sam hadn't got my joke. 'Rosie,' he said softly. 'There are protocols for this kind of thing. Aspects need to be researched thoroughly before any of it gets leaked to the public.'

'If it ever does,' added Monty. 'There's quite a few lengthy procedures we must go through before anything that drastic occurs.'

'Not to mention Health and Safety,' I said quite seriously. 'That scaffolding ...'

'Well, excellent,' said Monty, wrapping up the conversation. 'Thank you for your efforts with this one. Aunt Tabby and myself are extremely grateful.'

'Which reminds me,' I said. 'Did you get anywhere with those requests of mine? Not the whisky one.'

Monty blinked. His eyes hardened for a moment then he smiled. 'Yes,' he said. 'I succeeded with one of your, perhaps, foolhardy requirements.'

'Then you absolutely have my discretion regarding the tunnels,' I said. 'What time and when?'

'Tomorrow,' he said. 'Your appointment's at three.'

CHAPTER TWENTY-THREE

Araminta de Vere was pretty surprised to see me sitting at the dirty grey table in the visiting room, rather than Agent Walker. But at least she didn't turn round and demand to be returned to her cell.

Denied a regular appointment at the hairdressers, her hair had lost some of its colour and the squat Farrah-Fawcett style had been cut short and blunt so she'd now got more of a Susan-Boyle-prior-to-X-Factor look going on.

She settled her big horsey behind onto the bolted-down chair and grunted. 'I suppose you've come to find out if I'm sorry. To see me weep and wring my hands and get down on my knees and plead? Well, I'm afraid you've wasted your time. That's not Araminta de Vere's style,' she said and thumbed her grey sweatshirt.

I'd forgotten how she referred to herself in the third person. And how crazy she was. My hopes of getting any coherent information started to fade.

'No, actually,' I said with a sigh. 'I've already assumed you have no regrets. I bet you'd do the same again if you had to. Family reputation and all that malarkey.'

I thought she'd pick me up on my slang but she didn't. Prison life was making her less spiky.

'Oh right,' she said, and pulled down her sweatshirt and crossed her arms. 'What do you want then?'

'I want to know what happened when you chased Celeste that night. I want to know who the man was.'

'Right,' she said. 'I did wonder if you'd remember that part.' She tossed her Susan Boyle back and said to herself, 'Makes no odds I hazard. Araminta can tell. But cooperation will be looked upon favourably, one hopes.'

Oh blimey. This one hoped she hadn't actually lost the plot altogether.

'All right then,' she said and bared her teeth. 'What do you want to know?'

I thought about it and said, truthfully, 'Anything you can remember.'

'Will you tell your lawyer about me?' Her eyes narrowed, foxily.

'Oh yes,' I replied, not that I had a lawyer. But if I ever did, for whatever reason I engaged them, I would tell them that Araminta de Vere was a crazy old bat.

'Araminta, deal-broker,' she said, and her wonky smile widened. 'Well, you know what? I'd seen them together earlier in the week. Celeste and he. Outside the museum. Though it had been closed that day. I knew your grandfather was away.' She sent me a forehead full of frowns. 'No doubt on one of his barmy investigations, so Celeste had obviously taken the opportunity to get her fancy man in. Though that's not what she called him, when I stopped to say hello.'

'No?' I said feeling my heart beat a little faster.

'Called him her "partner". Ridiculous term, I always thought. Like it was a business enterprise.' She peered down her nose, waiting to deliver the motherload. 'He was pushing you in your pram.'

The image blew across my brain: Celeste laughing, long dark hair like Ethel-Rose, pink lips, her hand crooked through that of this man, who for some reason I had dressed in a gaberdine suit like the one I had found hanging in Septimus's wardrobe. In his hands the man was gripping the handle of a big old-fashioned pram with a pretty fabric hood. And he was smiling. I could have got lost in the picture but I didn't have long and needed to really stay on task. 'Did Celeste give him a name?'

Araminta paused, as if surprised by the question. Then she said, 'It was foreign. And when he greeted me he was exceptionally polite. He had an accent. Possibly French.'

Wow, I thought, but pushed on. 'And what was his name?'

I watched her squint her eyes and reach back into the past. 'It was possible it began with an "A",' she said and unfolded her arms so she could tap the side of her Boyle. 'Anton?' She looked up at the ceiling. 'Or Andre? Antoine? Something like that.'

I held my breath. 'Surname?'

Araminta's eyes snapped back to me. 'Oh she wouldn't have said that, oh no. Not one for formalities was your mother.'

It felt strange hearing her say those words: your mother. It had back in the summer when Araminta had been bashing my head on the floor. It did now, as she sat opposite me, an inmate.

'And what was he like?' I mused out loud, omitting the unvoiced 'my father', if that indeed was what he was. Not just some passing boyfriend. Or 'partner'.

For some reason this irritated her. 'Like?' she said, pushing her lips together like a stewed prune. 'Like? I don't know.' She shook her head in short sharp jabs. 'Can't recall,' she said flatly.

'Oh come on, Araminta,' I said in exasperation. 'You must remember. That day – it changed everything. It was memorable.'

'I suppose so.' She paused. I was surprised by her cooperation. 'Well, he was tall. And well-dressed. Dark hair. Quite fastidious I thought. Not the type you might think Celeste would go for, she had always had a taste for a wilder kind of man.'

'What colour eyes?' I asked, flashing my own at her to see if they prompted any memories.

'Oh I don't know. It was such a long time ago.'

'Okay,' I said. 'Well go on. What happened?'

'I didn't see them for long. Maybe a minute or two. But I had the impression they really weren't happy about seeing me.'

Completely understandable. I mean, who would be? I thought, then quashed it. I needed to keep her on side. 'So then later? Before the accident?'

She screwed her face up and sniffed. 'I think I told you about that in summer.'

'Tell me again,' I said. My voice sounded hard. But the command in it produced compliance.

'All right,' said Araminta. 'Well, you know, that afternoon, when I found out from padre what had gone on with the girl, Celeste, and he'd told me about the whole sordid story, well obviously, I was shocked, mortified really, you see. And when I realised he'd let the girl go ... Well, you can imagine, can't you, we couldn't have that. All our dirty linen ready to be aired by that, that,' she caught sight of my face and moderated her tone. 'That woman,' she said with more prudence than I would have imagined her capable of.

'So,' I kept the anger out of my voice and nudged her on. 'You got into the car to find her and went down to the Witch Museum?'

'That bloody place,' she said, lips stiffening. 'If only it had never been built at all!'

I was careful not to betray any more feeling so repeated. 'Did you get to the museum?'

'Not quite,' she said. 'As I was approaching, Celeste's car shot out of the drive. He was in the passenger seat. She was going very fast. I hung back, at first, then followed them down Hobleythick Lane. It was a terrible night. Oh, the weather was awful. One of the trees had already come down in the village near the vicarage. The wind was up and there were leaves flying all over the place.'

I nodded. Same as Dad had described.

Araminta sucked her teeth for a moment. 'It didn't take me long to see they were heading for Chelmsford. The new road hadn't been built then, and they were bombing down towards the brook. I guessed they were going to go into the police station to tell them what had happened. Couldn't let that happen, could I?'

Just to egg her on I shook my head. 'I understand.' Though it pained me.

'Now it might come as some surprise to you, but I did not have murder on my mind. I thought I would buy Celeste. Everyone has their price, as they say. Some more than others.'

Buy my mother indeed! Like she was something that could be owned. Like her silence was buyable! My lips pursed.

'As they were turning the bend on Piskey Lane, I put my foot down and accelerated. Booted them right up the bottom,' she said and laughed.

I clenched my teeth determined not to react, but wait and listen and learn.

'Only had to do it once,' she continued. 'That old banger wasn't much cop and went spinning round and round across the road. When it started careering over the grass, down towards the brook, I parked my own and got out. Started running towards it because I thought it might fall straight in. But it hit a tree. There was a tremendous bang and that's what stopped it. Smoke started coming out of the bonnet. I didn't know what to do. I just stood there. Then I heard you crying.' She nodded at me and for a moment her face looked less nutty than before. It reminded me she was a mother too. 'When I reached the car, I saw you in there. Still strapped in. You were all right. But both Celeste and the man were out for the count. And there was …' she paused, '… there was blood on the windscreen.'

'Did you check to see if they were alive?' I asked but she shook her head.

'Did think about it, but then I realised this might be a gift from God. A good way to solve the problem.'

My stomach turned over. How on earth could she think that divine intervention? She was deluded. Completely mad. Prison was where she belonged. For as long as possible.

'And I thought the car might blow up,' she went on oblivious to my dark machinations. 'So I got you out and then got Araminta out of there as soon as I could. Dropped you off, like I said, at the Witch Museum.'

I leant forwards on my elbows and rubbed my head. 'And that's it?' I wasn't sure I could cope with any more.

'And that's it.' She re-folded her arms.

'Not much to go on,' I said out loud and regretted it, for as I looked into her face I saw she knew instantly what my plan was.

'Oh no, no,' she said and wagged a finger at me. 'Not now. Not after all these years. You can't possibly think of finding him.'

'Might be my father,' I said and shrugged.

'You shouldn't do that,' she said with a sincerity that completely took me off my guard.

Why would she warn me off? I wondered. After all, like she'd said, she had nothing to lose. 'Why not?' I regarded her with close attention.

'Because your mother drowned in the brook,' she said simply.

'I know,' I returned.

'There was no one else there,' she said. 'After I left, there was only him.'

'What?' I said, as her meaning dawned. 'You think he might have pushed her in?'

She shrugged. 'He wasn't there when they found her, was he?'

CHAPTER TWENTY-FOUR

'Well?' said Sam when I got back to the museum. He had a nervous energy circling his body and was fidgeting even more than he had in The Griffin's beer cellar. 'How did it go?'

He came over and helped my coat off and then gave me a hug.

I wasn't really expecting it and I think if I hadn't been so mentally exhausted I might have given in to a blush. But it just wasn't in me. I hugged him back very briefly and then looked around for something to lean on. Sam didn't look like he was going anywhere.

I was exceedingly pleased the museum was closed, and went and propped myself against the ticket office ledge. 'It was informative and a bit of an ordeal. She's given me some info but I still need to see Big Ig.'

Sam picked up my bag. He had my jacket folded over his arm. 'Monty will keep his promise. You'll see him. You just have to be patient. Really. I know it's not your forte but try to keep tight.'

'I just want to know everything now,' I said. There was a bit of a pronounced pout in there.

'And you can,' Sam said and offered me his hand. 'But remember, now and then, what you're really looking for is often right under your nose. You just don't see it sometimes.'

I looked at him, standing there with his arm stretched out to me and I took it.

'Come on,' he said and led me into the darkness of the museum.

I wasn't sure where this was going, or what we were doing or where we were going to end up but I was so tired I gave up thinking and just went with the flow, past the torture instruments, the folklore, the poppets and the old hedgewitch.

I stopped at the foot of the stairs to our quarters – they seemed a long way up. But Sam tightened his grip on my hand and pulled me. He was strong, and I felt some of his strength pass into my body. Then with each step I took, a warmth began to build. Inside me my spirits were rising.

I was coming home.

I was back.

When Sam opened the door to the living room, I blinked hard: the place was full of light. A deeply autumnal amber coloured the room, flooding in through the west-facing windows.

And I stepped into it.

Outside, the sun was setting. The evergreen trees that bordered our museum dipped and bobbed, basking in the mellow glow, like it was some vast and dark emerald sea.

Sam led me into the middle of the room so I could feel the subtle warmth of the sun on my face, and shining on my hair.

'I retrieved it from amongst the jumble,' he said. Then he walked me over to the fire and sat me on the comfy chair. 'I hope you don't mind. It was in the box in your room. The notebook,' he said. 'I think it's time, don't you?'

Then he pointed to it, on the coffee table next to a glass of poured wine. As I stared, a slim shard of sunshine fell upon it, illuminating the mustard cover so that for a moment I had the sense the book itself was glittering.

'Your birthday is September twenty-first, isn't it?' Sam asked.

I nodded and reached for the slight and floppy paperback.

'Because this looks like Celeste's handwriting to me,' he said and with that, retreated quietly closing the door.

And so I took it onto my lap and opened the first page.

'*15th of December 1982*' the entry began.

AUTHOR'S NOTE

Astute Essexians may have deduced that my Damebury is very similar to Danbury, a small village on a hill three hundred and sixty-seven feet high. It was in the thirteenth-century church sited there, St John the Baptist, that a knight's tomb was indeed discovered. Another was discovered later. According to *The Gentleman Magazine* of 1779, that occupant was said to be without any signs of decay, pickled in a solution that, yep, tasted like ketchup. Those who are interested in finding out more about this most fascinating episode can find the article online.

The new discoveries have (sadly perhaps) come straight out of my imagination. However there have been stories of ghosts and secret tunnels leading from The Griffin to the church circulating for decades, though none to this day have been found. I should also add here that the cellars and their contents are products of my fancy. Though The Griffin itself is indeed a delightful pub with an excellent menu.

E. Nesbit's story helped fire my imagination and if you would like to read it, this too can also be found with a quick google. It is entitled *Man-Sized in Marble* and I would recommend it to those who like their stories full of suspense and superstition. As Tabby Walker attests, 'It's a damn good read.'

ACKNOWLEDGEMENTS

It was Martin Frampton, the headmaster of North Street Juniors, who first told me, many years ago, about the Pickled Knights of Danbury, so it is he who must be first thanked. Without that playground chat this book would never have happened and I'm very grateful to him for it – and also for educating my son!

Thanks must go, as always to Jenny Parrott, my editor, who is simply fantastic and a great support in all my 'strange' endeavours. Margot Weale, is nothing like Margot Lovelock. A more hard-working and lovely publicist, I swear, could not be found. Same goes for Thanhmai Bui-Van, my sales manager, who is irrepressible, full of good nature and energy. My gratitude also goes to Juliet Mabey, Novin Doostdar, Harriet Wade, Paul Nash, Laura McFarlane and all the team at Oneworld for making these books and their jackets so great.

I am also indebted to the eagle-eyed Francine Brody, who has helped me a lot with this script.

My husband, Sean, and son, Riley, are also to be praised for their unerring guidance and encouragement. This must be extended to my mum, dad, step-mum, step-dad, brother, sister, step-brother and step-sister, nieces, nephews, cousins, aunts, uncles and friends too many to mention. Special exceptions include Rachel Litchtenstein, Colette Bailey, Steph Roche and Kate Bradley.

I have had a few conversations with people who have helped my work to evolve: Sarah Ditum, Ros Green, Cathi Unsworth, Chris Simmons, Ben Nicholson and Jane Gull. Thank you for your input. It's always valuable.

And I must thank, super-fan, Birte Twissleman for her fantastic support and unstinting enthusiasm, and Mark Lancaster for his companionship and most excellent driving.

Jo Farrugia wanted her daughter named after a baddie, so I think I've nailed that one.

Big up to the Essex Girls Liberation Front – Jo, Elsa and Sarah. Check them out on Facebook.

If there's anyone I've forgotten to thank, please forgive the omission – the feeling is there even if the names elude me.

Final thanks, of course, go to my readers. *Strange Tombs* is, as always, for you.